IN VERITAS

2

He speaks secrets to her in the dark.

He speaks secrets to her when she least expects it—downstairs, lifting his gaze from his glowing screens, or in her ear as they board the bus. He tells her stories: he was fifteen and stole twenty dollars from his teacher's wallet. He was six and afraid of horses because of the one that stepped on his foot. He was eight and fell out of a tree, but was too proud to say anything, so he walked home and went to bed with a cracked rib that he nursed for a month.

When she knows everything about him that he can think to tell her, he whispers the colour of her hair or the sound of the rain on the windowpanes. He gifts her everything he is. He is terribly close—inches, a breath, the width of a dream—but his truths are cool on her skin.

She gives him few words, but sometimes she lets him curl his fingers into her palm. He tells his secrets to her navel and her breasts and the shadow of her clavicle.

She speaks with her hands. She keeps all his syllables safe.

SEPTEMBER

Continuing through the market, Verity sees a foot-long dragon, its tiny wings folded against the wind. There are gaps in its rusted scales and its tail lashes as it roots in the garbage by a news stand. The vendor says, "Fucking pigeons," and throws a rock at the bin. The dragon explodes in grey feathers and an edge of pointed yellow beak.

Verity doesn't blink. Instead she folds her arms, head lowered, and thinks *the dog is a snake is a dog,* over and over like a chorus or a puzzle.

The dog follows her.

She knows the dog follows her because it smells of lilac and coal, and there's a tingling at the edges of her lips. Verity keeps her head down and her hands in the pockets of her coat; she walks a little faster than usual, and her fingers are wrapped around her phone.

She stops once or twice, whirling, catching nothing but an indecipherable blur, and the swift turns threaten to give her a headache as the maelstrom of the city resettles around her. A taxi moves slowly past her on the street, pausing hopefully. Verity almost flags it, but then her chin goes up and her shoulders straighten, so the driver continues on.

Verity stares deliberately back at the corner where she last turned, but the sidewalk is empty in the afternoon's emerging sun.

Still, she smells lilac.

She pauses at a bakery window, gazing at a tower of cupcakes and the ripped corner of a concert flyer where she now notices a stylized black canine logo and bold letters for The Between. The paper has been torn halfway up, the date and locale lost. In the glass, she sees her own reflection, pale and clean. Just over her reflection's left shoulder, she spots the dog on the opposite side of the street. Its ears are perked jauntily; its tail is a waving banner.

She feels a brief stab of triumph, but when she turns, the dog is gone.

"It, um, isn't very nice to scare me," she says, more loudly than she is accustomed.

A passing courier gives Verity an odd look.

She shakes her head and continues walking.

"Okay," she says, this time halfway under her breath. "Then we're going to the store."

No one responds, so Verity paces another two city blocks with the scent of flowered coal in the back of her throat. She doesn't turn again, but once, she is certain she sees the dog slinking just across the street. It slides its belly low to the ground and a stubbled man in a baseball cap crouches to scratch its ears. Deliberately, she gazes down at her own careful steps and the raggedness of her scuffed white sneakers. Her thumb digs hard into the palm of her hand.

She doesn't need to look up when she reaches the corner store; she can feel the logos crawl across her skin. The faded paper advertisements stuck across the windows promise great savings, free coupons, special offers, and healthy snacks. Verity can hear the last one snicker; the taste of blood rises in her throat.

Swallowing, she fumbles for the door; her fingertips almost brush a small cardboard square advertising menthol cigarettes. *Fresh taste,* shrieks the square, just in time, and Verity's fingers jerk back and resettle on the barred glass of the door. The bottom pane has been shattered and plastered over with tinfoil and tape.

A bell above the door chimes a drip of cold clarity down the back of her spine as she enters. Verity shivers and is assaulted by a thousand tiny spikes of sensation; rows of cigarette packs and candy bars and chips waver in the dim lighting. The sun through the door is warm at her back.

In the ripple of cigarette symphony, the teen boy behind the cash register says something. It takes a moment for Verity to parse.

"You can't bring your dog in here," he says again; there is a hint of irritation beneath his general malaise.

"Um."

Verity draws a careful breath and turns; a foot behind her, the dog sits insouciant, its tail wagging slowly. Its golden eyes are bright, but the sun fails to penetrate the ink of its fur.

Verity frowns.

The dog flicks an ear.

"It's not my dog."

"Well, you can't *let* a dog in here." The teen folds his arms, frowning. The moustache he's trying to grow is coming in unevenly.

Verity would like to argue, but all she can think is *the dog is a snake is a dog is a snake.* She realizes that she can feel her heart pulsing.

She says to the dog, "Go away."

The dog wags its tail.

"Oh yeah," offers the teen. "That'll work."

His sarcasm throws a wave of black across Verity's eyes just as a new shadow looms in the doorway, falling across the dog. For a dizzying moment, she can't tell the difference, and she sees the dog and the shade squirm, the dog's fur running like wet paint. Then, the door chimes and the man in the baseball cap enters the store. His hat is pulled too low; his eyes are hidden, but he wears a tobacco-stained denim jacket and a concert t-shirt. The Between, it reads, in black and jagged silver. Toledo 1994.

The man smells of sweat and last night's beer. He looks as though someone has been gnawing on his edges. He makes Verity itch.

The dog's ears are attentive as the man pushes past Verity toward the counter.

"Uh, can I help you?" The teen slouches with arms folded, his shoulders pressed to a display of cigarettes. SMOKING WILL KILL YOU, repeat the warning labels behind him, little black squares on brightly coloured packages. Verity breathes them like a fresh drifting breeze.

"Yeah." The man in the hat shoves a hand in his jacket and pulls out a gun, so sharply that Verity barely registers the singing metal.

The dog's tongue lazes between its teeth. The boy at the cash has straightened, hands dropping and eyes going wide.

"Open the register," says the man with the gun. When the teen doesn't move, the man snarls, "I said *open* it." The gun is unwavering. Verity and the dog might as well not exist; the man stands with his back half turned.

The teen flashes a panicked look at Verity. Glancing in turn at the shelves nearest to hand, she sees only discordant boxes of chocolate bars and gum. She fingers the phone in her pocket as the boy's thin hands fumble with the register. The machine makes a cheerful chirping sound; the cash tray remains shut.

There is something wrong with the gun.

Verity doesn't realize it until the man in the hat snarls, "I swear to fuck I'll put a bullet in your head," and the metal whistles like a dying train in his hand. He keeps the barrel trained on the boy's head.

"He won't," she offers, swallowing. She wouldn't speak, normally, except that it's been that sort of morning and the shriek of the weapon offends her. She doesn't like the acrid taste of a boy who thinks he's about to die. Her words are almost lost beneath the chiming of the register and the frantic gasp of the boy's breath. The man in the hat whips a fierce glare in her direction, and Verity looks at the floor. She sees that the dog has glided further into the store, winding between her and the man; it stands there, its plumed tail erect as a shadowed flag.

"Shut up."

"He can't shoot you." Verity's fingers twist in her pocket.

"Shut *up*." The man steps forward; the barrel of the gun rests against Verity's forehead, and she draws a breath. She hears the teen make a choking sound. At her feet, the dog has flattened its ears.

The dog is a snake, she thinks, and *gun.* But the gun part is distant and whining at the back of her skull. She exhales very slowly, drawing one hand from her pocket, and she touches her fingers to the strange man's wrist. His skin is warmer than she had expected. She can feel his startled jerk.

She asks, "Do you have any bullets?"

"*No,*" snarls the man, too viciously for that confession; his eyes widen. His gaze is the green of spring grass, marred by the streaking red of a broken vein. "What the hell?" he adds; shades of genuine shock touch his anger. "I thought you were with the dog."

Verity drops her hand; she looks briefly to the teen, his hands clenched white-knuckled at the hard corners of the register. "He doesn't have any bullets," she offers, because the boy doesn't seem to have been listening. The whine of the gun has died.

She realizes too late that she has misjudged when the man's eyes narrow. He jerks his gun hand back, the butt of the weapon raised, and slams a blow down toward Verity's head.

There is an obsidian blur as the dog at her feet launches itself, in perfect silence, toward the man with the gun. Verity doesn't have time to more than half raise a defensive hand before man and dog tumble with a crash into the shelving—chocolate goes flying, jangling boxes scattered—and then something frigid brushes Verity's skin, a whirl of burning before a furred force shoves her roughly to the floor and the store's front window shatters outward.

When the taste of razors in sunlight clears, man and dog are gone.

Verity blinks several times at the half-crushed chocolate bar that lies on the linoleum just in front of her face. Its claim to be 'new and improved' bleeds slowly across the tile. She scents gasoline and dust; she realizes the smell is the breeze from the shattered window, an unseasonable autumn warmth that wars with the store's air conditioning.

She presses her palms to the floor and pushes herself up. When she turns her head to look at the broken pane, she sees only the glitter of glass edges and an empty sidewalk beyond. A car drives past and slows curiously. A torn advertising flyer waves nauseatingly in the breeze.

The boy behind the counter has pressed himself back into the corner, one shoulder mashing the crinkling display of cigarettes. His breath hitches loudly.

Verity's own lungs are not quite working properly; she wonders at the hint of constriction in her throat and the tremor that twitches the ends of her fingers. She bites once at her lower lip before she asks, as calmly as she can, "Could I, um, buy some milk?"

The teen's eyes are white-ringed. Verity knows what he will answer, even before he blurts, "Are you freaking insane?"

The question drifts behind Verity as the bell on the door chimes, then she's standing on the bright sidewalk with shattered glass crunching beneath her feet.

Verity looks up and down the street, but sees only cars and the drifting rot of the city. Closing her eyes, she sighs.

When she reaches for her phone, something in her pocket jabs at her finger. Her brows draw down as she pulls the object from her jacket, finding it folded in a piece of paper. It is a round black pin, inexpensive and incongruous, the kind easily affixed to a lapel or a backpack. It has come undone and the protruding needle is sharp. The logo on the pin's flat disc is a jagged silver B, matching the logo on the gunman's shirt. The pin is less than two inches wide, a circle made of plastic and sheet metal, but it feels oddly hollow in her hand. She holds it between two fingers, frowning, and unfolds the paper to reveal a crudely printed concert flyer. THE BETWEEN, it reads, LIVE IN CONCERT, but the date is two weeks ago and marked CANCELLED. The address of the venue is McLuhan's, a theatre on Bank Street that she vaguely remembers as crumbling.

Verity breathes in lilac and coal and the lingering scent of dust.

"Hang on," yells the teen, from inside the battered store. "You gotta talk to the cops."

Verity looks at the broken window—at the sharp-edged glass hole and the shadowed shelves where candy and ramen packages live. Then she tucks the pin and paper back into her coat, lowering her head as she walks down the street.

This time, she is moderately sure, she isn't followed.

She waits beneath a sign on the corner, until a bus comes like a red and white worm and she can sit in silence between a large man who smells of cheap cigars and a woman with a screaming baby and an empty stroller. At each stop the bus makes, the stroller rolls forward into Verity's ankle. She keeps her hands clasped tightly in her lap, and still finds them shaking.

The city glides past the window, shifting from the low awnings of the market to towering glass skyscrapers, and finally to gentrified streets with leafy trees and old, narrow houses. Verity nudges the stroller aside with her foot—earning herself a glare in the process—and disembarks. In the shelter of an oak, she pauses for breath, and to test for the oiled presence of the dog. Then, shaking her head, she walks up the stairs to the entry of a well-kept elderly grey townhouse. She crosses the small deck and pushes open the unlocked front door, on which frosted glass letters proclaim *FLÂNEURS, INC. ALL SERVICES FREE.*

Verity enters the foyer, her footsteps quiet on the antique hardwood as the door closes and shuts out the city. Familiarity settles around her, white walls like a cloak. To the left, just past an open archway, Jacob's unoccupied desk is cluttered with papers, his desktop computer, and two half-assembled laptops. Verity is grateful for the gossamer tease of the mess. She mounts the stairs to the right, fishing for her keys, and her hand brushes against the pin in her pocket.

Unlocking the door upstairs, she hears an electric whirring that brings with it the tastes of ginger and cut grass—a sensation that dives down the hall and slaps lightly at her skin. When she closes the door behind her, the sound cuts off, and Jacob's voice drifts from the kitchen.

"Vee?"

"Hi," says Verity. She keeps her coat on. Her eyes are on the floor—she traces a wisp of that elusive ginger, a sparking flash—and she frowns at the puffs of flour like clouds on the hardwood. Her sneakers leave prints as she walks.

"We're having pancakes! Maybe. I'm not making any guarantees."

Jacob has short black dreadlocks and cedar eyes and freckles sprinkled liberally across burnt sienna skin. The ease of his grin often distracts from the unfortunate length of his nose. Just now he is looming over Verity; she blinks at the flour on his t-shirt, and the smooth length of his collarbone outlined just beneath.

"I know I'm not a chef," he admits, "but I keep wanting to—hey, what's up?"

His palm hovers an inch from Verity's left shoulder. She shakes her head minutely and his fingers drop away.

"Vee?"

Verity frowns at the worn line of Jacob's collar, where the soft fabric is developing the first signs of a hole. "Wait," she says, and knows that he will. She tilts her head to the side, measuring the spiced brush of air against her cheek; she is silent for almost a full minute while she thinks. He stands there, though she knows by the taste that he is concerned.

Finally she says, "I saw a dog turn into a snake. Only it wasn't a dog. Or a snake." She measures each word for its furred weight on her tongue. She can see the syllables hang like icicles.

After a slight pause, the shadow of Jacob's hand crosses her face. He tucks back a strand of her hair, and when she doesn't flinch, he strokes his thumb just beneath the line of her jaw. "O-kay ... so I basically have no idea what you're saying."

Verity swallows.

Jacob sighs. "Is this like when they found that dead seal in the canal, and you told me it was a hippogriff?"

"It was *like* a hippogriff," she corrects, carefully. "It had a horse's head." She shakes her head, feeling Jacob's touch melodic on her skin. She knows there is something helpless in her voice; she can feel the stammer start in the back of her throat, where she wants to explain. She tries again: "No. The dog—the snake—wasn't the same. Except for some lilac, maybe."

"Like the dragons?"

"A little like the dragons." Verity rubs her palms at the thighs of her jeans. "There was a man in black."

"Are you okay?" Jacob shifts his hand, bringing two fingers lightly under Verity's chin; she ducks her head, though she knows he's trying to meet her eyes. Her vision is full of tiny flares.

"Vee," says Jacob again. "Do you need to talk to someone? I mean, I know we said—but if you needed to."

His concern is unexpected. It shoots lightning through her lungs. Verity does look up then, and her eyes flare. "No. We promised. No."

Jacob frowns down, his doubt etched between his brows. He has flour in the jagged locks of his hair. "If you're sure." The uncertainty hangs, but an instant later his gaze has brightened. "Oh, hey," he adds. "Did you get the milk?"

Verity thinks it's odd that his fingertips flutter against her skin, until she realizes that his hands are steady and she is trembling. *The dog is a snake,* she wants to say, and *he had a gun,* but her throat works and she doesn't have the words.

She shakes her head again; her eyes close and she sees only the dancing sparks of her world changing. She lets Jacob envelop her then—his long arms around her, his ragged shirt against her face, his chin very light on the top of her head.

Flour dusts the kitchen in the afternoon sunlight, golden motes flickering as they drift through the shadows cast by the tree outside the window. Verity and Jacob stand there and breathe; neither sees the dark snake in the branches of the tree, or the golden eyes watching.

"Nothing is poorer than a truth expressed as it was thought. Committed to writing in such cases, it is not even a bad photograph. Truth wants to be startled abruptly, at one stroke, from her self-immersion, whether by uproar, music or cries for help."
—Walter Benjamin

3

Ask around about Santiago, and you'll find all the answers are different. You'll hear that he is immortal and that the Ouroboros serves him. You'll hear that he fought his way to the centre of the world, where the great snake lay gnawing on its endless tail, and that he cowed the creature with a whip of shadow and blood.

You may hear, also, that he and his slavering beast were birthed of a she-wolf—that they were Romulus and Remus, the brothers twinned.

Others say that he was a warrior once, and fought in Rome. They claim he tamed a dog in the gladiator pits. Or else it was a snake.

Maybe he is the sorcerer who calls the darkness home.

Or perhaps he is the son of Death. He likes that one.

He likes all of those stories. He made them up himself.

SANTIAGO

Stefan Santiago was born in the back of an underfunded clinic, thrust bloody and small into the hands of a sweating nurse's aide when the ambulance was slow to arrive. The baby came into the world furious and writhing, his face already twisted in a scream.

His mother Laura was young. She had hard eyes, sculpted hair, and a smile that didn't forgive. She tried for a few months, and then she showed up on her brother Ignacio's doorstep and shoved the baby into his uncle's surprised arms. "I can't," she said. "Your turn."

Where Laura was hard, Ignacio was chipped at the edges—a lanky, restless man who made an unimpressive living selling pills out of his dresser drawer. He didn't know what to do with a baby. He would have protested, but his sister was already gone. Instead he stared down at the bundle of blankets, and offered, "Huh."

So Santiago grew up in two cramped rooms, surrounded by strangers, cigarette smoke, and the occasional dead rat. He slept on a narrow mattress in the corner of the living room, springs digging at his back. By the time he was three, he had learned to step around the needles on the floor. Long before he was four, he knew when to duck, and when the edge on a man's raucous laughter meant that he should lock himself in the bathroom and be very quiet. He could open a beer or roll a joint on command—quickly, so as not to anger any big hands. They didn't swipe at him often—not while his uncle was watching, and he was usually watching, but sometimes he was in the other room.

Santiago was scrawny for his age. He had a habit of baring his teeth. He was only afraid of three things.

First was the snake. The snake lived in a worn hardcover book that was one of four in the apartment—the other three were thick and full of tiny type, but the fourth was almost all pictures. *A Child's Guide to Nature*, it said on the front; the book was water-stained and the dust jacket was ripped, but the boy Santiago liked to sit with his back to the corner wall and flip through the sticky pages. He looked at lions and jackals and elephants. He liked the pictures of brightly coloured birds.

The snake's scales were mottled green and brown, except where it curled over itself and hints of its underside showed black and yellow. It lay swollen on a bed of broad jungle leaves, shining as though freshly excreted. Its tiny dark eyes were watching.

Santiago knew exactly where the snake was in the book: on a double spread of the sixteenth and seventeenth pages, between the elephant and a river full of crocodiles. Mostly, when he reached the photo of the elephant, its trunk jauntily waving, he made sure to grip the next two pages tightly between his fingers as he flipped, so he would skip the snake entirely and see only the crocodiles and the muddy water. But sometimes, when the noises from the next room were too loud, and he could hear yelling or moaning—or, once, the sharp report of a gun fired into the wall—he would huddle in his corner, open the book, and stare at the snake. He would force himself to brush his fingertips over the too-smooth scales, petting the page, tracing each moist-looking curve, until the apartment was silent and he could slam the book shut.

The second thing he feared was the dog that lived in the alley. The dog wore a spiked collar and was kept behind a chain link fence. It had deep brown-black fur, and perked ears, and pale yellow eyes that stared baleful and wild from the broken wooden crate where it liked to crouch. When Santiago walked to school in the mornings, he had to clutch his bag to his chest. But it didn't matter how careful he was, or if he walked to the other side of the street. The instant he set a toe on the sidewalk, the dog would lunge, barking, and the fence would rattle against its weight while Santiago ran with his heart in his throat and his skinny legs pumping.

He tried to toss the dog a sandwich once. The stale bread scattered in the alley, mustard-smeared, and the dog hurled itself so hard against the fence that Santiago thought he saw a chain link snap. He tripped and went sprawling, trying to get away; the knee of his torn pants was sticky crimson all day, and he had no lunch at school. After the final bell rang, he dealt with the four smug boys who followed him—he punched one in the nose, elbowed another in the gut, and bloodied his other knee on the pavement before they ran. Then he came home with his head high, and he tried to stay on the far side of the street, but the dog barked and barked until Santiago dashed past and fled upstairs.

The third thing that scared him was the dark.

At night, he would lie on his mattress on the floor and if the apartment were quiet, he would stare up at the blackness and imagine the dog crouching by the front door, or the snake gliding slowly closer across the linoleum. In the darkness, he was not alone, and all the hidden things were breathing. They whispered words he could never quite hear.

When he was very little, he would cry gasping sobs until his uncle came and turned the light on. Ignacio would bring him a stuffed bear, and if it was a good night, would sit with him until he slept. Ignacio's fingers were rough but careful in Santiago's hair; Ignacio smelled of smoke and something else that was decaying and sweet. His uncle's hips were too sharp to be pillows, but Santiago could weep his fear into the worn cotton of Ignacio's shirt.

"They talk at me," Santiago confessed once, sniffling. "All the shapes on the walls. They move. They want something."

"It's a dream, buddy. You're a big boy," Ignacio said, in his low gravel voice. "Don't listen, and they'll go away."

He was wrong.

When Santiago was older, the whispering was louder, but the stuffed bear was long gone and he was too proud to cry. He liked the nights when his uncle stayed awake; sometimes a crack of light would escape the other room and spill across the floor so he could see there were no snakes and nothing that slid and gibbered in the night. But when the light went off, he would huddle beneath his blanket, and his legs were wet and his mattress stank.

He was afraid of nothing else. Not the days when Ignacio stared into space; not the rough cuffs of the men who reeked of liquor and sweat. He was not afraid of thunder, or speeding cars, or the kids who stalked him after class to call him names and kick his shins. Some days his neck was wet with spit balls, but he didn't care. He kept to himself, and his eyes were flinted. They only dared to follow him in groups.

He liked his uncle's spiced cologne, and the quiet of the school library, and the tuneless humming of the old man who ran the café downstairs.

One night when Santiago was already in bed, feeling smug but faintly disquieted about unfinished math homework, a man came to the door with a wad of folded bills. His shoulders were broad and so was his jaw. His skin was smooth as a dolphin. He leaned against the jamb and smiled down at Santiago's uncle with an expression that Santiago didn't like.

Ignacio only looked at the bills with resigned eyes, then jerked his chin. "Other room," he said. "I try to keep it away from the kid, you know?"

"Oh, of course." The stranger watched Santiago and smiled. "And who is this?" Santiago glared back. He didn't want the man to step inside. The shadows in the corner of the room gurgled and moaned, but no one else seemed to notice.

"Leave him be." Ignacio shook his head, but stepped back and let the stranger in. The broad man followed Ignacio to the other room, but his gaze lingered on Santiago, and his broad-lipped smile was rubber pulled over crooked teeth.

The bedroom door closed.

Santiago lay quietly, knuckles white and blanket tucked, and waited for his uncle to finish with the man. He knew the pattern: Ignacio would unlock the dresser drawer. It would open and close, then there would be a murmur of voices. The stranger would leave and Ignacio would have money for groceries. Sometimes it would take longer, or they would come out and sit on the couch with beer and rolling papers, but Santiago couldn't think that Ignacio liked this man.

The drawer opened and closed.

The shadows were whispering. Santiago was good at ignoring them. He was a big boy now.

There was an exchange of voices.

Then there came a barrage of meaty sounds, pounding and wet.

Santiago heard his uncle cry out once, and then again; there was a new note in Ignacio's voice, one that swooped high and then choked off in a strange, low gurgle.

Santiago stared at the smoke-yellowed ceiling, clutching the blanket to his chest. He wondered if he should do something—he imagined himself getting up and pacing to the doorway. He imagined his knock.

Tio, are you okay?

He could take the baseball bat from behind the front door. He could charge through.

With a thrill, he imagined how the dog's teeth might rip at the stranger's throat, if it were there.

He thought of the snake, and how it would wind up the stranger's legs and choke him.

The sound of breathing came harsh and desperate from the other room, loud enough to be heard through the door. Santiago didn't think it was his uncle.

He heard something hit the wall with enough force to rattle the kitchen cupboards.

He tasted copper where he'd bitten his lip. His eyes were wide open and the light was on, but black streaks swirled across his vision; he thought he saw shapes, the dog's ears or the snake's sliding tail or the edges of sharp teeth. The darkness whined higher; past it, Santiago could still hear the breathing, faster and faster. He imagined it coming closer. He imagined the snake's cold eyes and the sinuous ribbon of its tongue.

The stranger in the next room grunted.

There was silence.

Santiago stared at the plain wood of the bedroom door and couldn't decide if it was worse not to hear anything at all. He kept his own breathing soft and careful. Air caught in an unwilling sob, somewhere deep; he willed it back. He didn't dare to twitch.

A spring creaked.

The bedroom door opened just a crack; the air that wafted out smelled like the toilet had backed up again, or like someone had been sick. Santiago saw the stranger's hand extend—itself very much like a snake—and trip the light switch with one deliberate finger. There was blood on the hand, and on the cuff of the man's suit.

The lights went out.

Santiago could not hear any footsteps across the floor. He could hear only the urgently gibbering darkness.

The boy yanked the blanket over his head, squirming down to the mattress. He couldn't keep the sob from escaping; he jammed the blanket between his teeth, and it was a rank fuzziness on his tongue. He tasted cotton and his own saliva. He couldn't breathe. He couldn't open his eyes. The shadows were roiling, their voices like spitting oil. A greater blackness loomed over him and he knew the man was standing there.

A rough hand closed on his ankle. Its fingers were sticky and hot.

There was no sound from the bedroom. The air was motionless.

The man jerked Santiago backward, off the mattress and onto the floor. The blanket tangled; it was no protection against the impact that slammed Santiago's shoulder. His teeth closed hard on the flannel corner and he gagged on a sudden rise of bile in his throat.

His eyes flew open and he saw only the dark.

He had never been more afraid.

Something inside of him cracked open. All of the darkness poured in, filling him to bursting. He thought of the dog, and the snake; he thought of all the horrors in the night, all the things that scared him the most, and he willed them all upon the stranger with the meaty hands. When a boot crunched against his side, he didn't feel it; he took that agony and he channelled it into terrified hate. The shadows were screaming at him, and for once he screamed back—a young boy, conjuring the worst thing he could imagine and shoving it straight at the stranger's chest.

Santiago called all his fears into being, and they answered.

It was as though he'd split himself in two.

He saw, as if from a distance, the stranger's grinning face, bloated as a slug. He cowered into a ball, arms raising to ward off the descent of the boot.

He was a boy and he was something else. He was the night taking form. He was a demon called. He leapt.

He scrunched his eyes shut.

He shut his eyes, but he could still see. He closed his jaws around the soft white neck; he tasted hot blood. His jump knocked the man away from the seizing boy on the floor and he ripped at quivering flesh.

There were sounds again: squelching and splattering, a choked cry and a gasp that cut off in a burble. Santiago felt thick wet warmth spray across his arm and his ear. He scrubbed his palm across his face, and blinked. His eyes were beginning to adjust to the dim light that crept around the edges of the grimy kitchen window. The bathroom smell was worse.

The shadows were silent, but not entirely so: the morass of whispering voices had become just one, and that one was familiar, echoing his own thoughts back to him. He could almost hear them bouncing. Santiago crouched on the mattress and also watched himself crouch. He could see the mop of his hair and the gangliness of his own knobby limbs. He felt suddenly, oddly calm. He looked up at the darkness and the darkness looked back. It had golden eyes and the same sharp ears as the dog downstairs. It stood proudly over the broken body on the linoleum.

Santiago could see now—better, he thought, than ever before. The shadows didn't seem so deep. Blood streaked the cracking walls; it stuck to the cheap plaster in gobbets, a great splashing wave that crossed the bedroom doorway and marred the carpet beyond. Santiago saw the curl of his uncle's hand, lying palm up and still. Ignacio's long fingers were shattered.

Something yawned open in Santiago's chest. He barely had time to puke on the sheets crumpled around him before he felt the darkness rush in there, too. It was soothing. It whispered now with one voice, and the voice was his. It would never leave him.

He wiped gore and vomit from his lips with the back of his hand, and looked again to the middle of the floor, where the great black beast crouched heaving over the body of its prey. The stranger's corpse was a mass of so much meat; the thing above it arched its back like a wolf, and writhed its snakelike tail. Its ebon fur was impenetrable to the flickering yellow of the ceiling bulb.

He was distantly aware of his own fragile form on the mattress. He tasted blood and liked it.

He looked at the beast.

He looked back at the boy.

The monster bared its teeth, its golden stare flat and bold.

Santiago straightened. The monster's nose came forward as the boy extended his hand.

Santiago was not afraid anymore.

[**IMAGE**: A boy and his dog, making friends in the remains of a battered apartment, next to a mattress on the floor. The boy is wearing a ragged t-shirt and pyjama bottoms. Shadows swirl in the corners, hinting at the shapes of snakes. The dog's tail is reptilian. The corpse on the floor is mangled beyond recognition, and the walls are sprayed with blood.]

Are you still reading?

yes

4

Sometimes she dreams she's killed a man.

She doesn't know his name or his face. She doesn't remember how it happened. She only dreams of the guilt—the frantic secret and the desperate desire to hide the body. In her dreams, no one knows what she's done, but they will find out in the instant they open the closet door or pick up the bloody towel or notice the knife is missing. Her nights are a blur of turning knobs and the rustle of the bag that holds the corpse. Sometimes, the body is already buried, but she runs through twisting halls with a shovel in her hand, grave mud dropping in clumps.

Those are the nights she tosses, steals the blankets, cannot rest.

She doesn't understand.

She has never killed anyone. If she did, she wouldn't lie.

OCTOBER

Jacob decides they should try catering, which means Verity comes downstairs one morning to find two sharply pressed black-and-white uniforms hanging from the staircase, and she and Jacob spend two weddings and a bar mitzvah distributing tiny trays of hors d'oeuvres to guests in various stages of slurring. They do not make the hors d'oeuvres themselves. They have learned better than that.

"Ehn," is Jacob's verdict. "Too loud, too sloppy. You didn't like it, did you? What if we were roadies? I got a call from this guy."

Verity is willing to try, but the next day she finds that Jacob has decided he wants to be a guitarist. He buys a red guitar and sits on the staircase plucking at strings; he downloads a tutorial to his computer and stares at the screen, his face lit in glowing blue as his hands fumble over mismatched chords. There is a yellow guitar for Verity if she wants it, but she rests her palm flat on the steel strings and frowns. "Cilantro," is all she says on the subject. She flicks the smallest string with her fingernail, and the narrow herbed sound makes her blink. She touches Jacob's cheek and leaves him to it.

While he plucks, she spends three weeks wandering the city, feeling the air turn cool and watching red and brown tint the fall leaves. She tastes the pavement with each footstep.

She tours her city from the flapping tarps of the market to the crumbling stone and weathered wood of her own Glebe neighbourhood. She inhales the clean glass lines of the Queen Street business district and the dustiness of the downtown cafés. She passes soda cans, cigarette butts, and discarded wrappers, evaluating each in turn. She even takes buses to Kanata and Orléans, where suburban miniature mansions line up in crowded rows, identical soldiers on bright green lawns.

Sometimes she catches a hint of shadow at the corner of her vision, or a drift of petal scent across her skin, but when she looks, she can find no trace of the dog. Though she checks each morning, the magician does not appear again at the market's edge. Verity stands in his place beneath the stone archway and smells perfume drifting when the wind catches at the flyers pasted to the red wall of the bookstore across the street. Recognizing the jagged edges of the cheaply printed logo spelling out The Between, she crosses to brush her fingertips over paper faded by sun and wrinkled by rain. The concert date is February 3, but a banner across the top reads CANCELLED. In the background is a black smear in the shape of a wolf—or a dog.

The flyers have a familiar hollow feel; Verity knocks once, but hears only the dullness of damp plywood. Her knuckle scratches against a rusted nail. She frowns. She glances back toward the market, but sees only a passing car.

The theatre listed on the flyers is McLuhan's, but Verity walks by the building on Bank Street and finds the windows boarded. She has passed it before—it is only a few blocks from her house—but she has tended to cross to the other side of the road, bothered by the flutter of papers affixed to the plywood and faux-Victorian columns at the building's front entrance. This time she stops directly in front of the doors and makes herself look. She sees a blur of advertisements for theatre groups, guitar lessons, and upcoming plays. She sees faded posters for movies long gone.

She sees, over and over, stapled pages with the logo for The Between and an image of the black dog, each with CANCELLED stamped across the grinning muzzle. Indeed, the marquee above the doors spells it out in unevenly spaced black and white: THE BETWEEN CANCELLED SOR Y.

The sign drones irritatingly in her ear; she shakes her head. She tries the doors and finds them locked. She stands on the street for a minute and then, on a whim, she takes the Between pin from her pocket and affixes it to the lapel of her jacket. She wonders whether it will change her life; she waits a moment to see if the wind reverses or the magician appears, but the doors remain closed. The fall air is crisp and clear.

She leaves the pin on.

Three days later, a long-haired young man approaches her as she is sitting at a small outdoor bistro, nudging a roll of avocado sushi with her index finger. He is panhandling on the corner. He has ripped off the sleeves of his vinyl jacket, and his face is a glitter of piercings. Something in the desolate slope of his shoulders reminds her of the magician—though if the man in black were fraying at the edges, this boy is worn to scraps. When he walks up to Verity, hands jammed in his pockets, she is already fishing for money.

What he says is: "You like their music, huh?"

Verity stares blankly until the boy motions toward the pin at her chest; she touches it with one bemused hand. "Oh. I've never heard them."

The twist of the boy's mouth brushes like sandpaper across her skin. "Oh." He half turns away and Verity sees The Between studded in steel pips across his back before he reconsiders enough to add, "Got any change?"

She can't find any coins, but she gives him a twenty-dollar bill from her wallet and he tugs three fingers at his greasy bangs when he backs away. She thinks he's being sarcastic.

A week later, she sits on a park bench watching a six-legged cat and wondering at the peculiar precision of its gait. The cat is stalking a pigeon, much to the chagrin of a flock of other pigeons and the displeasure of the small woman sitting on the other bench just to Verity's left. The woman is a wisp, her hair in a neat copper-grey bun. Her every worldly possession is apparently kept in a small shopping cart. She has half a loaf of bread in her lap, and she's tossing bits to the birds, but she pauses to throw one at the cat. "Shoo," she admonishes. A crumb bounces off the cat's ear and it hisses. Its tongue is forked; a tiny gout of flame escapes its teeth.

Verity tilts her head, watching the beast retreat. The pigeons that scatter before it are just pigeons; she hasn't seen a dragon in days.

"You leave my birds alone," says the woman, fiercely. She glares in the direction of where the hexapede cat has vanished behind a tree. "You're not special. All the more claws to hurt them with," she grumbles. "Go on before someone sees you."

Before Verity can say anything, the woman has turned to address her. Beneath sparse brows, the stranger has eyes like milky agates, sharply slanted at the edges. "Do you like their music, dear?"

When Verity is silent too long, the woman reaches a dry-soiled hand and taps at the bundle of her belongings in the metal cart and the edge of an ill-packed t-shirt dangling like a tattered flag. The Between.

Verity hesitates. "I, um ... their concert was cancelled."

"Hmph," sniffs the woman dubiously. Verity wants very much to ask about the cat, but then the woman rises—more spryly than her bowed form might suggest—and trundles her cart away down the path, her thin shoulders stiff. The cat is gone. The pigeons cluster hopefully around the now-absence of bread.

The third time Verity is approached, she has stopped at a flower cart on a corner of Sparks Street, the pedestrian mall cool in the shadow of government buildings. She is trying to decide whether the roses whistle like carnations or the carnations taste of nasturtium; it takes her some time to register the soft breath of surveillance across her skin.

She turns swiftly. The flowers have her expecting the dog, but she encounters instead the mocha eyes of a brown girl standing at her elbow. "Hi," says the girl, who might be sixteen or seventeen. Her thick black hair is drawn back with an elastic. She is wearing a red hoodie with a The Between logo silkscreened onto the upper right of her chest. Despite her small stature, she seems somehow more solid than anyone passing, as though she is a rock wearing against the edges of the city. "Great music, huh?"

Verity admits, hesitantly, "I've never heard them. But people don't seem to like that answer."

She expects the girl's lips to draw tight, but instead they curve in a grin. "You're supposed to say the second album was better than the third."

"Was it?"

The girl's smile is unrepentant. "No. But that's the countersign. I mean, such as it is. The system isn't great."

Verity finds the evenness of the girl's teeth reassuring; the white smile plays across the air, leaving a precise track of glowing green that Verity does her best not to stare at. She focuses on the girl's face—or at least, the smoothness of her hairline, because Verity is not particularly tall but the girl doesn't come past her shoulder.

"I won't say it if it's not true," Verity says, apologetically. "And I don't really understand. The pin—there was a dog...."

"Oh," replies the girl. "You're one of *his.*" She seems disappointed—one shoulder lifts in a shrug—but then she tilts her head. "And it's not *not* true. I mean, really. Also, it can be kind of funny. A guy argued with me once for ten minutes. He felt my musical tastes were lacking."

Verity doesn't know what to say to that, except, "I don't lie." She looks down at the sidewalk and expects that the girl will retreat like the others, but she finds herself staring down at her own sneakers and a pair of unmoving blue flats. The girl has a scuff on her right toe.

"Hm," says the girl. This time she looks at Verity more intently. "Really?"

"...I could say someone told me the second album was better? Is that close enough?"

"There you go!" All shoes are unmoving. Verity wants to shift her feet, but it would destroy the perfect balance of canvas and concrete. The girl's voice tastes like an apricot.

"I don't know what's going on," confesses Verity again.

The girl laughs. "My name's Privya. But listen—" and here her tone sharpens, "what colour is my voice?"

Silver, thinks Verity automatically, but she doesn't answer, because the shock of the girl's question has turned the air to static. There is a single moment where she looks up, surprised, and the girl—Privya—is still standing there, short and unassuming with her hair in a ponytail and her hands jammed in the pockets of her hoodie. Privya's gaze is both knowing and expectant.

Uncertain, Verity parts her lips.

That is the precise instant when the phone vibrates in her pocket. She palms it one-handed, the action so ingrained it barely registers. "Sorry," she says. "My—Jacob."

But Privya's face has gone blank. It is the expression Verity had expected before—the same as the magician's, shuttering and somehow betrayed. "Huh." Privya takes a step back. "No, I'll let you take that." The silver has leached from her tone; her words are etched with fallen leaves. "See you around, though."

The phone buzzes again and Verity glances down to see two new texts:

BROKE ALL THE G STRINGS

OK THAT SOUNDS WEIRD

As she watches, a third comes in:

IM TALKING ABOUT THE GUITAR

Words ripple across the screen. When Verity looks up, swallowing the lingering impression of sandpaper, the girl is gone, but there's a bright pink poster waving from the lamppost near where she was standing. THE BETWEEN, it says, LIVE AT LANSDOWNE PARK ABERDEEN PAVILION. The date is next spring: March 5.

The paper tastes like dust and empty spaces. Verity stands on the city street and feels the ghost of music drift across her skin.

5

OTTAWA (Oct. 3, 2013)—Officials at Agriculture
Canada are warning of an apparent outbreak of
Creutzfeldt–Jakob disease in Ontario, after a third
person has been reported dead. 62-year-old Ottawa
resident Manfred Rochester, along with Torontonian
Adnan Sayid, 36, and an unidentified Kingston
woman, has died of complications resulting from the
disease; two other cases in the Ottawa area have
been diagnosed.

While Creutzfeldt–Jakob disease (CJD) is closely
associated with bovine spongiform encephalopathy
("mad cow" disease) in cattle, officials say that no
source of contamination has yet been identified.

"Rest assured we are working closely with
representatives from the Centre for Disease Control
in order to resolve this issue," said the Honourable
Brigitte Maisonneuve, Minister of Agriculture. "Our
sincere condolences go out to the victims and their
families. We grieve the loss of Mr. Rochester, a
long-time employee of Ottawa's Chaudière Falls
power station, a loving husband, and a grandfather
of three. At this time, however, there is no evi-
dence that any food safety procedures have been
compromised."

"Remember that this disease may incubate for one to eight years," said Dr. Hans Mikaelsen, head of neuroscience at Ottawa University. "So it may be tricky to pin down the source. It's highly unlikely that we're discussing anything in the current food supply."

CJD attacks the brain and may manifest suddenly. Symptoms may include a rapid onset of dementia, with associated hallucinations and memory loss. Anyone experiencing such symptoms should seek medical help immediately.

No cases of mad cow disease have been identified in Canada since 2006. However, despite pleas from the government and representatives of the agriculture industry, sales of beef in the province have already dropped by fifteen per cent.

OCTOBER

Verity stretches as she wakes, feeling the sheets rub against her bare toes. It takes her a moment to let sight and sound and taste and touch and scent settle, until she is certain that the ceiling isn't melting and her mouth is not full of flowers. The blankets are tangled where Jacob left them. A sliver of daylight filters through the blinds and across the grey sheets.

There is a snake in her bed.

She thinks it should be a metaphor, but it's a reptile instead, curled thin and black in the indentation on Jacob's pillow. The snake has golden eyes and smells like charred lilac. It is smaller than she remembers.

Verity looks at the snake, and the snake looks back. She isn't sure if she should be frightened. It does not appear threatening.

When it flicks out a little black tongue, she almost has the impression it likes her.

"Not okay," she tells it, firmly. Folding back the blanket on her own side, she sets her feet on the floor and rises, tugging down the buttoned top of her pyjamas.

When she pads into the main room, it is the dog that follows. She doesn't see the change from scales to fur; she only knows that when she walks toward the coffee pot in the kitchen, there are four paws on the hardwood behind her. The dog's passage makes no sound, but Verity can smell it like velvet across the back of her neck.

She hears something thud downstairs, and something else that sounds like a child wailing. There's a square pink sticky note on her coffee mug; in Jacob's sloppy block print, it reads, WE'RE PHOTOGRAPHERS TODAY.

Verity detaches the note with two fingers and sets it down on the kitchen counter. She pours herself a cup of coffee from the mostly-full pot and curls her hands around the warmth of the mug. The dog plunks itself down in the middle of the kitchen floor and looks at her, its ears perked.

Verity stares at the dog and the dog stares back. It seems to her she is making no more headway than when it was a snake.

She doesn't mind, entirely. The jet of its coat mixes well with the taut bitterness of the coffee.

"Do you have a name?" she asks. Her voice is still rough-edged with sleep.

The dog doesn't answer, but there's a faint crashing sound from below and the subsequent drift of Jacob's voice is hopeful: "Vee?" It's hard to watch the dog when the sounds from downstairs waft crimson across the floor.

There are questions burning in her. She swallows them down with the coffee; she can hear Jacob talking, words muffled, tone bright.

"Stay," she tells the dog, firmly—feeling more than a little uncertain about the whole thing, but when she takes her mug into the bedroom and turns to close the door, the dog only cocks an ear in her direction. Its tongue lazes, black as its fur.

Verity finds a shirt and a pair of jeans. Her half of the dresser is neat and tidy, socks lined up in rows; Jacob's is an explosion, a plaid sleeve leaking to the floor. She changes and runs a brush through her hair. Glancing at the closed door, she draws a slow breath, then takes the time to make the bed. She draws her morning in neat cotton lines, tucking in each sheet corner before she straightens and picks the empty mug off the dresser, carrying it back to the kitchen sink.

The dog is still there.

"I don't know what you want," Verity says. "Maybe—maybe I should've said 'go'? I don't know what to say to dogs."

From below, she hears again, "Vee!"

The dog slides to a sprawl on the floor, placing its head on its crossed paws. It makes no sound—no breath, no whine, no scratch of claws. Its pupils are shining and reptile-reflective. In the familiar warmth of the kitchen, Verity breathes smoke and the ashes of dreams. Then, setting her mug in the sink, she shakes her head. "Don't...."

She pauses, wondering exactly what she wants the dog to do, or refrain from doing. She settles for a vague wave of her hand, her own hesitance trailing sparks in the morning dust. "I'm going downstairs," she says. "You aren't invited."

Exiting the apartment, she shuts the door carefully behind her—not that she really expects a lock to contain the dog, or the snake, which already found its way in. The noise of a shrieking child echoes from the office below, and Verity keeps two fingertips on the banister as she descends, the better to guide herself through the scent of shattered glass and the cloud of tension that ripples across the staircase.

Below, the foyer opens into the main office, where Jacob's desk is colonized by increasingly large electronic screens and piles of paper. The open area that would normally be the house's living room is cluttered with an impressive array of camera equipment. A tripod has been knocked over. Two small children are running in uncontrolled circles while a pinched-looking woman with curling red hair and a mint-green suit stands with her arms folded, casting frequent, irritated glances at Jacob, as though it were his children who were misbehaving. Everyone except Jacob is dressed for the occasion: there are shiny buttons and ribbons, half-tied.

Jacob is at the desk, leaning over his computer, shirt untucked and jeans stained with paint. His dreadlocks are on end and he runs his hand over them again; he looks up at Verity's entrance. He's gnawing slightly at the edge of his lip, but the set of his shoulders relaxes when he sees she's arrived. His relief is a palpable thing; his affection is the loose comfort of silk tangling in her lashes.

"Hey," he says. "I got this set up, I think. Grab a camera?"

There's a dog. The dog is a snake. There are so many things Verity would like to convey; the sound she makes mingles greeting and a familiar, helpless exasperation, discomfort fading in the jangled familiarity of his mess. She shrugs, and keeps a safe distance from the marauding children as she wanders to pick up the tripod. She finds a 'power' button on the camera and turns it on, grimacing as it adds to the faint, electric burr of Jacob's equipment. The room is taut with digital waves and the yelps of excited children.

They've never done this before and yet there is a rhythm, Verity at the camera and Jacob wrangling their subjects. The camera is not hard to use, though it is significantly harder to use well. Verity points the lens and keeps busy clicking whichever buttons seem least sour; the viewfinder is a kaleidoscope of pouting shrieks, so she concentrates on moulded plastic and the hum of energy at her fingertips. Around her, figures bustle and jostle and whine; she clicks, and hunches her shoulders, and lets time pass until she hears Jacob say her name again.

She shakes her head; she wants to say that she is not a photographer, but Jacob is bent over his computer screen and the woman in green is looking over his shoulder. The kids are playing tug of war with a stuffed pony, rolling against the pale blue of a hanging backdrop.

"These aren't very good," is the woman's flat verdict.

Jacob shrugs. "You aren't paying us," he points out, cheerfully enough. "Vee, what do you think?"

Verity leaves the camera, rubbing her fingertips against her thighs, and walks to look at Jacob's screen. She blinks the aura of red and gold away from her lashes and sees, first, that the woman is right: the images are ill-framed, brightly lit, blurry. Jacob scrolls through wild eyes, crooked teeth, a fuzzy close-up of the stuffed pony's tail, until one image jumps razor-clear and Verity says, "There."

It's a photograph of the little girl, just turning her head; her hair is tufted gold. There's a sparkle in her eye and a chip in her tooth. Her face is in the lower right corner of the picture; behind, her brother's shadow plays on the wall. She looks as if she's been caught by surprise.

The image sparks in Verity's ribs. "That one."

Jacob peers more closely, but the children's mother scowls immediately. "It makes her chin look fat."

Verity would protest, but Jacob has already done something to the image onscreen—a click of his mouse and something alters the girl's bone structure, shifts light and contrast. It gives Verity a headache.

"That's amazing!" gushes the woman.

Jacob is modest: "Thanks. I took a class in graphic design, once."

A dark glide of motion tugs at Verity's peripheral vision; she thinks it is the dog in the hallway, but when she looks over, it is gone, and Jacob is tapping at his keyboard while something flexes in the whining hum of the room. The morning light spills through the wooden slats of the blinds on the front window, illuminating the hardwood in bright tiger stripes.

"Okay, let me get these printed out for you, I think I have it working here—"

Verity and Jacob exchange her pleading glance for his quick grin, and she edges into the front hall while he is still talking; it takes only a moment to slip on her shoes and lift her jacket and a soft grey scarf from the coat rack near the landing. A moment later and she is out the door, sliding her hands into her pockets.

If the inside of the townhouse can be a well of confusion, marked by odd flurries of light and the snapping ozone of Jacob's ranging hobbies, then the city, as always, is a tornado. Verity stops on the front step and closes her eyes until she can reconcile the clouds that passing traffic sends snaking across her vision, and the way the sun's warmth smells of oil and cloves. Only when she finds her balance among the sounds of the street does she allow herself to look at the spreading leaves of the oak tree, which chime like bells and lightly sting her fingertips, or the slab of sidewalk that tastes of lint and soiled leather.

When the world resolves itself, the dog is waiting for her. It is a worn shred of shadow sitting patiently at the foot of the stairs, and yet it has a particular solidity, as though the earth might crumble and open beneath the weight of its feet. Verity feels the gravity pull of it, and she stills for a long breath before judging it safe to descend the steps. The dog remains sitting, its yellow eyes watching. It wags its tail once.

Verity tries to keep her gaze steady, but there's a bird in the tree chirping a streak of mauve. Then the door has opened behind her and the two children are streaming out and down the stairs. The young boy's squeals are a spike through her temple. The mother follows more sedately, hands clenched on her purse and an irritated sigh puffing her lips. She pays Verity no attention whatsoever.

"Puppy!" yells the girl. The black dog bares its teeth and she wisely detours in the opposite direction, her small feet barely wavering. She has been distracted by something crumpled and dry on the sidewalk, about ten feet away. Her brother follows. Verity just glimpses the sad remnants of a cracked dragon wing and a scaled, half-flattened tail.

"Neat!" crows the boy.

His sister runs back to the base of the spreading tree. "I need a stick," she proclaims. "Need a stick. I wanna poke it." She sets one hand against the bark of the tree's trunk and stands on tiptoe, reaching up for the branches several feet above her head.

"What are you—oh, leave that alone." The children's mother finds her voice, stepping forward, her heels clicking on the steps and then the concrete until she can get a view of the sidewalk and the crushed form that has caught her son's attention. "Don't touch that, honey. It's just a dead rat. It's full of germs." She ignores the dog, but she does cast a glare back over her shoulder at Verity. "*Someone* should keep the property cleaner."

Verity swallows the taste of cactus thorns—she wants to say *we have no rats*—but when she opens her mouth, the woman has already moved on, grabbing the little boy's hand and herding both children further down the block. Her arm is already waving as she hails a taxi.

When Verity looks back at the sidewalk, she doesn't see wings any-more—only matted fur and the stiff wormy twig of a broken tail now naked and pink.

The dog has paced several feet away down the sidewalk, where it sits once more, waiting attentively.

"You want me to go with you," she guesses slowly.

The dog waves its tail again.

"Where?"

The dog only cocks its head this time, one ear turning sideways.

Verity sees the world stretching jagged and uncertain before her; in the shadow-dog's attention, she feels the pull of the magician's gaze. In the maelstrom of the city, her balance shifts.

At her back is the familiar comfort of the townhouse—the careful spaces she would know blindfolded, the golden dust of the kitchen and the safety of Jacob's flashing grin. She could turn and take five short steps to refuge.

On impulse, she draws a breath and turns slightly to the side, ges-turing with her chin. "The, um, dead thing on the concrete," she says. "What is it? Did you see a rat, too?"

She is, she realizes, standing on a city street, talking to a dog.

The dog looks at her. Then it wags its tail again, deliberately, and lets its black tongue spill out over its teeth.

It is, she thinks, laughing at her.

Verity sighs, and steps forward.

6

I read that Jacques Derrida liked an idea called sous ratûre, which means "under erasure"; he would write a word and then cross it out, to try and communicate that his thought was incomplete—that language was insufficient for clarity and he'd only used the best word he had under the circumstances. Did you know that?

```
yes and he was right but also if i used sous ratûre
all the time everything i wrote would look like this
i couldnt talk and it wouldnt be any clearer and
you would be annoyed but i like that you read about
derrida so thanks

you havent written about colin
```

We're getting there.

OCTOBER

Verity follows the dog down her tree-lined Glebe avenue. She is not surprised when the shadow-creature turns on Bank Street, padding toward the old theatre. The city throws itself against her in whirls of scent and touch and taste, but the dog is a ripple of sable that waits patiently when she pauses.

Once, she ventures, "Where is your friend?," but the dog only prances on jaunty feet, sliding a look sidelong. Its eyes are slitted now, like a snake's. Verity thinks it looks amused.

The glitter taste of it sends a trickle of electricity down Verity's throat, contrasting with the richly spiced scent of the graffiti on the wall of the stationery store just to her right. Swerving, she almost walks into a mail-box. When the dog presses itself against her thigh, she says, "Don't," but kindly, and rights herself, brushing her fingers against dented metal as they pass.

The dog stops outside McLuhan's, as expected. Again, Verity is struck by the oddity of its shadow stretching across the pavement; she can discern no difference between the ink of its fur and the spill of darkness at its feet. It occurs to her that the dog is its own shadow. The thought gives her pause; she lets it melt over the back of her tongue and stares at the alien blot. It looks impatiently back at her with slitted golden eyes, and flattens an ear.

"Okay?" says Verity, helpfully. She looks over at the parade of ragged flyers plastered to the theatre's windows, then steps to the door. Above her, the marquee letters still spell out 'THE BETWEEN CANCELLED SOR Y.'

The front door pulls easily open. Verity pauses, the city looming familiar and cacophonous between her shoulder blades, then the dog slips past her in a wash of fur and she follows.

The papers plastered across the windows outside allow sunlight only in streaks and flutters cast across the threadbare red carpeting of the unlit lobby. Verity is cautious in new spaces; she lets the door close behind herself and waits until she can parse the dust singing lightly in her ears or the stale taste of abandoned brass trim. The lobby is shallow but wide, marked with faux Victorian columns where the paint has chipped to reveal plywood beneath. Against one such column, the magician leans, arms folded. The dog has gone to sit at his feet.

The magician asks, "What are you looking at?"

"Half an octave."

"Hm."

Verity notes that the collar of the magician's faded black t-shirt sports a round pin identical to her own. The Between, like an empty space in the stone of his silhouette.

Verity considers several possible things to say, then ventures, "What's your name?"

"Santiago," he says, and adds a flick of his fingers. "This is Ouroboros. Ouro, if you like." The dog seems larger now. Its narrow back is level with the magician's hip.

"Hi. Why...?" Verity can't think of a good way to end the question. It's too big. She ends up gesturing vaguely around the lobby, then to herself.

"Someone asked for you. It's—let's call it unusual. She generally doesn't ask for anything."

"Who—"

But the magician makes another motion, a graceful gesture that flattens his palm in her direction.

Verity sighs. "I don't need to stay here."

"Need, no. But you want to know, don't you? Everyone does." The magician is watching Verity; it is the same look he gave her in the market, wary and a little perplexed. The dog's head is canted at an identical angle, though it strikes Verity as friendlier. It might be the perky set of its ears.

"Not everyone," corrects Verity, who shakes her head, warding off discomfort like a bee. "But I do. Um. Want. I think you are some of the things I've never understood, and so is your dog, and I want the answers like breathing."

"And so?" Santiago raises an eyebrow, hands in his pockets. He withdraws the left, conjures three playing cards, and slides them away again before she can register more than the jack of clubs.

"So I think there are other ways. You gave them to me." Verity touches the pin on her jacket collar, and looks deliberately at the matching logo pinned to the magician's shirt. "Someone told me to say the second album is, um, better than the third."

She doesn't see his face change—there's a burst of violet obstructing her view. She hears, instead, a rippling whisper of uncertainty in the air.

"That way's slow going," he says; she know it's true because it tastes of mango, cool and sweet.

"A lot of things are, for me." Verity rubs her hand over the back of her neck, beneath the unbrushed fall of her hair. The scarf she wears is soft and a little too warm. She feels the precipice, the *wanting;* she sees, also, the edge to the magician's easy smile.

She is very alone inside the old theatre.

"You're surprisingly blasé about this whole thing." The magician's observation is half a question, his tone bemused.

"People who know me will tell you," says Verity, carefully, "that my world is a strange place."

The dog's eyes are gold and the magician's are like sparkling coal. While Santiago studies her, Verity looks at the dog, which is staring back. Its tail fluffs out, then smoothes to a reptilian whip.

Santiago offers, "We've been watching you. We can't figure it out. This company you work for—what do you do, exactly?"

Verity shrugs a shoulder. "We haven't decided yet."

"Hm."

Before Verity can ask, the magician adds, "You're interesting. But you're not one of us."

His words are mist to her; she shakes her head. "How do you know?"

"Your phone. I'm going to need that from you in a minute. Here— this way."

Santiago peels himself off the pillar and steps to the side, the dog following, but the magician's liquid motion fizzes in Verity's ears, and she tosses her head. When he turns back, one eyebrow raised (the dog with one ear perked), she can only frown at him.

He walks toward her again, the dog following, and that's when she sees the flicker-flow pattern of their steps across the sun-dappled carpet. "You have no shadow," she says, but it doesn't taste right, melding with the hint of gasoline on her tongue and Santiago's flash of wicked grin. Ouro, simultaneously, shows its teeth.

Verity blinks. "The dog is your shadow."

The magician's grin grows a little wider, then abruptly thins. Verity sees the dog's ears go back, and she thinks, *it could be less easy.* She wonders what he might do, this unknown man in a disused building where she is a little too far from help.

"This way," he says, simply. He runs a hand through his curling hair, and strides to a narrow door on the side wall. EMPLOYEES ONLY, says the handwritten sign. The paper is yellowing and torn at the corners. Below, in smaller letters, it reads, NO CELL PHONES, NO CAMERAS, NO COMPUTERS. Someone else has added, in hurried red ink, NO PACEMAKERS.

"Is it about the band?" Verity is bemused. "The show is cancelled."

"It's always cancelled."

Santiago opens the door and gestures Verity through. As she passes, she looks down at the dog, sitting now with its tail curled around its feet. It watches her before following her through.

Verity isn't sure what to expect, but the broom closet is unimpressive. The room is maybe four feet by four feet, two walls lined with shelves that are mostly empty save for a cardboard box and half a bottle of bleach. Three candles are burning in glass jars on the far shelf, adding to what little light filters in from the open doorway.

"Phone," says Santiago, and holds out his hand. Verity hesitates, but slitted yellow eyes stare up at her from the black streak that curls around the magician's wrist, and she realizes the dog has slipped in as the snake. She stares at it for a long moment—*the dog is a snake is a dog*—then fishes her phone from her pocket and drops it into the magician's outstretched palm.

He accepts with a disdainful wave of his fingers, conjuring the smooth piece of technology away and wiping his palm on the sleeve of his jacket. There's a plastic bucket of water to the side of the door; liquid splashes the leg of Verity's jeans and she glances down, startled, to see the rectangle of her cell phone settling to the bottom. She considers protesting, but it's already too late, so she lets out a slow breath and turns. The closet is tight. She sets her back against the rear shelves and sees Santiago's form silhouetted against the low light of the lobby before he shuts the door behind himself. The candlelight glitters, reflected from his gaze.

"Close your eyes," he says. When Verity hesitates again, he adds, "I'm not sure we can do this if you're watching. I won't hurt you."

There's grey in his words—the future, she thinks, foggy and undefined—but nothing that stabs at Verity's skull, so she closes her eyes. It doesn't make the little room less claustrophobic. She can still see the memory-echoes of candle flames and the swirling, deeper blackness of the magician's presence. Verity breathes lilac and wonders about the snake.

Santiago takes her hand—lightly, but firmly, his skin hot and dry. The world shivers. She hears a door close behind her and wonders that she didn't hear it open. Her hand is released and she stands alone in space that feels suddenly larger, air whispering around her. She hasn't moved.

"You can open your eyes," Santiago says, but she already has. Verity blinks and sees the lights of a hundred tiny flames—candles and lanterns both, spread out before her and stretching down the aged wooden planks that line the length of a seemingly endless hall. The hallway is only about six feet across but extends well into the darkness, and when she tilts her head back, she can find no ceiling, only wood-slatted walls going up and up into shadow, covered in patches of stucco and irregular splotches of brick. There's a door in the wall behind her, tall and broad, carved of planks that are thick but cracking with age. The magician still has his hand on the knob.

Verity feels splinters in her lungs and the impossible weight of plaster and brick bisecting her flesh. In that instant, she cannot breathe; she feels gravity beating against her bones. Even as she gasps, the crush fades and she can discern only the dusty space of the hall and the impossible height above.

Santiago says, "This way." When he touches her elbow, Verity flinches; his confidence is a frosted shroud. The air is hot. The magician curls his lip and then drops his left hand to his side; the whisper of snake-Ouro slides down his leg before it ripples larger and the dog presses lightly at Verity's leg. When she touches its ruff, she finds it furred, neutral, barely solid. She only shakes her head and lets her hand rest on the shadow-beast's back when she steps forward, uncertain of the floor beneath her feet.

"What?" she asks. It takes her two tries. She has to moisten her lips. Her sense of wonder wars with the faint smells of sweat and urine that pervade the stale air. "There was only one door." Her own words are sugared lye on her tongue—indeterminate as smog.

"One and a half. This is the *between*." Santiago gestures, palm up, a broad sweep that encompasses the expanse of the shadowed hall. "The space in the walls. Or what's left of it." He turns the wave into a pointing finger, indicating the way forward. "There."

Verity blinks, and thinks that perhaps one light is different from the others—a steadier glow, whiter, like the guiding twinkle of a distant star. "There," she echoes; her fingers tighten in the dog's fur. Santiago casts her a quick glance, but he doesn't touch her as they move forward. Ouro, on the other hand, stays close.

The hall remains inconveniently narrow. *Between,* she thinks, and tries to rectify the air she breathes with the sensation of brick dust weighting her lungs. As they pick their way forward, careful in the dark, Verity sees irregular shapes resolve into bits of piled furniture: an old wooden table, a pair of chairs, a rolled-up carpet. She sneezes and thinks of corner garage sales and dusty storage units. Twice, she has to press against the wall to slide by. The dog guides her.

She registers the low hum of voices and the impression of shadows up ahead, human forms vanishing just at the edges of lantern light. The lanterns themselves are scattered—some hang from sconces, while others dangle from iron stands. They are spaced irregularly, at odd angles. Verity, Santiago, and the dog walk a straight path down the long hall, picking past piles of abandoned furniture, breathing dust, guided by guttering candles and the soft pale glow in the beckoning distance. Their footsteps make little sound—Ouro is silent, as always—and Verity swallows back the taste of desiccation and the sensation of scales drying and cracking in the back of her throat. She tugs at her scarf, pulling it looser. No one approaches them.

Eventually, they pass a set of five chairs piled haphazardly, one on top of the other, wooden legs disjointed. Beyond this makeshift blockade, an empty area seems suddenly spacious, thick candles burning on stands in a loose ring around a well-swept floor. People are standing here, clustered in little groups; Verity doesn't know what she was expecting, exactly, but they are just people. She sees jeans and t-shirts, and worn running shoes that could be her own. A boy with a spiked mohawk sits cross-legged next to an older woman whose long brown hair is in hundreds of matted braids. They are talking quietly. A bald man in a threadbare suit is reading a paperback book, squinting at the ragged pages; in the soft light cast from above, his head is pale as an egg.

A man in a familiar ball cap leans against the wall, arms folded. He is glaring at Verity, and it takes her a moment to recognize him from the convenience store. He has no gun in his hand this time. When she shivers, the dog presses closer against her leg.

Someone giggles. With a start, Verity realizes there are children in the hall; a small clay top spins into view. A young girl and a young boy are chasing it. Neither is older than four. The girl's hair is in two blonde pigtails, held with yellow ribbons. The boy's shirt sports a cartoon bear. They hold hands at the edge of the light, and their laughter paints the stillness with glittering shards.

The bright glow is just ahead, and Verity looks there last, because she suspects the brilliance may blind her. The whiteness is not as sharp as she had thought, however; it resolves into a pale boy sprawled across a short, broken-down couch in an unfortunate shade of orange and brown plaid. Its cushions are worn and misshapen.

Verity thinks the boy is dying.

He is young, but not a child; he has the gangliness of adolescence and a frame like paper stretched over wire. He wears a white shirt and blue jeans. There is light under his skin; it spills from him in a soft, steady glow that illuminates his face and hands. His eyes glitter blue, lit from within by hidden constellations that shine through the thinness of his half-lowered lids. He is looking at nothing in particular. His hands are long-fingered and loose. Behind him, dark wings spread from his shoulders, pressed awkwardly into the couch and splayed raggedly across faded cushions.

Ouro leaves Verity's side and leaps gracefully up onto the couch, nosing at the boy.

The boy is holding a beer bottle in his right hand. He lifts it out of the way without protest, then sips at it and says, "You're back." A sleepy tenor, stretched thin. "So she's the one? Hi there."

Verity feels tears, shocking and unbidden, welling in the corners of her eyes. She wants to throw herself down in front of the boy. She wants to take his hand and run her fingers through his hair. She does neither of those things—she would never; she only blinks the moisture from her lashes—but the effort trembles from her spine to the tips of her fingers.

There is a pause, during which Verity realizes that a small group of the people they've passed has assembled behind her and Santiago and the dog. Their presence is a static tingle between her shoulder blades. Their silence is reverent. She drops her gaze to the floor, and the last drift of the boy's words. "Hi," she says, uncertainly.

"Hi," repeats the boy unnecessarily. "Thanks for coming. This is all pretty weird. I didn't even know she could write."

Verity must look blank, because the boy adds to Santiago, "You didn't tell her." It's not a question, though concern brushes the edges of his tone. His white lashes lower over the glitter of his gaze, a slow blink, then lift again. The light he casts illuminates the couch cushions, limning his skeletal fingers in an even paler white. The edges of his feathers gleam a little. Nothing of his halo touches Ouroboros, who remains an enigma of solid black.

The dog lowers an ear and Santiago shrugs one shoulder. "She came with Ouro. But no, it wasn't my most convincing argument." Even the magician speaks more gently to the boy; there's deference in the set of his jaw. Verity turns her head, casting a quick look toward his face, and he quirks the corner of his lips in what might be apology. It tastes like rosemary and the warm embers of a fire. He picks up a lantern stand, holding it like a staff, and swings it to the side.

The lantern sways, casting its dim glow across the block letters that have been crudely smeared across the wall. *VERITY,* they spell, where they haven't begun to drip down in clotting rivulets. Verity had thought the smell of blood was the boy and the boy's incandescent decay; she realizes she was wrong.

"Like I said," notes the boy, not unkindly. "It's a new one on me." He takes a pull of his beer and tilts his head, studying Verity with dazed, amiable curiosity. He sits slumped. His pale hair falls tangled in his eyes; she wants, again, to brush it aside, and doesn't. When he shifts on the couch, the lines of his wings pull behind him, long shapes with strange bones beneath. "What are we doing with you, then?"

Santiago continues to stand, holding the lantern stand quite still so the light can fall against the smeared wall. Verity only knows he is looking at her because the dog turns its head to do the same, golden eyes impassive. Behind her, the small group whispers.

She divides her attention between the boy's blue eyes and the seaglass glimmer of his words, sliding along the worn floorboards. "I don't know," she says, honestly, and hears her own voice waver. "I want to ask you about this—about spaces between walls. About your wings. About a dog being a snake. But also, um … whose blood is that?"

The boy's smile is bright but sad—the last flutter of a butterfly in winter. "Jihan's. So we guessed maybe she meant it." He turns his head, then, and calls to the blackness behind him, where the hall extends well past the fall of any tiny flame. "Hey! Your friend's here."

There are no footsteps.

The lamplight glimmers first on a long, thin kitchen knife, and then on the tall figure of the woman who emerges from the shadows. At first, Verity can't tell the difference between the woman and the knife she holds; both are cold, spare, precisely honed. The woman's eyes are a purer steel, lacking the old blade's spots of rust. Her hair falls in a single grey braid down her right shoulder, but her face is unlined. Her skin is dusky, her nose aquiline and sharp, though not quite straight; it might have been broken once. She wears a pale lavender cardigan, half-buttoned and too large; a grey shirt; a pair of torn jeans. One of her sneakers is untied. She doesn't appear to care.

The boy's fingers are tight around his bottle. Verity registers the sudden silence behind her, and the way the dog has gone stiff.

She stands quite motionless, and she tries her best to look at the woman who walks like a sword, but she cannot focus past the sense of burning coals scorching her spine, or the sweep of Ouroboros as it slides down off the couch cushions and crosses the floor to return to her side. She touches the dog's head and it ignores her, crouching slightly on its front paws as it stares up at the approaching woman.

Santiago sets the lantern stand down on the floor. It makes a small scraping sound, startling in the stillness. The glowing boy drinks his beer, slouching deeper into the couch as his wings stretch and fold awkwardly across furniture that wasn't meant to fit them. He is the only one not watching the woman as she passes; he is studying Verity, and stars glitter in his eyes.

Verity says, "Hi," again, because that seems appropriate. She adds, helpfully, "I'm Verity," and she gestures toward the smears on the wall with one uncertain hand. She hears her own tone turn up a little at the end, like a question, and thinks Jacob would poke fun (can hear him ask, *Are you?*).

It occurs to her that the strange woman is very close.

The boy's wings rustle as he leans forward to set the bottle down, struggling to rise. "Hey now, what are you doing with—"

He cuts off with a gasp, and Verity would look to see why, but there's a stinging pressure above her hip and she's staring straight into a pair of blank steel eyes. The woman's irises are reflective as a cracked mirror. Verity sees her own face pale and shocked, a thousand times repeated. In the broken gaps she sees something more, something cavernous and desperate, and for that yawning chasm, she has no words.

Jihan, she thinks. And, *She's afraid most of all.*

Fire twists in her gut; her hands close reflexively around the woman's, just where Jihan still grips the hilt of the knife that has slid seamlessly into the flesh between Verity's lowest ribs. She feels smooth skin, iron fingers, and the sticky heat of her own blood. She is frozen. Jihan's expression is stone.

They do not breathe.

Time resumes. Someone is yelling.

"It's okay," says Verity softly—she doesn't know why, but it doesn't feel like a lie. "It's just a knife." She doesn't know why she says that, either.

Jihan's grey brows twitch together in the moment before she steps back. Verity's hands clench around the knife's wooden hilt, and Jihan turns away, her smooth braid draping down like a whip as she walks soundlessly back into the dark.

Verity wonders if this blade in her organs should hurt more, but abruptly it does. She tries to gulp a breath and chokes on blood. The blood tastes of copper and salt but rings in her ears like a gong, and she cannot see at all because her late-flowering fear is blooming like poppies, red petals around the lantern lights.

She would fall, but there are arms around her—the scent of coal and lilac. It's a garden in a mine shaft.

She thinks Santiago is swearing.

The boy is there, then, mouthing something she can't hear; his eyes are a furious sapphire. The light that shines from within him turns his flesh to something alien and glows incandescent through the thin white fabric of his shirt. At his shoulders, the black wings spread slow and broad to block the light.

He is perfect. Verity would be stunned if she were not trying very hard to live.

The angel touches her, and the world goes white.

[**IMAGE:** Jihan and Verity, in the dark. They are close together, each leaning into the other, and Jihan is driving a knife between Verity's lower ribs. Verity is shocked. Jihan is expressionless. They are staring into each other's eyes.]

youre leaving it there?

Why?

its a ~~break stop~~ cliffhanger but i didnt die, anyone reading knows i didnt die its obvious from the way you started

It seemed like an appropriately dramatic break.

you should finish

All right, but I know part of it's not accurate, because you've never said.

none of its right the more you add the harder it is to read, words on words

What did you see when she looked at you?

~~fear hope a vicious sorrow nothing~~
~~everything~~
sous ratûre

You are a very irritating person.

Verity doesn't die.

She expects to; there is a long period where she loses track of time. The boy's palm rests just in the hollow beneath her throat, and his touch is effervescent—a light that brings with it a soothing warmth that goes beyond the flesh. He makes Verity think of safety and home and the feeling she gets when she wakes in the night and can hear Jacob breathing beside her. The boy is sunbeams; he is the scent and taste of honey, and each of these sensations is simple and perfectly pure.

He says things, but Verity doesn't remember later what they were. She remembers that his smile was broken and sweet. He crouches with his hand on her skin and his wings spread wide, sheltering them both in a cloak of jagged feathers. Some of the feathers are snapped short, or crooked; Verity is very close, so she looks at those wings for a long while. They are not completely black; they shine green and purple in the light, a sheen like oil or the feathers of a mallard duck. They flex as the boy keeps his balance.

He knits things back together inside her using nothing but his fingertips at the base of her throat, his glow spilling quiet joy. She only lies there, basking, while time passes and feathers spread for her amusement.

When he lifts his hand away, she could weep.

He leaves her with an indescribable clarity. Verity and the boy look at each other, and she sees the lights die in his eyes, leaving a colour like the night sky just past the horizon. The absence of his touch leaves her chilled, and she reaches for him, but he is already folding, dark wings and pale arms crumpling like crushed origami.

Over his shoulder, she sees the steel cold eyes of the woman Jihan, and Jihan's arms—sleeved in lumpy violet yarn—wrap around the boy's chest, a trap snapping shut from behind. For an instant, Verity expects the other woman will drag the boy away as though she is a cat with a toy or a dead mouse, but Jihan lifts him carefully enough, for all that her face is an empty mirror. The boy is slack, his eyes unseeing, when the woman carries him into the darkness. She doesn't turn her back. The last Verity sees is the gleam of her dispassionate gaze.

Verity takes a breath, and the last touch of the boy's purity has left her wonderfully, precisely at peace. It is the first time in her life that the world is not shouting at her; it takes her a moment to adjust to stillness as clear as a raindrop. She props herself on her elbows and knows without turning that there are exactly nine people clustered at the edges of the light behind her—she knows that the light *is* light, without any muddle of sound or taste, and she knows that the two children from before are huddled and frightened.

She is between walls. It is and is not possible.

She lies with her shirt covered in blood and no gash in her skin. The world around her hangs in perfect balance.

She reaches one hand to the side and buries her fingers in the dog's fur.

"Sorry about that," says Santiago. He is sitting on Ouro's other side, his elbow crooked around his upraised knee. Verity doesn't quite look at him; she savours her peace while she has it. She touches her free hand to her sticky, stiff shirt, and wiggles the fingers through the gash in the torn cotton.

"She would have killed me," she says. She is enchanted by the easy simplicity of her own voice.

"Apparently."

"Why?"

Frustration marks the line of Santiago's shoulders and the way he gestures—sharply, palm up. Verity suspects the stains on his hands would be blood in better lighting. "Who knows? Like the kid said, we didn't even know she could write."

"Will he be okay?"

"She won't hurt him."

Something vibrates in his tone, a hint of crimson that creeps back into the world as the first of the boy's perfection fades. It makes Verity sigh. "There are different kinds of hurt," she says. She realizes her hand is still resting on the dog, and takes it back, adding, "Sorry." Ouro's ears perk forward, yellow eyes watching.

Verity stands, and Santiago moves with her. The small crowd behind has melted away by the time she turns, though she catches the glitter of a child's gaze by lamplight. "My jacket," she says, but the magician is shaking his head.

"It's a mess."

"Oh." Verity folds her arms, gripping her elbows, and she looks at the floor, where the spreading stain of her own life has dried now. The world is still mostly clear, and without echoes in her ears or on her skin she can trace the edges of each smear that has soaked into the scuffed wood.

She should say something—*what* or *how* or even *how long*—but 'why' and 'where' have accomplished very little, and there are traces of vibrant fog creeping back at the edges of her senses. She closes her eyes instead.

Santiago says, "Are you okay?"

"Yes," answers Verity, with wonder and regret. "But it won't last." Even the sound of her own words is new to her—without colour, not scraping at the inside of her throat. She rubs her palm across the back of her neck, feeling the brush of her hair.

"I'll take you home." Santiago's tone is cool, though Verity thinks there's a hint of apology there. She feels the dog nudge against her thigh.

When she looks at the hall again, she sees lamplight and the empty couch. The boy's abandoned bottle is sitting on the floor.

Verity is awash in understanding—things that are and are not, things that can and cannot be. She can't see into the darkness, but she knows the hall stretches a long way before it turns at a near-perfect ninety-degree angle inside the wall of the old theatre. She knows that the same happens behind. "*Between*," Verity breathes.

The magician says only, "Yes."

Verity faces the spot on the wall where her name is still written in dripping gore. She frowns at the bare slats of wood; the light behind casts her own shadow in front of her. There is no matching outline for Santiago, though he isn't far from her left shoulder, but the shape of Ouroboros slides and winks on the wall. Verity shakes her head, then turns and walks back down the hall the way they first came. There are few figures to mark her passage; most have melted away, somewhere in the distance of the narrow space. The clay top lies abandoned on the floor. Verity steps carefully past it. She thinks she hears a child laughing somewhere behind her, but she walks only with the magician and the dog, and her path is lit by irregularly placed candles and the occasional mismatched sconce.

When Santiago would say something, Verity only murmurs, "Not yet." She barely keeps herself from begging. The hall is long and Santiago remains silent, though the dog brushes against her.

Finally, she reaches the door and stands before it. It has the look of a farmhouse door: broad wooden boards streaked with worn red paint, warm and incongruous in the dimness of the strange space. Verity touches two fingertips to a smooth knot in the wood, then shakes her head and shifts her index finger an inch and a half to the left, gripping the brass knob. "Here," she asks, but it isn't really a question. In the act of opening the door, she finds she has already slipped through. She has and has not moved.

There is a space there that she cannot describe. She knows there is a door in the wall. She knows also that the wall is solid, a mass of drywall and wood, wires and insulation. *Things that are and are not*, she thinks, and *the dog is a snake*.

When the world re-aligns, she stands in the dingy closet, only shelving behind her. Glowing candles illuminate the bucket of water where her cell phone drowned. The air is too close; Verity shoves at the door, finds it unlocked, and strides through the lobby. She suddenly wants nothing more than to be outside.

The glass doors are unlocked too, crusted with the whisper of paper flyers. Outside, it's night, and the air is chilled; Verity stops on the sidewalk. She has no jacket and no scarf, and her torn shirt is covered in crusting blood. She measures the black sky against the clotted stickiness of her buttons, and wonders what time it is. She has the fleeting impression of half a breath, or a star's lifetime.

A moment later, Santiago stands beside her. At first, she thinks Ouroboros has vanished, but in the glow of the nearest streetlight, the puddle of darkness at the magician's feet blinks golden eyes at her before settling into a perfect mimic, like any other shadow.

The magician settles his coat over her shoulders. The leather of his jacket is cracked, but warm and heavy. "You're going to get us arrested."

"Sorry." Verity is looking at the ground, where the length of her shadow crosses Santiago's boots, mingling with Ouro. She looks up and, briefly, meets the magician's gaze—directly, steadily. There are no streaks or sounds to distract her.

She thinks of the woman Jihan, with her steel hair and her eyes like mirrors of hell, and she wonders if the magician's secrets will be the same. She is curious, but in that moment, not afraid.

Santiago's dark illusion plays at his feet but his eyes are real enough—startled, irritated, with unexpected hints of auburn in their depths.

Verity meets Santiago's gaze and sees him falter.

"The boy made everything clear," she comments. "It won't last. But I've never—I see, now. You can't really be yourself out here."

The magician makes a choked, startled sound, but Verity is not looking anymore. She extends her hand again to touch the wall, where the theatre's old brick has been spray painted with a slash of bright but now-fading yellow. She adds, with puzzled certainty, "There are twelve thousand, three hundred and forty-five bricks in this building." And, "It's very quiet."

There are questions she should ask, but the city is crisp and still for the first time in her life, and she can feel the clean lines of her senses slipping from her with each word. So when Santiago might say something, Verity only shakes her head. Pulling the old leather jacket closed over the mess of her shirt, she walks slowly toward home.

"Tell all the Truth but tell it slant." –Emily Dickinson

7

Consider Jacob.

Imagine that he doesn't know where he fits or what he wants to do with his life. Imagine the only constant in his world seldom makes eye contact, seldom laughs, never says she loves him. She twitches; she reaches for things he can't see, steps around empty air, tells him there are hippogriffs in the canal and the dog down the street has six tails.

She holds him in the night; she listens to every word he says and tries everything he asks. She brings him soup when he's sick and coffee when he's tired. She keeps all his secrets. She has only ever asked him not to lie to her.

Imagine she comes home with an ocean of blood dried all down the front of her torn shirt. The buttons give way when he rips and he demands to know if she's okay and what happened. She isn't hurt. Her skin is smooth and he checks fifty times with his hands, then fifty-one, but she just stands there. All she'll tell him is that she found out tonight that she doesn't want to die. She sounds surprised about that, maybe a little pleased. His heart drops through the bottoms of his shoes and he grips her arms like she won't be real but she is, and she's smiling but she's looking at something that is maybe just over his left shoulder.

"Will you use the internet for me?" she asks.

She doesn't like the internet.

He wants to say what the fuck, Vee *or maybe* what happened again *or maybe even* no, *because her skin is stained red and now so are his hands. His palms are sticky with someone's blood.*

He says, "What do you need?" like it's normal, and he's kind of proud of how he isn't panicking right now. She touches his hand.

"The Between," she says. "I think it's a band."
Consider how Jacob feels at that moment. Even if this isn't about him.

COLIN

The story of the boy with the fractured smile starts before he was born.

His mother was an artist who lived in a commune in southern California. She inhabited a small tent at the edge of a forest, in a row of other small tents, close enough to the trees to hear each leaf rustle. She sold paintings to tourists; she read books and played music and enjoyed the sun on her skin. She avoided plastic and processed food and neoliberal capitalist systems. She didn't have a television. She didn't intend to have children.

She knew the exact day her son was conceived. It was May Day, and there was a great pole, wound round with ribbons, erected in the centre of the clearing in front of the little tent village. Someone had arranged for a busload of tourists to come through. Colin's mother—her name was Sarah—sold three watercolour landscapes and counted it a good day, then she lay in the grass and drank wine until the music started. A friend took her hand and coaxed her to dance around the maypole. She danced with a young man who drew her picture in the dirt with a sweep of his toe. She danced with a woman whose long red hair was the same shade as her own. And finally, she danced with a man who had the bluest eyes she'd ever seen, which was the only thing she ever said about him, later.

Blue eyes, she would tell young Colin, when he was a child at her knee. *Like the sky, like the sea, like yours. And he laughed like violin strings in the wind.* Colin always wanted to hear more, but that was when his mother's attention would drift elsewhere, and she would shiver.

The eyes were what she remembered best, but she thought the man had been beautiful. His skin was tanned; his hair was thick; the bones of him were lean and strong, and when he pulled her—laughing—toward the forest, many of the gazes that followed were jealous and knowing.

He took her into the trees and laid her down on a bed of moss. He whispered in her ear, and she wasn't sure of the language, but she knew it must be poetry somewhere. She laughed up at him and the light came through the branches and made a halo of his hair.

She remembered the quick flash of his teeth. "Living in tents. Do you people even know who you are?" She remembered the moment when she stiffened, afraid.

"It's okay," he told her. "I'm going to make an angel." (*He was sad*, she said years later, puzzled. *But laughing. He held me like I was a trophy, or a jewel, but I think, my darling, he meant that for you.*)

She didn't remember the rest of it; she only knew, she said, that the man whispered, "His name is Icarus." Then all her world went light.

She woke alone under waving tree branches, with dead leaves stuck to her skin and mosquito bites studding her reddened flesh. Her friends were calling her name.

It was two months before she felt the first stirrings inside, but she spread her palm across her bare stomach, there in the dirt on the forest floor, and she knew. (Or so she claimed later. At any rate, Colin liked that part of the story. He was less fond of the way his mother's hands shook when she told it.)

She took vitamins; she stopped drinking coffee. At first, she went to the doctor, but the doctor drew her blood and made her pee on a stick and then shook his head sadly. She went away with her hand cupped over her abdomen, her hair a little wild and her knees quivering.

"I'm pregnant," she whispered to her friend Véronique, who lived in the tent next door and who made some small living as a midwife. Véronique laid her hand on Sarah's flat stomach and frowned, but she brought Sarah flowers and little packets of tea.

At three months, Sarah could feel a swelling in her gut but her body was soft and lean as a prairie field. She went to the doctor again, and a man in plain nurse scrubs ran a wand over her belly. She thought she could see an oscillating image on the screen, some strange jellybean shape, but then the speakers squealed like a dying drum and the monitor faded to static. Calibration issues, the nurse told her, and he pecked at keys, but then he shook his head and sent her away once more.

Her stomach hurt. She didn't go back.

She retreated to her little tarpaulin home by the trees. She tended her garden and worked on her art. By six months, she was awkward, unbalanced by the hot weight she could feel nestled just under her ribs, kicking at her and turning restlessly beneath her palm—but her clothing still fit, and though she twisted and turned in front of her small mirror, she could see no bulge. "I'm pregnant," she told Véronique again. "The baby has hiccups. It's been driving me nuts all morning." Véronique brought her a posset for her trim belly.

The colours in Sarah's work grew wild and bright. She made wide slashes across the canvas. She sold a lot of paintings. She put the money into a college fund.

Véronique was a midwife again—for Sarah, on a chill winter's afternoon when the sun's light glared white and frost threatened at the edges of the forest. The entire affair was surprisingly painless, at least for the mother, who insisted afterward that she'd felt nothing but a butterfly flutter within, even when her still-slender flesh tore at the awkward, forceful passage of her young son's sharp body. He came into the world already breathless, tiny lungs labouring, tiny eyes squinched shut.

He had ten fingers and ten toes and two wings, curled tight and small to his shoulders like the plucked wings of a chicken. When his mother's panting exertions finally thrust him into the midwife's waiting hands, he came with one leg twisted, caught somewhere in the walls of the birth canal against an unforgiving pelvic bone. His skin was translucent, stretched over blue veins; he weighed almost nothing. *Like a sunbeam,* Véronique said later, her voice soft and her worn eyes suddenly dreamy. *Like a feather made of light.*

Véronique had no time to exclaim over impossible babies with curling wings, not with the boy's knee wrenched at such a sharp angle to the left and his skin going blue beneath his coating of blood and slime. She whispered a prayer to private gods and rubbed the child sharply down until he finally squalled, then she put his blanket-wrapped body in his mother's waiting arms and looked about for something to make a splint.

"His name is Colin," said Sarah, her fingertips gentle on the faded wool of the blanket, "after my grandfather." In her head, she heard *Icarus* and *I'm going to make an angel.* She bit her lip against the sudden, fearful taste of rebellion. She held the tiny bundle in her hands, and for a brief moment, she wanted very much to scream, or to laugh, or possibly both, but the baby opened his eyes just then and she was lost in a blue deeper than the sky.

Véronique said, "We should call an ambulance," because there was too much blood on the sheets and the little boy was too small and his bones weren't set right. There were limits to what she could do, there in a flapping tent at the edge of the trees.

"We can't." Sarah stuck her finger into the swaddle of blanket at the baby's shoulder, wriggling it into the space between soft folds and softer skin. The baby was sticky with the remnants of his birthing gore, and still felt like a whisper of springtime. She stroked, wonderingly, at the frail bone of his wing, featherless as a new-hatched bird's. "And we can't stay here."

She thought of the hospital, and scalpels, and the cold severity of needles and microscopes. She looked up to search the round nutmeg face of Véronique, who was her friend, and sometimes more.

Véronique was the one who tucked them into a rattling station wagon and drove them away in the night, Sarah bleeding and the tiny bundle of life gasping in her arms.

That was how Colin Icarus Warner came to grow up in a small house on a cliff's edge between the ocean and the woods, watched by two doting mothers, as far from tour buses and vacationing photographers as could possibly be arranged. He was a sweet baby; he never cried. At first, Véronique thought something was wrong with him, but she poked and prodded and studied, and eventually had to shrug, "I think he doesn't like to bother us." She smiled when she said it, though, and tiny white fingers were wrapped around her hand.

It wasn't easy having a child who never cried. They didn't know if he was hungry, or tired, or in need of changing. Sometimes Sarah would feel the wrench of memory tearing at the flesh inside her; after the baby, she was tired. She ached. She bled and never quite stopped bleeding. Still, she held her son and warmth suffused her; he would smile, and reach for her necklace, or the flower in her hair.

They waited for him to perform miracles. But Colin grew like any other baby, save that black feathers sprouted from his wings—downy at first, but inky and smooth by the time he could gurgle his first words. "Mama," he cooed, and the feathers at his shoulders glimmered with hints of greens and purples and blues in the light, like the sheen of gasoline on water. He was a pale, fragile child. His eyes stayed a deep, innocent blue, the shade of a newborn babe's, unchanged with the passage of time.

Sarah would lie at night with her back pressed to Véronique's, her womb aching inside her. She knew the stranger in the forest had torn something open, had planted his parasite where her life used to be. Still, when she couldn't stop shaking, she would get up and lift her angel child from his crib; he would smile the sweetest smile, and when she took him back to bed, he would snuggle into her shoulder and she would know he felt the warm glow of the connection between them. They would be soothed and safe.

"Do you think he'll fly?" asked Véronique idly one morning, when Colin was doing his very best to stand, his wings spread and his hands latched onto the edge of the kitchen chair. His leg, twisted at birth, remained so, the left foot curving in and the muscles withered. For the first few years of his life, he would pull himself along the floor or hop in a sort of tripod crawl, wings flapping like a wounded bird. He never complained. When he was a little more than two, he found a worn branch at the edge of the woods and used it as a crutch.

On the days when she wasn't too tired, Sarah taught him colour and laughter and history and math. Véronique buried her hands in the garden and taught him herbs and poetry and a little French, the rough Québecois of her homeland. They both taught him to hide from strangers, and to wear a big coat, so he could tuck his wings away on any rare moment when a car might wander up the unpaved road from town. Véronique made the first coat when he was three, and bigger ones as he grew; they were patchwork and ragged, but he knew the drill. An unexpected car, a hunter, a tourist, a family at the beach—Sarah lived in dread, imagining betrayal from every passing plane.

"But *why*?" asked her son, when he was old enough to ask. The childish exasperation in his tone was the closest he ever got to complaining.

"Because you're different," she said. "Because they wouldn't understand." She eyed the sailboat bobbing in the offshore distance. "Go!"

So Colin threw the coat over the folds of his wings and fled limping for the trees, where he would hide with his breath panting warmly and ants crawling across his sweaty skin.

Why was his favourite word. Scientists, he was told, and circuses. Sarah spoke of petri dishes and Véronique of microscopes; when little Colin woke crying, though, he said he dreamed of being caught in a birdcage, trapped behind unforgiving bars. He burrowed into Sarah's shoulder and clung there, tears soaking her chemise.

Colin was a sickly child; his fair skin blistered in the sun. When he was five, Sarah would watch as he limped his way over the grass and down the rocks to the shoreline; he spread his wings for balance at the ocean's edge, and beat them as hard as he could, but the waves washed cold over his bare feet and he only staggered in the wind.

When he was six years old, he managed to climb the gnarled oak on the bluff by the south side of the house and teeter along the widest branch, just above the fence and overhanging the surf below, arms and scraggly wings outstretched. Sarah, at the edge of the garden, had an easel in front of her, and her fingers were smeared with paint. She looked up too late, just in time to see her son balanced fearless there in the sunshine and the scattered shadows of the leaves overhead. He sucked in a great lungful of air and spread his wings as far as he could, until the very tips brushed the twigs a foot past his fingertips. Then he leapt into the sunlight.

For one glorious moment, he was free. His wings beat the air once, twice—he soared.

That was the instant before he fluttered awkwardly, fell ten feet in a down draft, then twenty more, then floated to the left and up, flapping desperately, just before he smashed directly into the boulders by the surf and broke his left wrist.

Sarah screamed.

Véronique was the one who bound him up, bustling, muttering imprecations under her breath. She was a large woman, soft, her hair in heavy braids and her hands gentler than her words. Sarah never saw her so angry as that day, when Colin came with silent tears rolling and his cracked arm cradled in his opposite hand.

"Did you think?" Véronique asked him roughly. "You are not a bird! Did you *think*? You could have died. You could have—we can't take you to the hospital." She broke the broom handle over her knee with a single, violent motion, and then again, so she could bind the pieces into a splint. "They'll see you. They'll take you away."

"But—" protested the boy, biting his lip.

Véronique snapped, "Stop that." She bound his wrist with stained cotton and wood—she pulled it tight, once, aligning the bone, and he shrieked without making a sound. That was the day they knew he really couldn't fly. He was a little boy with tears on his cheeks and snot on his upper lip. Sarah wrapped her arms around him and he burrowed close against her; where his cheek brushed her neck, she felt the golden joy of their contact, and heard him sigh.

"It's okay, baby," she told him. "You're okay."

He was a happy enough child; the birds in the woods were his friends, and the squirrels and rats and centipedes would come writhing to his touch. He had books and paints and two women who made sure he was safe and warm and fed. He played by the sea and under the shade of the trees, and if occasionally he watched longingly as some strange family picnicked in the distance, such moments weren't enough to trouble him.

He performed his first miracle when he was seven. "Mama," he said, "this bird is sick." He was standing in the kitchen doorway, one hand on a rough stick he'd brought from the woods. His other hand was cupped around a yellow-black ball of fluff.

Sarah looked up from the curtain she was inexpertly mending. "Put it outside. It could be diseased."

She saw him flinch. The guilt stabbing through her made her kinder when she added, "You don't want to get a fever again."

"She isn't that kind of sick," said Colin, with a flash of little-boy stubbornness. His lower lip jutted. He curled his fingers carefully, stroking the edge of a tiny beak. "She has a lump inside."

"Let me see." Sarah rose, walked over and peered down at the tiny bird nestled in Colin's hand. Maybe it was a little misshapen, or a little too round. Certainly its eyes were dull and its beak opened and shut, opened and shut, as though it were panting. "Maybe we can find it a box."

Her son's face was the picture of quiet agony. She would have done anything to soothe him. All she could do was reach for the bird, but Colin pulled his hand away, cupping the little creature close to his own thin chest. "No. I can fix her."

Something flared bright in the depths of his eyes. Sarah took her hand back.

Colin turned around and limped back through the open doorway, moving three steps into the garden. Then he tossed the little bird gently into the air, and it flew away.

The boy staggered slightly, or perhaps his crutch slid in the loose soil, but he laughed.

That was it; that was the miracle, or at least the first one Sarah noticed. She started to see it, after that: the fox kit scratched by barbed wire, the seagull with the broken leg, the frogs and robins and centipedes.

"Have you noticed the animals?" she asked Véronique, and Véronique chuckled.

"Oh, yes. I think bees wouldn't sting him. I asked him to keep the aphids out of the garden, but he said it didn't work that way."

"What way?"

"He says they don't talk." Véronique shrugged her shoulders. She was peeling carrots at the sink, tossing the long dirty skins into a colander. "Or he doesn't talk to them. I don't know, *cherie*. Maybe he's an angel after all."

"Hm," said Sarah. She peered out the window to where her son stood out on the bluff, an ungainly shape with his blanket-scrap coat too large over his wings and his weight leaning on the old branch. For a moment, she had the panicked thought he might jump again, but he was standing quite still, a score of yellow butterflies darting around him. His face was upturned to the sun.

A month later, he brought home an ancient squirrel. It was grey and mangy; its tail had been broken once and hadn't healed straight. "Just like me," said Colin, pleased. "Kind of." He fed it nuts and seeds and bits of his sandwich. He didn't often name the animals, but this one was 'Methuselah.' It seemed to Sarah that Methuselah was mostly leather stretched over bone, with odd spots of rough fur and long, yellowed teeth.

"Fleas," said Sarah, dubiously, but Colin chirped, "None!" and that was the end of that.

Like all living things, it seemed, Methuselah was happiest in the presence of a little boy with ragged dark feathers cresting at his shoulders. But when Colin went in the woods, Methuselah liked to stay around the cottage. She would perch at the top of Sarah's easel, nibbling at a seed; she would scramble up Véronique's back, stealing bits of vegetable from the kitchen counter. They got used to scritching the squirrel behind her ears. Véronique called her "old lady," and the squirrel's fur was maybe not so ratty after all.

Sometimes, if Sarah took a nap in the afternoons, the squirrel would come and sleep curled in the curve of her neck, and Sarah would wake to the scent of fur and forest. She got used to stretching out her hand at odd intervals and having a warm little head nudged into her palm.

"Squirrels don't act like that," noted Véronique, more amused than anything.

"Hush," said Sarah. "We're friends."

Still, it was Colin's squirrel, and he would hobble around the cottage with the skinny grey ghost on his shoulders.

Methuselah stayed for months—a constant amid Colin's parade of temporary pets and wounded creatures. Then Colin got sick again.

At first, it was the usual: he would stagger a little when he got up in the morning and the squirrel jumped from the crook of his arm to land in the tangle of blankets on his bed. "You okay, honey?" asked Sarah, and Colin shrugged.

After another week, his appetite failed. He would never eat much— and never meat—but now he picked listlessly at his salads. He fed the nuts to Methuselah, which kept the squirrel lurking, skeletal and ever-hopeful, at the edge of the kitchen table.

Colin lay on his cot for a week, the fever blooming in red flushes and wet streaks across his skin. Sarah and Véronique took turns laying cool cloths across his forehead. Methuselah clambered up and down the wall, cavorting like a young thing.

"What's a baby squirrel called?" Sarah wondered aloud.

Colin muttered, "Kit," and tossed his blanket off.

Sarah sat with her elbows on the armrests of her chair and her chin planted firmly in her hands. She stared at her sick son and silently counted every breath, every clench of his bony fingers. When the cloth on his forehead grew too warm and dry, she would reach for a fresh one on the table, then dip it in the bucket at her feet and wring it out. She switched cloths and touched her fingertips to her son's hair, still pale and baby-fine. It was not quite blond—it was translucent, rather, like an old man's.

"You'll be better soon, baby," she told him, because that was how it always worked. When she touched him, she felt golden reassurance bloom. She looked at her son and was satisfied and safe.

She was startled when Methuselah scrabbled wildly at the wall and then fell, tumbling down to roll across Colin's pyjama-clad chest. The little squirrel—ugly at the best of times—looked suddenly even more fossilized than usual, beady eyes glazed. She twitched stiffly, narrow claws scratching.

"Oh dear," said Sarah. "Not there."

She reached forward, thinking regretfully that the squirrel was very old, after all, and perhaps she could hold Methuselah through the last moments (and, more importantly, perhaps her son's wayward pet should not expire in his bed).

She saw it then: the way her son's eyelids lifted and the flare of light in his irises when he shuddered, raising a hand to rest his palm on the squirrel's knobby vertebrae. His pupils were pinpricks.

Methuselah writhed to life, suddenly energized, and ran across Colin's chest, then up the wall and onto the kitchen table.

Colin stopped breathing.

At least, Sarah thought so—she was frozen, a half-second's dismay before her boy was coughing and choking, his breath coming in loud whoops that had her rushing for a bowl to catch the watery stream of his vomit.

She was lost for a little while in the immediacy of his need. When he slept, though, she pulled the blanket back into place and sat with her hands in her lap, smoothing her palms over the wrinkles of her skirt. Methuselah darted across the floor and clambered up the back of the chair, nuzzling at Sarah's shoulder.

Sarah scratched the little head gently, three times. She stood and went to the kitchen nook, where she shook four unshelled peanuts from a jar onto the counter. The squirrel ran down her arm and sat snacking, yellowed teeth gnawing and mangy tail perked.

"Go on," said Sarah. She thought about it, and then she dumped the rest of the jar out, sending nuts rolling as Methuselah hopped and scrambled and whirled. When all of the food was gone and the squirrel's stomach and cheeks were firm and round, Sarah picked Methuselah up in one hand and walked outside, blinking in the sunlight. She looked, but didn't see Véronique—only the gulls over the ocean waves, and the yellow waving flowers in the garden.

Sarah held the squirrel against her chest and picked her way across the grass and down the rocky bluff to the sea. She stood at the edge of the water with the salt wind tossing her hair; she cradled the squirrel's frail body in her left hand and stroked, gently, with the right. She could feel the creature's ribs, thin as toothpicks, and the throbbing heartbeat just beneath the tattered old fur. Methuselah nestled trustingly in the hollow of Sarah's collarbone.

Sarah thought about her son and the light in his eyes.

She walked three steps into the ocean, to where the sharp chill of the water hit her knees and soaked the hem of her skirt. Then she tightened her grip on the squirrel—made sure it was firm—and felt Methuselah stiffen, squirming suddenly in the moment before Sarah plunged the tiny body into the sea.

She held the squirrel under for a long time. When she straightened, hands empty, her wrists were scratched with red lines. She left Methuselah floating for the gulls.

Colin's fever broke that night. The next morning, he wondered about his pet, and Véronique searched at the edges of the forest, calling.

"Squirrels aren't meant to be pets," Sarah told Colin. She felt a stab of guilt as her boy sighed, and then she shoved the feeling down, watching him eat a bowl of muesli and sliced banana. She fancied she could see a faint flush of pink creeping back to his cheeks.

After that, she was careful about the animals that Colin brought home. The ones that were too old or too broken—the ones with the growths or the pus-filled eyes—were shooed out the door while he slept. Some met quietly bloodier ends. Sarah grew hard about it; she watched her child, and her eyes were chill with resolve.

He was healthier after that.

He still wondered *why* he was different and *why* he had to hide (and why the sky was blue and water was wet and birds could fly, but not he). That was when Sarah sat him down and told him about angels.

The boy was not entirely sure what to make of the whole thing. "But *why*," he asked again.

"Well," said Sarah, "angels talk to God."

"You don't believe in God."

"That's true." Sarah pressed her fingers to her lips, and inhaled slowly, waiting for the pain in her gut to subside. Colin rested his thin fingers on her leg, and it did. "I don't know what to believe," she said, honestly. "Do you hear God? Does He—She—talk to you?"

Colin thought about that. "I hear your heart," he said, finally. "And the ocean. This morning I heard two foxes fighting over a bone. Was my father God?"

"I hope not."

"Why?"

"Because he was a—" Here, Sarah stopped, biting her lip against words she knew would only hurt the little boy at her knee. "Man," she said instead. She never cried anymore, thinking of the stranger in the forest, but there were times when she would cough, deep and wet. The blue-eyed monster had left her a wound that wouldn't heal.

He had left her a son that wouldn't heal as well, she reminded herself, and she covered her son's small hand with her own when she saw him wince. His skin always felt like sunshine.

"You're bleeding again," he said.

Startled, she looked down, spreading her legs as she poked at her skirt. The pale green fabric was almost worn through, and touched with the rusty ghosts of old stains. Her alarm gave way to equanimity. "No. It's all right."

"You will be bleeding," asserted the child, gravely. "It's okay. Hold still."

Sarah felt warmth rush through her—the pleasure she always felt at her strange child's touch. She smiled down at him and he smiled back, his little face trusting. In the blue depths of his eyes, she saw the faintest hint of starlight. "Your heartbeat is normal," he said. An instant later, he frowned as she froze.

"Honey?"

"Hold still." He was a little boy in a quilted green coat, with stains on the hem and a ragged patch of fuchsia on the shoulder where Véronique had last mended it with a dishrag from the kitchen. The sleeves were slightly too short and his knobby wrists stuck out at the cuffs. "I'm helping," he told Sarah earnestly.

He turned his palm up, curling his fingers around hers. His touch spread pleasure through her, but for the first time, it couldn't soften the ice that stabbed through. Sarah stared down at her strange angel child; she rested her free hand atop his head and felt the delicate bone of his scalp beneath the feathered strands of his hair. "Honey," she said again, and watched the light in his eyes flare before his lashes fluttered.

"It's okay," he said. "I stopped it." And, "Mommy, I'm tired."

She knew the signs well by then: the abrupt pallor of his already-pale skin, the tremble in his fingers, the way his breath hummed in the back of his throat as though each lungful were an almost-stifled cry. "Sure," she said. "Nap time, okay?"

Sarah freed her hand—any room was colder without her little boy's touch—and then she leaned down and scooped her baby up, cautious of the wings she knew were folded close against his shoulders. He weighed almost nothing, a frail body tucked into her arms; she picked up his walking stick in her other hand and carried him to his cot in the corner of the room, where the blankets and pillows were piled high and coloured brightly. She set down the stick and laid the boy down more carefully, tugging a blanket over him. He was already closing his eyes.

"Do you do that often?" she asked, though the answer was already a stone in her gut. "For me, I mean. When it bleeds." She kept her voice low, so as not to alarm her boy; she tucked another pillow beneath his head.

"Sometimes," he mumbled. "So it won't get worse." He frowned, his fluttering lids paper-thin. "But it gets worse."

"It's okay, baby." Sarah sat quietly until Colin slept, then she rose and smoothed her palms on the wrinkles of her skirt. She plucked her favourite orange shawl from the back of the chair and wrapped it around her shoulders, but felt no warmer. She walked outside, fingering the ragged tassels of silk. She strolled past the garden, past the oak tree, up the hill, to the highest point of the bluff, and stared out at the blue expanse of the sea below, where the seagulls were white specks dancing. When the sun was too bright in her eyes and the wind too sharp, she half-turned, one hand keeping the hair from her face as she looked back at the cottage. She could see Véronique's sturdy shoulders and the back of her grey-black hair as she knelt, weeding busily in the neatly kept garden.

Sarah looked at the cottage window for a long time, but all she saw were the curtains waving. She reached a hand into her skirt pocket and touched the feather she kept there.

She felt strong. She could breathe. The ache in her gut was a shadow of memory.

She thought about vanishing into the trees.

She thought about a life long and empty, without black feathers or blue eyes or the opiate warmth of a child's small hand.

She smiled, then, at the kitchen window and the boy she knew lay sleeping beyond. She smiled at Véronique's curved back and the memory of a velvet-rough voice. Then, without a word, she gathered an end of the shawl in each hand, spread her arms, and leapt.

She was flying.

The last thing she saw was the sea.

8

The Between
From IKD, the Internet Knowledge Database
This article is about the band. For the contraceptive device, click here.
{{Editorial note: Portions of this article need citation. Some assertions are in dispute.}}

The Between is the name of an indie rock band that tours in locations worldwide. While their discography is extensive, copies of their albums are rare even among collectors, and it is rumoured that pressings of their earliest releases number less than 100. Footage of their performances is equally rare, and aficionados are warned that files claiming to be MP3s or videos of The Between are frequently disguises for malware, trojans, and other viruses. {{Please provide a verified example of an existing album copy.}}

Reports conflict as to whether the band is from Norway, the United States, or Canada, or whether it has five members or four. A 2009 feature in *Rolling Stone* suggested the group was all-female, but the drummer and lead guitarist are known to be male. {{Please link to article.}}

Some people claim there is no band, or that there are multiple bands, and the entire thing is some weird piece of performance art. Those people are just disgruntled hipsters.

{{Citation needed.}}

Discography: *Matador* (1979), *Sharpshooter* (1988), *Walls* (2001), *Terminal* (2010). Track listings unavailable. {{Please update this information.}}

OCTOBER

Verity sits on the couch with a blanket over her shoulders. She isn't cold, but she holds the soft edges of the fleece because it will make Jacob feel better. Jacob is sitting in an armchair three feet away, staring at her, his hands twisting in his lap. He hasn't touched her since he brought her a clean shirt and tucked the blanket over her. She has a headache.

"I don't understand," he says, carefully, "what you're trying to tell me." She knows he thinks he is being patient. His words send citrus streaks down her vision. She shakes her head and the streaks go flying in droplets only she can see, so she squeezes her eyes shut and presses her palms against her closed lids.

"Between the walls of the old theatre. A woman stabbed me." She's been saying the same thing for hours.

"I don't—"

"I don't know how else to say it." Verity doesn't lie, and she most especially doesn't lie to Jacob. She knows it would be easier if she did. *I was mugged,* she could say, or *there was an accident*; the words would be tar, toxic and simple. She could bite them off with her teeth. Jacob would believe her.

She presses a knuckle into her temple and says, "Inside the walls," but she has tried that already.

She is momentarily confused by a bell that stabs her in the eye—or maybe the dig of her knuckle sounds like a bell—but then Jacob says, "It's the door." His explanation is automatic but curt. He gets up and vanishes through the door that leads downstairs.

Verity sits quietly, breathing in the fleece against her neck and the feel of Jacob's old blue t-shirt against her skin. Her legs are bare and she draws her knees up, curling her toes against the couch cushions.

It isn't very long before the door from the upstairs hallway opens again, and Jacob says, "Uh ... it's for you." He is taken aback, though he has not forgotten to be angry with her. His voice is flat.

Verity blinks. She draws the fleece closer yet and thinks of the magician. She waits for the scent of smoke and blossoms, and the smooth dark undulations of the dog.

It's the boy who enters, though—white haired, limping, his thin shoulders swimming in a big navy trench coat and half his weight resting on the cane in his left hand. He pauses three steps inside the living room, Jacob following, and looks around. Verity is abruptly self-conscious—not of her bare legs, but of the monochrome furniture, the white couches and empty walls. Jacob's eyes are fixed downward on the centre of the boy's shoulders. The boy's slight hunch suggests he can feel the stare.

"Ah...." says the boy, awkwardly.

"Jacob, could you, um...."

Jacob blinks, raising his incredulous attention to the couch. "You're joking."

"No. It's ... could you...?" Verity waves at the hall but she doesn't need to; Jacob emits a low, dissatisfied rumble and is already stalking out.

Verity wants to apologize, but she doesn't know what she would say; then he's gone, and there's an angel standing lost in the middle of the hardwood floor.

Verity still doesn't know what to say. She pulls the t-shirt more firmly over her knees.

"Sorry. For the whole mess, I mean. Here, let me see." The boy approaches, leaning on the cane. A hint of stale sweat clings to him, and his coat whispers against his ankles, the ragged hem brushing the floor. He's wearing hiking books. Verity can't see his wings, though she knows now that they're there. She has seen them graceful and spreading. She sees now the subtly curved lines beneath the folds of the coat, where bones shouldn't be. The pull of him is subdued, here in the linen-domesticity of her living room, but she feels her breath catch all the same.

The boy extends a hesitant hand toward her face and asks, "May I?" She breathes the cut-glass delicacy of his cheekbones. There are no lights in his eyes today; they are bottomless navy, circled with the sort of tiredness that leaves bruises. His face is alert but his fingers tremble with some slight palsy.

When Verity doesn't object, the boy cups her chin in his hand. The instant he touches her, she feels the light through her skin, though it's less than before; her headache eases. The room around her settles momentarily into clear, amazing relief. She draws one easy breath before it blurs.

"Knife wound's better," comments the boy, absently. "Not the rest of it. I knew you were built strange. Everything hurts you, doesn't it." His tone is too matter-of-fact for a question. Through his fingertips flows a weak trickle of purest joy.

Verity wants to wrap her hands around his wrist to hold him there. Instead, she turns her head and pulls her chin away. "You, too." She isn't surprised when the boy wavers. She curls her toes hard against the couch, bereft. "Please. Sit."

She gestures to the overstuffed white chair recently abandoned by Jacob. "Thank you," she adds. "You make the world ... a little clearer. Less, today. Are you okay?" Her own voice threatens to shatter the remnants of that tentative peace, but she inhales after speaking and waits while the boy sits.

The coat around his shoulders pulls, the lines of it all askew. She imagines the wings beneath. She wants to kneel on the floor and press her cheek against his knee like a child.

"I'm Colin," he says. "Yeah, sorry, I'm just not as strong out here. The air, I guess. So you're Verity, huh?"

"You can call me Vee."

Colin grins, like she's given him a gift. Verity supposes she has. The expression makes him look older; it draws lines along his mouth, and wrinkles at the edges of his eyes. "That guy your boyfriend?"

Verity shrugs—a little helpless, as she always is when faced with the question. "Jacob," she supplies.

"He's not one of us."

Verity wonders what *us* means. She would ask, but the boy continues, "Do you love him?" He asks as if it were a perfectly normal question—as though he'd asked her about a hometown, or a favourite book. He sounds sympathetic. In the aftermath of his touch, Verity hears the tenor of his voice unadulterated. She marvels at the sharpness of the room and the worn cushion fibres beneath her toes.

She hesitates again. "I don't understand that word."

"What?" Colin is startled. "Love?"

"People use it...." Verity shakes her head. "They love ice cream, or sunsets, or their children, or the scent of the shampoo in someone's hair. A word doesn't mean anything when you use it for everything. It tastes like week-old oatmeal." She considers, then concedes, "I think I might use 'love' for what you are. Jacob is—he's there in the morning."

"That doesn't sound like much."

"Then I'm not saying it right." Verity looks down at the long grains of the hardwood floor. "He makes me coffee, black, and he answers the door so I don't have to," she tries again. "He tells me things. He knows I won't lie to him. He's there in the morning. He's there at night. He's there when your magician frightens me, or when I come home covered in blood." The boy's touch has left her able to speak, words running like water. She doesn't mean the last of it to sound accusatory.

Still, Colin winces. "Sorry about that."

"It wasn't you. And, um, thank you." Verity flutters her fingers over the spot between her ribs. She is still startled with the wholeness of each breath she takes. "It costs you something for that. It costs Jacob something to ... listen. To live with me. But we have each other. No one else."

"You wouldn't call that love?" The boy is honestly intrigued. One pale hand fingers the head of his cane.

"Jacob is Jacob." Perhaps belatedly, Verity ventures, "Why?" It doesn't occur to her not to answer the broken angel with his porcelain face and his shoulders slumping in her living room chair.

"Oh. Just, it doesn't tend to go well, between us and them."

There must be a strange expression on Verity's face, because Colin flushes. The flash of pink across his cheekbones is bright and illuminates delicate spots—he might have had freckles, thinks Verity distantly, in another life.

She is beginning to lose track of her own life.

She wonders when, precisely, everything got so odd.

She thinks of the magician, but the angel is already saying, "No, I don't mean—look."

This time, something awkward and concerned lurks beneath the wry twist of his lips. "What'd you tell the guy? About last night?"

"That a magician with a dog that is sometimes a snake took me to a hall between the walls of a theatre, and a woman stabbed me." Verity hesitates. "Or a thought that resembles a woman. I'm—the words aren't right. Though when you touch me, it feels like they could be. Thank you for that."

"I'm not sure what you mean."

"Everything usually ... fractures. Fragments. You let me hold it, for a little while." Verity pauses again, and then she pushes her hair back, studying the boy. There are no sparks in her vision; she looks him directly in the eyes, revelling in the sheer simplicity of the act. When he flinches, she blinks away. "I'm sorry."

"Look through a guy, why don't you. Listen, did you tell him, uh," Colin shifts his shoulders, the vast coat flowing around him. "About my feathered friends?"

"The wings?" Verity pauses. "I don't—no. He kept asking about the blood."

"Okay." There's no mistaking the relief in the boy's voice. "I don't need anyone trying to sneak peeks."

"Maybe 'not yet'," confesses Verity. "I don't lie to him."

"Well, it's a noble choice, but wait until I'm gone. Or, you know, just *wait*, would be my advice. My pathetic plea, I guess."

Verity savours the translucent purity of Colin's hair. She fights the urge to go outside—to immerse herself in the sights and sounds of a city that briefly doesn't wound her, even as the hint of gossamer mint wafts across the back of her throat. She sits quietly and inhales the perfection of his worn work boots against the scratched floor.

"I don't understand what's happening."

"Yeah. I'm your guy." The corner of the angel's lips curls. "Or at least, Stefan's shit for straight answers, and good luck getting anything out of Jihan pretty much ever."

When Verity is silent, Colin looks puzzled. Then—as he registers her soundless expectation—he folds his palms together, fingers twining. "Ah. So how much do you know?"

"That a magician with a dog that is sometimes a snake took me to a hall between the walls of a theatre, and a woman stabbed me," repeats Verity, with a little shrug. "That the dog and the magician are the same. That doors can have only one side. That you healed me. And maybe you're an angel? Except that's very, um...."

"Judeo-Christian?" he suggests, wryly. "Yeah, I know. But I've never talked to any great being upstairs. I'm just an unlucky bastard most of the time. Sometimes I can help people. I'm glad I was there—although usually where she is, I am. Or vice versa." At Verity's parted lips, he adds, "No, she's not here right now. I told her to bug off. That'll be good for an hour or a day or, well, three weeks once, before she forgot and showed up with a pigeon wing and a fifth of bourbon." He rubs his hand across the back of his neck, then drops it back to clasp his wrist between his knees. "She's, ah, my fault. Sorry. That's kind of beside the real point, I guess."

Colin pauses, but Verity only waits, so eventually he ducks his head and says, "I don't really know how it works for you. I felt some of it, but the best I can figure—wait. Let me start with the door. You're right; it only has one side. And that's impossible, right?"

He seems to want an answer this time—his anticipation brings the faint scent of autumn leaves, which makes Verity exhale. She shakes her head. "No. Yes."

"Yeah. That's pretty much the hangup. Though you're pretty chill about the whole thing, I have to say. Stefan said, too." The boy's mouth twitches at the corner. He adds, not unkindly, "There's usually a lot of oh-my-god and this-can't-be-happening."

"Except it did." Verity spreads her hands. "I, um ... there are a lot of things," she says, slowly, "that are and are not. I know. I feel truth like ... fire, or light, or maybe the taste of honey. And if something is true...."

"No need to argue about it, then?"

His understanding is an unexpected relief. Verity flashes Colin another look; she doesn't meet his gaze this time. His words have left a faint silver mist barring the way.

"Right. Okay. So there are doors, we're clear on that, that exist but shouldn't, because they defy any law of physics. And laws of physics are real, right? Like, gravity is a thing that's true. And dimensions. And mass and time and ... okay, I'm actually terrible at physics. But that stuff's all legit, yes?"

"Yes," says Verity, puzzled. "And no. Mostly yes."

"This is not the easiest conversation I've ever had," notes the angel, gently. When she would apologize, he shrugs, shifting his weight in the chair. He drops one hand to massage his knee. "Right. Well. Take all those rules that everyone knows. Gravity. Electricity. Thermodynamics. Science words. Then imagine there's a type of person—a pretty unusual type—who's allergic."

Verity blinks.

"'Allergic' isn't really the right—words are important with you, huh? It's the best I've got. And all I have is what I've figured out, or what someone's told me about their grandmother's grandmother's grandmother. Anyway, let's say there are two ways of knowing the world, and one way has three dimensions and cell phone networks, and the other doesn't."

Verity hesitates. "Like magic?" The word is stiff on her tongue; she is not surprised when Colin shakes his head.

"That's their word for it," he says. "We've forgotten ours. I just ... Christ. How do you explain things there aren't words for? Do you know what that's—" He cuts off, looking at Verity. Leaning forward, he rests his elbows on his thighs and lets his long fingers dangle between his knees. "Yeah you do, don't you. That's your whole thing."

There's warmth in his voice. Verity lets herself smile at him, briefly, but she drops her gaze to the too-wide cuffs of his sleeves before the honeyed comfort of his tone can drip over her. She is trying to listen.

"The lazy thing to do is break it down to science or magic, but that's not—magic's a stupid word. It's their word."

Verity frowns. "It tastes like iron filings."

"Sure. Magic isn't real, right? That notion of 'magic' tells a story that says one thing is possible and the other thing isn't, like a wall can't be both solid and hollow or a door needs two sides. Ignore that word because it says we don't exist. Imagine, instead, two kinds of people who walk in the world. Thousands and thousands of years ago, both were just fine. One rode horses; one rode the wind. One built with stone; one built inside. Everyone was happy. Then the people with the horses and the stone, they started making wheels and writing and paper and mathematics. They started taking up more space—not on purpose, not to be evil. They worked with gravity and electricity and walls that were solid in the middle. They got strong—so strong they didn't know any other way was possible—or if they ever did, they forgot. The world was just as they made it. But anyone else got squeezed. I guess go back a few thousand years and there were whole cities with people who'd crawled inside the walls. I don't mean lost cities—I mean London, St. Petersburg, Damascus, anywhere you can think. Then the squeeze kept coming, and the people between, they got fewer and fewer. They lost their spaces, their histories, even their children. These days, most of the folks born to it never even know. They stumble through the world and they just can't quite function. Their computers don't work or their bank accounts get axed or their credit cards won't swipe. Little things. You follow?"

"I think so."

"Mostly they're just unlucky, or think they are." Colin grimaces. "Then generally at some point when they're young, they develop some kind of disease no one can identify. I mean, someone'll *say* it's cancer or lupus or autoimmune. It'll bounce from one diagnosis to another, if they've got the means. But the upshot of it is there're people born in this world who can't live in this world. The rules aren't made for them anymore."

"Made?" The word shines brightly in the room—brighter than the late morning light that filters through the window. Verity tilts her head, studying the shape of the boy's voice. She has no cause to disbelieve him; his explanations are sharp against her skin.

"Yeah, it's ... knowing, I guess. Common sense. It's not about belief. People out here *know* there's no such things as dragons, and no way a crowd of misfits fits inside a wall. People know doors need two sides. And the people who know that far outnumber the ones who don't, or who aren't made for it. I guess it was different, before. It's like there's a war no one ever declared, and the side that won didn't even realize what was going on. Still doesn't. Like your boyfriend, there."

Verity feels a piece of the world slide into place. Still, she ventures, "You have wings. He would see them, wouldn't he?"

The angel blanches, porcelain fading to bone. "Maybe. Might be he'd change them by looking. All the shit they think is impossible can't endure their looking—they know it isn't so, and the world is what they make it. Like how dragons aren't real. You ever see one of those little dragons half-warped, with pigeon feathers or a rat tail because someone stared too long? If he saw my shoulders, he'd want to know why, and the whole thing would end up with me in a lab or a zoo and probably someone would say something about genetic mutation or vestigial limbs. I can't do for him what I did for you, though—I can't 'prove' any of this shit is real. Going by past experience ... to him, I could be a freak with growths on my back, but I couldn't heal him if he had a knife in his gut—at least, not if he knew I were trying. He's not made for me to help."

"Can you fly?" Verity doesn't expect to ask the question, but it comes. It is tinged, somehow, with wonder, and her own curiosity is rich on her tongue.

"That'd be nice, wouldn't it?" Colin pulls a wry face and continues to knead his fingers around the knob of his knee. "No good. Gravity, mass, I don't know. Physics says no. The wings are stronger *between*, but there's no room to spread them in the walls. Can't fly, and if I'm God's messenger, hell if I know what He wants me to say. And I can't fix my own damn leg, but anyone else, sure. They come to me, see, with the sickness on them, the hole inside." The angel's shrug is nearly lost in the vast tent of his coat; the gesture is casual, though his eyes are pained. "My turn," he adds, cheerfully enough. "You're weird. I don't get you. I guess you're one of us but you're all right out here. What is it you do here? Or downstairs. Or wherever."

"Oh. Anything Jacob wants."

"Sorry?"

"He hasn't decided." Verity tugs at the edge of the blanket, orienting herself in the spare familiarity of the room. The angel's presence is a subtle disruption, like a lamp left shining in the wrong place. "We try things. We've been, um, photographers. Caterers. Accountants. Detectives." She shrugs. "Usually, we make mistakes. But I try what he wants."

"But what do you want?"

"I want Jacob to be happy."

"Ah." Colin looks down at the floor as though he might see through it to the man downstairs. Verity wonders if maybe he can.

When he doesn't continue, she blurts, on impulse, "I want to know. To understand. A door or a feather or the fall of a leaf. Anything."

"Ah." This time, the angel seems satisfied. "Well, look, you're pretty set up here. Food, place to sleep, that sort of thing. The theatre ... it's a bit of a shelter right now, for the ones who can't cope. If you need it, though, it's there. I guess you know how to get in now."

"The door that isn't," murmurs Verity. "Who built it?"

"Who knows?" The angel shrugs. "Some of the older buildings—here, other cities—they have these spaces carved out in them."

"The *between*."

"Yeah."

"There isn't really a band, is there?" It isn't quite a question. Verity feels the truth on her lips as she speaks it, like water over parched skin.

"Nah. I mean, sure, every so often a couple of us will bust out guitars or a cello or something for a night, keep the name alive, but really it's just the signal. Sign, countersign, whatever. Actually, that's kind of why I'm here. Something's off." Colin rubs a hand over his face, the other hand still kneading absently at his knee. The coat pulls over the long lines of the hidden wings tucked down the sides of his legs. Verity catches a glimpse of oiled black feathers. "Jihan wrote your name on the wall. I don't know what that means. And now she's wearing your scarf. It's got blood all over it. She picked it out of the puddle and knotted it around her arm like some kind of mourning band. I can't take the thing away. It's like fighting a cat."

"She attacked me." Verity thinks she is quite calm in pointing this out.

"I know." Colin sighs. "Look, she's ... not like us. She's not all there. She's the worst thing I've ever done to anyone."

"What did you do?" Verity finds it hard to believe anything ill of the boy. He sits tired and remorseful. She remembers the golden sunlight of his touch.

"I made her live." Colin's fingers press at the bridge of his nose. "It's a long story. Anyway. Like I said, she wrote your name on the wall, and she doesn't do that kind of thing. So I think you're important. And we've just started seeing these."

Verity supposes there are a number of responses she could make.

Instead, she sits quietly and waits for Colin to fish around in one of his giant pockets. He withdraws a crumpled piece of paper, folded into quarters, and unfolds it before leaning forward and extending it to Verity.

She accepts it cautiously, smoothing the rumpled paper against her knee. The thin photocopy is tattered at the edges, impenetrable ink block printed on a dubious shade of pale rose. The logo for The Between is splashed across the top, just above the stylized image of the dog. *Live in Concert*, promises the poster. *Lansdowne Park Aberdeen Pavilion. March 5.*

The paper makes Verity's fingertips tingle unpleasantly. It takes her a moment to figure out why. She traces the concert date lightly with her index finger. "It doesn't say cancelled."

"No. Damned if I have any idea why." Colin shakes his head, looking at the paper. "When we make those, they're just signals for gatherings and safe spaces—like, they tell people to go to McLuhan's. No one who's not in the know is going to show up for a cancelled event for a band that doesn't exist. Ouro's on ours so people will know to watch for the big black dog. But we didn't make that one. Apparently there are some in a few other cities. We've had folks trickle in from Toronto, Winnipeg, New York in the last few days—one guy almost killed himself taking a bus. Border crossings are a bitch, incidentally. Jihan had me stumbling through a forest in the dark when we came up. Still, whatever this poster is—there aren't a lot of us, but people are going to gather. Word's spreading."

"Hm." Verity turns the tattered poster in her hands. "Rotting gardenias," she observes. "That's probably not helpful. I'm not sure what I can...? I've seen one of these, though. There was a girl. Her name was Privya."

"Oh, Christ. Not her again." Colin is both startled and suddenly sad. His regret is gentle but unyielding, blending salt and the sound of a distant ocean.

"Vee?" Jacob's voice comes from downstairs, drifting thinly through the door. It isn't often that he shouts. There's something in the tone—some edge of iron and glass—that has Verity suddenly on her feet, puzzled.

"Um," is all she says, but she paces quickly to the door, and the angel puts his cane to the floor and levers himself up to follow.

Verity's feet are bare on the hardwood, but she hurries out to the hall and leans over the banister, Colin just behind her. She is, abruptly, overwhelmed by the scent of coal and blood—by a dust storm of static.

She closes her fingers around the smooth wood of the banister, squeezing, until her vision clears and she can gaze down into the town-house foyer. She sees Jacob, his hair mussed and his t-shirt untucked. She sees Jihan, two steps up from the landing, poised like a missile ready to launch. In the morning light, the woman from the walls is the same—spidery frame, misbuttoned lavender sweater, grey hair pulled back in a smooth braid. She is wearing Verity's formerly grey scarf tied unevenly around her left bicep; it is now a splash of rusted fabric with the ends gone stiff, mottled with dried brown stains. Her shoe is still untied, and now one of the laces is broken.

Jihan is half-turned toward Jacob and Jacob has one hand extended, as though he would have prevented her from ascending the stairs. He hasn't touched her, but she has stopped, regardless. She is staring at Jacob; profiled from above, her expression is hidden but her posture is that of a raptor waiting to strike, the planed bones of her face as smooth and streamlined as a bird's.

"Look, you can't just—" Jacob begins but does not finish. His eyes are wide, his expression wondering as he looks up at the woman.

To Verity, it tastes of sun and rain simultaneously. She is distantly aware that this expression on Jacob's face is new—that he has never looked at her that way. That he has, perhaps, never looked that way before.

She feels, entirely unexpectedly, a stabbing sense of loss.

"Shit," breathes the angel behind her, then he's lurching past and half-hopping down the stairs. "Don't touch her," he snaps. "You, don't touch *him,* and hell if I didn't say leave me alone this morning. For one goddamn morning. Sorry about this." It's not clear whether the apology is for Jihan or Jacob, but he pulls up next to Jihan and grasps her arm—smoothly, without fear, his cane in the other hand, his greatcoat dragging on the steps. "Sorry," he calls up, and that one is clearly for Verity.

The woman in Verity's stained scarf acknowledges nothing, but she bends her elbow when the angel touches her, easing the angle of his grip. She stares at Jacob for a hard moment longer. Jacob only holds himself brittle, as if the slightest breeze would crack him.

Verity, watching the angel and the woman in their vagabond clothes, swallows a misty morning that doesn't belong in the solidity of the staircase. She sees the impossibilities dancing around them. She tastes the wire familiarity of Jacob's hair and understands, suddenly, how well his loose grin fits with the plaster of the walls and the pull of gravity against his shoulders.

She tightens her hold on the banister.

By the time she descends the stairs, Colin has tugged Jihan past the unresisting Jacob, and is heading for the door. When Verity's bare foot hits the bottom step, Jihan turns her head and Verity sees that mirrored gaze again, blank and polished as a knife blade.

Verity presses her palm to her ribs, reflexively, but the taller woman shows no recognition and makes no move toward her—only glances at Jacob again and then allows Colin to tug her down the hall and outside. "I'll send Stefan—sorry, Santiago—by," says Colin, "for anything else you need. Crap, sorry again."

Jacob hasn't moved except to turn his head. He stands staring at the door as it closes, his hands loose at his sides. When Verity touches his wrist, he lifts his arm automatically, pulling her close. She turns her shoulder and fits just exactly into the curve beneath his. He smells of coffee and flannel.

"Who's your friend?"

"Colin." She answers without hesitation but knows that's not what he's asking.

"I meant—"

"I know. She isn't."

"Vee." There's a ragged edge threatening his patience that she's never heard—not even in the small hours, with blood and shivering and stories that can't be. His arm is warm across her shoulders.

"She isn't my friend," says Verity. "I don't know if she's his. I don't know if she's a person, or just shaped like a woman. But they call her Jihan."

Jacob doesn't answer. He's looking at the door.

Verity adds, "She's the one who stabbed me."

"Oh." Jacob frowns at that, then glances down at Verity sidelong, briefly tightening his fingers. "Well," he says. "You're okay now, right?"

Verity isn't sure how to answer, so she remains silent. She leans her head against Jacob and feels his lips brush her hair. She is very cold.

"Some guy called," he adds. "Wants us to look after his sister. I guess she caught that mad cow thing; flipped out overnight, just kind of stares at the wall."

"We don't do medical." Verity's response is automatic. "You're not a nurse."

"Well, no, but we could hire one. Help them out, you know. Give it a try."

"You could if you wanted to. I don't, um...." Verity gnaws at her lower lip. "No medical."

"Yeah. Yeah, you're probably right. Anyway, I was thinking we could be quantity surveyors, except I'm not sure yet what that is. I heard it somewhere, though." Jacob is rambling as he stares at the door; Verity finds the rumble in his chest comforting. He is not a large man, but she compares him to the delicate fragility of the boy breaking beneath the world.

"Hey," says Jacob. "Was that your scarf?"

Nestled against Jacob's side, in the stillness of the hall, Verity thinks about spaces that cannot be, and wonders at hollow walls. She is looking at her hand—at the sudden bloom of impossibility beneath her skin. It is a gleam like fireflies.

"Risk! Risk anything! Care no more for the opinions of others, for those voices. Do the hardest thing on Earth for you. Act for yourself. Face the truth." – Katherine Mansfield

9

She has lost something.

She lets him touch her, though the walls melt around her and his fingers ask questions she doesn't understand. His need is a puzzle she has never minded solving, but now she lets him close and regrets it. He kisses her neck; from behind, he runs his tongue along the edge of her ear. The sounds he whispers burn like bitterest poison. His hands are too tight on her hips.

"Stop," she says.

He does, though he's mystified and maybe a little hurt. He hesitates there with his breath hovering at her earlobe and his palms on her bare skin.

She offers, "I know what you're going to be. What you are, now."

She feels the curve of his mouth, the brush of stubble as he smiles. "Oh yeah? Lawyer? Rock star? Astronaut?"

"Hers," she murmurs, and he tenses against her back. "Don't," she adds. "Don't touch me and think of her. It's a lie."

"I wasn't—"

"Don't!" She doesn't mean to snap; it's defence against the shuddering cloud of his denial.

There is a pause. His arms slide around her, salt-sweat and sticky.

"I'm sorry," he says; he buries his face in her hair. "I'm sorry. I love you."

She tastes the word as she always does, mouldy and colourless. The apology is pure, though; she squirms in his arms, turning, and curls herself against him. It's warm there. She wonders how much longer that will last.

OCTOBER

"Did we get a dog?" Jacob asks Verity the next morning. She pauses, hands wrapped around the heat of her mug, not certain she's heard correctly.

"What?"

"Did we get a dog? I mean, it's cool if we did. It just probably needs to be walked or fed or something." Jacob pours milk into a bowl of cereal, then puts the bowl down on the floor. "Here, boy! Girl?"

Verity doesn't know how she's missed the sense of smoke; she breathes it in as Ouroboros glides in from the hall, tail plumed and feet silent on the hardwood floor. The dog sits in front of the cereal bowl, tongue lolling, and laughs at her (she is sure) while Jacob scratches it behind the ears.

"That's Ouroboros." Verity cranes her neck so she can watch over the back of the couch. "The dog that's a snake."

"Looks an awful lot like a dog." Jacob crouches, placing his hands on both sides of the dog's head, mashing back its ears with rough goodwill.

"That, um, might not be a good idea."

"He's a good boy. Isn't he? Aren't you a good boy?"

Ouroboros wags its tail. Jacob ruffles its fur; it stares at him, yellow eyes impassive.

"You know, I had a dog. When I was a kid, I mean. Are you a snake, dog? Come on. Show us what you got."

Jacob leans close, looking into the dog's face, wrapping a hand around its muzzle. It tosses its head, like any irritated but well-mannered beast, and looks toward Verity.

"Come on," says Jacob. "Be a snake."

They wait. The request hangs in the air. For all of Jacob's playful tone, everyone is suddenly still.

Verity is surprised to taste the bright citrus splash of Jacob's hope; she sees his shoulders sharpen, and she suspects he has startled even himself with the suddenness of possibility and the realization that he doesn't want Verity to be wrong.

She presses herself into the back of the couch. She says to Ouroboros, "Please."

She surprises herself, too, with her own hope, tentative and chest-tight.

The dog pulls its head free and grins, exposing too-white teeth. Jacob waits for half a breath longer, then puffs out air between his lips. He pats Ouro on the head one more time before he rises and steps back to the kitchen counter. He leaves the cereal for the dog (who ignores it) and pours two more bowls, adding milk and fishing two spoons from the drawer before he walks to the living room. He places Verity's bowl on the coffee table and drops down next to her on the couch, settling his breakfast on his stomach.

By then, Verity has had time to swallow back the sourness of her disappointment. She is not particularly shocked.

Jacob slides an arm around her shoulders and stirs the spoon in his cereal. He lifts the spoon a few inches to let milk and muesli dribble back into the bowl. "Here, boy. C'mere."

Ouroboros glides to the side of the coffee table, an oil-slick ghost. Verity looks at the floor, where she sees the shadows of the table and the faded armchair and Jacob's legs as he stretches them out. The dog's paws touch the hardwood and spread, inky and two-dimensional, no distinction between fur or shade.

"It's its own shadow," she says. "Look."

Ouroboros lays back its ears, molten gaze abruptly baleful.

Jacob sighs and turns his head, glancing at the dog. His gaze skims briefly over the black-furred form and then he focuses on his cereal again. "Listen." He tightens his arm around Verity just slightly, cupping her shoulder. "I was thinking we could make you an appointment."

"No."

"Vee—"

"No. We promised."

"Look, I know. But just to see someone—like an actual qualified someone, not one of those quacks. Nothing permanent, or drastic, or—babe, you came home with blood all over you and I don't know what to do."

Verity stares past Jacob's warm cedar eyes; she can smell his anxiety, a burning metallic overlap to the dog's perfumed smoke. The dog is on the floor watching them both, one ear now perked. Verity feels herself trapped by the weight of Jacob's arm. She squirms free and stands.

"Vee."

"We promised."

"*I don't know what to do.*"

"I know." Verity swallows. "I can taste it. But I'll leave."

"Vee." Jacob takes her hand. She doesn't look at him. There are red stars spinning in the corners of the room.

She says, "I know you're scared. I know it's strange. But I'm okay and if you try to—I'll walk out. And I'll miss you. But I won't come back."

"No." Jacob's response is immediate. He squeezes Verity's hand until she looks at him, or at least at the freckles splattered over his cheekbones. "I'm sorry."

"You'll be sorry for a while," predicts Verity. "And then you'll think of Jihan." She can hear her own voice gone thin and alien. When Jacob flinches, she shakes her head and pulls her hand away. "I'm sorry too." Apology tastes like nutmeg.

The dog hasn't moved. It sits on the floor with its tail curled around its feet, yellow gaze bright, head cocked to the side.

Verity says, "The dog and I are going outside." She walks to the door as though she expects Ouroboros to follow; she is relieved when it does, though its tongue still lolls with some secret joke.

"Want to be a welder tomorrow? There's a building going up on Lisgar. And a guy who promises not to let us burn ourselves."

She know it's a peace offering. Verity holds the door as the dog glides past her. "Okay. Tomorrow."

Ouroboros doesn't touch her on the way down the stairs. It walks a few steps ahead, pausing on the landing to wait for her. When she reaches the foyer, Verity sees Santiago's jacket hanging on the rack and remembers her own was lost on a bloody floor; she pauses, then takes Jacob's, checking his pockets until she locates the familiar jingle of his keys. His denim bomber is too large.

"I don't suppose you brought back my coat. Or, um, my wallet."

The dog flicks an ear, which is approximately all the response that Verity was expecting. She sighs, then unlocks the door to the office, entering the front room. Pulling open the bottom drawer of Jacob's desk, she reaches into a sea of crumpled money and removes a handful of randomly denominated bills, smoothing them against her thigh before folding them into her pocket.

Retrieving Santiago's leather jacket from its hook, she steps outside and the dog flows past.

The day is the sort of pale autumn brightness that brings light but no warmth. The tree in the front yard is bare, its yellow leaves scattered across the lawn.

Verity sees no dragons, but the magician is standing below, his back against the bottom of the porch railing; he has found a shady spot just where the house blocks the morning sun, slouched in jeans and his Between shirt. He has his head cocked to the side. "That's quite the drawer of cash." From around his wrist, the black snake rises up, its own head tilted at the same angle.

"It's Jacob's." Verity stops two stairs from the bottom, so she's slightly taller than Santiago. She can see the hair thinning on his head, and the silver strands glinting in it. She offers his jacket. "You couldn't do that inside?" she adds to Ouroboros. Her tone is resigned.

"He really couldn't." Neither Santiago nor the snake looks particularly apologetic. "Not with your boyfriend watching. Some mundane jerk thinks he's a dog, he's a dog for the duration." The magician accepts his jacket and tugs it on before gesturing with his free hand; conjuring a small red flower, he makes it vanish again. "We can only work it out here if I play like it's a magic trick. Otherwise it's like trying to go *between* and running face first into the wall."

"Jacob doesn't believe me. He knows I don't lie. But he, um ... thinks that I'm...."

"Crazy?"

"Wrong."

"Sorry." Santiago raises his hand, flashing his fingers outward to offer a glimpse of the king of clubs. "Can't help. Really—tell him it's a trick and then he'll believe it. He knows how his world works. No arguing with that."

It's not a lie—it tastes of cucumber and a certain insouciant hint of pepper—but Verity ventures, "You wind your shadow around your wrist like a bracelet. You don't cast one on the ground. Can't Jacob see that?"

Santiago and the snake both watch Verity for a moment, flat-eyed and considering, before the magician says, "Ouroboros winds himself, and you'll notice I'm standing in the shade. It's a risk, Ouro and me being separate out here. We usually just do it for sidewalk shows, and we only do that when we need the cash. Look, Feathers gave you the rundown, didn't he? It's the way it is. Out here, a snake is a snake. A dog is a dog. A snake can't turn into a dog, unless it's just a magic act. Everyone casts a shadow in the sun. And maybe some freak kid can be born with wings, but he sure as hell can't fly with them. It's all about what people know. Just common sense, right? We can't prove what honestly isn't real to them, and if we try ... well. There are plenty of doctors and drugs for that kind of thing. Lot of us learn that the hard way."

Verity flinches.

The magician, she suspects, pretends not to notice. "We got caught outside when I was about twelve—Ouro and I, I mean. Sun came out and I was in the middle of the street with my black dog and no shadow. Next thing I knew, a bunch of kids came around the corner and when the first one looked at me—just glanced my way, even—it was like some giant hand started stretching me out, yanking Ouro away. It's hard to describe."

"What happened?"

"Not sure how it came to me but right in the moment I stared down that first kid, dropped my jacket over Ouro and yelled 'abracadabra!'. It was the first time he was the incredible vanishing dog, meaning he slid right up my sleeve and out onto the ground, so it looked like I had regular old darkness at my feet and they bought it. Otherwise I'm pretty sure I would've been standing there with a new shadow on the dirt and some empty husk of a dog running off down the road. Some idiot can ruin us just by looking. So we try not to take chances anymore. What we have, that's for the dark, and the *between*. It's a chain around all of our necks." Santiago shakes his head, dropping his hands as Ouro vanishes into his sleeve. "And, P.S., if Ouro comes in to get you again, do not draw extra attention to him. That was a stupid move. Come on."

"Where are we going?"

"Some stuff I want to show you." The magician considers, then adds, "I'll see if I can get your ID back. No promises."

"You heard me say that?"

"Ouro did." Santiago turns to glance up the street; it's a quiet day. The sidewalk is empty and so is the road.

When the magician begins to walk, Verity falls in beside him. She keeps a safe distance. The wind is chill. As the magician steps out of the shade, his shadow stretches out along the ground, lengthening to eclipse Verity's. It winks at her once with a gold eye, and then settles into an easy mimic of Santiago's stride.

"Who is Jihan?" she asks.

"She doesn't talk, so we don't really know. She's older than she looks. She's got a weird way with knives—sorry—but she comes with the kid, and the kid is worth it."

Verity considers that. "She wrote my name on a wall in blood," she says, slowly, "and you came to fetch me."

"Yes."

"Just like that."

"Yes."

"So I think there's more."

If Santiago were the dog, his ears would flatten. Instead he goes silent, jaw tightening. When he lengthens his stride, Verity has to walk a little faster. It's difficult, with the little flashes of his irritation along the ground, red and a cascading blue that wraps around her ankle. Its soft cling carries an air of hope.

"Colin asked me," says the magician abruptly. "What he wants, he gets. He helps us and we're going to help him right back. Make his life a little better. You know truth, right? Tell me if that's true."

Verity sees in him, suddenly, the hint of vulnerability—something pugnacious, vicious, lethally uncertain. She is sorry when she says, "The future isn't truth or lie. It's only fog."

Santiago tosses his head. "We *can* help him, then."

"I think that's ... it's not a lie." Verity shakes her own head, sliding silver sparks from her hair. "Words are imprecise. How will you?"

"Hell if I know. Not yet. I follow his lead." Santiago's irritation has passed, brief and light as a summer storm; he pauses for half a step and glances down at Verity beside him. "Okay, first thing today. You saw me open the door *between* in the closet at McLuhan's. You did it from the other side. Think you can do it both ways?"

"Maybe. It tasted—there are things I understand, now that I know."

"Huh." Santiago sounds dubious (a prickle on her skin) but he veers right, dodging between two of the street's older duplex homes. They are tall, narrow, turn of the century. He runs his fingertips along worn wooden siding as Verity follows. Grass gives way to gravel beneath her feet.

Santiago stops just beneath a windowsill, paused beneath lace curtains and glass warped with age. "There are spaces all through this city. There's one here. Can you feel it?"

It takes Verity a few seconds to figure out what he's talking about. She glances over her shoulder, looking for neighbours, then tilts her head at the house's side. She touches her tongue to the back of her teeth, parsing the taste of dust and the hum of some distant energy. "Here," she says, and she raises her own hand, letting her palm hover over the spot where olive paint has just begun to chip and flake from the wood beneath.

"Good. All right, new trick." Santiago taps the siding lightly, just above the spot Verity has chosen. "You feel the door on the other side?"

Verity nods.

"Right. Open it."

Verity pauses. Her brow furrows. She presses her hand to the flaking paint and tries to look beyond it, but sees only green and the sunlight on the back of her hand. "It was easy," she says, "after Colin ... he made everything clear."

"He's got a gift. Still—you've seen it now. Just do it again. The trick is knowing. Don't doubt; don't overthink it. You know the door is there, so open it."

Verity frowns at the wall. Then, closing her eyes, she draws a breath, casting back for the sensation of impossible space. Remembering, she reaches (through the wall to the other side to the door that doesn't exist) and—*the world twists*—and then they stand in darkness. Nettles sting her throat but when she takes a breath, she inhales only dust.

She chokes and feels Santiago's hand on her shoulder.

"Wait," he says. "There's usually a lantern on the left. If it's still work-ing, it'll light when you touch it." Light blooms from a single flame in a glass-sided lantern that hangs from a hook. One of its panes is broken.

Verity coughs, blinking. Puffs of dirt fly with her breath. Three feet in front of her, she sees a brick wall. To her left, the wall seems to have fallen in, filling the space with crumbled clay. To her right is another slim hallway, extending with no ceiling or end in sight. There is at least an inch of dust on the floor. "Who made this?"

"No idea." Santiago stands with his arms folded. The snake is back, larger this time, draped across his shoulders. Both study the cramped space with an air of pained resignation. "Holes like this are mostly in older buildings—like, Victorian at least—and this isn't the city for it. I've heard Europe is riddled with hidden mazes. I don't know what they do in places without walls. A woman from Colorado once told me she found a little *between* in the side of an old army tent. This space isn't much but it'd be useful in an emergency—just don't try to use a door if anyone's watching you who doesn't belong."

"It won't work?"

"No. All right, now. Back outside." Santiago lifts the latch on the impossible door. It's just a rough slab of wood, really, notes Verity. There's nothing mysterious about it at all, until the magician touches her elbow and the world shifts. They stand in the bright autumn sunlight, blinking, and she pulls Jacob's coat closer around her shoulders.

"If someone—not one of us, I mean—had been standing in front of the door, it just wouldn't open. Sometimes, if they aren't watching, we can slide by." Santiago tilts his head back to squint up at the sun. Its glare deepens the lines around his eyes and casts his shadow in sharp contrast at his feet. The snake is gone again.

Verity studies Santiago's cracked leather boots and the puddle of shade, but she sees no sign of Ouroboros—the magician's shadow is, to all appearances, mundane. Still, the air carries a hint of cindered sweetness.

"All right," says the magician. "We have some walking to do. It isn't too far."

Verity means to watch the shifting darkness at Santiago's feet, but the butter-ripple of a passing car distracts her. By the time she adjusts, he is already at the sidewalk, waiting with one eyebrow raised.

She says, "Sorry."

"I don't get you." Santiago calls a rose to one hand, then ripples his fingers, replacing it with the queen of spades. "You live in that house above those computers, and you're pretty quick with a cell phone, and you take the bus without puking. But you're weird in your own way, huh."

It takes Verity some time to arrange the words in her mouth. By the time she is ready to speak, she has negotiated a block of screaming sidewalk and she's gratified to realize that Santiago has waited for her response. She offers, "Jacob sometimes thinks I am trying to make a metaphor—like I could describe the city as a fire, maybe, with smoke and ember and the taste of coal, and our house like the low blue flame of a match. Or maybe it could be an ocean and the glass of store windows could run in waves."

"But it's not a metaphor?" Santiago is shuffling cards now as he walks. The shadow at his feet is a perfect mimic of his movements, utterly normal.

Verity skirts a shallow pool of the magician's curiosity and tries not to step on Ouroboros in the process. "The licence plates of the cars that drive by are a sort of, um ... brittle peppermint, but the card in your hand has a high-pitched whistle and," she considers slowly, "the wind tastes like ... apple? It's everything all at once. I feel the traffic lights cool on my skin."

"That sounds confusing."

"Maybe if it were a metaphor it would be a tornado." Verity shakes her head. "True things are clear. Most things are grey. A lie is a hole or an oil slick or—" She nearly runs into a lamppost, then realizes Santiago has pulled her to a stop. He drops his hand from her elbow. Regrouping, she forges forward again, swallowing back the vaguely bitter windmills of brown leaves skittering across her path. "I don't know why."

"Huh."

Apparently that is all Santiago is prepared to say, because they walk in silence for several minutes. Bank Street is long and straight, and the sidewalk is relatively empty, though Verity flinches from both the creeping whine of window displays and the honking rumble of traffic. The slow incline of the ground ripples beneath her feet. "Where are we going?"

"The bus station. Since those new posters have gone up, I try to check for stragglers." Santiago adds, "Hold up. Here." He extends a hand, curled around something. When Verity moves to take it, he drops another pin for The Between into her palm. "We've got a few of these still floating around. Think of it like an 'ask me' button. We're out of shirts."

Verity stops and looks down at the little pin, then fixes its coal-mint needle to the lapel of Jacob's coat. She makes sure it's secure before she keeps walking. The magician stays just a little behind her; his sinuous languor reminds her of the dog, or the snake, though he lacks his creature's silence. She can smell his footsteps on the pavement.

"I'll be honest," says Santiago, and Verity wishes he would, but she doesn't interrupt, only works on picking her way through the swirl of the magician's words. He continues, "I'm taking you with me today because we hope you might start doing runs to the train station. It's a hell of a walk from here and it's hard even on those of us who can take the bus to get there. More specifically, it's hard on Colin—he's the one who ends up patching us up when we come in puking."

"I'm not sure I understand."

"Those posters—the ones that say the concert's a go? Apparently they're in other cities. Fredericton. Montréal. One guy came in from Baltimore. We're all crap at travelling—if we have to, we take buses or trains, but it's a lousy ride. If we're really unlucky, the thing breaks down just because we're riding in it. Even if not, we come out wanting to ralph. But word's been spreading, and we've had a few people trickle in. So I try to wander by in case anyone needs to be scooped."

"Where did you come from?"

"Toronto. Few months back. I had it relatively easy; the train made my skull want to crawl out my ears, but at least I wasn't coming over the border. Not many of us have passports."

Verity thinks about that. She tucks her hands into her pockets to protect her fingertips from the pricking of a cola advertisement on the side of a passing bus. "Colin said the posters—they just started going up, though?"

"Here, they did. A kid who came in from Winnipeg yesterday said they'd been up a few weeks." The magician shakes his head. "There aren't many of us here, but more than I've seen in one place before. Me and Ouro, it was gut instinct. We got up, I had breakfast, we skipped town. I figured it was something about Colin, calling us—something bone deep. Now I'm not so sure."

Verity considers, but doesn't answer; she is concentrating on the slow uphill walk toward the city centre. Ottawa is painted in whistling swirls around her. The logo on a discarded burger wrapper smells faintly of battery acid, and the mailbox she passes tastes like lukewarm pickles. Santiago is just behind her, both like and not *entirely* like the dog, a centre of tenebrous quiet that keeps her pace without complaint.

At the highway underpass, she hesitates, letting Santiago go ahead. The shadow of the arch looms high before her, and the whip of traffic above is a rumble that's tangible on her skin. She feels the threat of it, phantom gravel rattling hard enough to bruise. She shakes her head. There's saffron on her tongue.

She hears the whispered brush of lilac and coal, but holds herself still and takes a moment to sort through the city in her head before she says, "Say that again? Sorry."

"I said, okay? What's the holdup?"

"I just needed a minute." The magician is a carbon blur behind the streaks that mar Verity's vision, but she pegs his general direction and then walks forward carefully, the weight of passing traffic groaning above her head. It's a short passage; she's done it before, and she knows the bus station is just on the other side. When the underpass lifts itself from her shoulders—when she is free of it—she waits for her vision to clear and then crosses at the light, heading for the large, squat brown building just off the main road.

The bus station has never won any awards for architecture. It is a large ochre block striped with a line of narrow windows that are slightly sour in Verity's mouth. She keeps from making a face, only glances at Santiago and gestures for him to take the lead again. She trails his liquid darkness along the sidewalk. "Okay," she says slowly, "so what do we do?"

"Well, first," says the magician, "we look for the obvious." When he extends a finger, Verity follows the line of it toward the side wall of the station. She sees a young woman with curling red hair and a faded brown jacket, sitting cross-legged next to a rolled sleeping bag in front of a paper cup.

The woman is looking back, her lips pulled into a frown that rustles down Verity's legs.

Santiago says, "You look for the ones who are looking for you. Here."

He then sets off across the parking lot toward the red-haired girl. When he reaches her, he stops, conjuring a folded five-dollar bill with a practised swagger before dropping it into the cup. "There's a lot more foot traffic on Bank."

"Yeah." The redhead has a voice like smoke and rattling sand. "I'll move as soon as I quit wanting to blow chunks. Also, thanks." She is wearing a familiar band t-shirt, faded and torn at the collar. Her green eyes are hard, but she takes in Santiago's shirt and the pin on Verity's jacket, and the set of her spine relents a little.

"You a fan?" Santiago gestures to the logo on his chest.

"Sort of," the girl replies. Her answer is casual, perfunctory; she has already let herself relax against the wall. "Second album's a lot better than the third."

It's not a lie, thinks Verity, so much as a fiction. Still, it tingles on the side of her jaw.

The magician says, "Yeah. You know where to go?"

"Saw the posters. What's this about a real show? Like, not cancelled? And where's Lansdowne?"

"Got me. Never mind about Lansdowne—look for McLuhan's. Bank Street's right there, head down a few blocks that way. Old theatre on your left. Can't miss it. Band's on the marquee out front. If it's locked, hang on. I won't be long after you."

The girl plucks the money from the cup and rises, hooking her fingers through the shoe lace that ties the old sleeping bag. "People are coming in," she says. "Heard about this in Chicago. Hope you're ready for a crowd." She glances at Verity. "Thanks for the directions."

When Verity doesn't speak, Santiago cuts in, "You wouldn't need directions if someone hadn't been replacing our posters. You see anyone else today?"

"Old guy and a kid wandering around. He's, like, *weirdly* old. But I was thinking about talking to them. They have the look." The girl waves toward the doors of the bus station and shifts her feet, the loose untidiness of her sleeping roll bouncing at her hip. "You guys have food?"

"There are supplies at the theatre. Not a lot, but we're doing okay. Come here and I'll show you. Verity, hang on." Santiago leads the girl back toward the main street and gestures southward. Beneath the scraggly branches of an urban tree, he conjures a fan of cards, makes them vanish, and extends his other hand to the girl, who takes it. He says something Verity can't make out. She thinks he is being kind. The girl's smile lingers on the hollows of his face.

Verity tries to watch them, but the wind sends a battered newspaper page skittering across her vision, and she swallows back rancid soap as the world slides away from her. She thinks she sees the flutter of small wings overhead. Then the girl is gone, leaving nothing but the magician on the sidewalk with the slow crawl of afternoon traffic filling the street behind him.

As Santiago walks back, Verity watches the silhouette of his tall form splay across the pavement, as though he were anyone. She finds it strange that he seems lessened now with his shadow back where it belongs. When he reaches her, the darkness at his feet opens two golden eyes and winks. It's a twinkle of light. An instant later, the magician's shadow mirrors only curling hair and the exact shape of his ears.

"Leave Ouro alone," says Santiago, but he sounds amused. "Okay, let's go in. Keep an eye out for an old guy and a kid. You go first—I hate those doors."

Verity shifts three inches to the side to keep her sneaker clear of Ouroboros. There is, she is interested to note, no lie to the shadow. The shape of the man etched on the pavement is as easy as the shapes of the dog and the snake. She glances at the doors of the bus station, then approaches, Santiago two feet behind her. The glass panes hiss and stutter as they begin to open automatically, then hesitate before pulling back with a sudden jerk.

The magician eyes the panes warily, then sighs and steps through. "I always try to forget how this place smells."

To Verity it is burning plastic and rosemary, but when she tilts her head, she suspects the ringing in her ears has a subtext of fading vinyl and despondence.

"It's like this," says Santiago, his hands in the pockets of his jacket. He scans the rows of plastic seating laid out before them. "I don't know your deal, but we need any help we can get. The kid's already getting worn to shreds, and Ouro and I can't be everywhere. We just want you to stop by the train station every so often, see if you spot someone wearing a shirt or a pin. If you're not sure, just leave them alone."

"Sometimes you're not sure?"

"The band thing's a good signifier for anyone who knows what's going on, but honestly, it's less useful the more well known it gets—and most of us are just schmucks who don't ever know what's wrong with our lives or why our televisions keep fritzing. The ones like that might be pulled here by ... whatever seems to be doing that ... but they wouldn't have a clue about the theatre or how to get in. If you spot any of those, let me know. I'll do the explaining."

"Are you—" Verity begins, but then a small figure skips past the windows at the far wall of the station waiting room, outlined against the encroaching brightness of the day. "There," says Verity instead. It isn't hard. The child's bouncing form tastes like moonlight on snow.

Sure enough, coming around the corner by a wall of lockers, a taller man follows slowly after the girl. He is bundled sturdily against a cold that seems unlikely in the vaguely damp warmth of the station. His movements are marked with dogged patience, a loyal follower to the child's silver-quick brightness. A pom-pom perches saucily atop his knitted cap, and the light from the windows glimmers at the wild white bush of his beard.

"Excuse us." Santiago is surprisingly polite. He approaches the man with care, Verity trailing behind him.

The old man stops, turning by a row of vending machines. His eyes are a washed-out cerulean, the whites gone yellow, streaked with small red veins. A rip on the left sleeve of his stained winter coat releases a puff of cotton. He is as tall as Santiago, but has the stooped stature of a man shrinking with time. His wan smile marks itself in curving creases on his face; his skin has the quality of an old letter, folded too often and easily torn.

"Sweetheart," he says, "here's someone, now."

In the corner, the little girl has halted but is still prancing. When she turns, the tail of her shining black hair whips behind her. She is perhaps three years old, burnished where the old man is faded, and her gaze is brightly polished slate. Her attention lights on Santiago's shadow. Abandoning all pretence of high stepping, she toddles forward past the old man and past Verity, both hands reaching downward to pat at the man-shape of Ouroboros-in-disguise spilled on the floor. She ignores the magician entirely. The shadow falls across her skin.

"My Sanna," says the old man, proudly. He muffles a cough. "Sweetheart, come hold Grandpa's hand." The little girl pays him no attention; she is rubbing her fingertips along the filthy floor as though she is burying her fingers in Ouroboros's fur. She presses her cheek to the rubber mat, her inky hair mingling with the shade that now spills across her. Ouroboros continues to hold the shape of the magician, the overhead lighting casting Santiago's form squat and ill-proportioned on the ground and the little girl. Santiago regards the girl gravely.

"Your granddaughter?"

The word hums to Verity, slightly sharp; it lingers in the air, leaving a trail of butterfly vibrations.

The old man looks down at the child; she is nothing like him. Her toddling brown alertness contrasts with his wasted pallor. He smiles at her uncaring shoulders. "Close enough," he says. "She's with me. We have no one else. I'm Alan." He coughs. "Kids these days all go on about music. I see your shirt. You're the welcome wagon, are you?"

"Such as it is. We were looking for strays. You need a hand?"

"Be all right in a minute. That bus left me a little off." Alan's attention lights on Verity and lingers, sharp with sudden interest. She ducks her chin, a long-accustomed gesture, sending mousy hair in front of her face. A moment later, the man has moved on to address Santiago again: "We came in a few hours ago. You're the ones with the posters?"

"Some of them."

"Rock groups. In my time, one just wore a suitable flower on one's coat." The man sniffs, but the inhalation seems to send him off balance; he teeters momentarily backward before Santiago steps in to grasp his sleeve. "I'm all right, young man."

It isn't entirely true. Verity shakes her head against the buzzing and sees the girl doing the same; Sanna pushes herself off the floor and toddles in the direction of the door, which lets in a breeze as it hisses to let a man in a blue coat walk in, his eyes on the phone in his hands.

"We're leaving now," says the old man to the little girl. "Honey?" She doesn't look at him. She is pawing at the floor as though she expects it to give way like sand. The man's bushy eyebrows wriggle as he grimaces apologetically. "My Sanna—she's, ah, special. Your spaces will be all right for her?"

His concern is real enough; Verity can see it, wafting across the vinyl flooring in a ribbon of soft colours.

She is surprised when the little girl turns her head and laughs, light and brilliant as birdsong. Pushing away from Santiago's spilling shadow, Sanna skips toward the exit, hands outstretched to catch the floating rainbow of her grandfather's care. When the doors hiss open for her, the shreds of colour drift and separate between her fingers, and she smiles.

She sees truth, Verity wants to say, and doesn't. The shock of it is electric on her skin.

The old man and Santiago watch the girl with varying degrees of benign puzzlement.

"As I said," murmurs the grandfather, apologetically. "She's special."

"Huh." Santiago keeps his hand on the other man's elbow and helps him walk after Sanna, who twirls now between the open panes of the doors. "Well, we've got kids she can play with, and a resident angel. Maybe he can do something for her."

They emerge from the station into the crisp air outside, the breeze tugging at Verity's hair. Below her, Santiago's words spread like slow ripples on a pond. The girl Sanna jumps over one, then frowns when there's no splash.

The old man watches his granddaughter, but a sudden enthusiasm flares in the set of his shoulders when Santiago speaks. "Well then," he says, and bows—first to the magician, then to Verity. Verity wonders that he doesn't topple like a dried birch. "I look forward to meeting this ... angel. I'm old, but not so old I can't heed a call."

His words are a chime—the little girl smiles—but Santiago only gestures gracefully back toward the main street and the steady river of traffic. "Please." His eyebrows shoot up when Sanna twirls forward and reaches for his fingers; her gaze is on the dancing leaves of a tree, but she latches onto his hand and walks with him when he steps experimentally toward the sidewalk. She is careful not to tread on his shadow.

"I'm fairly certain," Alan confides to Verity, in a half-whisper, "that angels aren't real."

"His name is Colin. He might be an angel," Verity allows, thoughtfully, "if heaven is made of rag and bone."

Still, something brightens in the old man's eyes, and Verity thinks, *this is what Colin does.*

"Shall we?" Alan offers his arm. Verity blinks, but when she hears Santiago snort, she shakes her head and touches the old man's sleeve lightly with her fingertips.

She says, "This way."

They are perhaps a strange picture, Santiago and the girl ahead, the old man and Verity trailing. Santiago flips a quarter along the backs of his knuckles as he walks.

Alan leans down toward Verity's ear. "Did your friend's shadow just wink at us?"

Verity only shrugs. The old man chuckles and seems content to walk with her. The city is not silent—cars go by, pedestrians, a man on a whizzing bike—and Verity hears also the razored sound of rising buildings and the whisper of drifting clouds. She notices, ahead of her, the little girl turning to watch the spreading oil slick at the feet of a man in a tattered suit preaching on the corner. He quotes the Bible and his words drip with slow viscosity down to his worn leather shoes.

Alan says, "Thank you. It's nice to see young people taking an interest."

Verity doesn't know what to say. She touches her free hand lightly to the pin on her lapel and braces herself for the underpass.

10

what happened to the pictures

Did you like them? Were they worth a thousand words?

thats very

What?

Vee?

I will leave this whole thing hanging until you type something.

arbitrary

What would you like a picture of?

sometimes when santiago smiled it had an edge like
lemon, the way lemon stings on an open cut

Yeah, see, this is why I stopped.

[**IMAGE:** Privya leaning against a streetlight. She looks about sixteen, short and compact. She has a bouquet of flowers in one hand. She's wearing a winter vest over a t-shirt, a long loose skirt, and high chunky boots. Her hair is in a bun and her face is friendly. She is about to laugh.]

PRIVYA

Once upon a time, at the very centre of a lush jungle, flowers bloomed at the base of a great dead tree. No one knew how long ago the tree had died, or how many years it had spent growing. Its branches spread grey and twisted through the green canopies, and the monkeys and parrots left it bare. No butterflies sprang from the knots in its gnarled bark. Its trunk was so massive that three large men could not have encircled it with their arms. People spoke of it in curious whispers, but few knew how to find it, and fewer still knew the precise secret of locating the exact crack along its southern side. It was a tall crack, far too narrow for even the smallest child, but despite this, anyone who mastered the trick of it might be able to slip *between*. In the heart of this spreading husk, the right person might stand on a broad plain of sand spreading beneath a cloudless sky.

In the impossible desert at the heart of the tree at the centre of the jungle, a young girl named Privya lived with her father in a tall stone tower.

The desert has long since passed into legend, and the stone tower with it, because the world came to know that such things were not really possible after all. The desert was real to Privya, though. She knew where the lichen flowered at sunset, and how to suck the water from a cactus, and where the spiders dug tiny holes in the dust.

She had a gift; her father told her so. Every morning, she would rise and throw a plain cloak over her shoulders, then take the curve of sharp stone that hung by the door and slice it in a line along the inside of her elbow. She would stretch out her arm and walk the circumference of the tower's base, letting her blood drip in red splatters that would vanish in the golden grains of the thirsty sand. It hurt every morning, slicing her own muscle like ripe fruit, but she would smile a little and sing under her breath to the shifting sands and the worn stone. "Here," she whispered to the desert beneath her feet. "Take it and be strong."

When she was finished, her arm tingling and her skin sticky and hot, she would fetch the water bucket from the cactus bed and carry it up and up and up the winding stairs to the top of the tower. She would make tea in the cracked clay teapot, the old repair of its seal rough beneath her fingers. She would pour it into two cups, then take one to her father and set it on the desk just to the right of his hand. He would ask her, "Have you driven the jungle back today?" and she would nod, and he would smile proudly. He knew six uses for gold, and one of them was to mend her flesh anew. He pressed glittering dust into the gashes of her arm and made her whole.

The second cup of tea was hers; she would drink from it as she sat cross-legged on the floor and listened to the dusty scratch of his voice.

Most of her father's conversation was meant to teach her things. He taught her how to balance wood against iron, what symbols contained a fire, how to coax the form of one stone into another, and how to capture the starlight caught in drifts of desert sand. When he asked, Privya would echo his words back to him, or draw a quick sketch against the floor with her fingertip. When the pattern she mastered was exceptionally complex, he would smile. Sometimes her tea would get cold.

Every year or so, some staggering, wild-eyed stranger would come gasping to the foot of the tower in the hidden desert. It was Privya's task to descend the narrow staircase and open the tall door at the foot. She was never entirely sure whether the person pounding on the other side would be tall or short, woman or man or someone else, whether she would be met with exhaustion or bemusement or once, memorably, anger. She knew to step to the side, lest the stranger fall in and on top of her. She knew to wait for the pause while they blinked, surprised at the small girl with the bare feet and the neatly bound hair.

They would hand her bags of lentils or rice, sometimes a bit of sweet fruit, then follow her up the stairs, their eyes growing large as eggs, and though it was not a *terribly* tall tower, sweat would bead on their faces. The wanderers, who had come a very long way to see her father, often quailed at the first landing. Once there was a woman who marched behind Privya all the way up, so quickly that Privya herself almost tripped to stay ahead. Mostly, however, Privya knew to stop and wait until the visitor decided to follow, or (uncommonly, but occasionally) simply opted to turn and descend again, walking back to the desert with request unspoken.

Privya was not allowed to be in the room when her father talked to these strangers. She would go outside instead, and see if there was a horse or a mule she could water and pet. She liked the mules best. They were better company than the visitors.

The years passed mostly unmarked. Privya liked it when she grew old enough that her moon-blood came, and she could simply walk around the tower some mornings while warmth ran down her legs but her arm remained whole and the stone crescent hung untouched by the door. The sand drank that crimson as easily as the other. Her father would ask, "Have you driven the jungle back today?" and she would smile, and they would drink tea.

By then, the visitors were no longer surprised to see her at the door. "You're the daughter," they would say, and she would bow and show them upstairs. They never stayed long. Only some of them were happy when they left. One woman, who had laughed all the way up the stairs, cursed all the way down and kicked at Privya as she passed.

"Turn left at the scorpion," Privya called after, as she told them all. "Or you will walk, and keep on walking. The desert keeps what it likes."

The woman didn't answer. Privya never knew if she made it away, or what she had come for.

"The world wants things," her father told her. "Lead turned to gold, or water to wine, or the dead to the living. The world is also stupid and selfish. Tell me again of the five humours of metal."

She did. Then she washed the tea mugs and built up the fire for a stew.

It seemed as though her life had always been this way, and might always be, but outside the tower Privya could see the desert changing. The changes were small: the pebbles that had shone brightest in the moonlight lost their glow over time. One morning, she went to fetch water and saw that a strange moss had grown across the ground. She plucked a moist handful and took it to her father; seeing it, he shook his head.

"There is only so much of you to bleed. The jungle is getting bold; ignore it. Otherwise, it will only be encouraged."

Privya nodded. Resolute, then, she ignored the subsequent peppering of small creeping vines across the tower's base. A week later, she let the distant shrieking calls of some odd bird go unremarked—but every morning she bled herself, and she walked, and she let the crimson wardings splatter on the ground. The desert sands rolled hotter under her tough-soled feet.

Perhaps a month after that, when Privya was strolling around the tower's perimeter, her bleeding wrists downturned and her head tilted back to catch the brightness of the sun on her face, something sharp and wholly unexpected stung her ankle. She looked down to see a glossy black and red serpent writhing in the dust. She said, "Hello," but her breath caught at the fire running up through her veins. She took a step and her leg folded beneath her. She fell to the ground and the snake bit her again, just beneath her left eye.

She lay there for what seemed a long time, with her nerves burning and her lungs too small for her chest. She lost track of the snake. She wanted to cry out, but the only sound that escaped her was a sob. Her breath was no louder than the wind, and she knew her father would not hear her, would never come down from his vials and books and pots of ink.

A single bloom of yellow was growing on a vine just in front of her. She would have touched it—the petals looked soft—but her fingers felt fat and stiff, and her arm wouldn't move. Agony twisted her muscles, curling her body, but she smelled the desert heat and watched the flower until her tongue grew too large in her mouth and she couldn't breathe. That didn't hurt as much as she thought it would. The flower blurred and glowed, until Privya slept.

She was surprised to wake.

She found herself in her bed in the tower, with her familiar soft blanket pulled over her and a fire crackling against the morning chill. Her father was reading at his desk.

"It's late," she said, confused. "I'm sorry."

Her father didn't look up, but he gestured toward the table, where two cups of tea stood waiting. Privya shed her blanket and stood, adjusting the fit of her robe before she padded across the room to fetch the cups. They were lukewarm. She stared down at them in puzzlement, then carried them across to the cluttered desk, taking one for herself. She was thirsty.

"We will begin with reptiles." Her father touched his cup lightly, with two fingers. "And the six uses for the venom of a crimson-striped viper."

Privya hesitated—had there been something? She touched the skin beneath her left eye, but her fingertips encountered only the smooth warmth of her face. So she said only, "Yes," and knelt on the floor and sipped at her tea, which tasted bitter and unpleasant, but perhaps that was to be expected; her father did not often work at kitchen chores. She gave rote responses to his questions, but she felt as if she hadn't slept enough, and as though all the colours of the tower room were running together like candle wax. Everything was familiar: the wooden screen that shielded her father's bed, her own cot at the side, the well-kept hearth and the circular shelved walls full of glass and bone and books, scrolls piled high. The light that streamed through the arrow-slit windows was too bright, though, and her head hurt.

The world was a little strange to Privya after that, though her days continued in the same ceaseless, peaceful heat as before. She got up and blooded the tower and made the tea, sat through her lesson and swept the floor and made savoury hot stews, but nothing tasted quite right. She woke with copper in her mouth, and she could not remember her dreams.

Odd thoughts came to her; she dabbled her fingers at the entrance of a spider den and wondered whether its furred legs would make a crunching sound between her teeth.

"My moon-blood has stopped," she said one day, in sudden realization. She was puzzled, counting backward through obsidian nights and days that had grown somehow grey.

She caught herself staring idly at the pulse beating below and behind her father's ear. When he glanced over and met her eyes, she thought his lined features paled. He said only, "We will have a guest tomorrow."

She didn't ask how he knew—he always knew. She only bowed her head, then went to chop a few more potatoes for the stew.

The stranger arrived midway through the morning. He had a long scarf wrapped around his head, matted with sweat and dust, but in the slits of the fabric, his eyes were kind. He bowed to Privya and handed her a small sack of dried fruits. "I have come to see the Alchemist," he told her. Privately, she thought that last was a little unnecessary, but still, she accepted the fruit. On a whim, she gestured the man ahead of her rather than leading him up the stairs; she found she could study the line of his back as he ascended, and the little curl of hair against his neck, pleasantly vulnerable.

The stranger greeted her father, who clasped the other man's hand in both of his own. When Privya made to retire below, she was startled to see her father shake his head. "Stay," he told her. "I am performing an experiment. You will assist."

Obediently, she clasped her hands and stood still. The stranger coughed dust. "Sir," he said, "I have come very far. My brother is very ill, of a wasting sickness that steals his breath in the night. I beg you—"

"Sit," said the Alchemist, gesturing to the floor in front of the fire. "We will see what we can do to help. My daughter will join you, across the rug. I wish you to think of your brother's symptoms—keep them as an image in your head. Privya, you will set your hands upon his skull; you know the pressure points that best foment the transfer of thought? Attend."

Privya frowned, puzzled—why should she need pressure points to obtain a list the man was likely perfectly capable of reciting for himself? Her father's expression was implacable, though; he smoothed his moustache with one finger, then folded his hands within his ink-stained sleeves. So she knelt in front of the stranger, who was much taller. He bowed his head obligingly as she reached up; his lips were moving silently, doubtless as he recited his careful list of words. His eyes were narrowed in concentration, but he looked at her with tattered, vagabond hope.

The humours of human thought had never been her strongest area, but she caught the words *swollen* and *vomit* as she settled her fingertips into place. She saw a flashing image of a young man, scraggle-haired, strain etched deep in his narrow face, crooked teeth bared in pain. Then a rushing overtook her, as brutal and unexpected as a sandstorm; she gasped. She would have held the stranger's need like a weaving between her fingers, but the storm rose up and she lost it.

When she came back to herself, her fingers were still resting in the dry tangles of the stranger's hair. One of his eyes rolled a little, blankly, toward the right. His mouth was slack.

She drew a breath rich with life, and didn't have to ask her father why she felt suddenly strong, or why the room was so vivid. Horror was voiceless in her gut.

"Yes," said her father, with begrudging approval, as though she had precisely recited the twenty-six variations of turmeric love potion. "Exactly like that, from now on. You must pace yourself, though, or they will stop coming entirely."

She swallowed hard, and set her hands on the stranger's shoulders, shaking him as his head rocked loosely back and forth. He made no change in expression.

Privya dropped her hands to her lap and continued to kneel in front of the fire. The air was sweet in her lungs; the cramped room around her was brilliant with life, though she knew now that it was stolen. She imagined the stranger's accusing eyes had fallen on her, but when she looked, he was only drooling at the wall.

After a few minutes, her father went to sit at his desk. The quill of his pen scratched against parchment.

Finally she said, "There was a snake."

The pen stopped scratching.

In the ensuing silence, she shook her head. "You said it was stupid and selfish, when the outsiders asked you to—to bring back the dead." Her tongue tripped over the words. She couldn't help herself. She wished the stranger would smile at her again.

There was a long pause, then her father answered, "Take him into the desert and leave him. It is the kindest thing." His tone had an odd, diffident sort of gentleness, then he cleared his throat and the pen resumed its whispering calligraphy.

Privya studied her hands against her knees; she turned her palms upward, looking for some sign, seeing only neatly trimmed nails, the pale lines of gold-marked scars, and the furrows left by the hot sun. "Let me give it back. The essence of him. How do I—?"

She knew what he would answer. Still, she waited until he said, "It isn't possible. Outside, now."

Obedience was ingrained. She rose and took the stranger's hand, his skin warm and clammy in hers. He came when she tugged at him, though his gait was shambling and he wouldn't look at her. The stairs were difficult.

She took the man into the desert and let go of his hand. Then, standing beside him, she turned to look back at the improbable tower. The sun was still high overhead.

"He was wrong to do it," she told the stranger, who swayed loose-jawed and uncaring. "I didn't know. I'm sorry." Still, she sighed. "I will not take another," she told him. "What do I do? Stay here and eat my father? Or let him watch me starve and die again?" She waited, but the shell of a man before her offered no answers.

"Could I leave? If I do not feed the sand, the jungle will come."

Privya stood for a long time, gazing at the tall stone and the paths she had worn in the low dunes around it. She could see pale leaves encroaching. She rubbed a hand along the other arm and felt the slow pulse in her veins.

She looked at the slack-lipped stranger and thought of the moon-blood that wouldn't come.

She sighed again. "I can't leave you," she said to the drooling man. "The desert is not kind. I am sorry. I'm sorry for your brother, too." Leaning down, she scooped up a rock of medium size, with some heft, but not too large for her hand. Then, stretching up—for the man was very tall—she gripped the back of his neck with one hand, and bashed the side of his skull with the rock. The impact made a crunching sound.

He blinked once.

She was not strong enough, the first time, so she cracked him across the skull again.

A drop of brightest crimson ran down his left temple. His eyes were blank and drifting, and he never flinched, but he staggered forward and fell to his knees. She raised the rock two-handed, and hit him again, and then once more, until her hands were marked with blood and grey mush and bits of bone and the stranger lay in the sand, his face a pulp.

She could barely see the tower this time, through the water in her eyes, but she dropped the rock and turned to look at the sandy stone once more. Though the window slits were black, she fancied she could see her father's shadow.

She knelt to wipe her hands dry in the sand. Then, brushing granular gore from her fingers, she lifted her chin and walked away into the desert. The sun burned on her robed shoulders.

She walked, and kept walking. She didn't turn again, though she imagined the tower receding small and insignificant behind her. She passed a sprig of misplaced ivy, growing, and saw it stretch to cover her tracks. There was no end to the sand.

She knew the way out of the desert; she had told enough travellers before her, though she had never trod the steps herself. She walked until she found a brown scorpion squirming in the dust; she stood looking down at it, knowing that this was where the pilgrims turned. Then she continued straight on, toward the setting sun.

She walked through the night, her breath frosting in the air and her hands rubbing uselessly at her arms. In the morning, the sun rose behind her and a tiny cloud of sand rose before her, like a miniature storm; she looked down and saw the scorpion again, waving more furiously this time. Its tail flexed in agitation. "Thank you," she told it, "but no. I do not belong out there." She walked through the day, blisters rising on her skin. Her lips grew chapped, then cracked, then bled and dried to scabs.

She was staggering the third time the scorpion appeared, its barbed stinger almost frantically pointing left. "You are a kinder desert than I expected," she said, or tried to—her throat felt as though she had swallowed fire ants. She looked toward the sand to the left, and she hesitated. Then she wiped her palms against her thighs, remembering, and shook her head. She walked forward again.

The scorpion did not come to her a fourth time. She walked through another day, another night, another day after that. She recited to herself the fifty-six purposes for cardamom and the thirty-eight constellations. She wondered at her own reserves and the stolen strength that kept her marching, one foot in front of the other.

She had died once, she thought. She knew what to expect. She waited for the numbing dark.

But when she fell, finally, face in the sand, without the strength to blink the grains from her eyes, she felt only the conflagration in her throat, the cracking gorges of her lips, and the withering of her skin. A rushing overcame her; she would have screamed. She thought of her father, and cursed him, and called for him, and would have wept but knew her tears would be charcoal ruin.

She dreamed of the snake.

She woke with blood moistening her lips and broad leaves shading her face. Birds were calling in the distance and she was staring into the face of a boy no older than she. There was a hole in his throat and his eyes were empty, already filming over. Her hands were tight to his skull.

Somewhere in her head, his memories were flashing; she thought *he has a sister* and *he liked butterflies* and then the last of him was gone, slipping away from her as she drew stolen breath and stared down at the red on her hands. "No." She didn't know to whom she spoke—to herself, her father, the boy. "No. It was going to end in the desert."

Her robes were shredded rags; she wore a bloodstain across the curve of her stomach. She hesitated, but she took the boy's tunic and left him. She walked through verdant land, recognizing a flower here, a vine there—the bits and pieces of the world that had crept to the foot of her lonely tower thrived everywhere here. She found a river and washed her hands.

She followed the running water, marvelling at the way the mud sucked at her bare toes, but she took no joy in it. The boy's life coursed through her, and she was weeping.

When the river gave way to a rushing waterfall, its cascade falling a hundred feet of jagged cliff, Privya stood at the top and spread her arms before jumping.

A wet black boulder leapt to meet her.

Again there came the rushing, and a shrieking pain that crackled through her. She felt each bone break. She felt the water enter her lungs and bubble.

She waited desperately for nothingness.

She was terribly cold for a long time.

Then she was vaguely aware of screaming. It wasn't hers.

Her thumbs were jammed into the eye sockets of an old man holding a spear. Her fingers were lined along the pressure points of his skull; his body was limp between the crush of her palms.

Gasping, she dropped him and stepped back. She had a brief vision of his grandchildren—*a boy and a girl, laughing, with a ball*—and then turned to see those same children, a few years older now, lying blank and staring on a dry riverbank. The air was hot and wet. She was covered in mud and the rotted shreds of her stolen tunic. She was stricken with horror and the echoes of pain, but she couldn't remember her name, so she stood with her hands at her side and didn't move. The sun was low before *Privya* came to her, and the vision of a tower on the blasted plain.

The young girl's shift was made of some fine fabric that Privya didn't recognize. It was also too small. Privya took the grandfather's cloak instead, and walked away.

She found a road, carved through the jungle by horses and carts and the two-toed print of some strange beast. A soft glow in the evening distance suggested a nearby town, so she ducked her head and marched determinedly the other way. When the ground began to slope, she followed it upward.

She came eventually to a low cliff, and walked along its base until she found a crack that led to a cramped cave filled only with dust, dried droppings and gnawed animal bones. She rearranged the bones and the droppings at the cave's mouth, reciting the sixteen uses for bestial defecation under her breath. She added strips of leaf from a vine she recognized nearby. Then, stooping for a sharp rock, she stepped inside the cave and opened the vein of her wrist. She added three neat symbols to the leaves and retreated to the back wall, waiting for the rumble and the burst of howling vibration that would bring the cave mouth collapsing inward.

She choked on dust for a little while before she laid herself down in the dark and waited for the air to grow stale. "I only want to sleep," she told the rat skull lying just under her hand, "that the monster in me sleeps too. I don't want to hurt anyone anymore."

The skull was not sympathetic, though a trickle of blood from her wrist touched it and its teeth gnashed a few times in the dirt. She lay there tracing it with her fingertips, reciting bone-songs to herself and wishing for a peaceful death.

It took somewhat longer than she'd hoped. Her fingertips were growing numb and a little cold, but she gripped the rock again and sawed long slashes into her flesh, spilling power on the ground. She willed the cave to stay closed and thick.

The pain was throbbing, but it faded. Eventually, the air grew thin in her lungs and she felt herself gasping. She closed her eyes and smiled.

She thought she would drift, but she dreamed of fire and blood. Her muscles withered to screaming rope. Her throat dried to leather and she had nothing to drink; she could not groan.

When she gave in and would have scrambled toward the barest promise of light, raking her fingers at the rock wall, she was paralyzed. She dreamed only the rising tide of red.

She woke tasting hot blood, with visions in her head she didn't understand: light and glass and explosions of white powder. Her hands were clenched around the skull of a dead man wearing gold bars on his sleeves. She had seized him too harshly; his head had cracked open, his vacant eyes bulging. There were other bodies scattered around her: other men, young, with hair on their upper lips, and jackets to match the man in her hand. She was in the cave, with dust swirling in the air, illuminated by the beam of sunlight that entered through the wide crack in the rubble blocking the cavern mouth.

She dropped the dead man and staggered outside. At first, she only wept for relief and the ability to move her fingers. Like before, she did not remember her name. When the moon rose, though, *Privya* came to her, and she wept anew.

Her clothing—what had it been?—was rotting around her, but she no longer cared. There was a string of mules in the clearing, burdened with bags and now impatient and hungry. She took a hunting dagger from a fallen man's belt and cut all but one animal loose, then dragged the bags to the ground and slung herself on the back of the lead beast. It turned its ears back at her, but the dead man's language whispered through her mind; she uttered three words and commanded her mount back down through the jungle. Head down, it walked grudgingly.

She let it stop and eat and sleep, though otherwise she rode it for three plodding days. She found a river, and wasn't sure if it was the same river as before; if so, it was now too wide to cross, but she turned the mule and followed the water down to the coast.

With her toes in the white sand, she took the guide rope off the mule and patted it once on the rump. She tied the rope around her waist and tucked the knife into it, feeling the hilt hard against her hips. She turned to look at the sea. She drew a breath and flexed her toes, then hesitated.

She thought of red, and remembered timeless paralysis and the feel of her drying tendons snapping from her bones.

She thought of dead children by the river, and a young girl's curled hand.

She gritted her teeth and raised her chin, then picked up a long branch from the forest edge and walked into the water. It was colder than she'd expected, and the salt spray went up her nose.

She didn't know how to swim, but the branch floated, so she clung to it and kicked her feet, splashing away from the shore. She wasn't used to being wet, or chilled, and waves kept hitting her in the face and pushing her back toward the beach. But she had walked days through the desert; she kicked her feet again, and kept kicking, driving herself further into the water.

When the tide changed, it took her with it, pulling her out into the vast water as the land shrank to a sliver behind her and then vanished from view. When the moon rose, it sparkled on the waves. Privya was very thirsty, but when she tried to drink from the cold sea, she only choked up the salt again. Her legs hurt.

She took one hand off the floating branch so she could reach down for the knife tied to her waist. It stung her as she drew it free, but that didn't matter. She sliced more deeply, scoring across bone before her stiff fingers fumbled the hilt and the sharp metal fell away from her, somewhere down into the depths. That didn't matter either. All she needed was to bleed.

There was power in it, but the ocean was too big; it swallowed her essence, diluting what she was. She let go of the branch and meant to sink peacefully after the knife, letting the water claim her. But drowning was harder than she'd expected. When the water closed over her head, she was stricken with an abrupt terror. She flailed upward, gasping in a lungful of air; she reached for the branch and her hand slapped only waves before she sank again.

She wanted to focus, to remember staring eyes and the deaths she'd made. She wanted to remember a child's life cut short, but the flashes wouldn't come to her. Instead, she remembered the agony that had been her body rotting around her, and she struck out again, frantically, for the last bobbing hint of the branch.

Her blood leaked hot into the water. A wave closed over her head, strangling her, before something hard and rough bumped against her hip. It slid past, gone before she could react. She twisted. When she would have screamed, there was only cold salt in her mouth.

The hit came again, this time with teeth. Something ripped into her thigh and whipped away with a chunk of her. Her breath left her and the water rushed in. The bites continued: her back, her left arm, her right calf.

She felt herself shredded. She choked and fought and was ripped to pieces; she lost her fingers, her nose, her ears, her eyes.

When she couldn't breathe and she couldn't scream and her joints were pulled to strings of skin and vein, she knew that at least, finally, she would die.

She didn't. All the bits of her hurt and kept hurting, torn away from each other, drawing further and further away. She had no mouth to wail with, but she felt herself stretched impossibly thin. She was in pieces and she was drowned and she did not end.

Privya was red agony. She no longer had a mind with which to despair. She lost her name again.

When she came back to herself, her bare feet were planted on wet wooden flooring and she was clawing bloody-handed at an oak door that already bore the splintered marks of recent abuse. The door looked thick, but she thought she could hear a voice keening on the other side.

She rocked back and almost fell. When she put a hand out to the side, she encountered a wall and leaned against it, vomiting blood, bile, a bit of bone, something grey, something that looked like human hair. All she could taste was salt.

She screamed, and behind the door, the other voice screamed with her.

She had limbs again; she had hands, and she used them to clutch at herself, checking arms and legs, curling around her belly. She was frantic for touch and the sensation of her bones moving.

She was slimed with gore, but her skin was whole and bare beneath. Her nails were broken but grew as she watched. She scratched at her skin and the weals sealed in seconds.

She was teeming with other lives—she saw an old woman's swarthy face, a boy laughing with a wooden rattle, a man with a black eye smiling through bloody teeth. She stumbled back another step and shook her head. The voice was still shrieking through the door, but as she stayed silent, the stranger's wailing dissipated to sobs, and then to silence.

She was in a narrow hall of oak panelling, the battered door in front of her and stairs heading upward on her right side. Behind her was another door, this one shattered. Through it she saw shadows and a sprawled, lifeless hand.

The floor was rocking perceptibly beneath her feet: up and down, side to side. Up the staircase, she saw open air and the heavily clouded skies of a daytime storm that was either oncoming or just past. She could smell the salt of the ocean, but she wasn't certain if it was only the lingering impression of her nightmare.

Leaving the voice behind the door to its anguish, she ascended the stairs and found herself on a broad deck in the middle of an endless sea. She had seen drawings of ships in her father's books; she recognized the tall masts and taut sails. The air was quiet, but in the grim light of the distant storm, she saw the bodies scattered. They were mostly men, though some were barely adolescent, and she saw at least two women dressed in the same ragged shirts and trousers as anyone else. Their faces were wet. Some bodies were crushed; Privya stepped over a man with a missing jaw and had the vague memory of bone, cracking and brittle in her hands. When she paused to look down, she saw that his eyes were brown and vacant. His breath bubbled in his throat before he spewed out a mess of foaming blood. His stare didn't change.

"I'm sorry," she told him. She heard her own voice, rusted and resigned. She set her bare heel on the man's ravaged throat and crushed downward as she stepped over him.

Some of the others were already dead. She took care of the staring ones as she passed. When she was finished, she stood at the ship's rail and looked out at storm-tossed waves rising restless against the grey sky. She saw floating corpses—a wet mess of tasselled coats and sprawling arms mixed with pale, scaled bellies and bloated, finned creatures. She wondered if she'd done that, too. She was fairly certain she could guess.

The sight of the water made her shiver. She was growing tired of looting corpses for clothing, though, so she went back down the stairs into the room with the broken door. Stepping around the moustached man sprawled on the oak planking, she saw a bunk, a table, a chest. Inside the chest, under a brass astrolabe and a book in a language she didn't understand, she found trousers and a shirt. They were too big for her, and she mistrusted what might be living in their seams, but she put them on and rolled up the sleeves and legs.

The man with the moustache was still breathing, though his face was empty and drool pooled at the corner of his mouth. There was a circle of blood spreading slowly beneath him. Privya sighed and crushed his skull with the astrolabe on her way out. Then, making her way past the stairs to the door that was damaged but still holding, she knocked politely.

She thought that she heard rustling, and something suspiciously like a whimper.

"I won't hurt you," she said. "Where are we?"

This time, it was definitely a whimper.

She waited a minute or two, then she went up the stairs again and occupied herself with dragging the bodies to the rail and heaving them over the side. She still couldn't decide whether the storm overhead was oncoming; it seemed to have achieved a sort of stasis, looming clouds swirling restlessly over the tossing sea. The corpses she dropped floated up and down, bobbing into the side of the ship and away. She wished they would sink. She wondered how long it would take the sharks to eat them.

The tossing of the ship was making her feel ill.

When she had dragged even the moustached man to the railing and dropped him over—watching as he splashed in and then rose face down, limbs akimbo—she sighed at the gore on her stolen shirt and did her best to wash it out in a bucket of water. Then, dressing herself once more, she walked dripping back down the stairs and knocked at the door again. A voice (she thought it was male) screamed something she couldn't understand, then started sobbing.

"This isn't very productive," she said. She went back into the other room, looking for shoes, but found none. She supposed they wouldn't have fit her anyway. She spread her clothing on top of the sea chest to dry it, then clambered into a hammock near the wall and closed her eyes. She found herself feeling pleasantly sated. She relished each pain-free breath she took. She wondered how long it would be before the person on the other side of the door grew hungry.

When she woke, sunlight was streaming through the portal window and the ship's rocking, while still constant, had subsided somewhat. She rolled from the hammock and set her bare feet on the plank flooring, then retrieved her now-dry shirt and pulled it on, adjusting the fit of the too-large sleeves.

This time, when she knocked at the half-broken door, she heard a scuffling from inside. She waited. She took a moment to run her fingers through the salted tangles of her hair, which was a task more difficult than she had anticipated.

The door opened a crack. She shoved her hands behind her back and clasped her fingers together, doing her best to look as non-threatening as possible.

A darkly bloodshot eye peered out at her from a height significantly taller than her own. When it saw her, it flared wide, and the door slammed shut.

"I won't hurt you," she said again, quietly. "I don't mean to hurt anyone. I'm sorry. I can't kill myself again. It doesn't help, and whatever I become only makes things worse. But I'm me, now, and I'd just like you to help me sail this ship. We can't stay out here forever."

The door cracked open once more. The eye peered out at Privya. She did her best to look small and innocuous.

The door didn't open any further, but the man behind it said something in a language she didn't know. He spoke in a low bass gone raw with screaming.

Privya tilted her head. "Do you know what I'm saying?"

The man spoke again.

"Oh." Privya thought, feeling the weight of the stranger's desperate gaze upon her. He hadn't closed the door, but she could see the white ring around his iris.

Slowly, she unclasped her hands from behind her back and raised her right palm to her chest. "Privya," she offered, earnestly. "Privya."

Hesitantly, the man cracked the door a little wider. She saw that he was tall, raw-boned, and not much older than she. His brown hair was curling; his face was unshaven, sun-reddened skin pale with strain, and he had dried crimson splattered across the shoulder of his rough linen shirt.

She was careful not to move, except to tap beneath her collarbone a second time. "Privya."

The man swallowed. Finally, he touched the bob of the lump in his skinny throat. "Ibrahim," he said, or something like it. The name was foreign to her.

Privya stepped back to give the man room. She tapped her fingertips against the wooden wall beside her. "Wall," she said. Then again. She waited.

He answered with a syllable that came to her like a memory, swimming from familiar depths. She repeated it. He nodded. His eyes were empty with terror.

She walked up the short flight of stairs to the deck, beckoning him to follow. He shivered, shaking his head, but when she beckoned again, he apparently judged it best to obey. His attention darted around the broad deck, and she saw his shoulders relax slightly when the bodies of his shipmates were nowhere in view, though his gaze lit on a long smear of dried viscera and stayed there until she set her hand on a coil of rope. "Rope."

His head whipped around as he stared at her again. She repeated her request. They went around the deck—she asked about railings, sails, water. She had his language within her, awaking slowly. It was going to be a long process.

She had time.

Eventually, she would learn—she hoped before she was forced to turn on him. He seemed a nice man. She knew he would take her to land.

where did this story come from

Why? Is it not okay?

it buzzes on my skin some of this is pure though, the
sharks taste like cold vodka how do you know about
privya

She told Colin. I don't know when. You know he met her before.

okay

Which parts are wrong?

no

Vee? What makes the buzzing? I can rewrite.

no dont please dont ask me ill think about it and
all the syllables will burrow into me, ill burn your
stories like i burn mine i cant stop it hurts. all
words are wrong

Sorry. What about the sharks?

less wrong
keep leaving the pages on the desk
im trying

11

Jacob is not a man of routine.

He likes new things too much. He is too eager to play guitar or program a video game or weed a garden. He has tried managing a team of fifty; he has tried being their janitor. He likes to get up anywhere between five in the morning and four in the afternoon. Sometimes he adds Brussels sprouts to his sandwiches to see if maybe he's changed his mind about them (he hasn't, but he still tries).

He is used to sharing these experiments with Verity. In the days when she starts to leave him, though—when she roams the city to places he cannot follow, and tells him stories he doesn't understand—he finds himself sitting instead on the front steps, at some point a little bit just past lunch.

The hour of lunch varies. That doesn't seem to matter.

He makes two mugs of tea and takes them outside. He sets one on the bottom step, and then he slouches down at the top of the stairs, brushing off snow if he has to, bundled against the cold. If he waits, the woman with the mirrored eyes will appear.

He will spot her at first across the street, or half a block down. She isn't there and then she is—loosely balanced, feet wide, hands at her sides. She has Verity's scarf tied around her upper arm, stained with crusting remnants that might be better unidentified. Her pastel sweater is too large. She doesn't wear a coat. She never puts her hands in her pockets.

He makes no secret of watching her. On the good days, she comes closer, though he swears he never sees her move. He will blink, or cough, or watch a bird fly by, and then she will be standing on the sidewalk in front of him.

He is used to Verity and her habit of looking over his shoulder, or at his hands, or his knees, or something only she can see. He does not know what to make of this woman who stares at him and through him at the same time.

"Apparently, I have a thing for crazy," he tells her. Then, immediately and with regret, "Sorry, that was stupid. I'm an ass." She doesn't seem to mind, or to hear. He isn't entirely certain she understands him.

He sits and sips his tea, while the mug he's left for her sits untouched and cooling on the bottom step. He looks at her and sees himself reflected in her eyes; he sees her impassive face and the tiny images of his own stark, unexpected need.

"You have a little line at the corner of your mouth," he tells her. "Curved. Like you got it from smiling. And one just between your eyebrows, like maybe you frown sometimes when no one's watching. You could scowl at me. I can take it. I'll live. I feel like I might not, if you just stand there."

She doesn't respond. He watches her as though he can hold her through the strength of his curiosity. Sometimes she will stay until the tea is cold. Other times, a car will come down the street, or a dog will bark, or a siren will peal in the distance, and she will be gone.

Once—only once—he makes the mistake of getting up from his step and descending to greet her. He reaches for her hand. Then he is up against the banister with his arm twisted behind his back, sending hot spikes of pain to contrast with the ice cold breath at his throat. "Urgh," he chokes, and then he is alone.

He suspects that he should be afraid.

Instead, he makes cups of tea and waits.

DECEMBER

Verity develops a pattern of sorts.

It is, admittedly, difficult. Jacob wants her to come to cooking classes, and she tries it for a day, but she finds it hard to be a pastry chef when the flour whistles and the croissants turn blue in her hands. Then he wants to learn to skateboard, and she almost has the rhythm of that, but he's bored (and he almost breaks his wrist falling off, and it snows), so they serve ice cream from a cart until they realize that almost no one wants ice cream on the border of winter, and Jacob tries to eat sixty banana splits by himself.

Sometimes Jacob goes distant, quiet and untouchable as a photograph, and Verity knows there are things he isn't asking. She works harder. Hot fudge stains her sleeves.

When she has time, or when she sees a particular shadow move at the corner of her eye, she pulls on her coat and takes a bus to the train station looking for strays. Sometimes she goes to the bus station or the market and Santiago walks with her, his hands always busy, conjuring cards and buttons and coins. More often, it's the dog waiting for her at the bottom of the steps. She finds she likes Ouroboros as a companion. The black beast is always soundless, golden-eyed and somehow laughing, but it doesn't ask her for conversation or seem impatient if she stumbles over some hazy form only she can see.

She thinks often about the old man and the little girl. She wants to ask about the girl—about where Alan found her, or whether he knows what it is to see words strobe in the air. She wants to see the angel and feel the crooked warmth of his smile on her skin. She walks past the theatre, though, and keeps walking, her hands in her pockets and Ouro's cool gaze measuring her progress. "Jihan," she explains once, and the dog lowers its head, tail slinking. The theatre holds darkness and a woman with knife eyes. Verity remembers the cold blade between her ribs; she remembers the hot metal taste and the blood in her mouth. She shivers. She is grateful for the dog.

She grows to recognize the looks of the people who don't belong. They have a certain worry in their eyes, and a hesitance that tastes faintly of an ocean breeze. She doesn't encounter many. She sees a pudgy thirty-something man with blue hair and a worn denim jacket with a The Between patch on the sleeve; he's already picked a concert flyer off the bus station wall by the time she has a chance to explain. He borrows five dollars. She doesn't expect to get it back.

Not all the lost people know they're lost. Verity sees three teenagers in ratty sweaters gathered around a young man with a guitar; his songs are like wine poured over her skin, but she homes in on a girl with an unfortunately blurry neck tattoo and fingernails bitten to the quick. The girl keeps her brown hair in two braids, and she's never heard of The Between; she gnaws at the tip of her pinkie finger and backs away when Verity asks about invisible doors. Verity tells Santiago, but she doesn't see the girl again.

The ones wearing concert t-shirts and pins are grateful when Verity meets them. She tells them to go to McLuhan's and look for the angel. She shrugs at their thanks and feels helpless.

Some days, she wanders for hours and sees no one who smells of forgotten secrets and salt wind. She stares at the odd dragon or rainbow roach. When she goes home, Jacob is exasperated at the latest phone she's left behind, but he doesn't ask her where she's been, or why she has started taking cash in small but steady increments—the price of toilet paper, the cost of ten cans of soup. He puts more money in the drawer. In return, she doesn't ask him why he looks out the window, or whom he is thinking about when his smile is wistful but his gaze is somewhere else. He has stopped making her coffee when he gets up, though he still sleeps with an arm thrown across her and his breath in her hair.

One morning, Verity stands alone in the market by a light post decorated with plastic poinsettias and garlands of ivy. The air is cold and heavy with the promise of more snow; Christmas music plays tinnily from speakers on the wall of the low brown building that shelters the year-round craft stalls.

"Time flies, eh?"

The voice comes from behind her. Verity turns to see the girl Privya, who is wearing a puffy blue vest and holding two cardboard cups. Her black hair is pulled into a loose bun and her brown eyes are on Verity.

Verity pauses, uncertain, so the girl continues: "Seen you around. Where's the dog today?"

"Not here." It's the best response Verity can offer. She accompanies it with a slight shrug.

Privya laughs, which has more truth in it than the guileless youth of her face. Verity tastes winter sweetness at the back of her throat. Privya says, "Got that. Thanks. Guess they put you to work, huh? Here." She holds out one of the cups.

Verity takes it; the bitter-warm scent of coffee ripples across her skin. "Thank you. I try to show people the way. You aren't there? At the theatre."

"Not my thing." Privya sips her drink and stands with her free hand cupped under the opposite elbow. She regards Verity for a long moment. "It kind of sucks, doesn't it?"

The word seems to hover in the air for a breath before wafting. Verity tilts her head.

"My people live in a world where they don't quite fit," explains Privya. "Their credit cards fritz or their phones don't work. Computers give them headaches. They're miserable and don't know why. Some end up on the street. Some manage jobs or families. Always with that niggling sensation that something's off—that the world is flat and mean. But there's the fantasy, most of the time. That idea that they're someone special and something's gone wrong and all they need is that magic moment where someone else swoops in and explains. They dream that they're lost princesses or maybe wizards. You ever one of those?"

Verity hesitates, studying the waves of hair springing half-tamed from the nape of the girl's neck. "Maybe," she murmurs. "When I was very young. But I know both of these things are true: that I see things others don't. And that the world is, um … grey. And mean."

"And how," agrees Privya, equably. "Yeah. You're on the line. Those other kids, they grow up sad, maybe fending off parents or cops or shrinks. But they dream. Then one day, maybe they discover it really is true and they really are special. Except in this case, 'special' means their lives were screwed before they were born, and they're going to die young. You're sending them to the angel, right? He's an idiot. He means well. All he's doing is running triage, though."

Privya's words are building together now into a cloud that hovers over the sidewalk. Verity blinks, trying to parse one syllable from the other. "I'm, um, not sure I follow."

"I mean he's prolonging the inevitable. Maybe he'll buy someone a few weeks or months. Maybe someone else will get a sandwich out of it. Don't get me wrong; it's nice that they have somewhere safe and warm. It doesn't change the fact that we're a dying minority. Killing time. Treading water. Pick your metaphor, I guess. But you see it, don't you?"

"I see … dragons less often than I used to. And the last three were dead." Verity picks her words with care, letting her eyes drift to the velvet-festooned lamppost just behind Privya's right shoulder. Her voice is soft. "People kick at them like pigeons, or rats. People kick at them and they *are* pigeons or rats."

"Exactly."

"But … they don't know. They *can't*. I could say 'that's a dragon,' but it doesn't help."

"No. You'd say 'Hey, there's a dragon,' and someone would look over, and the second they set their eyes on it, the poor thing would sprout feathers or fur. How many things have you spoiled by accident, trying to show your partner, your parents, your friends?"

Verity swallows, then shakes her head. "I … I don't tell people. Usually. Sometimes Jacob. Mostly it's too hard. I tried when I was little."

"Yeah. Most of us do. There are consequences." Privya's voice is a ribbon, smooth and winding tighter. "To us or to them. Look up there." She takes a sip of her coffee and gestures with the other hand, pointing toward a streetlight just down the block.

Verity looks up, peering against the sun; the city dips and whirls around her, but she draws a breath and lets the urban morass flow through. Above a cheerful green banner, she sees what might be a bird, only it clings to the slender metal pole as though it were a newborn butterfly, wings shivering. She sees both ragged grey feathers and iridescent scales—the snub of an orange beak and the glint of a reptilian eye. The little creature's body is twisted around itself, jointed with bones that don't fit its skin. The sight tastes faintly of curdled milk and jagged glass edges that weep abandoned in the ozone of the city air.

Verity's lips part, but she only stands until her hesitation is marked with Privya's puff of a sigh. The dark-haired girl turns and flashes a sweetly curving smile at the next pedestrian to pass. He is a goateed man in a tan trench coat and a cheap suit. He has already averted his eyes, shaking his head, but Privya says, "Excuse me, sir. Do you notice anything strange about that bird?"

The man pauses in his spare-change denial and slides a look to Privya, startled. He takes her in, following her pointing finger, then shields his eyes with his left hand as he squints up to the lamppost. "What, up there?" His briefcase brushes his leg.

Verity blurts, "No." She finds herself taking half a step, as though she might jump or wave her arms—anything to seize the stranger's attention, to take the weight of his gaze from the little half-dragon's fragile, hunched form.

She doesn't even feel the world change. Maybe there's the slightest hint of peppermint leached from the air.

"It's a crow," harrumphs the man. "Are you—" He jerks his hand suddenly to the pocket of his coat, clapping his palm to what is presumably the lump of his wallet before he glares at Privya, whose expression of innocent curiosity has not wavered in the slightest. He rakes disdain across Verity, already distancing himself, and strides onward, case swinging.

Verity knows what she will see when she looks up: a crow, sickly and half-feathered, but a crow nonetheless, clinging now to its perch with thin gnarled feet. Its beak opens and closes; if it makes a sound, she can't hear it over the auburn rush of its executioner's departure. It flaps one wing and almost falls. Its trapped panic shines with the same desperate glint she's seen gliding behind Colin's starlit eyes. The thought makes her swallow bile.

"You didn't have to," she says. "I know what happens."

"That wasn't for you." Privya's regret is true, tinged with something like rosemary. She has moved closer; her arm brushes Verity's, but she too is looking up at the bird. "I hope the poor thing doesn't live," she muses. "Sometimes they do, for a while."

But the crow spasms—once, twice—and Privya breathes, "Ahhh," low and drawn out, as though all the air is leaving her in a single groan. Verity wants to fling her hands forward to catch the bird as it teeters from its perch, but she is too far, and it doesn't fall straight; it lurches in the air, wings flapping wildly, and careens drunkenly in the breeze before dropping to the sidewalk where it flops, exhausted, to its back. Its needle claws clutch at nothing. Verity sees its eye go wide—bold and wild, a dragon's eye—and then the creature shivers and goes finally, terribly stiff, its wings splayed and its beak clamped tight.

They are both quiet, watching, until Privya says, "Even that death is better for it than to be trapped halfway. I see them less and less over the years." She sighs; when Verity looks back to her, she waves a small hand, encompassing the city street. "These people—their way of knowing the world is more powerful than ours. There's no room left for us to exist, the moment anyone notices us trying. It wasn't always that way. Now speaking up's just a good way to ruin what's left."

Verity meets Privya's grave brown eyes for an instant before dropping her attention to the flicker of a broken dream on the sidewalk. "I'm not sure," she says, mildly, "what you're getting at. I mean ... Colin, or Santiago, or the theatre ... it, um, won't save anyone in the long run. But it helps. Should no one help?"

"There are other ways."

"You're the one who put up the new concert posters." Verity can taste the silver when she says it. She doesn't need Privya's shrug to confirm.

Privya does shrug, though—the slightest, unconcerned movement of one shoulder—and replies, "Sure. I started the whole Between thing in the first place. In Denver, not that it matters. For a while, it was a good signal. Now I'm mostly entertained by how willing people are to argue about the merits of a band that doesn't actually exist."

"Why, though? Why don't your posters say 'cancelled'? Won't people try to come? People who don't know, I mean."

"I'm sure they will," says Privya mildly. "It's the best signal we have. It's time for everyone to start gathering."

"Why?" Verity asks again.

"It's just time. Call it an equinox, or an alignment, or—there are times and places where the shades of what used to be are stronger. Where *we're* stronger. It's coming. You'll notice it, too. All those little phantom creatures are burning themselves out just to get here." Privya sips her coffee, turning her head to watch a passing bus as it splashes grey slush against the curb. She adds, casually, "Jihan knows. I hear she came at you with a knife."

Verity finds herself abruptly cold. Only the thin cardboard cup is warm in her hand; she stands in the winter chill and stares at Privya's sneakers—blue, laced with white. The girl has a hole above her left big toe where a blue woollen sock is poking through.

"I'm guessing it was revenge," says Privya, when Verity doesn't respond. "Not personal, really, as weird as that sounds. But I knew a woman like you, once, and she got that witch pretty nicely between the ribs. Maybe turnabout is fair play."

"A woman like me," echoes Verity, and she shakes her head. "When we met ... you asked me what colour your voice was. You knew."

"It's the way you hesitate at things I can't see. You remind me of her. She used to say my voice was like polished metal."

"Silver."

"Yeah." There is something in Privya's smile that tastes of cool tears and a particularly wistful shade of orange. When it fades, the expression lingers like its own ghost. "Then you pulled out a phone, and I figured you weren't one of us. I should've remembered the way Alethea always walked the line. She liked electricity. I caught her in a bare room once, a long time ago, just turning a light bulb off and on. Light bulbs were new, then. She said they tasted like lime peel. The bulb fried itself when I walked in; electricity was still fragile. I saw the look on her face. I was almost sorry."

"She was like me?" Verity thinks of a little girl skipping in a dingy bus station—a little girl who stepped over trickles of doubt on the floor—but she is not entirely certain why the mention dies on her lips.

"She was always ... seeing, hearing, touching things I couldn't. Telling me the world tasted like spring apples and abandoned wishes. She twitched like you do. I always thought she was permanently *between*, one foot here, one there. She had a theory she tried to explain to me once, that there were so many ways of being in the world and she couldn't perceive them all at once, but her body tried. It tried all the time. Sometimes it seemed like every blade of grass was screaming at her."

"What happened to her?"

"She died." Privya's voice is briefly arctic before she shrugs, softening. "She would have liked you. I don't think she did know anyone else like her. You know you're different? Not us, not them. *They* talk about science and physics, and we talk about dragons and one-sided doors. Most people can only experience one reality. Alethea always said everyone was right and also no one was right. I didn't get it, really. I've had some time to think about it since."

"Doors that are and are not there," agrees Verity. "Dragons that are rats. Cats that have four legs and six."

"God. It's been a long time since I've seen one of those cats." Privya sighs. Impatient, she fiddles with her hair and then pulls out the bun, letting the shoulder-length strands slide down. It makes her look younger—a teen girl killing time on the street, too small to be drinking coffee or feeling nostalgic about anything.

"You're like Colin. Older than you look."

Privya's lips quirk. "That kid doesn't know anything. I was there, the last time this happened. The time of gathering, I mean. They used to call it the Chalice. It's mostly a metaphor. Think of it like a cup into which all the power pours, and we come together when it's full enough to drink, or spill. Except it's not much power these days. It's weaker every time." She shrugs one shoulder. "I remember when the sky would brighten with stars we'd never seen before, and fires would burn underwater and leaves would fall upward into the air and the people would dance. That doesn't happen anymore. Now we might get a trickle of moonbeam or a few extra dragons. I can barely feel it now. I wonder if this time will be the last."

Verity feels a wisp of winter wind drift down the back of her coat collar. "Do they know? The others, I mean. Santiago. Colin."

"Not really. They've heard some of it, or at least the boy has. They're hanging around this city because it feels like the place to be—like they can make a stand here."

"I'm not sure I understand."

"Jihan knows." Privya glances down the street, then back to Verity. "I'm not sure they know she needs you. I'm guessing she doesn't even remember, what with the stabbing and all. She's not all there. You probably noticed."

Verity blinks and raises her gaze to meet Privya's again; she sees dark eyes, knowing and wry. "I don't—" she begins, and doesn't know how to end the sentence.

When the silence draws long, interrupted only by the sounds of passing traffic, Privya shrugs. "Last time, they thought there was a way out," she says. "Jihan almost killed us all. So, you know, I wouldn't necessarily advise that path. It's up to you, of course."

Verity stares at Privya, and then at the drift of Privya's words in the air; she tastes silver and the electrical sharpness of truth, and feels all the colder for the warmth of the coffee in her hand. She wants, abruptly, to talk to Santiago or to feel Colin's soft power across her skin. She wants Ouroboros under her hand, but she turns her head and sees only a woman and a baby stroller halfway down the block on an otherwise empty winter sidewalk.

"That was probably a lot to take in. Look, her way isn't the only way. And they're not the only group in town." Privya holds out a hand, offering a folded piece of paper. "Meet me at this address tomorrow night, around midnight, and I'll show you. I'll tell you what happened to Alethea."

Verity must look dubious, because Privya adds, "You know I'm not lying. Just meet me tomorrow. Don't bring the dog. And, you know, take another look at that theatre in the meantime. Think about what I said." She reaches forward and slips the paper into Verity's front pocket, then takes one more sip of her drink, tilting her head far back, exposing the slim young line of her throat. Then, dropping her cup in a trash can, she flashes Verity a quick smile and takes three steps back, vanishing into the alley.

"There are only two mistakes one can make along the road to truth: not going all the way, and not starting."
—Unknown (often attributed to Buddha)

12

Being Colin is a lot like drowning.

His lack of flight is an injustice. He has wanted to fly since he was a tod-dling child and first realized that the wings at his back stretched like a bird's. Some days, he can barely walk. The joint of his knee aches like an old war wound, a remnant of the battles his mother fought for him.

But Colin's real curse is love. He loves the grubby child who clutches at the hem of his coat; he loves the driver who nearly mows him down on the crosswalk. Each person he encounters carves a hole inside him like a teenaged crush. He wants to save them all. Everyone he meets is his lover and his dearest friend—even the ones who swear at him on the street or avert their eyes when he huddles choking in a doorway.

He loves even Jihan, though there are times when he screams at her blank face, or when he sends her away. He washes the blood from her hands time and time again. He touches her cheek and senses only the mercury whirl of her insanity. He feels her stroke his hair sometimes, in the night silence, and his love for her fountains in the emptiness of his gut.

They come to him in the shadows between walls. They come to him dying, with the outside world settled cancerous and subtle in their bones. He lays his hands on them. He enters them and makes them whole; he returns to himself lesser than he was before, knowing that they will only falter again. He heals them and he grieves for them. He wonders if it's his own unshed tears that pool inside his lungs and suffocate him: the swollen weight of the wounds he can't fix.

`youre using '`love`' a lot i dont like that word`

You said it was all right, for Colin.

`hes the only one but it still creeps off the page`

I'm sorry. I'm trying to explain. Can I keep going?

`yes sorry too`

Colin is never sure which pains are his own and which he coaxes from others. It all runs together after a while. It drips into his joints and swells there. Exhaustion drags wetly at the ragged feathers of his wings, until the tips drag on the ground and he staggers with the need for air and sleep. That is when a child will come to him with a sick puppy or a fevered mother. That was when Jihan plunged a knife into a startled, innocent woman with a face like a frightened ghost.

The lives around him are the waves that crash into him and the undertow that pulls him down and threatens to drag him out to sea. When he was small, it was the trickling need of an emaciated squirrel. When he grew, the seeping moisture of the wound within his mother's womb blocked his air. Now the cries of the dying come in sea foam flows that break against the thin fragility of his body.

Maybe the metaphor is too laboured. The point is that it sucks to be Colin because the begging never ends and he can never say no because he loves them all too much, but every touch kills him a tiny bit more. So he drowns in need, and then he drowns in whiskey or gin, until he can't stand and because he can't stand.

It's a hell of a life for an angel.

DECEMBER

Verity stands outside the old theatre just beneath the sign that reads MCLUHAN'S. She wraps her fingers tightly around the strap of her bag, looking at the posters for the cancelled concert. The faded papers that fill the admission window have been bolstered by new editions in bright greens and blues, stapled down the twin columns that line the entrance to the main doors.

Verity had hoped for Ouroboros, but there is no sign of dog or snake. She is alone except for the light wind that teases the flyers and tugs at the edges of her hair; even the traffic on Bank Street seems to have paused behind her.

Verity remembers the rusty kitchen knife in her gut. She remembers, also, whirling eyes and cracks of silver eternity. When she thinks of Privya's small smile, though, she sighs and takes three steps forward. She almost hopes the theatre door won't open, but today it swings easily outward at her pull. She slips inside, her boots quiet on the threadbare carpet, and she pauses to wait for a challenge that doesn't come. The ticket booth is boarded over, and since she last came inside, someone has painted a yellow anarchy symbol on the thin plywood. Daylight filters weakly through the papered windows behind her. Dimness rings in her ears.

She remembers the knife. It was dull and cold.

She takes a breath.

She walks to the door marked 'employees only' and turns the knob; it, too, is unlocked. The glow of the lit candle greets her as she enters, illuminating the dusty shelves and the bucket of water by the door.

It glimmers in the eyes of Jihan, who is waiting. Her silver gaze shines like a mirror when she lifts her head, and the candlelight gleams in the flyaway strands of her hair.

Verity freezes. The door swings shut behind her and the space of the little closet seems very small.

Jihan doesn't say anything. As before, she wears nothing she seems to care about—a mint-green sweater now, too large, pulled over stained jeans and solid brown boots that are laced and tied today. She still has Verity's scarf tied around her arm, its bloody edges stiffly protruding from their rough knot. In rags, she is regal. Beneath the shredding strands of knitted wool, the lines of her are sleek and unforgiving as a blade.

Silence stretches as Verity breathes and Jihan just stands there, watching.

"Hi," says Verity, finally. It comes out stammered. Her mouth is dry.

The other woman might as well be a statue. Her shoulders are as proud.

But they are there and the room is very small, so Verity says, "Please don't hurt me." Impulsively, she continues, "I don't know if I'm afraid or sad." She's surprised at her own words, leather and rain on her tongue. "There's a girl in the market. Privya. She says you want to escape, and you want me to—I don't know. I didn't know any of this. I didn't know about the *between* until Santiago showed me." Her words come tripping faster to fill the silence. She is aware of her own heartbeat drumming in her chest. "I'm sorry."

She is almost disappointed when Jihan fails to react. Verity isn't certain if she breathes.

Then the other woman has gone past to the theatre lobby, and the door is closing behind Verity, though Jihan's passage creates no wind and the candle's steady glow is unchanged. Verity stands alone in the dimly-lit closet and sighs. The whisper of air through her lips is not entirely steady; she brushes her fingertips across her side, just along her ribs, tracing the pucker of a scar that isn't there. Then, shaking her head, she steps forward toward the shelves, reaching for the door that only exists within the wall.

The world shivers around her, and she steps into the tall dark hallway *between* that reeks of sweat and worse things. The space is different than before. She realizes the prickles on her skin are voices rippling, and even an edge of drifting laughter.

The line of lights in the distance is unchanged, as are the burning candles that guide her way. She walks past piled boxes and bulky shapes draped with dusty sheets. The scent of lilac and coal comes to her, and she stops to wait for Ouroboros as the snake drops down from somewhere above, landing in a soundless, inky coil on the floor in front of her feet.

"Where were you?" she asks it. The snake only looks at her with flat golden eyes. It flicks a forked tongue and then wends its way apologetically around her ankle and up her leg, wrapping itself around her until its head rests at her shoulder. It's an odd sensation; Ouroboros is cool and rough. Its weight is transient, as though half-imagined, though she suspects it could be heavier if it tried. Today the snake is about three feet long, and narrower around her chest than it was on the ground.

"Hm," says Verity. She continues forward beneath the unsteady glow of the lights. Ouroboros brushes its head lightly against her ear.

The impossibly long hall is nowhere near full, its spaces still frequent and shadowed, but Verity sees shapes drifting ahead. There are more people here than the last time. They don't shrink from her as before. Someone says, "Hey, Vee," as she passes; she blinks, and recognizes a purple-mohawked young man from three weeks before. He is slouched beside a table beneath an array of four candles, a worn paperback book in his hands. She waves uncertainly as she steps over his legs.

Verity walks on, the snake across her shoulders. She passes a garland of tinsel that someone has hung along the wooden slats of the wall. She passes a mural of a starlit field newly painted in pinks and blues, the strokes rough and dimly illuminated by the lantern that sits on the table a few feet away. The streaks of colour sing in her ears.

She passes the worn couch where Colin sat the last time she was there, and she doesn't look at the stain on the floor, though she steps around it and her boots feel heavy on the planks. She doesn't see a grouping of empty beer bottles in time and kicks one, freezing as it rattles and clinks across the floor. Her shoulders pull in and she realizes it is Ouroboros tightening. She wonders if the snake means to be reassuring.

She bends and puts the bottle back, lining it up neatly before she carries on.

The area that was lost to darkness before is lit now with a continued and irregular line of candles, the wax in all sizes and shapes. The tiny flames are lined on small tables, set on chairs, or perched in wall sconces.

Verity can still hear voices, but she is alone with the snake when a bare, seemingly infinitely tall wall looms in front of her, and the hall- way—which has, until now, been perfectly straight—turns a sharp ninety degrees to the left. She touches her fingertips against the wood and turns, following the trail of candles. There's a stronger glow ahead, nearly eclipsed by the scent of pine and the constant high-pitched whine the walls leave in her ears.

There are people here, too, clustered in the close quarters. "Hey, Vee," someone says again. "Did you hear?" Verity isn't sure what to answer; she vaguely recognizes a pair of weathered cowboy boots and the series of red flowers someone has drawn in marker on the leg of a pair of denim jeans.

Bodies make way for her as people press against walls; Verity whispers thanks. On her right, she passes modest piles of food, mostly boxed cer- eals and granola bars. Leering cartoon mascots seem out of place, printed on cardboard over brightly coloured breakfast bowls.

Ouroboros stretches slightly—Verity suspects the snake has actu- ally grown physically longer—and winds its way up through Verity's hair. "Stop that," she tries, to little effect. "Sorry," she adds, to a woman squeezing from her path, "not you."

As she walks, the flotsam in the hall becomes noticeably older; she slips past the remnants of a miniature horse-drawn carriage, its doors missing and its roof gaping open. It was once painted red and gilded with strips of something long since pried off.

A river of conversation surrounds Verity now, and she can see chil- dren's laughter dancing golden among the dust motes and candle flames. She approaches a circle of lanterns blocking her path, arranged on tall, heavy iron stands—flames kept safely out of the way of tiny fingers, and a space cleared where faded pillows are tossed on the narrow floor. Six children, ranging in age from perhaps two to twelve, sit playing with a small number of toys; Verity sees a porcelain doll with curling hair, a wooden top, and a carved rocking horse.

The little girl Sanna kneels separately, facing the wall, and has her right hand extended, playing with the misty taste of wild grass.

"Be still," murmurs Verity to Ouroboros. The snake wraps itself lightly around her neck.

Verity crouches next to the girl and turns her own hand palm up, catching the whiff of grass between her fingers.

The little girl doesn't look up, but she pauses. Verity holds her breath, unmoving, and the snake takes her cue, until Sanna reaches out and strokes the bit of flavour with one small fingertip.

"It's from the rocking horse," Verity says. "The taste of its tail. It was a living horse's hair, once. Maybe this is ... phantom? A memory. A bit of its field."

"It's no good," says the pillowy-looking boy who was previously spinning the wooden top. His plaid shirt is worn but carefully mended. "She doesn't talk. Doesn't play. Just sits there, mostly."

"She might play," offers Verity, gently, "if you are slow, and let her figure out one thing at a time. A sight, a scent, the sound of your voice. It's all the same to her until she learns. She'll talk one day."

"Huh." The kid sounds unconvinced. His compatriots have stopped playing and are looking curiously at Verity and Sanna.

"What are you looking at?" asks a girl wearing a superhero t-shirt and a denim skirt.

All the words are pecking at the green on Verity's palm, chasing it with sparkles and a texture like worn shag carpeting. Sanna takes her fingers away, looking back to the wall.

Verity straightens, feeling the light cool weight of the snake around her neck. "Is Colin here?"

The boy with the wooden top waves further down the hall. "Can I touch Ouro?" he asks, interested.

Verity is startled. "Maybe?" It's as much a question for the snake as a response to the boy. She walks over, feeling the eyes of the children on her, bright and interested. She waits to see what Ouroboros will do, but feels it slide down from her neck as it winds down her right arm, tracing rings down to her wrist. It blinks golden eyes at the boy, rearing its head three or four inches in the air. It seems to have gotten smaller; it is barely more than a ribbon.

Verity raises her arm and waits as the boy lifts a tentative finger. She watches the look of awe on his face—feels his anticipation shiver across her cheekbones—and wonders if this is how Santiago feels, with the impossible shadow at his beck and call. She has no control over the snake, but she and Ouro are both patient as the boy strokes black scales.

"Cool," breathes the boy.

The other children cluster in Verity's space suddenly, their small hands cayenne-scented on her hips and her arms as they, too, reach for the snake. Ouro arches its neck, looking generally pleased with the attention.

Verity looks to the side, but she only sees Sanna's hunched shoulders; the little girl is still turned away at the edge of the light.

So Verity tells the boy, "If you play with Sanna a little, carefully, he might let you touch him again later." She is being daring—she feels the snake nip at her wrist—but the shadow-creature's touch is light and no teeth break her skin, so she thinks she has done well enough. She adds, apologetically, "We should find Colin now."

The children's disappointment flashes in little lightning strikes of regret, which Verity blinks through in order to cast one more glance at the girl. She sees Sanna turn toward one of the tiny sparks.

Saying nothing, Verity hitches her bag up on her shoulder and continues down the hall. She hears the whirring of the top start up again behind her. Ouroboros slides back up her arm, winding itself to her shoulder and perching there, cool and nearly insubstantial. "I'm still not afraid of snakes," she observes, but the snake only darts its tongue perilously close to her ear.

The hall is dark for perhaps ten feet here, a spill of shadows that leads to a renewed flurry of candles and glowing lamps. Here, the furnishings, such as they are, seem more modern, or at least the scratched old coffee table that houses the first candle collection might easily have come from a recent garage sale. A broken recliner comes next, its footrest apparently caught at a crooked, half-extended angle, the right side higher than the left. A spring is visibly eating through the worn seat.

Ahead, Verity hears moaning, and then a scream. A hint of stale tobacco in the back of her throat speaks to a man's voice stretched thin. She can hear a number of groans now rising to blend together, as though triggered by the first. Sound whispers and ripples around her, agonies breathed as discordantly as the wheeze of an off-key organ.

Light blooms to life somewhere deeper in the dusty length of the hall. It is pure and achingly sweet. The screaming stops, though the whispers remain.

The snake raises its head alertly, watching.

Verity walks forward and sees the first of several narrow beds lined up against the side of the wall. Like the rest of the furniture, they are haphazardly eccentric: an army cot, a mattress on the floor, a sleeping bag on a foam pad. Each is occupied by a huddled figure covered in blankets. Verity does not make out faces as she passes, but she is aware of a pale hand that extrudes from wrinkled sheets and plucks spasmodically at the edge of its own flannel sleeve.

She walks toward the light as though she were following a star.

As she grows closer, she sees that Colin is a constellation unto himself; brilliance spills from his skin, the trinity of glowing face and hands, all else blocked by the thick coat that cloaks him. One of his hands rests on the brow of a mountainous man lying prone on two mattresses, one makeshift bed piled on the other and both bowed beneath the weight of their occupant. Colin's other hand grips Santiago's sleeve; the dusky man in black is nigh invisible in the dim hall, but the angel's light gleams in the wild whites of his eyes.

If Verity were uncomfortable or afraid, there in the shadowed interior of the impossible wall with groans echoing around her, she could not sustain discomfort with Colin's glow reaching out for her. When she is close enough for his power to illuminate her skin, she feels the warm caress of his care. When the angel is there, she is safe.

She is perhaps five paces away when Colin grunts, his light glittering. He sags, going dull—the barest memory of power glows in him, like the afterimage of a bulb just gone out.

Verity quickens her steps, but Santiago growls, "Don't," and scoops the angel into his arms. In the sudden dimness, he is shadow against shadow, though there's still a lantern burning low in a wall sconce. He lifts his armload of tattered grace as though it weighed nothing, and Verity thinks that nothing about Colin suffering should be beautiful or reassuring, but the angel's lashes flutter gracefully against the fragile bones of his face. His skeleton hand clutches and releases at his coat collar.

A distant part of Verity feels pity, and still all she wants to do is touch. She curls her hands into fists and shoves them deep into the pockets of her coat, feeling the remnant of bliss sleek and glistening in her throat.

Santiago says, "Wait." His gaze momentarily reflects a candle flame, gleaming gold as the snake's, and then he turns away. The next cot against the wall is empty—a spare military affair, or perhaps leftover camping equipment, with a small flat pillow and a blanket folded at one end.

The magician bends and sets the angel down; Verity catches a glimpse of broken feathers beneath the wrinkled coat before Santiago pulls the blanket over. His voice is cool when he says, "Give him a minute. You need something?"

The snake is still wrapped around Verity's shoulders. It makes no move to return to its master, and she touches a light finger to its scales as she looks for words. "There's a girl in the market. Privya."

"Oh. Yeah." Santiago's teeth flash as he grimaces. It is remarkably similar to his smile. When he straightens, he too looks tired, fine lines threatening at the edges of his eyes. "Colin said. Should've told you to stay away from her. She doesn't strike me as all that stable."

"Jihan drove a knife into me," murmurs Verity, not entirely without asperity.

"Okay, point. Privya's different, though. I think she wants a war." Santiago nudges past Verity to check on the massive man now silent beside her. "Most of us aren't very good soldiers. Have you met Matt? This is Matt."

"Hello," says Verity obligingly. Matt, in turn, lifts his right hand and waggles his fingers listlessly in the air as Santiago tries to take the pulse at his wrist. Up close, the stranger is even more imposing, his form dominating the mattresses on which he lies. His skin is the shade of burnished walnut, smooth and shining. He is hairless. The edges of his eyes narrow to sharp points, and he seems to want to look at Verity, but his gaze rolls helplessly beneath flickering lids.

"It's okay, man," says Santiago, calmly. He's lying, and Verity does her best not to choke on it, though she can't keep her fingers from curling against her throat. She feels the snake flex around her shoulders and thinks it is an apology.

The magician adjusts the blankets as the other man's hand falls back to curl over the mound of his stomach. "Matt just arrived from London," adds Santiago. "He came by plane. He's an insurance broker. Managed all right with cars and computers. Has a passport photo. His whole life, though, he's been diagnosed with allergies—to cats, dogs, latex, strawberries, dairy, dust ... I can't remember what else you said?" Matt's hand waves again, weak but dismissive. "Yeah," agrees the magician. "Everything. A few years ago, they told him it was cancer, only they couldn't figure out what kind. Upshot is, he's like a lot of us now: this world has been killing him in increments."

"Thanks," grunts the man on the mattress. "That's very encouraging."

His accent is marked with smog and the sort of history that gathers in ancient stones. There's a rasp in his throat that keeps his words at a whisper. His sarcasm makes Verity shake her head quickly, in a vain attempt to dislodge the scrape across her skin.

"Sorry," says the magician, who isn't, because the word threatens to creep tangled and thorny down Verity's throat. She edges a step to the side.

"Stop it," mutters Colin, from beneath his blanket and the shroud of his coat. "You're both hurting her. I can feel it from here. C'mon over, Vee."

Verity hesitates, but Santiago steps aside, shooting her a warning glance as he presses closer to Matt's mattress. He gestures her toward Colin—a magician's graceful stage presentation, awaiting applause—but his gaze is flat. Verity only shakes her head, shifting past, careful not to step in the puddle of red sarcasm still wriggling on the floor. She almost walks into a low coffee table; the knock of her shin sets a light tilting dangerously. She feels Ouro slide from her arm, quicker than any reptile should move. The snake wraps itself around the teetering candle in less than an instant, steadying the flame. Its coils stripe the translucent glow of the yellow wax, leaving bands of dim light below the fire's shine.

Verity says, "Thank you." Ouroboros looks up at her with bland reptile eyes. She takes a moment to get her bearings, then takes two certain steps to the left and rests her fingertips against the shoulder of Colin's coat. The fabric is heavy and coarser than she expected. His bones are razor thin beneath.

"Take my hand." Colin's fingers flex invitingly against the flat pillow. The blankets partially obscure his face, but the messy fall of his hair gives off its own moonlight sheen. One white-lashed eye peers up at Verity, filled with a swirl of starlight.

"No," says Verity. "It hurts you."

The angel smells of stale vomit and the crisp perfection of a spring breeze. His grin is both bitter and fragile. "So does your pain," he says, hopelessly, but he wraps his hand around the pillow instead, clutching it close to his face. "Nice to see you. Surprised you're here. Where's her majesty? Not giving you any trouble?"

"She went outside. I passed her on my way in. I'm not sure she knew me."

"She *left*? Christ—" Colin's fingers flex convulsively before he starts to shift, one wing flailing outward beneath the blanket as he pushes himself up. Black feathers escape the worn grey flannel and the coat beneath, shining green and gold before they are eclipsed by a larger darkness and Santiago pushes Verity aside, moving to press the angel back down.

"Lie there," he says, without apparent sympathy, though Verity notes the speed of his intervention. She wonders how much time the magician must spend tending to the wounded. She inhales the wood dust of the air, and it tastes of cemeteries and mould.

"Not if she's wandering around—"

"She's probably outside Vee's place again." Santiago jerks a thumb in Verity's direction. "Sorry," he adds to her, and though his tone is flat, he does mean it this time. It's a velvet caress on the inside of her wrist.

Verity blinks. "She's stalking me?" She is abruptly cold.

"Don't think so. We would've warned you. Ouro's managed to follow her a few times; mostly, she stands on your steps and your boyfriend talks to her. Or at her. Maybe *he* needs a warning."

Verity doesn't feel any warmer. She crosses her arms, rubbing her hands up and down her biceps, and she's quiet for long enough that the angel's eyes flare bright with glittering power. When Colin would stir again, she lifts a hand, palm out. Santiago, too, is watching her.

"Privya," she says, swallowing back the sick taste of betrayal—is it betrayal? It isn't surprise. Ginger and bitterness. "She says you want to ... find a way out? That you need me for that?"

"Do we?" Santiago sounds genuinely surprised. "Yeah, though. That's what Alan's saying. If we hang in, maybe Princess Chuckles can get us the hell out of here."

"When? Is it March 5th? That's Privya; the new posters are hers."

"What is she even—Lansdowne is a dead zone." The magician spreads his hands. "Why would she send everyone there?"

"That's the million-dollar question," mutters Colin into his pillow. "Jihan's not much for talking, and you may've noticed Privya hates me."

"Jihan'll open the door," chimes in Matt unexpectedly. His voice is a whispering reed. "She's the one who'll take us home. I heard stories, when I was a kid. Now the old man says she's the one. Thanks, mate—I can breathe again. You all right?"

"I'll live. Give me a minute." Colin burrows deeper under the blanket, for all the world like a teenager who doesn't want to get up in the morning. Verity can see the white bone of his wrist.

"What does it mean?" she asks. "That someone could take you 'home'?"

Santiago is the one who answers. "Don't know. Seems like anything's better than here." He steps back from both cots, giving Verity a clear berth as he leans against the opposite wall, near the table where Ouroboros still wraps itself around the candle. "You should talk to the old guy. He says he recognizes Jihan. Who knows? She stares through him like she does everyone."

"It's all rumour," says Colin, pushing himself up on his palms. "Folks are getting excited. I'll admit, I'd love to believe it myself. Problem is, we've lost so much of what was. I'm thirty-two. Stefan's twenty-eight. We're old for what we are, but not old enough to remember whatever came before."

Thirty-two, the boy says. Verity looks at the fragile lines of his hands as he sits up, settling his feet on the floor and his fingers in his lap. His shoulders are stooped like a very old man's. She knows he speaks truth, and his bruised eyes are a punch at the centre of her chest.

Those same eyes flare as she drops her gaze.

"Don't," says Colin. "Don't pity me. You feel bad, and then it pulls me, and all I can think of is making it better, which makes me sick, which makes you feel bad. It's a shitty cycle."

"I'm sorry."

"Don't be sorry, either." The angel is half rueful and half irritated. Even his annoyance is gentle. "Seriously. I'd appreciate it."

Verity makes a concerted effort to ignore the slight figure in front of her; she focuses instead on the faint glow resurrecting in his skin, and the way it sends motes of pleasant humming dancing across her toes. She looks down at her sneakers and contemplates the drift of divinity over snow-stained canvas.

"Thanks." Colin stretches, the long bones of his wings shifting beneath the coat, then he rests a hand on Santiago's extended forearm and rises. He grasps at the magician, finding his balance. Santiago stands stoic, though his face is stern and disapproving.

"Thanks," offers Matt again, still unmoving. "Feels a little easier now."

"Great." Colin stretches his other hand to touch Matt's toes where they poke up beneath the blanket. "Hang in there." He straightens then and lets go of the magician, swaying as he scrubs a hand through the mess of his hair. "Is that it for now?" He surveys the wall and the line of makeshift beds where ragged forms toss and groan. He sighs; the lights flare in his eyes. "Christ. Get me another beer?"

"Fresh out." Santiago manages to sound mildly apologetic. It stains the blackness of his shirt as Verity watches, dripping down the fabric and leaving a darkness as impenetrable as the fine line of Ouroboros, still encircling the candle. The magician's eyes are as flinted as the snake's are bright. They both look hard as diamond.

"Hell," is Colin's verdict. "Right, well. When you can." His hair is a soft feather down, in static disarray. He steps unsteadily past Verity and pats at her arm—not touching her skin, but only the worn wool of her coat. "Come on and talk to Alan. I'd like to know what you make of this. Tell us whether it's real."

Verity finds her fingers have lifted of their own volition, reaching toward the faintly glowing skin, the angel's pulse beating just at the base of his throat. He pauses, turning toward her slightly, his chin lifting to expose the delicacy of his Adam's apple, and she understands that he will not stop her.

Still, she curls her nails into her palm, feeling the sting with the sudden directness of the clarity that even the brush of Colin's light brings her. His breath sucks in at the same time as hers; though her hand is an inch away, she knows that she has taken from him. She drops her hand, feeling a flush of warmth spread across her cheeks and savouring, despite herself, the silence of it. Around her, the dim hall settles into a ghost of clarity—it's ephemeral, only for that lungful of air as she sighs it slowly out.

"I'm sorry. I didn't mean to do that."

"There are a lot of damn apologies going around here today." Colin just sounds tired. He takes two limping steps further, then leans to pluck his cane from where it's been leaning forgotten against a crack in the wall.

"There are forty-six lives in these walls," says Verity, in the moment before the certainty leaves her. Even as she speaks, she can feel reality slipping back into chaos around her, the sense of individual lives dissipating beneath yellowed candle wax and the weight of her own words. The air tastes of sweat and despair. "What comes next?"

"We keep as many alive as we can." Santiago's voice is overcast velvet, edged with disapproval.

"Alan has them buzzing in the hall, but the truth is, we've never had a plan. We have survival. Plans were for a hundred years ago, maybe, or five hundred, or a thousand. Before we had to hide in walls." Colin's hand is white-knuckled on the handle of the cane, the ivory shade of bone leaking through the papier-mâché of his skin. "I don't mean to snap. I did say to stay away from Privya, though. She's dangerous. This about her?"

"Maybe." Verity fidgets with the strap of her bag; she has a hard time holding herself still as the hall trembles and resettles around her. Matt coughs, and the sound settles in tiny sparks that burn the skin just beneath her left eye. "I want to help."

"You are helping." Santiago's irritation has apparently relented now that Colin stands alone. The magician touches his fingertips lightly to the low table, so that Ouroboros can slide off the candle and vanish into his sleeve. "You've sent seven people here, by my count. If you'd like to help more, we could use cereal and toilet paper."

"Also some gummi bears, and a six-pack." Colin thinks about that, then amends, "All right, probably toilet paper first. Look, Privya—I don't know much about her, except that she's old, and angry. I've only met her once." Stars glitter and dance in his eyes. "A few of us have seen her around lately. A few more have joined her."

Santiago nods. "She watched one of my shows a while back. She dropped a twenty in the hat and told me it was better to fight for dignity than to dance for change on the corner. I'm still not entirely convinced she was wrong." His voice is wry; there's chlorine in it, but his hand is already half-raised against Colin's look.

Verity says, "She knows Jihan."

"They knew each other back in the day. They weren't friends. I don't know much." Colin sighs, blowing fine hair from his face in the process. "I knew they had power once—maybe still do. Real power. Not the ghosts of it that haunt this place. If something's coming, they'll be at the heart of it. And if Jihan actually can ... take us 'home,' whatever that means—if she can take us *anywhere* else—I'd really like to know about it."

Verity hears Privya's voice echoing, *Jihan almost killed everyone,* but finds she can't say it yet, without knowing; she doesn't want to see the barbs of the words sinking into Colin's hopeful flesh. She looks at the floor, but the angel is watching her. His voice is barely louder than the rustles of his patients: "You want answers. So do we all. There's a reason Jihan wrote your name on the wall."

Verity stands silently, and the scents and sounds of coming death surround her in a clingy miasma, slick and dusty on her skin. She isn't sure if it's Colin or the magician or the bodies in their beds—or all of these things—but the impossibly tall walls are too close. She meets Santiago's eyes for an instant; the magician is leaning with his arms folded and one shoulder against the wall. Shadows play around him, there at the edge of the candle's gleam, but Verity can see the crooked bulge of his nose and the worry lines at the edges of his gaze. Her bemusement must show on her face, because he shrugs.

She looks away, back to where Colin's blue exhaustion is sliding across the worn planks of the floor. "There are a lot of questions."

"We hear a few stories, here and there, that fill in some blanks. It's hard; apparently, no one freakin' well wrote anything down. We've found a few bits of stuff on a table—a broken sword, a ripped bit of lace, a blue marble. Someone scrawled 'library' on the wall over top, because that's helpful. Stefan'll show you, if you like. But mostly, we just have people. It's hard to separate wishes from real history, so I'm glad we have you. Come on." Colin holds his free hand out toward Verity this time; after a moment's surprise, she offers him the crook of her jacket-covered arm, and he takes it. His light is quiet now, offering only the faintest promise of peace in the slow desiccation of the hollowed walls. His weight is nearly indiscernible on her sleeve. "Right over here." His cane clicks lightly on the floor, and she moves with him as carefully as though he were made of spun glass.

Alan turns out to be a small huddled lump on one of the cots Verity has already walked by. The lump resolves itself into the shrivelled length of a man who is familiar, now that she takes the time to breathe in the blizzard wisps of hair that brush the tops of his ears. Despite his blankets, he is shivering.

"There now," says Colin, who lets go of Verity in order to bend over and rest his palm on the old man's skull. Alan's shaking stops almost immediately. He opens his eyes, and the blue of them is bright and pure with the angel's light; his smile is sweet as a baby's. "Alan, this is Verity. Alan's quite special."

"The girl from the bus station," says Alan, comfortably. The hoarseness of his voice comes easier here in the dim hall. "I'm not very special anymore; he just means I'm old. Not very many of us get old. Let go of me, son. Don't waste yourself on me."

"Not a waste at all. You're all right. Keep resting here." Colin's eyes are glowing again. Verity thinks he can't help it. He smoothes the man's hair back one more time and then reaches again for Verity's arm. "Vee," he continues, "was wondering about our lady of the fractured eyes. You said you'd known her?"

"Oh. Yes. When I was a child, she looked much the same. Seems ridiculous, doesn't it?" Alan coughs lightly and smiles. Verity tries to watch the man's wizened face, though really all she can see are the soporific afterimages of the angel's power. Colin has damped himself down again, or just lacks the strength to glow. She can feel him trembling against her.

She considers, then says to Alan, "Your memory is dust shining in the sunlight. I mean, um … yes. Okay."

"Oh, I do remember her. I—have you seen Sanna? My granddaughter—"

"She's okay," says Verity hastily, before Alan can move—before he does move, and breaks something in Colin beside her. "I asked some of the children to play with her."

"Oh." Alan settles back against the pillows; he is bones drifting downward, much like the skeleton of the angel on Verity's arm. "Thank you. What were we—yes, Jihan. Is she here? When we came in, she was sitting by the wall. Her hair was all in a tangle and her head was down, but she glanced up, just for a second, and I knew." He frowns. "I couldn't remember her name at first. I would have spoken to her, but I hesitated, and then she just got up and left. But I'm sure. I never knew her well, but I was a little boy and she was the same. She used to smile more. She had a fierce smile, but a raspy voice. She was with a woman who had eyes the colour of fog—and there was a girl, I think, from somewhere far." Alan blinks rheumily, robin's-egg eyes focused at some vision of his distant past. "My mother said they were going to save us. We all gathered in the city walls, waiting for the right time. A door was going to open."

Verity is exquisitely conscious of Colin balancing against her. She doesn't have to turn her head to know that Santiago is hovering not far behind. The sense of responsibility is strikingly unfamiliar and not entirely unwelcome. Still, she concentrates on Alan's story and the wisps of syllable drifting by. "What happened?"

"The earthquake happened." Alan's smile vanishes, his tone going sober. "All the walls fell in."

"San Francisco," supplies Colin. "1906."

"A long time ago," agrees the old man, sadly. "I should be dead now, and I certainly should've been dead then. The city crumbled to pieces, and the rescuers, they weren't looking for people *inside* the walls. There weren't many of us to start, and so much fewer since then. But I remember. The woman with fog eyes, she gave me a piece of taffy once, and said everything would be all right."

"Do you remember anything," asks Verity, "about the door?"

"I was only a boy. I thought it would be like the *between*—like crafting a door with only one side that led somewhere wonderful, and the lady with the sword was going to slice it open for us. Like she was fighting a gryphon. She was strong and tall." Alan sighs. His words come with care, but also a sort of breathless speed, each lungful of air used to best effect. "She doesn't know me now," he says again. "Of course, I am older than I have any right to be, and she looks just the same. But she didn't used to just drift past everyone like that."

"Don't tire yourself," the angel interjects.

The man snorts. "You're one to talk. Let me tell the girl what I can." He coughs, rolling his head so he can look at Verity. "Can you imagine if we could all just … leave? All I remember is the promise, and that it didn't work. My mother talked about a chalice. I imagined there was a cup those women would drink from, like a big goblet, and then they would open the door. I don't know. I wish I did. We waited, and most of us died in the dark."

Verity doesn't say anything. She stands in the gloom of the poorly-lit hall, and the angel on her arm reeks of exhausted decay. Alan, on the cot, sighs and snuffles and the sounds are marked with cobwebbed time.

"Yes." Santiago's voice winds, sardonic velvet, along Verity's shoulder blades. "We're all dying in the dark."

"She wasn't going to say it." Colin's thin fingers squeeze through Verity's sleeve. She is surprised at the strength of his grip.

"But she doesn't lie, does she?"

Verity turns her head to see Santiago silhouetted against the faint glow of candlelight behind him. The weariness in his voice belies the arrogant line of his shoulders. The contrast is an unpleasant vibration mingled with the general despair of the old theatre. She can see no sign of Ouroboros.

Verity says, "No."

Alan wheezes again with what might be laughter. Colin touches his cheek and then makes a choking sound. At first, Verity mistakes it for dry amusement, but the choking comes again, and it's wet and harsh. When the angel doubles over, a clot of blood drips from his lips.

Santiago is a charcoal blur pushing Verity aside. "Enough. Save your questions for later." He slides his arm around the smaller man's chest from behind.

Colin coughs, and the bubbling hack of it is echoed by someone in a bed further down the hall. The groans come again, whispering, and Verity freezes as the death-webs brush cold across her face and the backs of her hands.

Santiago snarls, "Go." He looms over Colin; in his arms, the angel's light gutters.

Verity swallows, then turns, hitching her bag over her shoulder. Though the floorboards seem to ripple in front of her, she quickens her steps.

"Life is an unfoldment, and the further we travel, the more truth we can comprehend. To understand the things that are at our door is the best preparation for understanding those that lie beyond." —Hypatia

13

Here's the thing about the dragons: they aren't.

This is how Verity explained it once: the word isn't right. They might look like little reptiles with wings, at least to anyone who isn't mistaking them for rats or pigeons or a stale city breeze. But that word, dragon, it was created by people outside the walls. Dragons are mythical; they aren't real, and the people who know that don't believe in things they can't see.

The people inside the walls, though, they've lost everything. All the pieces of their history have been shredded and scattered, and that includes words for things they used to know. So they forget their old terms and they use the closest one they can think of: 'dragon.' They were raised with that word, too. Anyone seen any dragons lately? Watch it, there's a dragon on that branch. Lousy dragon just stole my sandwich. They forget the ways in which their creatures are distinct.

Dragon is an easy word. The problem is that it comes with its own connotations: dragons don't exist. And those unnamed creatures that aren't really 'dragons'—they get that imposed on them, little by little, creeping over the years. We push them into the shape of a container that doesn't quite fit. Language remakes the world.

If there were more people inside the walls, fewer people outside, then maybe the connotations would change. But the ones who are dying don't have that power. They just get stuck using words that reinforce the world that's killing them. It's killing the dragons, too.

(See, I'm doing it too. I don't know what the word should be, either. Vee?)

```
i only know the spaces where the syllables used to
be
```

even thats wrong though; no sound is ever perfect. one
word isnt enough. also not everyone speaks english.

*What if we made up some new words? Never mind what they used to be. Call
them kuffles or skjmkk.*

how do you pronounce skjmkk

Did you actually just make a joke?

maybe

the answer is i think its too late; you could try
making a new word but not enough people would use
it. there are realities drowning in silence, in the
wrong phrasings.

think of it this way: youre telling this story and
you could say 'skjmkk' but a reader wouldn't understand and youd say 'like a dragon' and you have the
same problem

Is this why writing gives you a headache?

yes
mislabelling like a scream
keep going

DECEMBER

Verity does not sleep.

She lies quietly, letting the sound of Jacob's steady breathing trickle
down the back of her left hand, and the soft bell of the moonlight filter
through the slats in the window blinds. She has been nursing a faint hope
of the snake, but smells only the smooth texture of the blanket against
her legs. There are no golden eyes in the night.

She rises carefully, taking jeans and an old cotton sweater from the
dresser. Behind her, Jacob is still sprawled across the bed, his arm crooked
beneath a pillow and his face half-buried. His hair sticks up in clumps that
spark unexpected warmth somewhere inside her chest. Verity gnaws at her
bottom lip, then glances at the window. She pulls the sweater over her head.

Minutes later, she is closing the cash drawer, tucking a wad of crumpled bills into her pocket, and locking the office door behind her. The air

is bitterly, burningly cold, and her breath frosts as she pulls on a pair of woollen gloves and descends the icy stairs to the street.

The city's cacophony is muted in the late hour, though colours still waver in front of Verity's eyes and the light snowfall is a low-pitched hum just at the edges of her hearing. She takes a breath or two to adjust, then turns right and walks two blocks down toward Bank. She passes beneath snow-laden branches, footsteps cautious on a sidewalk streaked with ice. It is rough with the frozen imprints of prior boots. Streetlights gleam refracted from the half-frosted windows of parked cars. Ahead, she can see the occasional glowing streaks of passing traffic; she swallows the prickling scent of a signal changing from red to green. Her boots crunch in soft whiteness.

She stops at the corner of Bank and Second and fishes the folded piece of paper from her pocket, checking the address Privya has given her. The letters are neatly written in blue ink that only wriggles minimally on its white background. Verity appreciates the simplicity. She raises her hand to flag a taxi.

She hands the slip of paper to the driver and settles into the back seat, her attention absently on the window. He says something to her, but the words flow past like so many streaming fish. *Little Italy*, she thinks. Eventually, she says it. He adds, "Don't speak English?" and she only rests her gloved fingertips on the strap of her seatbelt. When the car starts moving, she is relieved that further conversation is not forthcoming. She notices the driver's golf cap, khaki green, stained with wear along the back of his neck. Outside is the quicksilver chaos of the sleeping city.

When the taxi slows to a halt again, the man at the wheel says, "This is Preston. You sure? At this time of night?" Verity pulls the bills from her pocket and sees the driver's eyes widen slightly in the rear-view mirror. His meter is an indistinct drum beat of green, but she peels two twenties from her roll and holds them forward until she feels them slide from her hand.

"Hey, thanks," he says, and she offers him a smile, but she's already drifting from the back seat, closing the car door behind her. The street is quieter here, though illuminated signs still advertise a bakery, a sandwich shop, an Italian grocery. Half a block down, a bar is still open; light and music spill briefly into the winter cold as a bundled couple scuttles inside, laughing.

The taxi rolls away; next to Verity, the nearest streetlight abruptly dies.

"Sorry. That's me." Privya is a shadow several feet away, standing with her hands in the pockets of a puffy and surprisingly practical winter coat. She has a knitted cap pulled low over her ears, little strands of hair escaping across her forehead. A scarf covers the lower half of her face; her breath has settled on it in crusts of ice. "Hi. Come on, it's freezing." Without waiting, she starts down the street, heading south to the end of the block.

"Where are we going?" Verity hesitates, but follows. They both walk quickly in the cold. They pass one lone man huddled in a shop doorway, a sleeping bag pulled tightly around himself. His beard is grey with frost and he shivers as he sleeps. Verity pauses to fish another twenty dollars from her coat and tuck the bill into a pocket of his soiled pack.

Privya pauses obligingly, though she only watches. "We're going to the river. Did you visit the theatre?"

"Yes." Verity blinks; there are tiny spots of white drifting between her and the smaller girl. She realizes that it is only snow, floating flakes glowing in the streetlights and humming in random but pleasant medley. "They're dying."

"Exactly." Privya shakes her head, then turns again to walk toward Wellington and the broad expanse where the city block ends. "My people. Yours, maybe—I don't know. I was never sure about Alethea; I'm not sure about you. It must be lonely. Even that broken doll of an angel has figured out where he belongs. You're somewhere...."

"Between," supplies Verity, and Privya snorts.

"Yeah."

"It seems like you must be lonely too. I, um—think that not many people like you get old. And you are very old."

"I should probably be offended. But no, you're right. It's pretty much down to me and Jihan and a bunch of sick kids, and Jihan and I are not friends. But I have my crew too. You're about to meet a few."

"Were you there? In San Francisco?"

Privya misses a step, then half-turns, walking sideways so she can watch Verity. Her face is hidden beneath the scarf. Snowflakes are gathering on her hat. "Yeah. What did he say about it?"

"Alan?"

"Who's Alan? Colin."

"Was he in the quake too?"

"Oh. No. Wait. The *quake*? You seriously had a survivor come in?"

"Just one." Verity's boot slips on slick pavement and she catches herself, fingers spread for balance, then shakes her head. "He was a boy then."

"Huh. He would've had to be. Even so, he's done well to make it this long. We used to live longer, but for most of us, those times have passed." Privya pauses at the corner of Preston and Booth, watching as a single car pulls slowly by. "Did he tell them about Jihan's supposed door?"

"Yes ... so did I."

"Mm." When the street is empty again, Privya crosses, ignoring the red light that dulls briefly as she passes beneath. Before them is a parking lot; farther are trees, and the lights of the buildings far across the broad expanse of the river. Verity trails after. Privya continues, "You should warn them about the rest of it. It's you I want to talk to, though. I'm going to tell you a story, and I won't lie to you. You would know, anyway. I got used to that, mostly, with Alethea. Telling the truth. I'd tell her tales of the desert, and she would rest her head in my lap and let me brush her hair."

"I won't do that," murmurs Verity.

Privya makes that snorting sound again, an amused puff that sparkles in the night air. "No. You can just listen and try not to lose any appendages to frostbite. I told you about the Chalice, right?"

"The, um, gathering time. Alan mentioned it too."

"Right. The last time it happened was San Francisco. We were ready. Jihan was going to open some sort of new portal, or make a new world, or—I don't know. The great escape. Alethea was going to help her. It was a bad time. The industrial revolution killed so many of us. There were just ... factories everywhere. Machines. Cars. The air changed. I'm used to it now, mostly, but I remember how many of us fell under the weight of it. The stragglers still came. They were dusty and bloody and hurting, but they came. They gathered in the walls of the city and thought they were safe. They had so much hope in their eyes." Privya shakes her head, eyes glittering. She leads Verity over the parking lot and through a stand of trees, down a short side road toward the rough banks of the river. Ahead and to the right, the lights of the Chaudière bridge gleam through a curtain of white flakes, snow drifting across the expanse of ice below. Verity can see hints of low islands and the gleam of the power plant. Past those markers, only darkness reigns—Parliament is lost, and even the next bridge is barely visible. Across the ice, the tall windows of Gatineau now haunt the snow's steady swirls.

Privya says, "The thing you have to understand about the Chalice— it's not entirely a metaphor. It's a reservoir of energy that fills over time, all these dribs and drabs of power trickling in until it spills over. It comes in strange cycles. It's older than I am. It's a remnant, I think—some heirloom rippling down the years from our ancestors, back when we had a heritage to speak of."

Behind Verity, the city seems to vibrate softly, each brick shuddering. There's a cola sign, still lit in a closed diner a block back, that is a stab through her temple. Ahead, she sees two distant figures huddled and waiting on the riverbank.

Privya raises a gloved hand in the air; through the fall of snow, one of the figures waves back. "These are my people up here. No one's here to hurt you."

Verity has to force herself to keep pace through swirls of winter and the gnat-like nag of the sleeping downtown core. Above, she can just make out a sliver of moon. Their footsteps crunch in snow and a thin layer of ice. "Should I be worried? About people hurting me?"

"Well, you already got knifed once. I thought you might be nervous. Okay; let's get this organized."

As the river looms closer, Verity must pick her steps more carefully; a path has been trod, but when she strays off it, the snow comes to her knee. As the people standing by the bank materialize more clearly in the frosted night, Verity makes out a tall, very thin man with a moon-pale face beneath his chunky knitted toque, and a shorter, stockier woman almost as black as the sky. The woman's face is screwed tight, mouth pinched at the corners; it is a look Verity has grown to recognize, the sign of illness eating from within. "This is Brian," says Privya, and the tall man nods. "And Shauna."

The look Brian is giving her prickles across the back of her shoulders. Shauna doesn't move at all. Still, Verity says, "Hi. I'm Vee," and tilts her head to look up at the lonely moon. A cloud is beginning to obscure the lower half of its crescent. The snow is falling faster now. She blinks white flakes from her lashes.

"Nice." Privya sounds approving. "Okay. Bring it harder."

At first, Verity doesn't understand, but then Brian turns his hands palm up and looks up at the sky, a strained smile stretching cheek to cheek. The wind comes up immediately, burning with cold; the snow it whips grows thick, obscuring and refracting the city lights in a fog of diamonds.

"Some of us," notes Privya, "still have a little power, now and then in the dark and the quiet, when no one is around to deny us. It's getting easier, with the Chalice approaching. Our heritage—the three of us you see here—is stronger than most. Imagine what your magician would have been, a few thousand years ago. Or that long-lived man. Or everyone's precious Mr. Warner."

Verity doesn't need to feel the word *everyone* slinking down her spine to observe, "You don't like Colin very much."

"I would rip his lungs out with my teeth if I could," says Privya. Her voice is light and pleasant, and it tastes of truth like strawberries. "But he's keeping half of that sad little colony alive. In fact, our little excursion tonight is going to help him. That should please you."

Verity takes an uncertain breath, but looks to Brian, whose eyes are still closed and whose hands coax the wind higher, bringing snow that rises in a slow cyclone of white around them. If Verity lets her own gaze go a little unfocused, she thinks she can see what the man is doing—casting glittering strands of energy out in a sort of spider web tornado, drawing the white flakes in. She realizes, with something of a start, that Shauna has vanished.

"Okay." Privya takes Brian by the arm, guiding the man carefully toward the banks of the river. "Careful. Everyone all right?"

Verity tucks her own gloved hands into her pockets, then reconsiders and takes them out again, keeping her arms wide for balance. She paces after the man and girl and finds that the snow makes it easier; the falling whiteness obscures Ottawa's chrome-stone sliding. They are safe in a cocoon of growing storm.

They cross over a guard railing, and snow whirls past the sign that reads: NO SKATING. DANGER THIN ICE. It repeats again in French. Verity hesitates.

"No worries. Brian has it covered." Privya's words are warm tea and marmalade, so Verity follows. Even through the gloves, her fingers are cold. She turns to look behind, but the blizzard has already half-obscured the late-night glow of Little Italy. There is no sign of Shauna.

"Um." Verity half-slides down the bank, catching herself on the dry snap of winter-dead reeds. She hesitates at the edge of the ice. "Your friend?"

"She's running an errand for me. Or did you mean Brian? He's fine." Privya is graceful, even in her quilted coat. She is already three feet out on the river, her hands in Brian's. "Stay close, Vee. We're just taking a quick hike out on the river."

There's more to it, of course—Verity can taste spring pollen, entirely unlikely in the night's chill, but she sucks in a frigid lungful and edges forward through the snow. She is startled when Brian opens his eyes and turns his head; the man's eyes are frosted over, as though death had crystallized in his lashes. It isn't clear that Brian can see anything, with ice creeping in shining lines through the crow's feet creasing his face.

"None of *them* can see us right now," murmurs Privya. "Not in our little storm. No people, no cameras. This is a little of what it used to be like." When she is finished speaking, she starts humming instead; it follows some tune Verity can't quite catch.

Privya keeps hold of one of Brian's hands and leads the man forward. The crystals on Brian's face are still spreading, a slow icy mould that runs over his eyebrows and down to his mouth. Verity pulls her hood up and follows. The wind blows unforgiving across the broad expanse of the river.

The ice is black beneath their boots, covered in places by drifts of feathered snow that alternately breezes at their footsteps and crunches beneath their feet. To Verity, it's a cinnamon distraction, but she is looking at the river—or rather trying to, as the storm dances in flurries around them. Where they walk is peaceful but for softly falling flakes; they move in the eye of a winter hurricane. Verity thinks she can see Brian's weaving drawing the flakes in and twisting them in a steady, thick circle. She is not certain how far out the snowfall extends.

The ice beneath her feet cracks suddenly, loud as a gunshot, continuing in several short, sharp echoes around them. "Hold up," says Privya, but it isn't really necessary, because Verity is standing very still. Her breath clouds half-expelled, misting the seize of her heart.

Brian lifts his free hand; the man wears no mittens, and his fingers are frosted as white as his eyes. They look as though they should splinter off and fall at the slightest motion, but he gestures easily, and the ice groans around them.

Only Verity flinches. Privya's smile is a dancing flash.

Small shapes ghost by in the snow; it takes Verity a moment to recognize the darting shadows of dragons, circling. She counts three, then five. "I didn't think they liked cold."

"They don't. They like power."

"Where are we going?"

"To the middle, or so." Privya continues to balance easily as the surface of the river thickens beneath them; Verity isn't certain what to make of the sensation, but she can breathe the heaviness of the ice that firms beneath Brian's outstretched hand. The river goes white at the edges of her boots, spreading outward in a widely frosted trail toward the centre.

Privya steps forward without the least hint of concern, Brian lumbering at her side, and continues, "Anyway, San Francisco. Jihan talked a good talk then. She thought she could use the Chalice to get us somewhere else. Separate the worlds. Make everyone happy. Alethea was going to help her. She was the one who could see what was true—which truths belonged where, was what she told me. Whose was whose. She believed in Jihan. I believed in her."

"You helped them?"

"I should have known better. We were desperate. Desperate and very tired."

"What happened?" Verity is careful to plant her feet where Brian has left tracks in the snow. She is beginning to feel the cold as a slow burn up her thighs.

"The Chalice happened, and I led them—down, through the walls, under the ground, to a cavern so deep and vast it was lit by algae that climbed the stone. I don't know who built it—or carved it, or first found it. It was a lot older than any of us."

The storm tingles at the back of Verity's throat, an electric promise that lingers when she exhales.

Privya peers forward into night snow and phantom dragons. "So Jihan was going to open the way," continues the girl mildly. "Alethea was going to show her the right path. There were a few thousand more in the city, clustered in the walls, waiting and hoping. Jihan plunged her hands into the pool, started gathering all that power into herself—then the earthquake started."

"Bad timing?" The frigid wind snatches Verity's voice and whips across her cheeks.

"No." Privya's grim tone tastes of ashes and a cobwebby regret. "This is the part where I want you to listen. Nothing I've said to you is a lie. Right?"

"Shades of grey." Verity shakes her head. "Words and connotations and shadows, no more than most."

"Okay then. So listen: when Jihan tried to open a door, she started the quake. And the quake just ... grew. The cave shook. There were all these cracks—a few at first, and then we couldn't keep our feet. It was like a hole opened and tried to suck the city in. It was spreading, and it was going to keep spreading, everywhere, forever, and *she couldn't stop it.*"

Privya looks very small holding Brian's arm, her boots braced for balance. Beneath her snow-spotted scarf, the lift of her chin is resolute. "I was there. I saw it happen. Am I lying?"

Verity wants to be clear. She offers, "Red. Crimson and the taste of cut diamonds."

Brian's entire face is ice now, rigid as a sculpture. He plods stiffly forward, paying Verity no attention at all. Privya moves with him, and continues, "I wasn't close enough. I tried to run forward and the ground threw me back. Everything was shaking. Rocks were falling. Someone was screaming. A stalactite fell; there was a crash, and the screaming stopped. I had blood in my eyes, but I still saw Jihan standing there, all that power pouring out of her. She couldn't control it. I saw it break her, and break *through* her. I knew the world would end."

"What happened?" Dragons swirl in the storm around them; the river ice beneath is frozen in low, wind-whipped ripples. Verity has lost track of the riverbank and the city lights, though she moves forward steadily, keeping close to the two figures that threaten to vanish in the night-blizzard blur.

"Alethea happened." Privya's voice is muffled by wind, but there is pride in it, and a grief not wholly suppressed. "She was right there. I saw her take Jihan's sword and drive it right into that idiot. It was the last thing she ever did. The earthquake died, but not in time to save the city. We lost so many when the walls fell in. There were thousands of us in San Francisco. Are there even a hundred here now?"

"I don't ... how is Jihan alive?" There's something missing; Verity wraps her tongue around the ache of its absence. Nothing Privya has told her is wrong; the conversation is smooth on her skin, contrasted with the burning of the cold air.

"She's the angel's now." This time, Privya cannot conceal her bitterness. "Or whatever mad part of her he dragged from death. I won't weep if she disembowels him in his sleep. The terrifying thing I'm trying to tell you is that she almost destroyed us all, and she could do it again."

Verity stares at the night and the pirouetting snow. She thinks more dragons have joined the storm; she counts at least seven, maybe eight. Lights loom very suddenly out of the gloom, glowing electric amber. She makes out the vague shape of the power station on its island downriver. She can see the lines of the bridges, free of traffic at this late hour. An instant later, the blizzard surges anew, obscuring her vision.

Verity realizes that Privya is expecting an answer. "You are saying," she offers, slowly, "that I shouldn't help her. Whatever it is she wants me for."

"I'm saying you're not Alethea." Privya's grip is still securely on Brian, who staggers slightly. The storm continues to whirl, touched by dragons.

"Alethea told me she walked in a maelstrom, and I tried to understand. I can see it more with you, though. The little tics—the way you twitch. I can't always feel the wind, but I can see you brace against it. You're not as strong as she was. And Jihan is even less sane than before. I'm terrified the two of you will implode the whole planet. So you can see the stakes are pretty high here. Come on, just a little further."

Verity wraps her arms around herself. Swallowing the taste of iron, she follows Privya and Brian. She glances once behind, but the snow has obscured the shore. She has the sense she is much farther from solid ground than she might like. "Jihan wrote my name and then she cut me. She hasn't asked me for anything."

"Maybe she forgets. Maybe there isn't enough of her left. Either way, it's like this: Jihan's way was almost the apocalypse, for everyone. Doing nothing—well, this might be our last chance to do *anything*. The Chalice doesn't fill itself often. Its power is less every time. *We* are less every time. So let's say, do nothing, and we're dead. The last of us will wither. I was immortal once. Now I wake in the mornings and I feel hollow and old. Okay, here. We're far enough, I think." Privya tugs at Brian's arm and the tall man obligingly stops. When he turns, his hair is solid, his features immobile; beneath his hood, his face has acquired a cool translucence, as though he himself were made of winter.

Verity stares a beat longer than she means to, then attempts to huddle closer in her coat and remembers to answer Privya. "So you don't want me to help her and you don't want me to *not* help her."

"There's another option. It's not anything you'll like. It's not anything *we* like. It's just the only choice left." Privya has none of Brian's icy opalescence, though her black hair is frosted at the tips with clinging snowflakes. She adjusts her hat as she turns in a slow circle, gazing at the storm and the diving dragons. She unzips her coat; she is wearing an orange cardigan that's slightly too long for her, over black corduroy pants and heeled boots that lace halfway up her calves. Verity notices she is not wearing gloves. It doesn't seem to bother the girl, whose hands are steady as she shrugs the coat away, letting it fall to the ice as she drops her hat with it and pushes up the sleeves of her sweater. "Here's good."

Brian moves stiffly, a hypothermic marionette who tilts his head to look down at the snow drifting across the blackness of the river ice. Verity inhales the crisp scent of pine and isn't certain whether it's the man or the storm. "Wait." She tries to speak quickly. She feels the syllables clinging sloppily to her frozen lips. "What's the other option? Don't—"

"It's okay. Right now, we're doing something else. The way our people are struggling, most of them won't make it to the Chalice—even with your Colin helping. Bri, you're doing great. Just over here. Yeah." Privya fishes in her pocket with one hand, and jerks her chin toward the hidden bridges. "Vee, you know what's down there? I know it's hard to see just now."

"Islands. The bridges." Verity speaks slowly. She pushes hair out of her face and gazes at the wall of slowly circling whiteness. "Parliament Hill on the right. Gatineau on the left. The art gallery."

"Closer. That way. On the water."

The rushing rumble is low but steady. Verity frowns and feels it slide from her like green from a first leaf. "The waterfall," she offers, hesitantly. "Or its ghost. Tamed. It curves like a hoof print in the river."

"Yeah, it's right over there. Don't worry—I think this is as close as we're getting. Look, we debated about what to show you tonight, but I made that mistake with Alethea: trying to protect her. I'm showing you everything I can. Brian, how's it coming?" Privya's hair is gathering flakes of white that drift to her shoulders and sleeves. A dragon darts from the blizzard and circles her twice, fragile wings flapping. Its iridescent scales are uneven, marred by scars, and she sends it a tense smile before it darts away.

Brian is rigid and brittle beneath the odd normalcy of his winter clothing. His formerly pasty features now glitter in the very faint light that manages to penetrate the whirling snow. If it weren't for the deliberate steadiness of his movements, he would look as if someone had put a scarf on an ice sculpture. He kneels and places the palm of his hand on the frozen river.

"Don't move," advises Privya.

Verity doesn't.

The ice in front of Brian gives, not with a gunshot crack this time, but with a hissing bubble as it vomits a cloud of steam into the air and melts away, leaving a neatly-edged hole in a slightly skewed circle. Verity feels the mist of it on her skin, a lukewarm drizzle that turns to pinpricks of frost across her cheeks and inside her nose.

Verity takes an involuntary step backward, but Privya says, "We're okay," and another dragon—a different one, Verity is fairly sure, this one with pigeon feathers just edging its wings—swoops its way gleefully into the hole and up again.

The river is a steady rushing now; in the hole, it froths against the foot of ice that edges it. In the night, it is bottomless. Verity can feel its merciless wriggle through her bones. She wraps her arms around herself and looks futilely back toward the shore she cannot see.

"I said don't move." Privya's voice is a little sharper this time, though she softens it when she adds, "Brian keeps everything safe for us where we're standing. I can't make guarantees if you wander off."

"I—I still don't know what we're doing." Verity looks at Brian, but the man hasn't shifted. He crouches there, his knees in the snow and his palms on the ice, his flesh indistinguishable from frost.

"I wanted you to see a little of what it used to be like, back when we had a place in the world." Privya, too, crouches at the edge of the river hole, facing the storm-lost bridges. Ill-dressed in her bright sweater, she nevertheless keeps her sleeves pushed to the elbows. She looks young again, the wind tugging loose strands of her hair, her bones delicate beneath dusky skin. She is pulling things from her pockets and laying them beside her: a folded penknife, a tiny glass tequila bottle, a sprig of something unseasonably green placed just under the anchoring weight of her knee. "Alethea always wanted to know things. Are you so different?"

Verity looks at the slim figure of the girl in the blackness, and she finds herself unexpectedly wishing for the dog, or Jacob, or blue eyes and the spread of tattered feathers. But there is only the circle of blowing snow, filled with dragons.

Privya waits through the next few beats, then nods once and focuses her attention on the gleam of dark water. She picks up the knife and folds it open carefully, dextrous despite the cold. "Like I said, the Chalice is filling; there's energy in this city for the taking, for the few of us who remember how. It's the only reason your angel isn't dead yet, though I doubt if he realizes it. It's how Brian can give us a little privacy tonight. Now. I met a man several weeks ago—just an average man, not one of us, but I learned some things I hadn't thought about before. Down this river are the falls, and past the falls there are power collection stations. Do you know how a power plant works?"

"Not really." Verity tilts her head, frowning. She can feel the energy if she thinks about it—the same harsh vibration she gets from Jacob's computers, pulling, circling, somewhere out of sight.

Privya waves a hand. "The water turns some turbines, and—honestly that's all I had from him that I could process. Outsider science will suck the years from my veins if I let it. Of course it works. A million people in this city know it. They don't give it a second thought. But there are things we can do here, where no one notices." Knife now held in her right hand, she turns her left palm up and calmly nicks the blade across the ball of her thumb—not deeply, but enough for a line of blood to bloom there and pool between her fingers. In the darkness, it too is black.

Verity inhales rotting cranberry and the slide of something long and warm across the backs of her calves. "What are you doing?"

Brian, undisturbed, continues to kneel. Verity has the impression he is holding the ice still beneath them.

"Setting starlight in opposition to steel. It's not enough—it won't last forever, but it will hold for a time. There are too many people around us who wouldn't believe that this works. Is 'believe' the right word? Alethea never quite liked it." Privya fishes the sprig of improbably green herb from the snow and lays it across her bleeding palm, then reaches down for the little tequila bottle. She unscrews its lid with one hand and something blooms to tiny glowing life within the glass.

"It's ... furry," says Verity after a short pause. "Vague against the top of my mouth. Things are possible or they are not; I don't think it's a matter of faith."

"True. There's a whole city here full of people who *know* that the river runs, and power comes from the river, then something makes electricity." Privya's face is smooth in the whirling dimness. "I, on the other hand, know that lightning is balanced with blood and sage and—" she pauses to spit downward— "water, and starlight. There are a hundred and sixteen uses for sage, by the way. I hope to share them with you someday."

The blizzard falters momentarily; Verity sees the glitter of the downtown core and, above, a sliver of moon obscured by a dragon's wing. She takes a half step forward. "Wait—"

"No." Privya tilts the little bottle and pours what looks like a trickle of glowing sand into the ice hole. She drops the sage at the same time and curls her left hand into a fist over the water, letting blood drip. Taking up the knife again, she cuts with savage precision into her own flesh. Blood gushes anew, running down her wrist and racing along the inside of her forearm, tracing oddly glittering golden lines before staining the edges of her sleeve.

Later, Verity will say there was a flash, but she will falter on the word, and make a sour-lemon face before she explains that she felt a flash, a glissando of sugar and insect wings that briefly made her blink. She did, she will add hesitantly, taste a hint of sage.

Nothing visibly happens. The river runs on. Privya keeps her fist outstretched, and her blood streams eagerly; some splashes messily at the edge of the ice, freezing in abstract patterns, though most drips into the water and is swept away. The wind catches stray droplets and flings them in the air. A dragon flits gleefully through and away, spattered in a fine dark mist.

Brian moves, finally—he throws his head back, both hands slapping down hard, and he draws in a breath that crackles in his chest. Verity is reminded of cubes being freed from a tray.

"It's okay, Bri. You can let the snow go now. Just don't let us fall in the river." Privya squeezes her fist, lowering it to the knee of her jeans. The blood has slowed but still runs, staining the denim. Her voice is strained but calm. She is looking toward the bridges that glitter between now-uneven gusts of snow. "Vee, you asked about the other option. When Jihan came, all those years ago—her idea of a door out was new. The Chalice's power has been used at many points in human history, but never for escape. We use it for survival."

Verity watches the word 'survival' pass in front of her as though carved with a scalpel. Its crimson settles in the stains on Privya's hands.

Verity ventures, "I don't understand."

"I know. Watch, though." Privya pushes her sleeves back down to her wrists and sits back on her heels, now squeezing her wounded arm tightly with the opposite hand. Sweat beads on her upper lip.

Brian mirrors her posture, sucking in another rattling-cold breath as some of the hoarfrost fades from his skin. The ice on the river groans but holds as the slow cyclone of snow lowers and drifts to a light dusting, revealing again the lights of the city—the tall buildings on either shore, and the graceful sweep of the bridges. Above, the crescent moon seems to have grown brighter.

Privya notes, "It might not have been necessary—the snow, I mean, but better safe, and thank you, my dear. Waning as we all are, I can only work when they don't know what I'm doing. It should be any—"

Verity sees the city die.

Not literally. I know, Vee.

She feels part of the omnipresent weight of it lift from her shoulders—a frenetic, constant energy goes suddenly still. It is not dramatic; there is no sound, no explosion, no earthquake. The lights simply go out in Ottawa's downtown core. The great clock tower at Parliament Hill vanishes and takes the copper green roof of the Château Laurier with it. The nearer bridge goes dark, and then the farther. In a wave, the lights die, east and north and south. Verity whirls; behind her, she sees offices and streetlights blinking out. She can see the headlights of cars as they slow, and the red of their confused brakes, inconsequential as fireflies.

It is, thinks Verity with mild amazement, wonderfully quiet.

"Ahhhhhhhhhh." Privya's exhale is low and soft; her shoulders straighten as she, too, is divested of some great burden. She is only a shape now, illuminated by pale moonlight.

Verity realizes the dragons have gone.

Someone touches her elbow; she shivers past the gravel feel of it and turns her head, startled to find Brian there. The tall man has mostly reverted to pallid humanity, though ice crystals remain in his uncombed hair and his eyes are glittering white.

"The river's restless now. I can't keep us safe much longer."

"Right," says Privya. "Let's head back." She pushes herself up with a tired groan; for a moment, she wavers at the edge of the ice hole, but when Verity would dart forward, Brian is still at her elbow, pulling her back.

"Don't touch her."

"Stay back."

The two snap simultaneously; Verity freezes in confusion, and it seems to her that Privya's eyes are briefly bloody, a sullen red that flickers like the brake lights of the cars on shore.

"Walk with me," says Brian, more gently, and he tugs Verity with him, back toward shore. "Privya's cranky when she's tired. I, on the other hand, am a saint."

Verity wants to tell Brian not to exaggerate—that she almost misses a step because of it, the hyperbole slippery and yellow under her boot—but she didn't expect the man to sound kind, and she is re-orienting herself against a city that has dropped several unexpected decibels in her mouth. She says, blankly, "You broke the hydroelectricity?"

"I poisoned the well," says Privya behind her, low-voiced and uncharacteristically hoarse. "Don't turn around. Keep walking. But yes, there are things we can do in the dark, in the moments when our truth is strongest. It won't hold. It'll buy our people a little time. Is it the same for you as for us? Do you have more room to breathe?"

"It's cold," says Verity. "People need heat."

"They'll live."

The lie slides down Verity's cheek and she shakes her head, but before she can object, Privya has already amended, "Most of them." There is no regret in her correction. "I said *don't turn around.*"

Verity, faltering, doesn't. "Is this what you mean by using the Chalice for survival? You're going to hurt people."

"Jihan would have run instead. But we have always fought back."

Verity says, quietly, "You mean war."

"It's *always* war—even now, when we scurry in the walls like rats. It's a war the other side doesn't know about and wouldn't believe in if it did. But there are times, like I said, in history, when we have had power to push back. The Black Death. The Plague of Justinian. The bodies that lay in the streets of Athens, or Marseilles. The Chalice can be a weapon you help me wield. It seems cruel, I know—it *is* cruel—but when there are fewer of them, that leaves more air for us, more space in this world. If this is our last chance, we haven't been fighting hard enough. We need that to change."

"How else do we survive?" Brian's voice is bitter. "If we tell them that we exist, that we suffer, they laugh and say we've heard too many children's stories. We scream and they do nothing."

"They're innocent." Verity wishes Brian's hand weren't under her elbow, but the guidance makes it easier to navigate the words littering the otherwise empty ice. On the shore, she sees a single light, small and white, turn in their direction. A dog barks.

Privya is still somewhere just behind, just close enough that Verity itches between her shoulder blades. "So are the people dying in that theatre. Remember that Alethea tried to be noble; the Chalice was wasted, and a city fell. So did she. Shhh—keep walking. I'd say Shauna's ready for us."

Verity's eyes are starting to adjust to the sudden blackness of the city, but the white light shines into her face as she approaches, and she lifts her free hand in squinting protest. The dog barks again. She can see it, a small creature wriggling at the feet of two figures who wait at the shore. One of them is holding a flashlight. The light dies, and a man's unfamiliar voice curses genially as he shakes it back to life. "Sorry, this damn thing—well, the whole city's broken tonight, isn't it? Are you okay? Your friend said one of you is sick?"

"Me," says Privya, before Verity can answer. "Thank you so much." It tastes like raw meat, but when Verity would turn, Brian tugs at her again, implacable.

"You folks really shouldn't be out on the ice." The man plays his flashlight across the DANGER sign in demonstration, then steps over the barrier at the edge of the walkway, leaning down the bank and extending a hand. "I have a car. Let's get you to a doctor." His other hand holds the flashlight and, Verity sees now, the leash of his indeterminately furred companion. Behind him, Shauna stands with her thick arms folded, her features indistinct.

Verity does not entirely follow everything that happens next: the way Privya brushes past, feather-light and swift, hands outstretched, or the way the flashlight plays across the girl's stumbling form. She has the abrupt impression that Privya's fingers have gone thin and brittle as winter twigs, and that the light illuminating Privya's hair plays across hints of bare scalp and streaks of white and grey among the blackness of her now-untidy bun. Verity thinks of indescribable weightlessness, a power worn to bone, and dreams of navy and starlit eyes, but Privya has no wings—only hands that reach forward and up, twisting in claws before the flashlight dies a final time and the riverbank, too, is plunged into night.

The dog whimpers.

There is a heavy crunch as a body hits snow.

Brian lets Verity go. It takes her a moment to realize she is released, and even then she only stands. The night is cold in her chest. She can see her breath frost.

"Vee," says Privya, mildly. "Come on." She sounds herself again, young and unbothered.

Verity's boots crunch as she steps slowly toward the bank. Closer, she sees Privya crouched before a goose-fleshed, loose-faced man in his middle years. His thinning hair is brown, streaked with grey, and badly combed over. He is wearing a beige overcoat over flannel pyjama bottoms and furred winter boots. He has fallen at the river's edge and slid to a stop, half-sitting. A line of drool runs from his half-parted lips to streak his chin, and he stares straight ahead, eyes rolling very slightly in his head.

He is still holding the leash. Above him at the railing, the dog whines.

Privya turns her head to look at Verity, and her eyes are feral even in the dimness. She has gained a new sharpness to her movements; when she rises, she cleaves the air. Her teeth flash. Verity thinks of Santiago's Cheshire smile and misses the snake.

"What did you do?" She keeps her voice a whisper and hears it waver.

"What I had to. Let's go."

But Verity has stepped to the man on the ground; she leans down, putting her hand on his shoulder. His muscles are slack beneath her palm. In the chill night, he is boneless and warm.

"I know," Privya says, standing with arms folded. "It sucks." The regret is gentle in her tone, but Verity sees the cheap veneer of it chip and crackle in the air between them. "It's like I just said. This is war."

"Will he recover?"

"No." Privya exchanges a glance with Shauna. "I promised not to lie to you. I wanted you to see everything—every part of tonight. You have to know what war means. But you can't help this guy, and you can't make it better. We really do have to go."

Tasting lime and ashes, Verity straightens, wiping her palm on her thigh as though some residue clings there. She looks down at the drooling man as he twitches, his head rolling forward and then flopping to the left. She says, quietly, "This isn't okay."

"Nothing is. Nothing has been in a very long time."

"We don't like it either," adds Shauna. Above her, Brian nods; he has leaned down to scoop up the dog, holding it tucked under his arm as it whines. Shauna moves around Verity and reaches up to the railing, hauling herself up the bank and over. "We need Privya, though. I'd really like to live past forty."

"It's worse for everyone if I don't take some of them," says Privya, accepting Shauna's hand up. She scrambles lightly in the snow. "I wish it weren't, but it is. Come on. We'll explain as much as you want."

"We shouldn't leave him here." Verity kneels next to the stranger. She touches his forehead with one gloved hand. Above, the dog growls and wriggles in Brian's grasp.

Privya hisses between her teeth, but she only stands with her feet braced and her arms close around her body. "You can't help him."

"I can take care of it," offers Shauna. "Borrow your knife, Priv?"

Verity says, sharply, "No." The stranger's right eye rolls to the white. Brian shrugs. "It'd be kinder."

He is not necessarily wrong. Verity filters through layers of grey, and shakes her head, clearing the wisps decisively from her hair. "No," she says again. And, "We shouldn't leave him. He'll freeze."

"What would you have us do? Call a doctor? What would you tell them?" Privya shakes her head. "He's one person, and you should balance that against the ones in the walls. We just bought your idiot angel's life. I won't excuse how it was done. I don't think you expect me to. That's all Alethea ever wanted: the truth."

Verity wipes at the man's lips with the end of her scarf before his saliva can freeze on his skin. Crouching, she looks up at the three figures above her and hesitates. Finally, she says, "I'll stay with him. You should go."

Privya's sigh is explosive this time. "Vee—"

"I just—I have to think about it. I don't know what—you should go."

In the distance comes the sound of sirens. Shauna reaches for Privya's arm. Shaking his head, Brian puts the dog down and steps back; all three melt away in the night.

The dog scrambles down the snowy bank, whimpering, and licks at its owner's face. Its curly tail wags hopefully, then droops.

Verity says, "I know." The dog's grief is a shining white.

[IMAGE: an aerial map of the Ottawa river where it flows past Centretown. It is accurate and to scale. Just above the falls, someone has drawn an 'X' in the middle of the water.]

14

OTTAWA (December 18, 2013)—A breakdown in the Hydro Ontario system has left approximately 100,000 people in downtown Ottawa without power. Affected areas include the Byward Market, Centretown, Sandy Hill, and the Glebe, as well as portions of Gatineau. While some facilities are running on emergency generators, the federal government has announced that all affected offices are shut down. Citizens without power are urged to proceed to local support centres or, if possible, relocate to the Orléans or Kanata suburbs, where power is still functioning. Children and senior citizens are especially at risk from the cold.

Early reports suggest the breakdown began in one of the generating plants at Chaudière Falls, less than two kilometres west of the downtown region, at approximately 2:13 am on December 17. However, attempts to transfer additional electrical load from Québec or New York have proven unsuccessful.

Technicians are reportedly having issues identifying the exact nature of the damage. "I've honestly never seen anything like it," said Marjorie Grant, one of Hydro Ontario's chief engineers. "It's like a hardware virus. Like it started at one station and then just spread. We're going to need to physically replace a lot of equipment."

It is not known how long repairs to the power station will take. The local police have received numerous calls suggesting a terrorist attack or electro-magnetic pulse, but they urge the public to remain calm.

JACOB

Jacob Shepard never knew his parents, though he was told his mother had been a famous inventor, and his father had been good with investments. Certainly there was money; he didn't think about it at the time. He lived in a very large house with a butler, a cook, a chauffeur, and three maids. There was a large painting on the wall of his mother Georgina and his father Geoffrey. His mother had his freckles and his father had the same wide-lipped smile, and they made Jacob a little wistful sometimes, but he wasn't lonely: he had Stevens the butler and Marcie the cook.

Sometimes he would lie in his bed and think about what he wanted to be when he grew up. He could build a studio full of robots that would fetch him things. He could be an astronaut and glide between the stars. He could be a chef, a firefighter, or a ballet dancer.

"What will I be?" he asked Stevens, one late night when he was sipping cocoa by the fire. He was still young; he had to hold his mug carefully, with two hands.

The butler paused in his careful arrangement of the silver. "What do you mean?"

"When I grow up. What will I be?"

"Your parents' company is being held for you in trust."

Jacob swallowed a mouthful of cocoa. It was warm and marshmallowy, just the way he liked it. He was frowning, though. "What do *you* mean?"

"It means that when you're eighteen, you will inherit controlling interest. You will be a financier."

"What's a financier?"

"Someone who works in an office and controls a lot of money."

Jacob thought about that. "What if I don't want to work in an office?"

"Well," said the butler, "you may feel differently when you're eighteen."

Years passed. Jacob went away to school and took the classes he was supposed to—math and computer programming and business communications—and the classes he wanted to: Latin and auto mechanics and visual arts and introduction to landscape architecture. Once, he sat in the principal's office while she tapped the tip of her pencil on the desk. "Latin is a dead language," she told him. "You're a bright boy and I'm sure you'd do well in the class, but perhaps you should be concentrating more on your future career?"

"I don't know what that is yet."

"I understand your parents founded—"

"I'd like to take Latin, please." Jacob always got what he wanted. The year he topped his math class was the year he learned how to dance.

When he was seventeen, all gangly limbs and frizzy hair, three men came to see him at school. They wore expensive suits. Their sallow ivory faces were humourless and deeply lined.

Jacob was brought into an empty classroom where the three men sat, rather awkwardly, in three small desks in the front row. He stood in front of the blackboard and wondered if he were supposed to give a presentation no one had warned him about. On impulse, he offered an arabesque, followed by a smooth plié. The men didn't laugh.

"We see," said one man, "you are doing well in your marketing classes."

Jacob had a hard time telling the men apart. They looked like pale dried reeds.

He said, "I guess."

"But only a C minus in international commerce." That was the man in the middle.

"That one was boring." Jacob folded his arms. "I aced art history, though. Is this about my average?"

"No. You are soon to inherit a very large company."

"I know! I've been thinking about that."

Jacob had the sense that the men were suddenly more attentive, though their shoulders were stooped. He refused to quail beneath the weight of their silence.

When they said nothing, he continued, "I've looked at the portfolio and the last ten years of quarterly reports. I'd like to branch out the product base."

The men remained silent.

Fumbling, Jacob said, "We can talk about it. But haven't you ever thought about making balloons, or marshmallows, or sheet music? Also, who exactly are you guys?"

After exchanging slow glances with his brethren, the man on the left suggested, "Perhaps you might sell it to us instead? We can give you a fair price. You could do whatever you wanted."

"I thought about that, actually—selling the company, I mean. Not specifically to you. Thanks, but it was my parents'. And I won't know if I like running it until I try it."

The men looked at each other. Finally one of them said, "Thank you for your ideas," and the three of them got up and filed one by one through the door. They left Jacob alone in the empty classroom, staring.

A week later, he was out on the field playing soccer when the principal came walking out, accompanied by a man and a woman with short hair and white coats. She had a letter crumpled between her fingers, and she was frowning. "Mr. Shepard," she said.

Jacob turned away from the goal he was supposed to be guarding. "Miss?" He heard the ball whisk into the net behind him, and the catcalls of the other players, but he didn't like the way the principal's face was pulled more tautly than the bun in her hair.

"You must go with these people."

"Miss?" He didn't think he'd heard her right. He didn't like the way the strangers were watching him, or the crisp colourless pallor of their uniforms. "Am I in trouble?"

"Go on."

The man and woman each took one of Jacob's arms. Startled, he looked between them. "I'm in my gym clothes."

"That's okay," said the woman. "Come with us." They had strong grips. They marched Jacob off the field and through the halls, out the front steps of the school to a waiting white ambulance. Its lights were flashing.

"Get in the back."

"I'm not sick." Jacob tried to stop walking but the strangers' hands were locked around his arms, dragging him onward.

"Just get in the back, kid." The man sounded kind—a little tired, maybe, like Stevens after Jacob had been asking too many questions. It was oddly reassuring. So Jacob climbed into the back of the ambulance and sat on a cot while the man and woman closed the doors and got in the front. He folded his hands and looked at an array of blinking lights and red hard hats striped with yellow safety tape. When the ambulance began to move, no one spoke.

Jacob wished he could change his clothes, and maybe read the book on Roman history that he'd been keeping in his room, but having no options, he stretched out on the cot and stared up at the ceiling. He thought about being an EMT. "Hey," he said, "you guys like this job?"

No one answered.

Eventually, the ambulance stopped, and the man came to the back to open the doors. Jacob hopped out and blinked around at what looked like an ordinary street in a tree-lined neighbourhood, next to a very tall brick wall with iron spikes on top. The woman muttered something into an electronic panel, and a gate in the wall swung open.

Jacob briefly considering running, but all he saw were trees and the pristine sidewalk. He didn't know where he was. The man was standing too close.

He reminded himself that the principal had said he was supposed to be here. It wasn't as reassuring a thought as he'd hoped. Then the man's hand dropped heavily onto his shoulder, and it was too late, anyway.

Jacob found himself marched through the gate and down a long driveway. He saw a green, well-manicured lawn, with benches placed along winding gravel paths. He saw a large white house with a low front veranda and white iron bars on the windows. There were a few people wandering around or sitting on the benches; they also wore white. They had bathrobes on, and slippers, like they'd forgotten to get dressed that morning.

"Is this a hospital?" It seemed small for a hospital. "I'm not sick," added Jacob again, but it made no difference. He was escorted through the doors and into a foyer where a grand staircase curved above him. The chairs here were small, elegant, and Victorian. The wallpaper was a rich satin patterned in roses. It reminded him a little bit of home.

"Mr. Shepard." A red-haired woman in a navy business suit was waiting for him, her smile rigid. "We've been waiting for you. Your uncle thought it best that you join us for a while."

"I don't have an uncle," said Jacob. Then something pricked him sharply in the arm, and the elegant house blurred.

He dreamed about whiteness: white that surrounded him, walls and sheets and rays of light through barred windows. He dreamed of trays full of soft foods, and little cardboard cups of pills. In the dream, people told him to get up, sit down, walk there, drink this. He did. He couldn't think of a reason not to. When he took the pills, rough fingers followed and pried his teeth apart so someone could peer into his mouth, as though he were a horse.

He wore a white shirt and a white robe because they were given to him and he was told to put them on. He spent some time staring at walls. He developed a certain appreciation for patterned wallpaper and the predictable repetition of flowers.

Sometimes he would find himself in a room where a bald dark man sat behind a desk. The man had horn-rimmed glasses and a thick pen he would tap against the notebook in front of him. He would ask things like, "Are you hearing voices now?"

The first time he was asked this, Jacob was confused. "Just yours."

The man made a note. "When was the last time you heard voices?"

"I don't understand. I'm not sick." Jacob's tongue was thick in his mouth. Then the orderlies came and took him by the arms until someone stuck him with a needle again.

He ate and slept and dreamed. Sometimes someone would ask him about voices or visions or whether he'd been touched in terrible places. He would say, "I'm not sick," but no one let him go. He started looking forward to the pleasant warmth of the pills.

One day, he found himself sitting on one of the benches in the garden outside, his hands loose in his lap. His white robe was soft. He sat in the half-clouded sunlight and tasted salt.

A hand brushed his face. Startled, he realized there was a girl sitting cross-legged next to him. She was thin, drab, hair a sort of indeterminate shade of taupe against the pallor of her skin and her own terrycloth robe. He thought she might be a few years older than he was. Her eyes were grey and abstracted; when she drew her hand back, she tilted her head to watch the glitter of moisture on her fingertips.

Jacob swallowed. "I'm not crying," he explained. "My eyes are just leaking tears."

The girl didn't look up, but she appeared to consider. She shivered, though the day was pleasant enough, and then she nodded. She wiped her hand on her flannel pants and then drew her knees up, wrapping her arms around her calves.

Jacob looked around at the garden. There were people here and there; he was vaguely surprised to find some of them were familiar. He studied an old man with a walker and thought, *we sat together at breakfast.* He wondered how long he'd been there.

"I'm Jacob," he offered, but the girl had turned her face away from him as she tracked something quite intently through the air.

He waited a minute, cotton wrapped around all his thoughts, but the girl was still ignoring him, so he tried again. "What are you looking at?"

The girl glanced in the general direction of his right earlobe, then she looked down at the ground. He noticed her fingers twitching before she smoothed them against her leg.

Just when he'd decided she wouldn't answer that either, she said, "A dragon. I think it's sick. Most of them are."

He liked her voice, though she was very quiet. He had the impression she formed each word with care. The delicacy of her consonants reminded him of an origami bird.

He squinted, wondering how long the sun had been so bright. He had to blink through a layer of blur before he could focus on the bit of air the girl was watching. He stared hard. For a moment, he almost thought he saw a hint of gossamer, a jet of tiny flame, but then the colours resolved into the deep crimson of darting feathers before the creature dashed away.

"It's just a hummingbird. It looks okay." He tried to sound reassuring. If the girl was here, he thought, she was probably crazy.

She didn't look at him, but he had the sense she was disappointed in him all the same. Her left shoulder dropped, and then she slid away, setting her slippered feet on the ground and standing.

"Hey." Jacob was alarmed. "Don't—it's nice to talk to someone. I'm sorry. I'm only half awake. I'm Jacob."

The girl didn't say anything, but she stayed where she was. Wrapping her arms around herself, she looked down, roughly in the direction of his feet. He followed the line of her gaze and was vaguely surprised to find he was wearing slippers, too.

He tried again: "What's your name?"

The girl's lips moved, but he heard nothing. She shook her head then, the ragged ends of her hair drifting around her shoulders.

"Hi anyway, I guess." There was a pounding at the backs of his eyes. He rubbed at the bridge of his nose, relieved when the gesture cast soothing shadows across his vision. He found himself adding, plaintively, "I'm not sick." It was a refrain by then. He shuddered with it.

The girl paused, her fingers stretched against the air as though she were playing cat's cradle. She studied the backs of her nails.

He sighed. "You don't believe me."

She flinched again at that; the invisible cradle collapsed as she swatted the air, chasing some equally invisible insect. For an instant, she glanced at Jacob's face; her grey eyes were terrifyingly clear. Then she walked away, slippers scuffing across the stones of the path. She didn't look back.

Jacob sat for a little while in the sunlight, until a large man came with a handful of pills in a paper cup. He swallowed them obligingly, waited while the man's fingers—impersonal but remorseless—explored his gums, and then tilted his head back against the bench, waiting for the welcome drift of oblivion.

Instead, he was pulled up, then pushed, then half-dragged down a short series of halls until he found himself plunked into a chair, facing a deeply tanned woman with short brown hair and a clipboard. She peered at him over her half-moon glasses and across a desk. "Mr. Shepard," she said, pleasantly. Her teeth were white and very even. "How are we today?"

He had a strong sense of déjà vu. He didn't say anything. The woman waited for a moment, then made a note on her clipboard. "Your uncle phoned," she added. "He's quite worried about you."

Jacob said, wearily, "I don't have an uncle."

The woman wrote something down again.

If he sat very still, the room acquired a sort of pleasant floatiness. "I'm sure I told you," he explained to the woman, not without a certain sense of futility, "I'm pretty sure those old men sent me here."

"Mmm." The woman jotted down another notation. "Which men would those be?"

"I think," Jacob said foggily, "they probably run my parents' company. My company. There's a company and I'm supposed to run it. I didn't want it *that* much. They didn't have to put me here."

"I see. And how long have you known these men?"

"I don't. I don't know them." He wanted to explain about the school and the principal and the empty classroom, but the walls were sliding and the dingy office was fading into a soothing golden light.

When he woke, he found himself sitting at a long low dining table, a bowl of oatmeal in front of him. He had a plastic spoon in his right hand. The girl from the bench was across from him; her oatmeal had strawberries on top. Her spoon was on the table. Her hands were in her lap, and she was gazing somewhere in the direction of the far wall.

"Hey," said Jacob, somewhat muzzily. "How come you get fruit?"

The girl didn't answer him. This time, he was expecting it. He was surprised, though, when she picked up her spoon from the table, scooped a strawberry delicately off her breakfast, and leaned forward to deposit it in his bowl. She was still watching the middle distance; her fingers fumbled, smoothing their way across the shining surface of the spoon.

"Thanks." He picked up his own spoon and plunged it dubiously into the morass of oats. It was soggy and tasteless, but the burst of straw-berry helped.

As he chewed, he looked around, working hard to focus on the room around him. The far wall was fuzzy, but he could make out slouched figures in white terry robes like—yes—he himself was still wearing. At the next table over, an elderly man with a face the shape and colour of an unripe radish was hunched over his own half-empty bowl, drooling slightly.

Jacob ventured, "Terrible stuff, huh?"

He was not surprised when the man failed to respond. He sighed. He looked back at the girl across the table, still stroking her spoon like a pet. "Do you even have a name?"

The girl's fingers paused. Then she nodded.

Jacob laughed. He couldn't help it. He thought he actually saw the girl's lips twitch.

She held up two fingers of her left hand. *Wait,* the gesture said.

So Jacob said, "Okay," and he waited with a patience borne—he suspected—of rather pharmaceutically inspired curiosity while the girl adjusted the angle of the spoon and fidgeted in her chair.

The room drifted pleasantly around him.

"My name," said the girl, with exquisite care, "is Verity." She appeared to be studying the tablecloth as she spoke. The skin at the base of her throat trembled, framed by the thin cotton of her gown beneath the terrycloth.

"Hi, Ver. Veri. Verty." Jacob found his tongue tangling, his lips moving of their own volition. He shook his head. "Vee."

Verity didn't seem to mind. She shrugged one shoulder; the gesture turned into an awkward roll, as though she were trying to free herself from some invisible strap. Jacob thought he knew the feeling. "Why...." Her voice was still quiet, her words hesitant. "Why are you, um, here?"

"Iunno." Jacob sighed and tried again, cautiously. "I don't know."

Verity's attention shifted to his hands, and he thought that she dis-approved of his response. He slid his index finger along the length of the table's edge.

"I guess I'm eighteen by now," he said. "I was supposed to own a company. I think someone didn't want me to. I'm really not sick."

This time, Verity nodded. Something relaxed in the line of her shoul-ders; her hair fell in her face as she ducked her chin. "Okay." She tugged lightly at the edge of the navy linen tablecloth. "'Sick' is subjective."

"What?"

"You could say 'insane,' which is mostly what they call us, and, um, you're not that, I think, but mostly everyone is just 'different' maybe, or...." Once she got started, it was like a landslide, words tumbling over one another as though she was just trying to get them over with as quickly as possible. Verity sighed. Not looking up, she gestured toward the right, taking in the side of the room with a ragged sweep of her hand. "This house is private. Not a hospital. It's expensive. Our families send us here, mostly, when we make them uncomfortable. The woman in the corner with the yellow hair, she cries a lot. She sees her dead son and she cries."

"Her dead son?"

"Yes."

"You think so?"

"She sees him. They tell her it isn't real. What's 'real'? It is to her. She is sad, though. Maybe if she stops seeing him, she can be less sad."

"Hm." Jacob glanced to the side, to the woman with the streaks of grey in her corn-silk hair who hunched softly weeping over her plate.

"The man next to her, he's, um, here because he asked to be."

Jacob paused. "Why?"

"He's afraid. Of the outside, of people, of himself. He says he likes the quiet."

"Why are *you* here?"

Verity shrugged a shoulder again. Her motions were a little bit jerky, he noticed through his haze. Her fingertips twitched. He was growing used to the stilted cadence of her speech; when she wasn't speaking in torrents, she hesitated over words like his language wasn't her own. "Because," she said finally, and left it there. He tried to object, but his tongue chose that moment to go thick again.

In the next moment, big hands closed around his upper arms from behind, and he was hauled to his feet. A voice said in his ear, "Therapy time."

It was always the same. A small room. Someone behind a desk.

He didn't have an uncle.

He was starting to wonder if maybe he had an uncle.

He started screaming at the woman behind the desk. He heard himself—the hoarse animal sounds. Then someone jabbed him with a needle, and he slept.

He woke in near-darkness. He didn't have to stretch to know he was lying on a cot. When he shifted, he felt loose bands of untethered straps sliding over his chest. Startled, he blinked in the faint moonlight from the barred window and rolled to his side.

He made an inadvertent sound when he realized he was not alone. His pulse leapt, but then he recognized the shape of the girl sitting on the floor. She was slouched against the wall with her knees pulled up to her chest. She wore the usual thin, hospital-style pyjamas, robe nowhere in sight. She was looking at something long and slender in her hands, turning it over and rolling it between her palms.

Jacob said, hoarsely, "What is it?"

Verity's hands jerked, then paused. She then held up the object for his inspection; he squinted until he could make it out. It was just a pen— generic, probably ball-point, with a plastic cap.

Jacob sat up, throwing aside the straps that slipped across him. He, too, found himself in hospital clothes. The thin cotton did little to protect against the chill of the room. "Okay. What's with the pen? And, uh ... should you be in here?"

Verity spread her hands, quick and nervous, palms up and fingers open. She kept the pen tucked into the crook of her thumb. In the darkness, it should have been less unnerving that she wouldn't look at him. He discovered it really wasn't.

Jacob said, "Do I have an uncle?" And, a minute later, "Look, we already established that you can talk."

The girl dropped the pen; it skittered lightly on the floor, and she only wrapped her arms around her knees instead, staring ahead and rocking a little.

"Hey." Jacob froze, uncertain, then slid off the cot, finding his feet somewhat unwieldy beneath him. He set a palm against the wall and lowered himself down to sit next to Verity. He didn't touch her, but he watched, waiting quietly, letting his vision clear.

Verity sat rocking; she was strange, and a stranger, though her presence was still better than waking alone and strapped down.

Maybe an hour passed. He wasn't sure. He didn't have anywhere better to go, and he was inclined to drift, his head against the wall. He was startled awake again when the girl finally spoke.

"I—" she said. She had stopped rocking, but then she jerked her chin down, setting her thumbs against her temples and pressing hard.

"Hey." Jacob had already tried that. Still, he didn't know what else to say. He reached down and picked up the pen from the floor.

"Words," murmured the girl then. Her voice was tense and low;

her fingers were outstretched in razor lines. "Buzzing." She swallowed a breath. "Burning. I. Am. Sorry." Her tone was quite even, marked with regret and a hint of embarrassment. She added, "Headache."

"It's okay. I honestly don't have a lot of friends in here. I can't afford to be picky."

He thought maybe she laughed a little. Verity curled herself smaller, pressing her forehead to the tops of her knees. "Tell me something true," she said, muffled.

"What?"

She only sat with her face buried and her back pressed to the wall behind her.

"Something true," said Jacob, puzzled. "Uh." He thought for a moment. "I don't know how long I've been here. I'm really fucking scared." He tightened his hand around the pen and added, more confidently, "I don't have an uncle."

The girl was quiet, unmoving. Jacob wondered if he'd given her what she wanted. He found himself wanting to brush back her hair, but he didn't touch her. She was curled too tightly against the world. He thought she might break.

She gasped in a lungful of air, though, and raised her head again. She was looking straight ahead, but she said, "Okay."

"...Okay?"

"You don't have an uncle." Verity was tense, but her words came easier.

"Just like that? You believe me?"

"I believe you."

"I really wish you were my therapist. Uh. Is she a therapist? Does anyone here have a licence?"

"Some. Some of them do want to help people. Others want money, or petty power."

Since Verity looked less like she was made of glass, Jacob lifted a hand and set the backs of two fingers against her sleeve. The gesture was sloppier than he'd intended. Still, she didn't flinch that time. He wondered if she noticed him at all.

His head, he was discovering, still had a tendency to roll against the wall. He closed his eyes.

"How'd you get in here?"

"They don't lock my door."

His hand was still touching her arm. He moved his fingers a little, feeling the warm solidity beneath. He reflected that he probably shouldn't have closed his eyes. "Not an answer."

The girl's fingertips brushed the inside of his wrist, quick and light as a butterfly, and then she moved away. The cotton of her pyjamas rustled.

Jacob thought she said, "I'll help you," but he was losing himself again.

He dreamed of the pen, writing loops and whorls across his skin in a language he didn't understand. When he woke, it was still in his hand, and the morning guard was prodding him awake with one toe. "You don't stay in bed, buddy, we're going to have to strap you in."

He didn't see Verity that morning. When he was allowed out after breakfast, he went to sit in the garden, though the sky was cloudy and the wind nipped at his bare ankles. He sat listlessly, waiting for his pills, vaguely satisfied that no one was interrogating him about relatives he may or may not have had. It occurred to him to wonder about Stevens. He felt a distant pang for home—even for school. He wondered if he'd graduated.

When the guard came with the little paper cup, the pills were white instead of blue. Jacob paused with the little capsules an inch from his lips. "Are these right?"

"Yes."

"Maybe 'right' is the wrong word. I'm not sick," Jacob reminded the guard.

The man said, "Look, they're fine," and it seemed like there was a flush running up his neck. He swiped the cup back and walked off without checking to see if Jacob had swallowed.

Jacob swallowed anyway. He had a morning of therapy to get through.

He had given up on telling the person behind the desk—it wasn't always the same person, though he'd seen the woman with the glasses more than once—about his family arrangements. He had almost given up on asking for a phone. That morning, he asked to talk to Stevens, then sat quietly after he'd been refused. It was a man that morning, who wanted to know if he heard voices or what he remembered about his father. Jacob stared at the wall. He wasn't really paying attention, but neither was he managing to find his usual wave of comfortable apathy. He found himself rather distressingly awake.

"That twitchy girl," he said, interrupting a question about his deepest childhood fears. "Verity. What's her deal?"

The man behind the desk was hazel-skinned and thick-bearded. His age was indeterminate, but lines tightened around his eyes. He tapped a finger against the edge of his keyboard.

"That young lady has been here for some time. If you wish to avoid the same circumstance, I might suggest treating this session more seriously."

Jacob rubbed at the bridge of his nose. His skin felt annoyingly constrictive. "You're not going to let me out of here," he said, irritably. "Can we just stop pretending? Look, maybe you're really a shrink. Maybe you have a lousy job. But you can't really think anyone's going to let me go."

"Mr. Shepard—"

"Seriously. Stop it."

The man was staring at Jacob with an air of bland but palpable disapproval. Jacob didn't particularly care. He continued, "I'm not sick."

"Mr. Shepard. Until we can begin addressing the root of your problems, we're never going to progress."

"What happens if we progress?"

"Well, then we'll consider different types of ther—"

"No. I mean, what do I have to do to get out of here?"

Jacob thought he saw the corner of the therapist's eye tic.

He sighed. "Can I *please* make a phone call?" He didn't really have to wait to see the other man's frown. "Listen. I'm gonna go outside."

He rose and walked into the hall. Somewhat to his surprise, no one stopped him. He tugged at his robe, pulling it close, and moved in the direction he thought the garden was in.

The halls seemed like less of a blur than usual. He went out the front steps and squinted in sunlight that was too harsh on his eyes.

He wasn't surprised to find Verity outside. She wasn't on a bench, but she was sitting next to one, legs crossed, palms pressed to the grass beneath her.

Jacob considered, then he sat down on the bench. Verity ignored him; she had her eyes closed. He nudged her shoulder with his knee. It didn't make a discernible difference. He was pleased, though, that she felt solid.

"That guy hates me," he said. "My skin feels like it's crawling off."

"Eric changed your pills," she murmured. "Placebos. I'm sorry it will be uncomfortable for a while."

"You're kidding me."

She cringed slightly. "No."

Jacob muttered something he had not been allowed to say in school. He scrubbed his hands through his hair. His scalp irritated him. "I can't think."

"You will."

"How did you—how can you change my meds?"

Verity only sat there, her palms resting in the green grass, a breeze ruffling the ragged edges of her hair. Just when Jacob had decided she wouldn't answer, she said, "I know things. About the orderlies, the doctors. They tell me when they touch me. They know I know."

"So what—you blackmail them?"

One of her shoulders rose, then fell. It was an uncharacteristically normal gesture, though a moment later, her fingers spasmed, her chin jerking to one side. Her shoulder bumped against his leg, but she didn't move away. "It's, um—a fine line. I can ask for little things. More, and...."

"You'll piss them off?"

"Maybe they don't lock me in at night." The girl said it under her breath, like a confession. He had to strain to hear her. "Or maybe they don't let me out at all. It's a balance."

He leaned forward, then back, his skin itching. "Are you feeling better today?" He wanted to grind his palms into the hollows just under his eyes. He forbore.

Verity raised her right hand and rocked it slightly in the air, palm down. She opened her eyes, glancing at Jacob's knee before turning her head to watch what might have been the passage of some invisible bird. "Everything's too loud sometimes. I get headaches."

"Yeah. I have one right now." Jacob hissed in air through his teeth. "Look, thanks, but—I think I like the pills. Gotta pass the time somehow."

"No." She was low-voiced but implacable. He fought the urge to kick her. He fought the equal urge to hug her. He shook his head.

"Please—"

"No. It will be better, um, tomorrow. The day after. They aren't helping you."

"You're killing me."

"No," she said instantly; her spine bowed. She pulled away from him with an unexpected violence, as though he *had* kicked her. "Don't."

"Hey." Jacob reached out, then thought better of it. His fingers quivered, outstretched, not touching. "What'd I do? Look, I am in a shitty mood. Hey. You're the only friend I have in here."

Verity whispered, "Don't lie to me."

Jacob was taken aback. "About what?"

"I'm not killing you," she said. She reached up, barely glancing in his direction, and touched her fingertips to his wrist as though she were checking his pulse. That single connection was fragile as a bird's wing. "Do you want to go home?"

Irritation roiled at the question. He meant to say something flip. Instead, he said, "More than I can possibly say," and Verity dropped her hand back to the grass.

"Okay. Then Eric switched your meds, and, um, I'm not sorry."

"Yeah. Okay. I gotta—I don't even know." He couldn't sit still. Jacob rose and left the girl sitting on the ground. He paced the garden for a couple of minutes, but the sun was too bright and the wind was rough on his skin. He passed other patients—an old man, a young woman, a boy who might not have been more than six—and was struck by the man's staring slackness, the woman's tentative smile, and the boy's intense engagement with a small plastic truck.

He walked back inside and would've gone to his room, but suddenly realized that he wasn't sure where it was. He was not about to ask the orderly, who was glaring at him. Instead, he picked a door to the right of the lobby that looked vaguely familiar, and found himself in the empty dining hall.

He stared at tables lined with plastic trays and flimsy utensils, then he tried the next door and found himself in a downstairs hall that seemed right. It was lined with doors on one side and a bay of windows on the other. Sunlight streamed in as he walked past names handwritten on whiteboards: Larouche, Richards, Pereira. He stopped at Shepard and turned the knob, opening the door to find a cramped room and the cot with straps dangling. There was a dresser he'd never noticed before. He opened the top drawer and found it empty.

He threw himself down on the bed and wrapped his arms around himself. He wanted to sleep. After a while, he started to shiver.

Time passed. He dreamed, maybe, of the girl who came in the night. He dreamed of straps and men swearing. He wasn't hungry, but he tasted vomit. His insides tried to crawl out his throat.

He woke with a peculiar sense of timelessness; he wasn't certain whether days had passed, or only minutes. His hospital gown was damp, and his skin was sweat-sticky. He stared at the ceiling, the popcorn plaster and the small water stain in the corner, and he found himself angry. It came to him with a shaking clarity. He wasn't certain how he hadn't felt it before.

He rose on trembling legs and looked in the second drawer of the dresser, then the third, until he found a white robe he could pull around himself. Then he stepped out into the hall. The light coming through the windows was greyer now, filtered by clouds, but it had the pale brightness of morning.

He walked into the foyer and heard a quiet hum of voices from the dining room, which he ignored in favour of ascending the curving staircase. On the landing at the top, he found a set of double doors that were locked and sealed with an electronic keypad. Glancing back over the banister, he drew out of sight when two orderlies crossed below. Then, checking carefully, he snuck back down and dodged into the hall on the far side of the lobby from the patient rooms.

There were fewer doors here—one to the right and another ahead. When the door ahead opened, Jacob slipped right, relieved when the knob twisted easily in his hand. He shut the door behind himself and looked at the office he was so familiar with: the desk, the chairs, the filing cabinet, and—most importantly—the phone. It was an old plastic office phone, spiral cord dangling. Its grey was grimed with years of use. It was the most beautiful thing he'd seen in ... he wasn't sure. Weeks?

He picked up the handset and held it to his ear, his hand shaking.

There might have been a sound in the hall; he flashed a panicked look at the door and dialled the number for home.

"The number you have dialled is a long-distance number," a woman's recorded voice told him primly. "Please hang up and—" He jammed his finger on the release, then lifted and tried again, this time with a one in front.

He heard it ring once, twice, then— "The number you have dialled is no longer in service," said the same woman. He thought she sounded inordinately judgmental that time.

He did hear a sound in the hall. Footsteps went passing by. He jammed his finger into the phone again and stared longingly at the door. It had no lock. For a wild instant, he wanted to wedge a chair under the knob, but the chairs were too low, and all he needed to do was make one call.

He gritted his teeth and dialled Stevens's cell phone; his hands were trembling. He hit the seven instead of the six and had to stop and try again. He wanted to puke. His mouth tasted like a steel brush.

The phone rang once, and then again.

"Hello?" The voice was tired but familiar.

Jacob could have cried. Instead, he hissed, "Stevens!"

There was a pause.

Jacob said again, "Stevens! It's me!"

"...Jacob?" Stevens sounded incredulous.

"You have to come get me!"

There were footsteps in the hall again. Jacob tried to keep his voice to a whisper, which was difficult when he could hear it breaking. He wanted very much to go home. With one familiar voice, the ever-present need of it rose up, broke in a wave, and threatened to drown him.

"They wouldn't tell me—are you all right? Where are you?"

"I don't know. A house. This is long distance."

The doorknob turned.

"They drug me," Jacob blurted. "They think I have an uncle—"

The door opened; he saw the woman with the glasses and the tight bun, an orderly just behind her. He wanted to duck down behind the desk, as though it would help. Her eyes were already flaring open in angry shock.

"Jacob—" Stevens was saying something.

"Trace the call and call the cops—call a lawyer!" The phone was yanked from his hand; Jacob was slammed against the desk, his face pressed down against the cheap wood veneer. He tried to struggle, and someone twisted his arm cruelly behind his back; he cried out, but they didn't stop. The woman with the glasses was yelling something out in the hall.

He felt the prick in his arm, and then everything went away.

Time got fluid again after that, but he wasn't dreaming like before. He was strapped to the bed. There was a plastic guard between his teeth and there were electrodes taped to his skin. They shocked him with them. He felt his muscles lock; his jaw clamped down. He couldn't scream. He could only stare at the ceiling and pant half-breaths through his nose.

"Patient is uncooperative and delusional" was what he heard. There were comments often repeated to him: "This is for your own good." "It'll be over soon." "Your uncle will be disappointed to hear about this."

I'm sorry, he wanted to tell them. *I'm sorry. Make it stop. I'll be good. I'll be good.* He couldn't tell them. His teeth were closed tightly on the plastic. Sweat was wet and cold on his skin.

"Tell me about your uncle," a woman said, and then the electricity came arcing through him. The straps cut into his skin. He bled and he cried. More than once, he felt the warmth of urine spreading down his thigh. He couldn't keep from shaking.

They fed him with a tube.

They shocked him some more.

When they finally unstrapped him, he didn't know what to do. He lay there, trembling and paralyzed with disbelief, while a man said, "You can go now." After a while, they put him in a wheelchair and pushed him out to the garden. It was a light sort of frigid: not bitingly cold, but there was a thin layer of snow on the ground, like foam on the short waves of the grass.

The orderly tucked a blanket around Jacob's shoulders, and Jacob wanted to laugh—he could feel it lurking at the back of his throat, harsh and barking—but he only said, "Thank you." His voice rasped. He sounded like a stranger.

He felt a hand pat him on the shoulder—as though the orderly were sympathetic, as though he cared. Again, Jacob didn't laugh. He only wanted to. He sat quietly until the man went away and left him alone. He was enjoying the bracing sensation of the breeze on his face.

It occurred to him to wonder about the girl. The garden seemed empty without her.

He thought about it for a while. Eventually, he pushed himself up; it wasn't easy. He fell back into the chair the first time, and the second. On the third try, though, he stood with the blanket clutched around his shoulders, then he turned and shuffled carefully back down the path and through the doors. No one stopped him, though when he made his painful way into the lobby, he felt the eyes on him.

He shuffled down the hall where the patient rooms were, and he stared somewhat helplessly at the whiteboards with the printed names: Larouche, Richards, Pereira, Shepard. Three or four more, further down. He realized he didn't know Verity's last name.

It was daytime, so the doors were unlocked and open. He looked in the first room and saw only an empty space identical to his own, complete with dresser and cot. There were no straps.

He stopped to lean against the wall and breathe. He ached all over.

He found her in the second room. There were straps on her cot, but she was just sitting on it, her back to the wall and her arms wrapped around her knees. He was starting to know the way she curled in around herself, staring forward, eyes shifting slightly to watch something he couldn't see. Her left shoulder twitched upward, then dropped, and he knew she knew he was there.

"God, I'm tired," he told her. She had a bruise on her neck and angry red marks on her wrists. He knew those. His arms looked much the same.

Jacob lowered himself to sit next to Verity, carefully and with some hissing of breath. He slid back on the narrow cot and slumped against the wall. He didn't touch her, but he looked at the scabs on her arms. He could see where her fingers had scratched.

"Thanks," he said. "For trying."

For a minute, he didn't think she was going to respond, which was all right; he had his eyes half closed for a nap when he saw her chin jerk. It could've been a spasm. He took it as encouragement. Taking half the blanket from his shoulders, he draped it over her. She didn't look, but she fingered the edge of it.

"This place is sixteen kinds of lawsuit." Jacob did close his eyes. It was nice, there on the cot with the girl beside him. No one was shocking him. He didn't have any pieces of plastic wedged between his teeth. "I'm not sick. Or I wasn't sick. Maybe I am now. Do you feel sick?"

Verity didn't answer.

"You're a hard person to have a conversation with. Anyway, this isn't what I figured I'd be doing at eighteen. I think I'm eighteen. I hope it isn't nineteen already. How old are you?" His voice was a rusty ruin, but he was enjoying the sheer luxury of talking.

He gave her a little time to see if she'd answer. When she didn't, he continued, "I was gonna travel. Maybe make things. Maybe sell the company eventually. I have money, you know. I just don't know what I want to do with it, or—I wanted to try things out. Be a butcher. A baker. A candlestick maker. Whatever. What did you want to do?"

He was expecting silence. He was not offended when it came. He was busy adjusting his half of the blanket.

"It's okay if you don't know, either. You can come with me, when we get out of here. I think—maybe if we just keep our heads down. If we just give them what they want." There was an edge of desperation to his own voice that Jacob found foreign. He could hear the echoes of his own aborted screams. He swallowed. "Maybe if I just sit tight and take the pills, my uncle will come for me. And I'll ask him to take you, too."

There was such a relief to saying it. He felt hope bloom in his chest, warm and sweet. He tilted his head back against the wall and let himself smile for what felt like the first time in weeks. His muscles ached and his temples were throbbing and the stubble on his face was long and itching, but they could get out, if they just waited. If they just did what they were told.

Verity's hand closed over his. Her fingers were small and cool. Startled, he looked over to find she was watching him. She had shadows under her eyes, and her lips were chapped and bitten, but her gaze still had that unexpectedly grey clarity. She said, "You don't have an uncle."

Jacob paused. "Oh. Yeah. You're right."

He sat there with the girl's hand on his and turned his palm up, curling his fingers over hers. He continued to sit when his breath caught in his throat; he heard his own voice, an inarticulate sob. It would have taken him off guard, but he was too tired. He felt like he was back in the chair, in the straps; he could only shake while the tears welled in his eyes and ran streaming down his face.

He wasn't entirely sure whether Verity drew him down or whether he was only permitted, but he found himself wrapped around her, his head in her terryclothed lap and his arms around her waist. He wept. He could do nothing but weep.

He felt her stiffen, and even in the midst of his ragged anguish, he would have moved away, maybe managed some sort of gasping apology, but before her rigid discomfort had time to register, he also felt her relent. She touched his shoulder. Her hand brushed slowly and quite tentatively across his hair, without rhythm, as though carefully measuring the texture of each strand.

He clung to her and cried. The walls around them were sterile and cold.

A week later, the lawyer came.

`thats enough`

What?

`thats enough the lawyer came it ended`

Is this part not okay?

`stop asking its never okay it burns i see the paper on fire i feel it on my skin the wrists the soft part`

Like that's not a worrisome comparison. Sorry. I'm trying to get it right.

`just keep going it cant sit here forever i cant sleep because its crying its important though just finish it`

15

Province of Ontario
Psychological Evaluation Report—Confidential

Patient: Richards, Verity Amelia
Date of Birth: June 3, 1982
Supervising Physician: B. N. Nichols
Date of Evaluation: October 16, 1991

Patient has history of treatment for multiple diagnoses (see attached). Poor verbal ability, failure to engage socially, little eye contact. Can react catatonically to excessive audiovisual stimulation. Suspected autism, possible early onset schizophrenia.

Patient has been enrolled in public school system but struggles with both social requirements and academic material. Recommend continuing current course of medication. Also recommend transferring patient to temporary residence in children's hospital, awaiting more permanent psychiatric placement; mother consents and indicates she is ill-equipped to deal with Verity's special needs in a home environment. Patient requires constant supervision and is prone to hallucination. Home care is likely to result in continued safety hazards and disruptions to routine.

Performance on intelligence tests indicates low IQ (<70). Chance of future recovery unlikely, if not impossible. Long-term goals should centre on stabilization and control of symptoms.

DECEMBER

Verity knows people are yelling at her. The words smell like an electrical burn.

She is surrounded by the maelstrom. There was a table in front of her for a while, plain stainless metal; she had concentrated on a long dented scratch in its surface, but then a smear of red obscured her vision and she lost track.

Now she sits and rocks, back and forth, though she cannot hear the chair and there is no rhythm to the world around her. She stares at a whirl of cinnamon anger and tries to will her way past it, seeking some hint of the familiar. She isn't certain how much time has passed since the city went dark and she lost herself in the snow holding a stranger's sleeve.

When she sees the brittle Morse code of the tap-tap-tap against her palm, she could weep with relief. She doesn't. It is a pattern she knows, though, and she can think of *touch* and separate the sight of it from the sensation on her skin. She sits in chaos and clings to the single familiar thing until she can resolve the room around her.

A particle board desk solidifies before her, and she closes her fingers around Jacob's hand. He stops the tapping and jerks away.

"Vee, what the fuck?" He is behind her. His voice is stiff.

She doesn't answer.

"I know you can hear me. What the *fuck*. Where were you? You just leave in the middle of the night now?"

She says, "I'm sorry." The air is taut with his anger; braided within, stretched almost to snapping, she can see the fierce delicacy of his unspoken terror. She wants to apologize again, and doesn't; she thinks they are not alone, though she is having a hard time making sense of the world past the desk. She is sitting. The metal table is gone and her hands are free. She has an impression of badges and antiseptic. The room seems oddly dim.

As she has that thought, a white flash rings in her ears. She loses the table, the anger, the feel of the chair—the moment she almost panics, she feels Jacob's fingers on her palm again, tapping. She fixates on the familiar pattern.

"—the damn flashlight out of her face! Look, how long was she here before someone even called me? I'm her legal guardian. You can't just keep her here."

"We just need her to answer a few questions." It's a woman's voice, cool and unforgiving. Verity sees a uniform stripe and a flash of police shield. The officer puts the flashlight down on the desk and then leaves, shutting the door behind herself.

The room is small and sterile. The desk is a smooth expanse unmarred by paperwork. Verity is sitting in a metal chair with worn padding. There's a tall plant in one corner, and a painting on one wall that is studiously, blandly abstract. Verity sighs. "Hospital smell." She is grateful to find herself still in her own sweater and jeans. She can feel Jacob's frustrated stare crawling on the back of her neck.

"Ms. Richards." There's a strange suit still present—a man, blond-and-silver hair, eggshell skin, incongruously bushy sideburns. He has kind eyes, but his mouth is pursed; the flashlight carves deep crags in his face, lighting his chin as though he were telling a campfire horror story. He sits at the opposite side of the desk, setting a briefcase in front of him. "This is a hospital evaluation room. My name is Joseph Graves. Mr. Shepard has called me in as your attorney in this matter. Rest assured, anything we discuss here is confidential."

She knows he means it because the words taste like oregano. Verity tries belatedly to catch Jacob's hand again, but Jacob has already pulled away. He stalks to a far corner of the room and leans there in the shadows, arms folded. He's glaring at her. She wants to meet his eyes, but as hard as she tries, his tension streaks ruby. She knows he has crossed his arms so his hands won't shake. His restraint vibrates across her cheek.

"Ms. Richards."

Verity licks the taste of cold from her lips and casts her attention back to the lawyer. She watches the mottled whiteness of his fingers on the files he is drawing from his case. "Yes," she says quietly. "I hear you."

"Are you okay? What the hell?" Jacob hasn't moved, but his voice is a whip. She can see it lash the desk.

Graves inclines his head. "I understand you saved a man's life tonight. The police would like more details, but I'm told you were unresponsive. Were you in shock? Did you know him?"

It takes Verity a long minute to gather her words in the right order. "No. He had a dog."

The lawyer's pause is nearly infinitesimal. Only a twitch of his right eyebrow betrays him. "Did he collapse before you found him?"

Graves's voice is patient, even interested. Verity looks at the plant in the corner. She suspects it is plastic. She can taste it in the back of her throat, ragged and a little rusty. She shakes her head.

"Ms. Richards. I'm here to help you. The officers who found you have been very concerned—partly for you and your friend, but also for the trail of blood they found leading onto the river."

"Hang on," interjects Jacob, "What?"

"Well, that's why we're here. It's not illegal to help a man who fell in the snow. I'm told there was a trail of footprints, though—three people—and a significant amount of blood by a large hole that had been cut in the ice. I understand they found clothing as well."

"Vee, what the—were you on the ice? Did someone dump a *body?*"

"Mr. Shepard, please." Graves begins to set his papers down on the desk.

"Don't," says Verity quickly, and his hands pause.

"Ms. Richards?"

"The files." Jacob's voice is still tight, stretching from somewhere behind Verity's shoulder. "Printouts give her a headache."

Graves's eyebrow writhes once more, holding still for a beat before he obligingly slides the papers back into his case. He keeps a small yellow pad and a pen.

"No one dumped a body," says Verity; the assurance is as clear as a drink of water. "No one I was with." She realizes she's thirsty. She shakes her head. "I didn't know. Nothing I tell you—no truth I tell you—will make sense to you. May I have something to drink?"

"Probably not right now. I don't say that for lack of sympathy: the emergency room is flooded with people trying to take advantage of the hospital's generator. I'm hoping we can get you released because no one has time to deal with you. Did you know there was a power outage?"

"I—" Verity swallows, processing anew the dimness of the room and the severity of Graves's cheekbones in the flashlight beam. She picks her words slowly, trying to avoid any taste of grey bile. "I know. The man with the dog—I sat with him. I didn't want him to freeze."

"Why didn't you call someone? Why won't you just carry your phone?" There's a crack in Jacob's voice now. His frustration is turning brittle. "Why were you even *there?*"

"I, um ... I don't know how to tell you. Not with words you'll believe, or understand."

"Try." There's so much texture in Jacob's single word.

Verity hesitates. "Dust soaked in starlight. Blood. Hydrokinesis?"

The pause in the room carries the scent of the winter storm outside.

"Ah," says the lawyer. "I see. Well then, our best approach is to point out to the police that the hospital staff are currently too busy for any non-emergencies, Ms. Richards is not in immediate distress, and of course, she has done nothing wrong."

The word 'wrong' reverberates in Verity's skull, molasses and angry bees. She swallows. She forces herself to sit still.

The lawyer's fingers rifle through the pages of the file. "I think we're fine here. At most, they have the suggestion of a nearby crime scene, but no indication that Ms. Richards was involved or even a witness. She was found saving a man's life. While I'm sure they would like to interview her, even if she did see anything, her status as your ward—and her medical history—would make any potential testimony highly suspect." Somehow, he has shifted to address his comments to Jacob.

His dismissal is familiar to her; Verity hunches in her seat. She would wrap herself in invisibility if she could, but she has only the shadows playing in the flashlit room. She smells disinfectant and sweat.

"So all they know is she was there?" Jacob wanted to be a lawyer once. Verity is grateful he isn't taking the opportunity to practice.

"Exactly. And presence is not guilt, particularly in a case where no clear crime has occurred. Her safety is an issue, though, if she's out alone so late. Ms. Richards." This time Graves speaks slowly and clearly, with deliberate care. Verity is familiar with that, too. He is saying, "I am fairly certain I can arrange for you to go home now, but there will be follow-up—by the police, or a hospital psychologist, or both. People are concerned about you. It's not safe for you to go out without telling Mr. Shepard. There was blood on the ice. Do you understand?"

When Verity is silent, Jacob says, "She understands."

Graves sighs slightly. He opens the folder and runs a finger down the pages of his file. "Given that Ms. Richards was near catatonic until a few minutes ago, I might also see if there is space available for admission to the psychiatric wa—"

"*No.*"

They speak at the same time. Verity closes her eyes and ducks her head, savouring the skitter of Jacob's voice cutting in with her own. She is sorry for the tin flavour of his impotent frustration. She is incredibly grateful. She takes a breath and tries to unclench her fingers.

Jacob says, "Not in the hospital. She can't stay here. They can't make her." He is wrong, though; Verity knows because the assertion drips in the air, splattering on the floor and leaving behind the lingering sheen of dirty oil. Still, she is warm with it, until he continues, "She'll see a shrink, though. I'll sign a contract if they need it. She'll take medication."

Verity shakes her head—more wildly than she intends, and she makes a sound she didn't expect, a trapped-animal whimper she didn't make in the police car or the dark interrogation. She knows she isn't impressing the lawyer.

"Don't even." Jacob hasn't left his station in the corner. His arms are still folded tightly over his chest. "I don't know what's going on with you anymore. You're going to see the doctor. A real doctor. A good one. I promise." He turns his attention to the lawyer. His voice is tired now. "If she said she didn't ... dump a body or whatever the fuck, though, she didn't. She was trying to help that guy. If the cops *do* find a crime scene, just play her up as a victim. Fell in with a bad crowd. Didn't know any better. So easy for her to not understand what's happening."

Verity says, "That's not true." She isn't sure. It's cotton in her mouth.

"Just don't, okay? I don't even know what to say to you right now."

Graves is still addressing Jacob. "Yes, certainly, that's our best strategy. I assume you are willing to maintain responsibility for Ms. Richards? If you prefer, I can handle any non-urgent paperwork later this week; my day rate is significantly lower."

"Do it now. The money doesn't matter." Jacob's voice comes muffled this time. He's rubbing his hands over his face. "Just get her out of here. Vee, you could have frozen out there, or gotten hurt, or ... what were you even *doing*?"

"I'll see about getting everything taken care of," Graves says, setting his folder back in the briefcase. "The power outage is likely to create some delay."

"Do whatever you can. Just do it now. Vee, look at me."

It's hard. The tension in the room smears the air in front of her, glittering blue as the angel's eyes; it takes her a moment to turn her head and focus past, on Jacob's strained face and the stubble lining his chin.

"I'm sorry. I don't know what else to do. Do you understand how freaked I am? You're going to go to a shrink," he repeats. "It won't be like before. We'll be careful. We'll find someone nice. But you're going to go, and you're going to take pills again. You promise?"

His anger is impure. It's the weight of his worry that presses against her shoulders.

She looks at him—at his slumped posture and his narrow fingers and the old coat that he threw on over his pyjamas because he got a call in the middle of the night. He stares at her, and she can only feel the crush of his need.

She says, "I promise."

It tastes like cleaning fluid or a smoker's lungs. Verity doesn't flinch, and the pretending compounds the lie, burning her from within, starting somewhere just beneath her collarbone and spreading to her fingertips, fire running down to her toes. She fights to stay motionless.

"Don't cry."

Jacob has moved. His hands brush back her hair; he touches the back of her neck. Her skin feels as though it is sloughing, leaving only the nerves embedded in her raw flesh. Her throat is full of bile.

She whispers, "I want to go home." Truth, cold and clear, to wash the deception away.

"Sure," he says. "We're on it."

She tastes rancid metal, but she lets him hold her hand.

"The truth is rarely pure and never simple." —Oscar Wilde

16

OTTAWA (January 25, 2014)—Crime rates are up 23% in the city's downtown core since the blackout began, say local police. Violent crime has increased 14% in the past four weeks.

"We've seen nine muggings in the last week," said Sgt. Melanie Reynolds of the Ottawa City Police. "People are stealing wallets, but they're also looking for winter clothing and blankets. The Mission shelter downtown was held up on Monday. We are encouraging anyone with extra winter supplies to bring them by the station, where we have volunteers who can organize donations. Anyone who can relocate is urged to do so; we're offering free shuttles out to the suburbs." Sgt. Reynolds refused comment on the ongoing investigation of the blackout, saying only, "We are working hard to pursue credible leads."

Technicians from Ontario Hydro have been working around the clock at the Chaudière Falls power station, gradually restoring electricity to portions of downtown Ottawa and Gatineau. So far, they have been unable to identify the originating problem. Sources have speculated that an unknown electromagnetic pulse may have destroyed the plant technology, and multiple pieces of equipment are currently being replaced.

"We've had success rewiring or replacing the systems," said Regina Souchard, one of the head electrical engineers on site. "We know people need power. We'll have the full grid online again as soon as we're able to complete and test our repairs." She declined to give a precise deadline, and denied media speculation that key equipment malfunctioned and Ontario Hydro is seeking to avoid a lawsuit.

Shelters are overflowing, and the Canadian military has established additional temporary living quarters in Confederation Park, as well as Orléans and Kanata. The federal government has promised aid as long as is required—indeed, House of Commons MPs are similarly affected by the city's current hardship.

In the meantime, residents refuse to let Ottawa come to a standstill. The annual Winterlude festival, though delayed, will launch on Friday. The Senators have rescheduled their hockey season to away games until further notice, but are continuing to hold practice at the Palladium. And ticket sales have resumed for the upcoming concert from The Between, to be held at Lansdowne Park.

FEBRUARY

Cold has different tastes, Verity discovers, and different textures. When she sleeps at night, huddled under blankets with three layers of socks on her feet and her breath frosting, the cold is edged and brittle, like sugar glass spun against her skin. When she rises in the morning and puts on flannel long johns and two sweaters and ventures into the kitchen to find a bottle of prescription pills next to a granola bar and a glass of ice water, the cold is a hollow in her gut that creeps up the back of her throat like heartburn. She can hear the cilantro sound of Jacob's guitar wafting up the stairs, plunked off-key with stiff, angry hands. She thinks he's improving.

She eats the granola bar. She can't flush the pills down the toilet since the pipes froze, but she grinds them to a fine white powder and throws them out the window, where the remnants are invisible against the drifts. That cold is transient, the breezy touch of regret across her face before she twitches it away with her fingers.

When she goes downstairs, Jacob is in the front room, which is now mostly empty except for a wooden stool and a music stand. There are three broken generators by the back wall, which he has tried and failed to keep working. Jacob keeps his gaze on the sheet music, which she knows he can't read, and says, "You take your meds?"

"Yes." She lies to him, smoothly, acridly, as brutally easy as a knife in the gut. She knows now what such a knife would feel like, and the comparison is nearly exact: her deception sliding into the meat of his remaining trust. It is the coldest moment of all. He doesn't question her further. She steps into the room just far enough to get to the desk and open the drawer full of crumpled bills—it's only half full now, but she pulls out some cash and folds it into her pocket. Jacob keeps plucking at his guitar. Verity puts on her coat and boots and slinks outside.

Once there was a reporter there, asking questions, shoving his phone at her face. She stared at his snowy boots until he gave up and went away. She knows she is lucky there aren't more.

Now the day is grey and quiet, though she sees a figure shift on a covered porch across the street; she freezes, then recognizes Shauna's stout silhouette. She moves to cross, but is only one foot off the curb when the other woman gives her a flat look, pulling two steps back.

Verity pulls her hood up against the frigid winter instead; her breath frosts in the air, and she walks down the block, past the old house with the hidden space in the walls. Shauna doesn't follow. Verity turns onto Bank and sees Brian, long limbs folded like a mantis as he leans next to a shop window. She thinks he nods to her as she passes, but she's watching the cracked pattern of the ice on the sidewalk.

The corner store has a handmade sign on the door saying 'CASH ONLY.' The sign tastes like copper, a bright penny tang against the oily sludge of the coloured logos plastered in the window. Verity bites her lip and ducks inside, bracing herself against the onslaught of branding.

It's as cold inside the store as anywhere else, though the glass cuts the cruelty of the breeze. The sun filtering in gives Verity enough vision to sort through half-empty shelves. There are only three packages of toilet paper. She takes them to the counter, where a man in a down coat is standing with his arms folded. He has a trucker hat pulled over his toque.

The toilet paper costs her most of Jacob's cash, but not all, so she adds five cans of soup and then emerges into the street with rivulets of duplicity and greed still running into her eyes. She clutches her purchase, the plastic-wrapped packages awkward but not heavy, one bag dangling from her arm. It's difficult not to touch the acid rainbow of the slogans on the sides.

She's half-tempted to walk back half a block and get Brian to help her, but a quick glance shows that he's not there anymore. Instead, Verity hefts the paper and turns toward the theatre.

She tastes flowered coal and says, "Hello," before Ouro's canine head nudges under her elbow. "My hands are busy," she says. "I, um, don't suppose you're good with carrying." Apparently, she is correct. Pointedly, she notes, "Santiago could help," but the dog sits on the sidewalk and laughs at her silently as she walks by.

A moment later, unexpected hands whisk the bulky packages away from her. Verity blinks, her fingers tightening too late, but before she can protest, Santiago says, "He could, actually. You can even let Ouro take the bag. Are these more supplies?"

It takes Verity a beat, not only to sort through falling syllables, but also to check the clouded sky, then stare bemusedly from dog to magician. Both are smiling at her—Ouro's tilted grin matching Santiago's crooked pleasure. On the sidewalk, she can see the faint impression of an additional shadow at Santiago's feet; to her eyes, it wriggles like an excited puppy before settling into a mundane patch of grey on the ice.

Santiago hefts the toilet paper, cellophane crinkling against his leather jacket. "Yeah. If the sun comes out, you'll see me duck inside pretty quick, but we're liking this new trick. Don't know if it's the power being out, the Chalice getting closer, or what, but no complaints."

Verity averts her eyes from the discordant screech of the packaging and feels Ouroboros's nose nudge her hand. The dog takes the handle of the soup bag delicately between its jaws and waits for Verity to relinquish the weight.

Santiago says, "For the theatre?" When Verity nods, he adds, "Great," and begins walking, the dog flowing past with inky grace. "We really appreciate this stuff. Is it not turning into a lot of money for you?"

"For Jacob. He doesn't care. I mean—he wants to know what I'm doing, and he doesn't understand, but he thinks it's for the homeless. The cash isn't important."

Santiago grunts. "Must be nice. Boyfriend still making you see a shrink?"

"Yes." Verity does not let herself recoil, though she can feel the weight of the magician's casual amusement at her throat. She follows Santiago, careful of the ice-crusted sidewalk.

"Don't worry about it. A lot of us have had people think we were insane. Most of us assumed it was true."

Verity doesn't answer; she isn't sure how to explain the lie that still lingers like tar on the back of her tongue. Ouro winds back, bag dangling from its teeth, and presses lightly against her leg. When the virulent drip of the cellophane in Santiago's arms nearly obscures a garbage can in front of her, the dog nudges her to the left, guiding her through the cumin-gasoline scent of the city. She drops a hand to touch the shadow's fur and feel the vagueness of the texture that isn't there.

When they reach McLuhan's, she is expecting the distant swell of voices when she steps into the *between* of the old theatre. To the left, the light in the old hall is much the same, endless candles burning, their glow cast upward into the gloom of a ceiling so far distant that it's invisible.

To the right, a shape stirs in the depths of a worn old recliner, and Verity starts—but Ouroboros is unalarmed at her side, and the shape leans forward to reveal stooped shoulders and Alan's friendly, wizened face. "Oh," he says. "Hello, there."

Verity feels Ouroboros press at her thigh until she steps forward, raising a palm to the opposite wall as the door opens behind her and Santiago slips through, muttering a curse as he nearly fumbles a package.

"And you too, Stefan. Brought us more of the necessaries?" Alan smiles at the magician, too, who nods back.

"These ones are on Vee. Entertain her for a minute and we'll add them to the stash."

"Hello, Vee," says Alan, obligingly, as Santiago and Ouro take the parcels away into the distance of the hall. "Thank you for that kindness. It's getting tight in here—more trickling in, and not many folks inclined to throw money to Stefan these days. Gather he was the big earner. Now it's a few doing odd jobs. Cold out there, too. How are you, dear?"

"Um."

"Sorry." Alan's blue eyes are keen. "I'm going too quickly?" He pauses then, waiting patiently until Verity has had a chance to parse through the rainbow of his conversation. Eventually, he says again, "How are you?"

She has to think about her answer. "Sad," she says finally, and shrugs a shoulder. "Cold. How are you? You look better."

"Thanks to Mr. Warner. I haven't felt this good in twenty years." Alan smiles, a wreath of wrinkles tracing across his face. "I swear the air's lighter. I can almost be myself again." Resting his elbows on the arm rests of the old chair, he steeples his fingers, looking thoroughly pleased.

"What are you doing now? Are you the greeter?"

Alan chuckles. "I doubt my old face is the first thing someone wants to see, coming through. No, I'm looking at the door and trying to remember. There used to be better ways of opening one of those."

"A door?" Verity turns to look, gazing blankly at the worn wood. The door doesn't taste any different to her than the last time.

"Mmm." Alan clears his throat. "In my younger days, I could open spaces *between*. Not just enter them. I made the doors. That was my gift. I'd find a nice old building with secrets locked inside and find my way into spaces a lot like this one. We've lost the knack of it; you won't find room in any of these new buildings. But that was how I survived the quake, when it came. I would've been trapped in the walls, but I opened my own way out."

"Could you still...?"

"Not anymore. What power I had to create things, I used up years ago." Alan doesn't sound perturbed, though a whisper of regret lingers leafily in the air around him—Verity ducks it like a low-hanging branch. The old man peers at Verity. "Maybe that's how I've lived so long. Once I burned through everything I had, there was nothing left the world would kill me for. Still, I swore I almost felt it again, yesterday or the day before: a little spark. We're all gaining something back of what we were, or what we could be. And there was another way to open these doors—the sturdy ones, the very old ones. They connect, if you know the trick of it. The *between* here joins to another hall that joins to, say, another building blocks away. I knew a woman who swore she could wind from one city to the next. Some of us lived half our lives without going outside. If I could only remember how, you all would do a lot less walking."

A serpentine shadow flows back down the hall, dark even in the poorly-lit spaces between candles. Its golden eyes glimmer like two matching flames before it slides seamlessly back to the furred shape of the dog, nudging its head beneath Verity's hand before it blurs itself reptilian once more and she feels the narrow length of it wend its way up her arm. Stopping at her shoulder, snake-Ouroboros studies her opaquely. She looks back for a moment, thoughtful, but it's Alan she answers: "I wonder if Privya knows. She met me by the river. It's a long walk from the market."

"Ah, well, she would, if anyone does. Jihan knew once, too. I think they came from somewhere far." Alan taps a fingertip against his lips and the wispy cloud of his beard. "Jihan, and the girl, and the other woman."

"Alethea," supplies Verity.

Alan's face clears. "Alethea. She was wonderful. Intelligent. Kind. I was young, but I remember her like I remember the sun. Eyes that looked right through you—much like yours, my dear, if I'm being honest—but such a smile. The other two circled her like moons. Or wolves. I'm not entirely sure."

"They wanted her to make a choice." Verity is quiet. On her arm, the snake regards her intently.

"In more ways than one." Alan nods. "But yes, beyond that, we had a choice. Fight or flight. My mother told me. We all gathered in San Francisco looking for a magic door. All we got were the walls falling in."

"Do you think you're—they're—doing the same here?"

Verity feels Ouroboros writhe along her upper arm; Alan, too, shoots her a look. She drops her attention to the wooden planks of the floor, where frequent traffic has replaced the dust with muddy footprints and scattered stains.

"That's the question, isn't it? Where Jihan is leading us? If she even *is* leading us?" Alan sighs. "She used to speak. She used to smile. I saw her weep once. How do we trust an apparition?"

"She isn't," says Verity automatically, to get the scratch of it away from her skin.

"Perhaps she's still a little more. But does she even know who we are? What dreams are we projecting onto her? And then there's the other young woman—still the girl she was. I'm told she coaxes some of us, here and there; some would like very much to fight back." The lines around Alan's mouth deepen. "It's just treading water, though. At most. Why kill so many innocents—and they *are* innocent—just to give our own people another few what, decades? A century? A war? We're dying so quickly already."

"Privya said this could be the last Chalice. But also that Jihan caused the earthquake—that if she tries again, and it's wrong, she could destroy everyone." Verity shakes her head. "I don't know if she even wants to try."

"If only we could just get some of those blind people out there to see. If they could understand, if they could remember, maybe they'd stop killing us." The old man's gaze is sharp. "I'm told you know truth. Can you tell me? Is the dust of some ancient choice really all we have?"

The snake slides itself into the strands of Verity's hair; she feels it loop around her neck. "It's grey," she replies, with hesitation. "Conjecture. The future isn't real yet. But it's not a lie that Jihan nearly broke the world. It has the weight of salt earth. And it's not a lie that Privya has killed, and would kill more if she could."

"There must be another way," says Alan again, and Verity thinks it's his confidence that edges the words in green. Or it could be hope, like the fresh bloom of spring in the dry chill of the winter walls. The scent of irises comes to her, ephemeral, and is gone.

"Yes," she murmurs. "We could do nothing. I don't think that's what you mean."

Alan chuckles. "No. I've never been one to let nature take its course." He shakes his head; momentarily, he studies the snake tangled in Verity's hair, the yellow eyes glittering just at the curve of her neck. "Thank you," he adds, abruptly, "for what you did for Sanna. The children talk to her now."

"It's okay. I wish when I was younger I'd, um, had someone who understood." Verity is silent for a long, careful moment, then she raises a hand to brush her fingertips against Ouroboros, to ensure the snake—and Santiago—is paying attention. "I think maybe she's like me."

Ouroboros winds itself loosely around her neck.

Alan's fingers toy with his beard again, winding through the ends. His eyes are cerulean and bright. "I had suspected."

"She's like me," says Verity, "but she doesn't know yet. The world is a mash of colours and tastes and the sounds of…." She pauses, then waves her hand a little helplessly. "I can't tell you. Only it took me a long time to know what was real, or true, and she's still lost. But if Privya hears, she may come for her."

"She won't." Santiago is grim, coming back down the hall. He's shed his jacket. His Between shirt is long-sleeved but ragged, with a hole above the hem. The darkness of the hall seems to cling to him, playing tricks in the hollows of his face, and for a fleeting instant, his eyes gleam as yellow as the snake's.

"I protect her." Alan's jaw firms. "She will be protected. She wouldn't go with a stranger. I don't think she would even understand a word that girl said." His voice is calm, but there's a hint of spiders lurking beneath.

Verity reaches to her throat and touches the snake where it still curls like a half-tangible necklace. It seems smaller than before. She sees Santiago shift his weight when Ouro moves against her hand. "It isn't easy," she says slowly, "to make sense of a world where logos scream at you, or syllables burn your skin, and other people don't know. She'll learn to use her words. I was seven. I think … maybe Sanna comes next, if there is a Chalice again? Maybe—I'm sorry. I don't know what will be. But I hope your granddaughter is well and safe, and I'm glad you're gentle with her."

"She's a good girl."

"She's a nice kid," Santiago concedes, folding his arms. "She's quiet. Ouro's not entirely sold on letting the boys touch him, but the bribery seems less necessary lately. They were colouring with her this morning."

"Thank you, Ouroboros," Verity murmurs, but Santiago is the one who flashes his teeth. She ducks her head. "I wanted to see Colin. Is he— does it still help him, the power being out? Privya said it would."

"Privya has lots of ideas about what's helpful," interjects Alan, dryly. "It's true the boy does better when half of us aren't dying of electrical poisoning, but balance that out with half of us freezing, and he still has his work cut out for him. Not much change since the last time you were in. I got him to eat some of that cereal. Anyway, you two go ahead—not enough room for three of us. It's getting cramped over there. I should find Sanna in a few minutes. I'll make sure we keep a closer watch. Stop and see her on your way out." The old man nods to Santiago, then smiles at Verity, the lines etching deep and familiar into his fragile skin.

Verity brushes her fingertips over the arm of Alan's chair, just near his knobby hand. The worn velour tastes of faintly bitter chocolate. She holds the sensation in her mouth and leaves the man staring at the door again as she turns away to follow Santiago down the hall.

There's a chill in the air here, too, the winter creeping in from the world outside. The narrow length of the *between* has grown more crowded, with bits of baggage and random pieces of furniture piled against the walls. Verity steps around an old wooden crate and walks toward the hum of voices somewhere past the magician's black-clad shoulders. Ouroboros is still twined lightly around her neck, and she feels the snake glide against her skin as it wraps around itself.

"Are we the only ones?" she asks Santiago. Her tone is both hesitant and pensive.

He raises an eyebrow when he turns. Simultaneously, the snake stills. "Sorry?"

"I didn't know there was anyone like me. Now there's a little girl. There was Alethea, before. I...." Verity waves one hand, letting her fingers come to rest on Ouroboros again. The snake is thin and cool. "Are we many?"

"I'm the wrong one to ask. For what it's worth, though, I don't get whatever it is you do, and I don't know anyone else who trips over a light breeze."

"Okay." Verity stands. When Santiago would turn again, she doesn't move, and the magician pauses, watching her curiously. Thoughtfully, she continues, "Only…."

His eyebrow climbs an inch higher. "Yes?"

"Whatever is happening … it seems like it could happen anywhere? In the world, I mean. And it's a big world. But you're blocks from my house."

"Yeah." Santiago shrugs. "I don't know. Are we here because you're here? Are you here because the Chalice is here? Is it one big coincidence? Colin says coincidence is an outside thing—that events just *happen*, and then fit, or not. I guess he takes things on faith." Santiago's smile is crooked, overcast with shadows that creep across his features. Verity feels Ouroboros slide across her shoulder and wind down her arm, but in the candle-lit hall, blackness undulates slowly at the magician's feet. She shivers and looks away, but the breath she draws in hums with energy that crackles faintly in the air.

On Verity's wrist, Ouro's eyes have a golden gleam that seems more than reflected candlelight. She watches rainbow traces of barely heard conversation swirl with the fog of her breath. It grows warmer as Santiago turns away again and they walk. The hall is cluttered with a neat pile of cereal boxes and a low table scattered with water bottles and fruit cups.

A small group of people is clustered around the corner; they press themselves to the walls, shifting away and down in a seemingly accustomed shuffle to make room as Santiago and Verity pass. Verity recognizes most of them. The numbers in the walls have grown a little in the past weeks, but not by many. Tones have grown easier, more familiar. The refugees call each other by name.

"Hey."

Verity registers the peppered hoarseness of the voice even as a flare of robin's egg blue leaps up her arm. She halts, startled, as Ouroboros rears up from her opposite wrist, suddenly hooded like a flaring cobra. Its eyes are narrow, its long fangs gleaming, and she realizes belatedly that whomever grabbed her arm has released her in the light of the snake's glare.

"Don't touch her." Santiago's voice is velvet cool.

"Sorry! Look. Sorry. I just wanted to—I don't know if you remember me."

Verity processes a faded ball cap over an equally worn face—a man a little taller than she is, his half-shaven face marked by salt-and-pepper stubble and sunless skin. His worried stare is a high-pitched hum in her ears, but the beaded intensity of his eyes is familiar.

She pauses. "The corner store," she offers, slowly.

The tinnitus stops as his face clears. "Yeah. Look. That was a lousy day. I didn't know who you were. I just saw Ouro and—"

"And thought I would understand," sighs Verity. "I do now. I mean ... it's not okay to rob people. To scare them with guns. But I know why you did."

"Colin ripped me a new one over it, anyway. He was right. And I haven't—I mean, I'm Rick. And I'm sorry. That's all. Thanks for helping us—with the food and everything."

Verity isn't entirely certain what to say, but it doesn't matter; Rick only bobs his head to her, jerkily, and brushes past, heading back the way they just came. When she turns to watch him, he too is weaving his way through the small crowd.

"That's new. You don't smile very often." Santiago's voice is as smooth as the snake around her neck. "We've noticed that."

"You smile when you don't mean it. It tastes of old olives." Verity says it gently. Her observation only makes the magician's mouth twitch, and she sighs. "Who is 'we'? You and Ouro, or you and others here?"

"Me and Ouro." Santiago pauses, considering. "And the kid made a comment the other day. Don't be sad at him, okay? That's a deal breaker these days."

"I don't want to hurt him."

"I know." Santiago extends a hand toward Verity's shoulder. She holds still, uncertain, wondering if he, too, means to pat awkwardly at her coat, but she feels Ouroboros glide from its necklaced perch as it wraps into its customary position around the magician's wrist. Santiago's fingertips brush her throat, then he flashes her the queen of diamonds and makes it vanish before he lets his hand drop. "Is that why? The thing with the power plant. Were you really trying to help him?"

"Privya said it would. But I didn't, um—I didn't know. I didn't make it happen. I was just there." The words trip off her tongue.

"Yeah. Well. Maybe it helped." The magician offers her a slight bow. "Thanks for trying." Turning, he leads her farther down the hall, past bits of furniture and three empty milk cartons, toward the glittering candle-light that marks Colin's makeshift clinic. There are more cots than before;

people sleep on mattresses and on the floor, huddled in ragged blankets. The sick have spread to the area where the children used to play. The *between* has narrowed to a hospital hallway filled with slumped bodies groaning on sagging mattresses. There are faces Verity doesn't recognize. Yellowed eyes stare dully from beneath dimly glowing lanterns.

The angel is no longer a fallen star. Now his gleam is that of a candle, and Verity would almost have missed it except for the taste of honey, warm and sweet in her mouth. The shadows deepen and the hall widens as space is left between the last of the mattresses and Colin's faint glow farther down, just where the next sharp turning presumably marks the corner of the building outside.

When the line of beds stops blocking half the floor, Santiago steps to the side, gesturing Verity ahead. He is scanning the hall behind her; she sees the way his gaze rests on each blanketed form in turn, and the way his shoulders tense. She has lost track of the snake.

She walks forward, only to freeze as silver eyes flare; too late, she spots Jihan in the darkness. Colin lies prone on his broken-down couch, which has apparently been moved for the purpose. He is gaunt, wrapped in a blanket and the big navy trench coat that is increasingly too large for him. His starlit eyes are half open, and his breath comes in soft pants. Above him, the woman with steel hair looms like a gargoyle, improbably clad in a pink sweatshirt and ripped jeans, perched on the back of the cushions. She has a notched hunting knife in one hand—newer than the kitchen knife, though nicked twice along the edge—and a cloth in the other. The cloth has half gone to shreds; it takes Verity a second to recognize the remnants of her bloodstained scarf.

Pulling to an immediate stop, she raises her hands. "I'm not," she says, and "I don't," but she doesn't know what she wants to convey. It doesn't matter, anyway, because the other woman's gaze is a bottomless void.

Verity swallows. She feels Santiago behind her, and his presence at her shoulder is as subtly familiar as Ouroboros, though her fingers twitch and she touches only air instead of the comforting insubstantiality of the dog.

"S'okay. She's leaving." Colin's face is empty and drawn, his pale skin marked with a sheen of sweat; he only moves enough to raise one hand and pat familiarly at Jihan's knee. "About time for you, isn't it? Go on. We can't stop you, anyway."

Verity wonders if she only imagines seeing the other woman's hand tighten on the knife's hilt, though she is certain she can taste the sudden prickle of a rope gone dry and frayed. Jihan rises, picks her way smoothly off the couch, and then slips past both Verity and Santiago, moving swiftly, touching neither. She is a flash of ragged grace and ill-fitting clothing, and then she's gone.

Verity whirls, but there's only Santiago behind her. His expression is unreadable. Shadows pool down his cheekbones and along his nose, a caressing darkness that deepens each line in his face. She wonders if that is Ouroboros crawling across his skin.

"She's gone to visit your boyfriend again," Santiago notes. One winged eyebrow lifts.

"Christ," breathes Colin, "don't—she's already frightened, now you want to—"

"I'm sorry." The magician's apology is quick and tastes of cranberry, tart but sincere. Verity isn't sure whom it's meant for. She only shakes her head and turns back to the angel on his couch.

"It's okay. I knew."

"Right." Colin closes his eyes, long fingers plucking at the blanket someone's thrown across him. "Do you know *why*? Honest question. It's the weirdest thing."

"I don't—I should ask him. I know. But we aren't talking much. I lie to him, and it's a cloud of hornets or rattlesnake stings, it's...." Verity sees Colin's fingers twitch again, his glow dimming, and she swallows, looking away. "Poison," she concludes. "Maybe it's a metaphor? It doesn't taste like one."

"Understand I'm not upset when I say this. Or, Christ, jealous. But mostly, her royal highness looks around a room—she looks *through* a room—and the only one she recognizes is me."

"Is Jacob in danger?"

Santiago's voice comes velvet in the dimness. "We don't think so. Ouro keeps checking, but she still just ... stands on your street, staring. I admit I don't get the appeal."

"I don't know what she wants. If she wants." Verity folds her arms, looking down at Colin on his battered couch. His eyes are lit only by occasional sparks of falling star. He closes them.

"I know," he mutters. "She's a damn cipher."

"You're sick," she says. "I'm sorry. And I'm sorry that I'm sorry because it makes things worse, so ... um. I wanted to—I still don't understand. About Jihan, and you, and—the Chalice. I mean, if it's a cup or not a cup, or what's in it, or...."

"We've lost the words for it," agrees Colin. The sparks of his gaze are still visible through his paper-thin lids. "Shit, I don't know, either. Chalice seems like an awkward word. I saw a cave, once, and a lot of rock. I know something's building here, and people are straggling in as sure as those poor little dragons are gathering on rooftops. But we're just ... enduring." The white lashes lift, and he looks up at Verity. "If we're sitting around waiting for Jihan to find some miracle way out of here, well ... she hasn't done squat. I asked her about it. She walked away and came back an hour later to give me a dead rat."

"What Privya said is true—that Jihan could destroy the world. I can smell the earthquake, like dust and some terrible deep ... I want to help you, but she scares me. And she's lost."

Colin coughs, but there's glitter in it. "Shit, yeah, that's about right. Stefan and I keep going in circles about it. I knew Privya blamed Jihan for something. I thought it was Alethea. I mean, it is, but I didn't know about a whole damn city."

"Whatever escape Jihan might know about—she opened the earth, almost too wide. You must care about that."

"That a walking bomb brings me rats? Oh, god, yeah, I care." The angel sighs. He looks like a fevered child, his hair damp with sweat, but his grimace is old.

"If it matters to you," Verity offers, as mildly as she can, "should she be just...?" She waves a hand back toward the shadows where Jihan last departed.

"I care," says Colin again. "What are we going to do, though? We're not going to tie her down based on something we hear she might be thinking of. I don't think we could, or that she even *makes* plans. There's not enough left of her."

"Anyway, it's worth the chance." Santiago speaks with arms folded, one shoulder leaning against the wall.

The angel blanches. "Stefan—"

"What's the worst that could happen?" murmurs the magician. "Death? Maybe nothingness is better than living crammed like roaches in a wall. You can't say you haven't been thinking about it."

"I can, but Vee'll know I'm lying." Colin's concession is wry, but there's a salt edge to it. His voice is thin. "No. I don't wish death on the world. What am I supposed to believe, though? That all this shit's for nothing? That we're all just going to waste away in here? Or Jihan blows us all to hell, or Privya blows *them* to hell?"

"Anything's better than this." Santiago's voice is soft and serpent-scaled. "Look, I'm not saying we should all throw in with Privya. But maybe Jihan'll get it right this time. She knows things. She doesn't talk, but she knows. Like when she wrote Vee's name on the wall."

"Like when she stabbed me?"

"She didn't kill you. You're here. Maybe that's part of the plan."

On the couch, Colin sighs. "She does know things. The days Stefan doesn't make any money in the market, she'll have already come in with a box of chocolate or a bag of apples or—a half-full pizza box, God knows where she got that one from. She'll pull me back on a sidewalk before a car speeds around the corner. She stood out on the street one day, staring at the damn alley until I went to check on her, and just as I got there, some truck came by and two men dropped off this couch by the garbage. It isn't big, you know? It isn't all the time. It's not like she'll answer to her name. But if she starts dragging a cot together, we can start getting ready for a new arrival."

"That's, um, a lot to bet on a maybe."

"She follows me around like a lost child or a lonely wolverine. Why?" The angel's scrawny fingers tighten on the blanket's edge. "She knows something. Aren't you the one who can tell what's true?"

"The future is grey." Verity sighs. "The past tastes like ... smoke and oregano. I know what she almost did. Privya says Jihan needs me— or Privya does. I don't know what that means, or how, except Alethea stopped Jihan, last time."

"Stopped her from what?" Santiago's voice is cold. "The quake, fine, but otherwise ... what? An apocalypse or a door? We don't know because she didn't finish. Now she can't tell us."

Verity turns her head; the magician is a trick at the corner of her vision, quick as the playing cards he shuffles. "The earthquake is true," she says. "And Alethea, who was like me. But the 'why' is all bound in 'maybe' and 'I think'—or you think, or Privya does. I think the danger is true, but—it's all possibility. What she might do. What Privya would do. Whatever they want from me—I don't like to see you fading here." She sighs. "I think the power will come back on today. I think time is running forward. How long do we have before the Chalice?"

"Christ." Colin burrows a little further under his blankets. "Weeks, if we can believe the posters. If she published the exact friggin' date. But look—" His eyes are open, flaring like falling stars. "You're right, of course. As utterly beautiful as it would be to have some miracle way out of this hell—if there's a chance Jihan could hurt anyone, we can't risk it. Don't know if there's a fucking thing we can do about Privya." He shifts, and Verity can almost hear his bones creak, his skin rattling like dry paper. He extends a hand toward her, his fingers outstretched and his shirt sleeve far too loose. "Take my hand."

It's a flickering moment of temptation. Santiago's attention jerks up to her, dark and disapproving. "No," says Verity anyway, startled.

Colin coughs. "It's not for you. I mean, shit, yeah, I want to help, I can feel that ache behind your eyes—but I want to know what you say without the world screaming at you. What's real, Vee? *Can* we get out of here? What—what do we do next?"

"I'm not," murmurs Verity, and "I don't—" but the angel is watching her with broken, glittering eyes.

She puffs air between her lips and tries to take a moment to think, but a wave of sound laps at her calves—whispers and exclamations carrying faintly down the long hall of the *between*, heralded by the frothing impact of a shout.

A length of shadow flows from Santiago's sleeve and leaps into the shape of the dog, Ouroboros whipping back down the corridor even as Verity, Colin, and the magician turn to see Rick running into view, his hat askew and his shoulder bumping the wall as he presses to the side, trying to avoid huddled figures on cots.

Beacon blue flares from Colin's eyes. "Christ, what—"

"The girl." Rick skids to a halt, narrowly missing a rickety wooden side table and waving his hand back in the direction he came from.

Simultaneously, Santiago says, "Privya." The magician's tone is grim, his gaze gone distant as he looks through the eyes of his shadow.

"Oh," says Colin. "Crap." His hand snakes out again, knobby-wristed; he wraps thin fingers around Verity's sleeve. "Help me up. Stefan, go on, see what she wants."

Santiago shoots Verity a single fierce glance, then moves nearly as fast as Ouroboros, grabbing Rick and pulling the scrawnier man with him, back toward the mounting cloud of consternation. Verity, meanwhile, holds still, letting Colin get a grip as the angel grabs up his cane and rises. He lets the coat slide away, despite the winter bite; his wings rustle and flex as he steadies himself. She is careful not to touch him, though light glimmers in the veins just under his skin, threatening to soothe.

"I love her, too, you know. That's the hell of it." Colin sighs, spider-fingers locking around Verity's sleeve. "All right. Let's find out what's going on."

She is careful, but the boy at her side seems reinvigorated by the commotion, and their main difficulty is navigating the tight space of the hall. Colin pulls his feathers to his shoulders, dropping just slightly behind Verity so that she can balance him while still avoiding the sea of beds, tables, and small food piles that block parts of the worn floor. The rest of the long hall is empty now; they make their way past discarded books and a scattered group of ragged plush toys. They move quickly, but Colin's steps falter at intervals, and Verity must occasionally pause as the growing mutters blind her, like rolling clouds of fog or an oncoming storm.

It isn't long before there are people blocking the corridor, necks craning as they cluster, but they press themselves to the walls to give way before Colin—and Verity by proxy. A girl with blue hair sends rolls of toilet paper scattering when she kicks them, scrambling to pile them up again while still keeping half her attention on what has become a confrontation just inside the door from the theatre.

The first thing Verity sees is Santiago standing with his arms folded, black on black in the dimness of the narrow walls. The small light burning just behind him details the edges of Ouroboros's bristling fur, the dog pressed to the magician's thigh. Its head is lowered, its ears back.

"It's really not necessary," Privya is saying. Her hair is pulled back in a loose knot, barely contained by a faded green ribbon. She is wearing a puffed winter vest over a bulky wool sweater and a skirt that falls in wild rainbow layers over tight-laced military boots. She looks like any teenager.

Verity, with a start of alarm, looks past Privya to see that Alan is in his armchair, Sanna's small form cuddled in his lap. The little girl is playing with an old bear that even from a distance tastes of fresh sea air. She is paying the newest visitor no attention whatsoever, though her grandfather's arms are around her and the old man's gaze is intent on Privya.

Privya, for her part, is studying Santiago, but her gaze shifts to the crowd down the hall; she offers Verity a quick smile that vanishes as she looks to Colin. "I'm not here to hurt anyone," she says. "Why would I? We're all in this together. Even you, Warner. You make stupid choices, but at least you're keeping these people alive. Tell your dogs to stand down. If you want to keep your refuge a secret, maybe don't print it on posters."

Santiago and Ouroboros both bare their teeth, but Colin says, "Stefan," and the magician and his shadow-beast go still, their hackles raised. The magician's fingers fidget deftly with a handful of cards. The dog's tail lashes in tandem.

Colin sighs, keeping one hand just below Verity's elbow as he adjusts his weight, leaning on the cane. His wings rustle at his shoulders, but behind them, Verity can feel the small crowd pressing. They are quiet now, the whispered waves fading to an anticipatory tide that laps low at her ankles.

"Why are you here?" Colin asks, and the sorrow of it drags like a stone warmed by the sun. "Vee told us what you did to that man by the river. Is that what you're about?"

"About?" Privya is genuinely perplexed; Verity can taste it in a flash of pomegranate, phantom seeds scattering in the air. "I am what I am. If I didn't feed when I needed to, it would be much worse in the end. There was a time when I mourned their losses, but that was before I knew what their numbers were doing to us. Would anyone here," and she raises her voice to carry down the hall, "choose one of them over one of us? You don't need to celebrate death. But if you had to pick? I mean, as it turns out, you do actually have to pick."

Verity hears the stirrings behind her and feels the angel's fingers tighten around her sleeve. Past the unmoving sentinels of Santiago and Ouro, she sees Sanna squirm in Alan's lap, reaching for a gleaming strand of uneasy fear, and the old man stroking his granddaughter's hair.

Privya says, "I'm sorry."

Verity is startled to realize that she's being addressed. Privya watches her, continuing, "I could have warned you. I just wanted you to see—all of it, what it's like, everything we could show you. I hope you weren't afraid."

Verity is just as startled to hear herself admit, "No." She is trying to look at Privya, but she catches Santiago and Ouroboros tensing, ready as whips. Colin only squeezes her arm.

Privya's voice is lower now. An old rage is fossilized in the depths of her gaze, and it gives the lie to her young face more than the faint scent of water and brimstone ever could. Her grief is older and deeper than Colin's, and no shining sparks rise to lighten the burnished mahogany of her eyes. "I was made. I didn't choose. Ask Mr. Warner what that feels like. Do you know he'd die for me right now if he had to, even knowing that I hate him? None of this is about what I am."

Verity swallows. "Did Alethea know?"

"Of course. She knew me inside out." Privya tilts her head slightly to the side, studying Verity. The green ribbon is jaunty in her hair. "Have you decided?"

Suddenly, everyone is watching her. Verity wants to quail beneath the weight of it, but the angel is leaning on her arm, and she holds herself rigid. She swallows and looks at the floor to keep the wash from her tongue and skin—the darkly flowered attention of Santiago and the dog, the peppered breeze of Privya's expectations, the honey-gold comfort of Colin's silent hope. She is aware of Sanna squirming, and the crowd breathing in the wood-splintered hall. Alan is walnuts and leather; she isn't sure why, but she can't look to him, either.

She tries to speak, but succeeds only in wetting her lips. The sound she makes is something like half of a hum.

"Leave her be," says Colin—sharply, for him.

"I can't," replies Privya, equably. "None of us can. She's the one who stands on the borderline, but she can't stay there. Even doing nothing is a choice."

Colin's presence is sweet in her throat, and Verity swallows again. "You want me to help you hurt people," she says then. "I ... I don't think I can."

She doesn't think Privya is surprised. When she risks a glance upward, the girl only stands, arms folded, melted snow glittering in her hair and the slow death of centuries somewhere behind the youth of her face. "It's self-defence. Do you think you'd be incapable of that, if I attacked you? If I came for your feathered friend? Oh, keep the dog *back*, I'm not threatening any of you."

Santiago and Ouroboros have both advanced two steps, the magician's stride as silent and gliding as the dog's. "Get out."

"She's given you an answer," says Colin, mildly, a rasp in his voice. "Is that what you came for?"

"Not entirely." Privya rolls her eyes at the magician looming over her. Not only does he cast a shadow over her face, even with the dog beside him, but the hall around him darkens, obscuring Alan and the shivering Sanna. Verity is relieved to see the little girl appears to have escaped Privya's attention entirely, though Alan is watchful. His expression is hidden in the bush of his beard.

Privya deliberately looks away from Santiago, apparently unmindful of how close Ouroboros's jaws are to her calf. Instead, she directs her words to the press of people grouped behind Verity and Colin. "If you're sick, stay here. If you can manage the outside, don't leave us to do all the work ourselves. Come find me in the market when you get tired of sitting and rotting."

"Get *out.*" Shadows pool in Santiago's eye sockets; the dog lashes a serpentine tail. Verity hears mutters from behind; she feels feathers brush her back.

Privya is serene. "A thousand years ago, you might have been something to reckon with. Now … I've seen your street corner tricks. You won't even touch me at all with your angel watching." She reaches for the knob of the old door, and adds to Verity, "You're making the wrong choice. I know the look on your face, though—I remember it on hers."

The moment of Verity's hesitation is enough for Privya to touch the door and slip through. There's a spark to it—a distinct, static charge of impossibility when the *between* opens outward and the girl exits via the door with one side.

Alan stiffens immediately. "That's it!" His exclamation is lost in the sudden hubbub that fills the narrow hall. Colin staggers, but Santiago has swooped in before Verity can react; the angel is braced between the magician and Ouroboros, letting go of Verity as he winds his fingers in the dog's fur.

"That's it," crows Alan again, his arms around his granddaughter, but his focus entirely on the door. "Vee, did you see? I almost had it. She knows the quick way, all right."

"I saw," says Verity, "but I don't—"

"Christ, what the fuck was that about? Stefan, don't fuss." Colin shakes his head, straightening, adjusting his weight on the cane as he leaves the other hand on Ouroboros. His wings flex behind him, long enough to brush both walls. "Everyone move back for a bit, will you? Not you, Vee. Alan, you're fine."

The waves of sound are back, pulsing in low rumbles and washing up to Verity's chest now, a rising tide that fades into drifts; she knows when the group behind her has broken, scattering farther down the hall.

"She and Jihan," murmurs Alan, "just as I remember. They look right past me—I'm not that little boy anymore—but I know them, just the same. How curious, to feel the years fall away." Sanna curls in his lap, watching the remnants of his youth wind through the pale bush of his beard.

"What was she after?" Santiago still stands with Colin, a hovering shadow over the angel's faint, skeletal glow. The dog is gone; the snake undulates up the magician's sleeve.

"Hell if I know. Look, Vee. What I was asking—please. We need the truth. Where do we go from here?" The hand Colin extends is trembling and just slightly translucent. The glow of his skin is not even strong enough to reach her, but Verity feels the warmth when she relents and touches her fingertips to the back of his hand, as delicately as she can. Light floods her. Colin shivers, and she jerks her hand back, looking away before she can see her guilt lash him. The hallway settles to stillness around her, and she can breathe. She focuses on the line of the magician's shoulders.

"It's an ember," she offers, after some thought. The clarity of her own voice is flat to her, all sound, no colour or texture across her skin. "Jihan may give you the flame you want, or a conflagration. Privya ... she can only breathe on it, to coax a flare before it dies."

"We knew that," says Santiago, impatient. "What kind of conflagration? How bad is this game?"

"I'm not a fortune teller." Verity looks Santiago in the eye for a moment, and she sees him flinch. The shadows that creep on his face mark an exhaustion half set to rival the angel's. "There are seventy-four lives in these walls, and they're dying more quickly than most, and you're all, um, playing with fire." She rubs at the bridge of her nose. "I don't like metaphors, usually. I'm sorry. Jihan is...."

She trails off. In her silence, she sees a length of darkness wind itself around Santiago's throat and open golden eyes.

Colin says, "What?"

"Possibilities." Verity watches Ouroboros. The snake is tiny now. It might as easily be a strip of leather. "She had a knife again," she says slowly. "In her hand today. Does she often have a knife?"

The angel frowns. "She always *has* one. Last time I saw it out—well, I'm guessing you remember."

Santiago's brows have drawn downward. Ouro's tongue flicks.

"She was going to see Jacob."

"You think she's going to hurt him?"

"I think Privya's people were watching the house today."

There is a pregnant pause.

"Ah," says Colin. "Hell."

[**IMAGE:** Jihan, perched on the back of an old broken couch. She's sharpening a knife. She looks straight out at the reader, expressionless. Below her, Colin is a mess of blankets, but light is visible glowing from his hands and any parts of his face that are visible.]

17

I'm not sure how to tell this part.

```
i probably cant help you sorry i want to which part
```

Jihan. I'm trying to fill in all the details, but then there's Jihan. What was it you saw when you looked in her eyes?

```
sorrow and a setting sunset all the sunsets on water
glistening but also a black hole and a single per-
fect leaf
nothing everything
every leaf and the exact pattern of its fall
```

...I have no idea what to do with that.

```
i said i probably couldnt help
```

COLIN (SAN FRANCISCO)

Colin followed a strange girl and her lantern through the dark. The more the walls solidified around him, the more the girl's quiet anguish splintered his bones. Her pain swept him as surely as the tide, and since he could not touch her, he stumbled onward in her wake. His coat was heavy and dragged at his wings. His walking stick was light and he leaned on it, balancing against the ache of his leg.

The girl looked younger than he did, but it had been a while since he'd been sixteen, and he was pretty sure the same was true for her, too. She still moved like a child—easy, thoughtless. She kept a few paces ahead.

The four people following bled auras tainted with the sickly sweetness of the dying, though they were stronger in the *between*. Colin had seen spaces like this only a few times before, and although he could breathe more easily, he didn't like the way the walls rose seemingly forever, their narrowness pressing in on him.

Piles of brick made the way difficult. Everything was brick here—it rose endlessly on either side and paved the floor beneath. Sometimes, the walls bowed inward, and the way was so tight it made Colin swallow, but the girl was no larger than he, and they both slipped through. Behind, more than once, he heard someone swear.

His wings flexed beneath the folds of his coat, but there was no room to stretch them. He would have liked to shed the heavy fabric, but the set of the girl's shoulders screamed need and pulled him on. His stomach roiled, and his cane slipped on unexpected bits of wood and broken stone.

The girl's lantern burned with a steady pale flame. Colin's world extended only to shadows and the tricky footing of the crumbling floor. He had a headache. His mouth tasted like a cotton ball soaked in bourbon and bile.

When the girl stopped walking and raised her lantern high to expose the mess of fallen beams that blocked their path, Colin limped up beside her. The raw impetus of her need was worms writhing under his skin. He raised a hand, unable to stop himself, but when his slight glow fell across the back of her neck, she gave him a sharp look. Her eyes were as glossy as agates.

He stopped himself. He let his hand drop back to his side and clenched his other hand around the head of the cane, mentally casting back to a hazed conversation in an ill-lit bar. "Okay," he said, awkwardly. "Look. This doesn't seem like the best spot for your sick friend. Why are we here?"

"It's the right place." The girl's voice was light. She studied the mass of fallen wood and shattered brick, lifting her lantern high, then she stepped back, gesturing to the figures following. "You may want to move out of the way." She continued to hold the light up for her people as they came forward. Colin saw ragged coats and soiled hats. He smelled oil, urine, and dust. Otherwise, he had only impressions: two men, he thought, and two women, but he wasn't sure. He wanted to lay hands on their dying bones. They dug at the blockage like moles.

"How did you find me?" he asked, standing again next to the girl. Her name was Privya—syllables uttered as she'd smiled at him in a booth that smelled of stale beer and ancient smoke. "I mean, you said Nathan. But Nate's not a chatty guy."

"I know people." Privya shrugged one shoulder. "I hear things." She glanced at him sidelong. The perfect smoothness of her bun was coming unravelled in the crowded dust. "I've been waiting a very long time. I wasn't sure we had any healers anymore." It was hard to hear her over the sound of hatchets in wood, and rock crumbling. "Not one who could help, anyway. How much do you know about San Francisco?"

"Only been here a week or two. Where are we?"

"In the ruins of the *between* that was."

A deafening rumble heralded the collapse of the barrier; Colin stumbled back three steps, coughing on dust. Privya didn't move, except to catch his elbow when he might have fallen. Her grip was implacable, but not cruel. The lantern was steady in her other hand. "Careful. This hall hasn't been stable in a century."

"No shit." Colin coughed again and muffled the sound in his sleeve. Privya's grip fell away from his arm. He could see the shadows of her people scatter in the murk, though motes of sawdust glittered in the lantern light and obscured his view. More importantly, he could feel that their alarm was only faint. He sensed no spikes of pain, only determination. The yawning need of the girl next to him was more agonizing.

"Let me help you," he said, impulsively. He lifted his hand again, palm up. He could see her shiver as his gleam touched her, though it was less than the light in her hand.

"Help me by helping her." Privya turned away from him and walked to the narrow gap in the collapsed hall. Her people made way before her, pressing themselves to the wall. She touched them, one by one, as she passed. Then, casting her light ahead into the gap, she said to Colin, "This way."

There was really only one direction, unless he wanted to head back. Colin wasn't sure whether he did, or whether he'd even be allowed. It didn't matter. Privya's anguish wrapped invisible strings around his lungs and pulled him forward. He was careful on the rubble. His own growing glow almost gave him enough light to see.

He stopped to offer his hand to a tawny girl whose short hair was mostly hidden under a giant woollen hat. She was shivering. "Let me help you," he said. She blinked at him; her eyes were puffy in the bare light. Her gloves were fingerless and, hesitantly, she touched the back of his hand.

Colin had never really found words to explain to people what he did. He simply reached into the girl—threw himself, really, into her—and found the things that were wrong. Her palm was cut. Her arms were bruised from the digging; her ragged nails were bleeding at the edges. More than that, the grey mass curling in her liver was reaching smoking tendrils through her body; it wasn't enough, yet, to kill her. He trimmed it back. He couldn't excise it—he never could, as much as he wanted. It had taken him a long time to learn to do what he could and slide back into himself, leaving the girl flawed but better. He soothed her trepidation with a thought, leaving her dreamlike, coming back to his own body with a ragged cough. He dropped her hand and gripped the cane as a wave of nausea took him.

The girl blinked again and said, "Thanks." It was the first time she'd spoken to him. He nodded and coughed again, then raised his head to find Privya still waiting by the hole, her lantern raised high.

Privya's lips were drawn sharp with impatience, but she nodded to him, even as every line of her leaned toward the gaping ruin and the shadows.

He hobbled forward. His knee was killing him, and now his organs felt too small. Privya's silent need wailed its clarion call.

Privya would have moved back to allow him room, but Colin said, "Lady with the light goes first," and she shrugged, ducking ahead.

She warned him, "Stairs." He moved forward cautiously, both hearing and feeling the followers gathering in behind him; the girl he'd healed was a soothing pulse of wonder.

After he passed through the excavation, not without a dust-filled cough, he found the walls curving for the first time as a smooth set of grey stone stairs opened up and curled downward before him. If anything, it was more claustrophobic than before. He couldn't keep the wings beneath his coat from rubbing the walls.

Privya walked before him, her light tread muffled by the dust she stirred up with every step.

Colin pulled a scarf out of his pocket, wrapping it around his mouth and nose. It didn't help. "Christ. How long since someone was here?"

"It was 1906." Privya stepped without hesitation, but she was careful to cast her light so Colin could see. Behind him, a man in a worn leather jacket carried another lantern. Their shadows all crept along the walls, distorted by the haze in the air. The staircase continued down. Piles of fallen rock made the going awkward, but the way was passable. They were silent, except when pebbles dislodged or Colin swore under his breath.

He found the stairs uneven, worn smooth by countless feet that had gone before, and he wondered at stone so much older than the brick and broken beams above. The descent was a growing agony on his knee; he felt bones grate with each step and already dreaded the upward return. The walls were too tight, and he had to hold his wings too close to his shoulders. He wanted to protest, but it died in his throat. The girl's need pulled him.

The texture of the rock grew rougher. The steps became smaller and more shallow until eventually, Colin found himself following Privya and her lantern down a steep slope. He braced a hand against the wall and found rough stone there, too.

"Where are we?" he asked.

Privya's shoulders screamed her desire for haste, but she paused for him. The steady flame of her lantern illuminated her young skin and the shining darkness of her bound hair. "This is a way that opens for the Chalice—it appears where it wills. It happens rarely. This passage is meant to close again behind the last who leave."

"All right," said Colin, slowly. There was a hint of an echo to their conversation here, words bouncing from walls long silent. Even the dust had faded, as if it didn't penetrate this far, leaving the air empty and clear. "Why's it still open?"

"She's still here. Come on. She's been waiting a long time." Privya turned away again. For the first time, as she moved forward, the walls veered away as the narrow passage widened to a tunnel, and a little further to a cavern. There, Colin stopped again, because even with the light spilling from Privya's lantern, he could see only a circle of rough stone floor and beyond it, a seemingly endless blackness that stretched above, ahead, and to either side.

He was moderately sure his knee was on fire. He savoured the moment to catch his breath.

"Stay here."

In a grateful burst, Colin thought Privya was talking to him, but he felt the shimmering hope of the girl he'd healed and heard Privya's people pressing behind him. One of them muttered a quiet oath.

Privya beckoned him, but it was her need that drove him forward; she burned, and he stumbled with it. Control lent her voice a preternatural calm. "They should be just up here, healer. This is why I brought you." Her lantern was low at her side now, spilling light across the ground—Colin saw cracked stone, loose rock, and, finally, the rising ghosts of slender stalagmites.

Privya touched his arm again, lightly, just at the sleeve. It was a polite gesture, but also peremptory; he stepped forward.

She walked with him. He was careful, his cane uncertain on the uneven stone and her quiet desperation threatening to pull him off-balance. Resisting the urge to lay his hands on her brought beads of sweat to his forehead.

A small part of him did enjoy the fact that she was an inch shorter than he. It wasn't something that happened often. He concentrated on that small and incongruous pleasure while the ground sloped upward beneath his feet and he found himself climbing what appeared to be some low, underground hill.

Privya's hand was still on his sleeve, and now she pulled him faster, mindless of his awkward balance. Her light was raised high, a single star except for the glow of Colin's own skin.

Thankfully, it wasn't a long climb, or a steep one. The ground merely rose several slow feet until it abruptly plateaued and they could walk easily again.

"There." The lantern trembled slightly in Privya's hand, creating a ghostlike shiver of light across the two figures that emerged abruptly from the concealing darkness.

"Christ!" Colin drew back; beneath his coat, his wings spread from reflex, but Privya's grip was tight. After a breathless moment, he realized the people in front of him weren't moving, and he could sense no life except the frantic conflagration of the girl beside him. "Christ," he muttered again. He shook his head, then drew a breath, studying the newly illuminated tableau.

The rock floor of the cavern rose again at what was apparently the centre of the unnatural mesa, culminating in a broken stalagmite column perhaps two feet wide and four feet high. Beside it, the figures of two women were locked together, motionless and just on the brink of falling. They were too lifelike to be statues, but the rigidity of their perfect imbalance was as solid as the rock of the cavern floor.

As he moved closer, the top of the stone column came into view, and he saw it formed an empty basin, the edges irregularly rounded. The women were off-centre, as though they'd been first positioned on either side but one had lunged forward, pushing the other back.

Privya hung back, almost a statue herself. Her mouth was set, but her eyes were black with wanting. Colin ignored the burning of her desire and leaned on his cane, letting his wings spread slightly as he shifted, taking his time to look.

The first woman he studied was the one who had lunged; she had skin dark as sable, and her hair was a wild mane of tangled black, streaming back as frozen as the rest of her. She wore a thin white blouse over a long grey skirt, threadbare and torn at the hem. Her face was not old, but it was mature and knowing, beginning to crease at the edges of eyes and mouth.

Her eyes were peculiarly clear, colourless as ocean spray on a cloudy morning; her lips were full but closed tightly, thinned in a grimace. She had a round nose and a round face to match the sturdy curves of her body. Her eyebrows were furrowed with determination, and the tears on her lashes looked fresh and wet, just on the verge of falling. She had a narrow sword in her hand, and she was stabbing it straight through the gut of the woman on the other side of the basin.

This second woman—the one stabbed—was the figure most clearly off-balance, her knees buckling, her hands latched around the wrist of her attacker and the hilt of the weapon buried in her abdomen. The attacker's muscles were tight beneath the thin linen of her sleeves, and she had not held back. Colin couldn't tell exactly what kind of blade it was, except that it emerged from the victim's back single-edged, slender and shining with viscera. He wasn't very good with swords. He could see that, distinct from the wet sheen of the sticky-looking metal, a smattering of stains on the ground marked the long-dried spatter of impact. It was black in the pale light of the lantern, but when Colin stretched out a hovering hand, his own gleam illuminated shades of red in the mess.

Privya made a sound. When Colin looked back, she was only a shadow holding a bright light. She said, "Help her."

The woman impaled had aquiline features—olive skin, high cheekbones, a nose that was sharp and slightly curved. Her age was indeterminate. Her hair was held in a single long ebony braid. Her eyes were black, or a very deep brown, and they were locked on the face of her attacker. Her lips were parted as though she were about to speak, or as though she had just begun to smile, and had been interrupted by the blade driving through her.

She had an athlete's spare frame. She wore plain rags in various shades of brown and grey—a shirt mended too many times, a vest, a pair of charcoal pants over sturdy leather boots. A knife was strapped to her leg, and an empty scabbard hung at her belt. Where she grasped her attacker's wrist, her knuckles were pale.

The two women were locked in place, intently staring, each focused on the other's face. Colin looked at them, and then he looked at Privya and saw something ancient and long-buried stirring beneath the girl's eyes. He felt, abruptly, the childhood urge to beat his wings frantically, desperately, until he couldn't breathe—until, maybe, he could soar. But there was nowhere to fly, and his coat was heavy on his body. He swallowed. "I don't think they're alive."

"They're alive. Help her."

"Which one?"

"Alethea." Privya spoke the name as an invocation. "The one wielding the sword. The other is a madwoman. Alethea is the one who saved us all."

"I don't think they're alive," said Colin again, gently—so gently, because Privya's wanting was a conflagration that threatened to burn his skin away. To alleviate it, he raised a hand and touched the forearm of the woman Alethea.

He wasn't entirely certain what to expect, with the figures in front of him frozen so expressively alive, though he had the fleeting fear that he might somehow be trapped with them, unmoving in the dark. He found Alethea's arm to be as cold and impenetrable as stone.

"They aren't—" he began. Then he paused, frowning, because there was almost something there. "Could you step back a little?"

"I'm hardly—"

"I can feel you. It's making this harder. And it's not very easy to start with. Here—hold my coat."

He felt guilt even as he shed the heavy fabric at his shoulders; he was grateful when Privya apparently took no offence. She only took his coat and drew back, the controlled blaze of her desperation abating a little with distance. It was a relief to stretch his wings. Before him and beneath his hand, he felt a ghost like a guttering candle.

It was a peculiar sensation, this life that flitted within a rock-cold corpse. Colin could not sense any pain or desire. If anything, he thought perhaps the woman Alethea was dreaming, but any visions she might have had were gossamer in his fingers. *Wake,* he willed her, but he was barely certain she was there.

He dreaded what he might sense from the woman with the braided hair, but laying his other hand against the plane of her cheek, he had no impression of pain; wherever she was, it was not trapped in a frozen moment with a blade in her intestines. She, too, was cold and impenetrable, though he was captured by the look on her face. She continued to stare straight at Alethea. He saw only determination and a broken hint of a smile. He thought the line between her eyebrows was the beginning of a wince.

"This one," he said. "Who is she?"

"Jihan. Leave her."

"Hm."

He could feel them both, the ghosts of life drifting maddeningly just within the statues of their bodies. Though their eyes were on each other, he didn't think they were aware—of themselves or of him. He reached for them, and they slipped away so easily that he was left unsure he'd encountered anything at all.

The blackness inside them was a precipice he could hurl himself over, seeking. The urge was strong.

He braced himself and remembered he couldn't fly.

"Come on, then," he murmured. He took a long, slow breath and let his essence dive into the stillness beneath his hands. He lost the sense of the cavern looming around him and Privya's furious hope beating at his back.

Colin usually had an instinct for wounds; he knew the pale searing of a weak heart or the hot shard of a broken limb. He knew how to wind his own energy around someone else's and coax bones and veins back to life, or how to soothe pain or weeping rage. He had never before encountered bodies that were almost—but not quite—the silent nothingness of a granite vacuum. He cast his awareness forward and felt his own self stretch thin.

He reached for Alethea first; the threads of her were pure, unmarred by blood or the echo of impending death. She was rivers of grey mist. *Come home,* he told her as he traced the lines and gathered her close. She was somewhere beyond sleep, though the sense of her life grew more solid as he drew her in.

His breath was coming hard in his chest. He ignored it.

He could almost curl his fingers around Alethea—not just the physicality of her arm, but the veins in her lungs, the lines of her bones, and the deathly stillness of her heart. He was losing the other woman, though; she dreamed in fading will-o'-the-wisp. His left hand held Alethea and his right hand touched Jihan's face and extended ineffectually into the void of her frozen death.

He could still hear Privya—*the other is a madwoman*—but he could see the ferocity of the hope in the stranger's eyes; he could see her smile at the woman who killed her. He worried she might feel pain.

He was getting slightly dizzy. He ignored it.

The shreds of the woman Jihan were ephemeral and bronze. He coaxed the sensation of her around his fingers, gathering the phantom strands, seeking the shape of her veins and the curving sweep of her skull. She had a multitude of scars; he almost knew the way they sliced and puckered on her skin. He could just begin to feel the gaping hot wetness of the sword wound.

He realized Alethea had become barely a whisper of thought in his other palm. He breathed life into her again, hurriedly, pulling at her dreams.

The stranger's bronze delicacy shivered and threatened to collapse. He threw his energy into her. He nearly lost his grasp on Alethea again.

A searing pain spiked through his right temple.

"They're somewhere else," he said. "They're almost gone. I can't—"

"*Bring her back.*" Even at the periphery of his awareness, Privya was roasting him.

There were times, later, when he wondered what would have happened if she'd been standing closer—if her grieving need had swallowed his will, or if he did not have such a close impression of that scarred stranger with the shattering smile. But Privya's fire burned at a distance, and Colin stood with one hand around Alethea's arm and the other cupping the stranger's face. He clung to spirits in grey and bronze, and fed his own life into their sleeping souls. They were cold and unresponsive to his touch; their eyes remained locked on each other. Within, they were ghostly tangles, and he drowned in a blackness far darker than the echoing cavern.

He reached for one, and the other faded. He almost had Alethea; he flowed through her, feeling the strength of her limbs and the sturdy ease of her body. Her hand gripped the sword hilt with granite determination. He mentally dove into dark stillness, seeking the sense of her—betrayal? anger? remorse? was that *love*?—but her mind was lost and drifting. The effort almost cost him Jihan's bronze strands; he jerked his attention to the other woman instead, tugging at the petrified blood in her veins as he willed her to return. Alethea's presence decayed.

The spikes of pain shot through his skull with regularity now. His teeth were gritted.

There was an instant when he almost had them both, though sparks flared in his vision and the ache of his knee thrummed with the same beat as the pressure in his head. The grey and bronze were a braid in his fingers; they were blood and flesh, muscles bound to stillness, but ready again for life. He felt Alethea's heart stir once, then again. It was a peculiar sensation. There was no hurt in her for him to heal, but he almost had her attention.

Simultaneously, he sought Jihan. He was careful—so careful—to keep Alethea in balance. He tasted blood at the back of his throat.

That was when he felt Jihan's pulse flutter once, then twice, before it caught on a ghostly flare of pain. He knew in that moment exactly where the sword ran through; it had sliced the edge of her bowel on its way up through her lung. He felt the poison of her innards and the way it would spread through her the instant he forced her to life.

That sort of pain was easy. He didn't think about it. He just reached out and fixed it.

He'd had his hand on Alethea, still—he had a flashing sensation of movement, of guiding her to draw out the blade, of a single haunting smile, then he lost it all. His vision went white.

He couldn't see for a long time. He could hear someone screaming—a high, shrill keen of agony. It wasn't his. His lungs were empty. Grief and anguish ripped at him from at least two different directions.

There was cold rock under his knees and his palms. He tasted blood. When the snow-static of his vision cleared, he saw darkness; even his own glow was guttering.

Privya snarled, *"Just kill them."*

He heard footsteps echoing to his left, and then a sudden, meaty gurgle. Beneath the maelstrom that already tore through him, he felt a terrified life flare and then die. It was familiar. He shuddered for the girl with the cut palm.

Death surrounded him then—one, two, three lives ending in fear and slicing pain. He clutched the rocky earth, desperate to do something, but he only vomited bloody bile. His wings flailed outward with each heave of his shoulders.

Privya's rage flared again and cut off, quite suddenly. If he'd been standing, Colin would have staggered with relief. As it was, he could only close his eyes and gulp for air. The abrupt stillness was a balm, even as his bones burned with the pain he'd failed to heal.

A single other life remained in the cavern, marked by a furious, wounded confusion. He could have traced it in ribbons of bronze.

He saw light, first as a glow through his eyelids, then through tears that reflected the shine like a multitude of jewels. Inhaling roughly, he raised his head and froze to find the lantern just in front of him, illuminating rough boots. He knew who stood there. He could still feel the whirl of her outraged loss, even as the psychic sense of her faded. She was pulling in on herself.

He looked up. She was watching him. Her eyes gleamed silver, emotionless, no more than mirrors reflecting the light she held in her left hand. In her right, improbably, she clutched the folds of his coat, the hem trailing on the dusty cavern floor. The untroubled planes of her features held neither anger nor pity. She stood very still, and he felt her now like an ache, like his joints swelling in the winter.

"I'm sorry," he said. He wasn't certain why.

He thought he should probably be afraid, but he was infinitely tired. His skin was raw with other people's deaths. He knelt on the rock and waited for her to kill him, too.

The stranger stood there looking at him—or perhaps only looking in his direction. He wasn't sure. The light didn't waver in her hand; she was much like the statue she'd been moments before. He looked back: he knew her now. He knew the hooked shape of her nose and the slightly aquiline slope of her face. He knew the scars he couldn't see.

"Christ," he said. She didn't answer that, either. She did hold out his coat.

"Oh. Well ... thanks." Pulling the familiar weight back over his shoulders, Colin turned his head to look at Alethea. With a stab of remorse, he saw she was no longer there. The lantern's glow spread far enough to illuminate the column of stone and the ragged pile of crumbled rock that no longer resembled a woman at all. He sighed. "I would have brought you both back, if I could." His voice was rough in his own ears and liquid with blood. "I don't understand. What happened?"

The stranger—Jihan, he reminded himself—was motionless. The lantern's light gleamed in her mad eyes and picked up the uneven edges of the rent in her shirt. There was more blood on her than before. It smeared her hands and shone in wet splashes across her neck.

"What happened?" Colin asked again, and he knew—of course he knew—but still he felt a creeping dread. Cautiously, he looked down to find his fallen cane, a little distance from his left hand. He grasped at it, slowly, watching the stranger again from beneath the hood of his lashes. She didn't react.

When he set the tip of the cane against the ground and gathered himself to rise, Jihan took a step forward. He was too tired to recoil.

He stared in exhausted disbelief at her outstretched arm. She had bent down, extending her hand to him. Her features were empty and cool in the lantern glow.

"You're friggin' kidding."

In her eyes, he saw only the pale hollows of his own reflection.

Colin considered, then grasped the woman's forearm. He meant to only touch her sleeve, which was sticky and wet with death, but his fingers brushed a rip, and through it, he felt her skin and the yawning abyss of her being.

He wavered; he could have fallen into her again. Jihan was a pit, and his wings spread again on sheer instinct, but then she'd pulled him up with a smooth, surprising gentleness and stepped back. He let go as soon as she pulled away; that, too, was instinct. He had never in his life held to anyone who didn't want him to.

"Let me help you," he said. Again, she only stood, holding the lantern. She was looking somewhere into the hidden distance. It made it easier to study her. He fixed on the steel of her hair—her braid was grey now where it wasn't soaked with blood, though he remembered it as black. She somehow appeared both older and younger than before. Her hair might have been covered with dust, or the remnant of a fire.

Colin could hear nothing but his own harsh breath and the pounding of his heart in his ears. He clenched his grip on the cane and stood swaying, while Jihan ignored him and held the light that spilled across the ground. His own skin had lost its illumination.

When the cavern stopped dancing around him, Colin hobbled carefully back across the mesa and began following the slope of the ground down toward the entrance. He didn't hurry. His knee was stabbing at him, and he was sick already with what he knew he would find.

The woman followed him. Her footsteps were soundless, unlike his sliding shuffle, but the light remained steady behind his left shoulder. His shadow staggered in front of him, long across the rocky ground. It stretched over pale pebbles and scraggly stalagmites. It stretched over Privya's upturned hand and then blotted the light that reflected from her staring eyes.

Colin's breath caught, but he didn't hesitate; he only continued his careful progress, stopping at the fallen girl's side. Her gaze was already filming over. The wound that had killed her was self-evident; the sword was still in her. The slash started at the join of neck and shoulder and then bit deeply into her chest. The angle of her head was impossible. Her brows were still drawn down, her teeth bared in horrified rage.

"I'm sorry." He said it to her, too, even though it didn't matter anymore. Her blood was still pooling, and it ran along the edge of his right boot. He studied the girl's body while her murderer held the lantern high.

He'd barely known her. He thought he felt a last drift of her desire, a stirring ghost of life and need. She was cooling meat now, and he could have wept for the innocent softness of her skin.

He turned his head and saw silver eyes, impassive in the lantern glow. Fury curled in him, and for just a second, he could spit, "Why?" But no response came, and in the next breath, he was overwhelmed with the need to pour his golden essence into the chasm of her madness. He almost fell.

He gripped the cane and closed his eyes until the impulse passed, then he moved toward what he hoped was the exit. He was still following the tug of recent death. He spared a last look for Privya, but he didn't trust himself to straighten again if he bent to close her eyes.

The way in front of him was dark, but Jihan followed just behind, illuminating the rough rock. He saw the slow blood pooling ahead before he saw the bodies. Grief stabbed through him again. His knee was close to giving out. His lungs felt as though they were filling with glue.

"Why?" he asked again, this time without hope. He could see, though: outstretched hands and the gleam of weapons. He saw a switchblade fallen in the spreading blood just before he saw the crumpled body of the girl whose hand he'd healed. Now her fingers were curled around a smeared pair of brass knuckles. Unlike Privya, she only looked surprised, the tip of her tongue between her teeth and her wide eyes glazing.

Next, a moustached man in a plaid shirt had fallen next to the baseball bat he'd been carrying all morning; he was missing an eye where Jihan's blade had entered his skull. Colin hadn't spoken two words to the man, but sorrow suffused him anyway. He stumbled onward to the dead woman with the short blonde hair and the hunting knife who'd bled out all over the ground. He sighed, looking down at her.

"I get it," he said over his shoulder. "They attacked you. You didn't have to *kill* them."

But the woman with the lantern only watched him silently; when he glanced back, he saw her eyes gleaming cold as a wild beast's. He swallowed. She made no move toward him, though, and when he walked, she followed.

He almost missed the tunnel out, but the light behind him veered to the left and then paused, waiting off to the side. "What?" he asked her; then he saw the curve of the stone at the exit and adjusted his path.

The slope of old rock beneath his boots gave way to the rise of stone steps as the walls narrowed inward. The stairs were as difficult as he'd feared, going up. He felt sweat bead on his temples and pool in the spaces between his wings.

He stopped to vomit. He didn't fall; he stood there with one hand against the wall and the other braced on the cane, leaning to the side as he tried not to puke where he was about to step. "What just happened?" he panted, staring at the froth running down the stone wall. "And I don't suppose you know how to get out of here?" He slid a look back at Jihan. He would have laughed, if death hadn't lingered in his memory and in the impassivity of her blood-splattered face. "We're in a cave. In a wall. What the fuck is my life today?"

He closed his eyes then and stood breathing, swallowing back the taste of bile and the ache of the stranger's madness at his back. He almost missed the pull of Privya's desperate need. He almost thought he could still feel it. He wasn't sure his knee was going to take any more stairs.

He sighed and shifted to the far side of the staircase, moving away from the wall and stretching his freed hand out to the side. "Right," he said. "If you're not going to kill me, I could really use some help."

He could have died in that moment, he supposed, if she'd chosen to attack him, too. If she'd even tried to take his hand, skin to skin, he might have lost himself in her spinning depths. He might have just fallen backward on the stairs.

He didn't care.

He felt the bloody mess of her sleeve under his hand (a whisper of death again, the memory of terror). When he closed his fingers around her forearm, she bore him upward. They walked two steps. She paused for him on the third.

"My name's Colin," he offered, between gasps. "Not that you care."

They walked upward together as the stairs smoothed out and then finally opened to the narrow corridor between walls. Colin stopped only a moment, to catch his breath and look at the tunnel and sigh.

It didn't occur to him until much later that the stairway didn't seal itself behind them.

[**IMAGE:** Colin and Jihan, standing together; she has a hand under his elbow. He is small and skeletal; she is nearly a foot taller and muscled like a gymnast. He's wearing his oversized coat and leaning on an old, battered cane. He's looking up at Jihan; his eyes are glowing, sparkling like stars. She's wearing ill-fitting clothing—an old sweater, jeans, boots. She has Verity's stained and crusted scarf tied around her upper arm. She has a knife in her free hand. She's staring at something unseen.]

18

Session Transcript February 2, 2014 (from manual notes; recording not working due to persistent power blackouts)

SJ: How are you feeling today?

VR: Cold.

SJ: I'm sorry; the heat isn't working. Can I offer you another blanket?

VR: No. It's okay. I'm sorry it's cold.

SJ: Did you do something to cause it?

VR: (pause—significant?) No.

SJ: Why do you think the power is out?

VR: I don't know how power plants work. The turbines stopped.

SJ: Yes, they did. The police want to know if you saw anything happen before the lights went out. You're my patient, though. Anything you tell me will be safe.

VR: No.

SJ: Excuse me?

VR: That isn't true.

SJ: What makes you say that?

VR: (no response)

SJ: You understand you need to speak with me as a condition of your continued release? Your guardian ordered these visits.

VR: Yes.

SJ: All right. Let's start again.

FEBRUARY

It isn't easy to rush when Verity and Santiago must wait for Colin, but someone has already handed the angel a crumpled mass of fabric, and he pulls the vast coat to his shoulders, wings folding expertly beneath before he lurches to the wall. He turns to Alan, his sapphire-star gaze swirling bright despite the bruises around his eyes. "Can you do it? Can we follow her?"

Alan is staring at the door; thought folds his forehead as he frowns. "I almost had it," he says again. "It's almost in me. I'm not what I was."

"So that's a no." Santiago slips past Colin in one sinuous motion and sets his hand on the doorknob. "We'll run it. Vee's place isn't far."

"Everyone stay here," adds Colin, raising his voice to carry, reed thin, down the hall. "I'm not dealing with anyone else puking outside." More quietly, he adds, "Christ, what's she doing now?"

Verity isn't sure if he means Privya or Jihan, but she doesn't have time to ask before Santiago opens the door that isn't. They all three slide through, footsteps quick, into the cramped utility closet and then the dim lobby beyond. Verity has lost track of Ouroboros, but the shadow creature emerges from Santiago's sleeve and drops in an inky line to the floor, where it expands in a smooth rush to the long, furred form of the dog.

Verity pushes the door open and braces herself for the city outside. Bank Street is an assault on her senses. A passing car is a scream, its tires gliding on dirty snow.

Behind, Colin makes a sound as though he's been punched just beneath the ribs. Verity knows how he feels. He chokes, "What are we even—are you sure?"

Verity can feel the last shreds of clarity ripped from her, delicate and irretrievable as spider webs torn in the wind. The city street trembles around her. "You asked me," she says, somewhat helplessly. "I *was* sure." When she looks back, Colin and Santiago are framed by the tattered edges of concert posters plastering the theatre windows. In the clouded daylight, Colin is the colour of frozen wheat. The lines around his mouth are savagely carved, and he leans against the taller magician, his hand clutching the head of his cane. Santiago is paralyzed by an uncharacteristic uncertainty, his dark gaze darting from the angel to the street and back again.

Verity feels the dog sliding by her thigh, neither warm nor weighted, but somehow substantial all the same.

"Go with Ouro," says Santiago finally, looking to Verity as he sets a hand under Colin's elbow. "We'll be behind."

"You'll be faster," concedes Colin. "But be careful. I don't—Jihan takes care of herself. But if Privya wanted to keep us away, something's damn well wrong." He shakes his head.

Verity is already jogging down the street. From behind her, she hears the angel call, "Be careful!" again, and she almost trips on it, but she keeps one hand wrapped in shadow fur and lets Ouroboros guide her. The city passes in streaks around them, whipping hot and cold across Verity's face. She has to dodge the discordant whine of a passing bus; the advertisements along its side shriek, and she can taste the condescension lodged in the number of a local dentist. A radio station's logo slimes itself across her skin. She isn't as fast as she'd like. Urgency pools in her lungs.

"I don't know what we're supposed to do," she confesses, gasps punctuating her words. Ouroboros doesn't answer her. She isn't surprised. Her boots crunch in dirty snow, and the dog is deathly silent. They half-slide around the corner.

A storm has come up on Second Avenue. Verity recognizes the feel of it: thick, quiet, filled with dragons. There are wings gathered around her, and flashing spots of eyes in the snowflakes, wild and dying.

Unlike the storm on the river, this one is spotty; it comes in rolling clouds of sleet. There are holes in it that Verity can see through like ragged patchwork—a white whirl, a beating wing, then an instant's clarity and the familiar line of the houses down the street before snow swallows them up again. The wind heaves sickeningly against her and then is replaced by Ouroboros as the dog presses against her leg. She drops her palm to the dog's head as she walks, and wishes she'd taken time to put on gloves.

The air tastes of ice and the salt sweat of desperation. Somewhere behind her, half dreamed, she can hear the low fierce whisper of the angel swearing.

Potential stings in the air—power, edged with the faded richness of the approaching Chalice. Here, the storm rages against the full weight of the afternoon city, hurling itself improbably against shingles and tree trunks and the alien smoothness of the cars parked along the meters by the sidewalk. As before, it circles. As Verity walks further down the street, she moves into the calmer eye. For just that quarter of a block, she sees no moving traffic, hears no blasting radios; the windows and doors of the houses are frosted thickly shut. She breathes the frail perfection of the moment.

Verity stands with snow whirling at her back and is not surprised to find that her house is at the epicentre of the twisting flakes. At the steps of the house, battling figures surge like the storm in miniature. Several are Privya's people, or at least Verity assumes so, judging by the presence of Shauna; the others she doesn't know, and she can process little except an array of coloured winter jackets, knitted toques and the flash of long knives. At the eye of that blade-cyclone is Jihan, moving almost too quickly to follow. She still wears an old pink sweatshirt and jeans, plain brown boots, her hair smoothly braided, Verity's scarf around her arm. She has her newly sharpened knife in one hand, now splattered with red. Her face is emotionless, but her booted feet are quick in the snow as she ducks a fist, half-turns, and parries a switchblade as it comes in. She moves without practice or style, but rather with a peculiar precision, milliseconds in advance of every falling blow. Her knife slashes across the inside of a young man's wrist, but she's already shifting away, sweeping her foot to catch at Shauna's ankle.

It feels like a dying coal smouldering at the base of Verity's spine. She fights the urge to remove her coat in the middle of the winter gale. She feels dragons whip past her back, and then Ouroboros tears silently away from her fingers and past her, launching itself at a quilted red jacket and a tangle of braided brown hair.

The whirl of figures on the step surges—Jihan again, a knee to someone's solar plexus, a low slice following. The heat is streaks of red in Verity's eyes; she strains to look through and past for gangly limbs and a familiar thatch of short dreadlocks. She doesn't realize she's holding her breath until she tastes a hint of golden spark and sees Jacob half-sprawled on the porch by the front door. He's sitting legs splayed, a hand to his forehead, blood running down his face.

Shauna lunges for those same front steps but Jihan is already in motion. Her kick lands directly in the centre of the other woman's lower back, propelling Shauna forward into the staircase banister. The old wood splinters but holds, and Shauna collapses in a fold of faded down jacket. Jihan has already launched herself toward a scowling redheaded teenaged girl.

At first, Verity doesn't understand why anyone would attack Jacob, but when she turns her attention across the street, she sees Brian standing rigid with concentration, his eyes and lips already lined with hoarfrost. Privya is next to him, two feet shorter, her hand laced through Brian's frozen fingers. All Privya's attention is on the fight across the way, but she makes no move toward the violence. The fist of her free hand is clenched, dripping a steady stream of blood to the ground at her feet.

Verity can taste Brian's strain; she can feel, too, the strands of Privya's bloody power reinforcing the storm and warring with the electric shock of Jacob's presence, a jarring rumble through the smooth copper whirl of the blizzard. Her breath is a struggling bird.

Privya's people are patchwork and threadbare; they taste of desolation and life unravelling. They are very much like the refugees in the walls of the theatre. In fact, Verity is fairly certain she recognizes a young man with a buzz cut and a face the same colour and texture as a fresh date. He is lined before his time. His bared teeth are yellow.

Ouro slams into the buzz-cut boy; its long snake tail whips out, wrapping around his neck and jerking him to the ground as the dog darts away. The prone figure is still, but lacks the chill static of death. Jihan is a whirl showing no such mercy. There is blood on her knife; there are bodies on the steps. The crowd of attackers is down to six.

At the top of the steps, Jacob is shuddering and trying to get his long legs under himself, one hand pressed to his bleeding head, the other grasping for the wooden porch railing as he pulls himself upward, his back against the door. His foot slides and he falls back, cringing. It is nearly palpable, the way the storm trembles uncertainly around him. The twist of his mouth is both pained and incredulous.

Verity casts a quick glance again toward Privya and Brian, then circles toward Jacob, trying to make her way to the porch steps by moving along the outskirts of the fight. Violence and dragon wings sing in the air, making the sidewalk heave beneath her feet.

No one pays attention to her. The remaining assailants are now warily circling Jihan and Ouroboros. Jihan stands at the ready, seemingly watching no one as she gazes into the middle distance. Slaughter is smeared on her sweatshirt and across the flawless line of one cheekbone. She holds her knife loosely in her right hand; if she breathes at all heavily, it doesn't show. The dog tracks its own circle around her, pacing counter to the attackers. Verity skirts carefully around, heading for the steps. Shauna, who has regained her feet and is noticeably limping, casts her one quick glance and then dismisses her, turning her attention back to Jihan's crimson-drenched weapon.

The storm whirls and hums in patchwork imperfection. Verity almost can't see past the flare of Jacob's blood and the sharp taste of the snow against her skin. She grasps the banister and keeps one hand free, fingers spread, as though she might somehow fend off one of the combatants on the lawn. Facing the fight, she manoeuvres herself around the post at the bottom of the stairs.

The instant before the heel of Verity's boot touches the lowest step, Jihan whirls. Her knife traces a low, brutal slash through the air that sends a sallow boy in a ragged camouflage vest tumbling backward in panic, though he is a good three feet away. Jihan ignores him, and the way Ouroboros lunges to protect her from a roundhouse punch when the woman to her left thinks she has an opening. The dog only goes for the woman's wrist. Verity suspects Jihan would have been less kind.

Verity only has the time for that fleeting thought before Jihan's mirror-steel eyes are focused on her—direct, blank, tainted with cracks of yawning madness. In the singular space between heartbeats, she thinks Jihan might throw the knife. She remembers—*always she remembers*—the helpless, frozen feel of metal sliding between her ribs. Her free hand shields her gut.

"I only want to help him." Verity blurts the first thing she thinks of.

"Vee?" That's Jacob from behind her, slurring and stunned. His voice is like a bruised apple.

Jihan doesn't move. She only watches Verity. The rest of the street might as well not exist. Then she shifts her weight and closes her left hand into a fist, a half-second before the boy in camouflage comes barrelling back into her range. The steel eyes whip away.

Verity can breathe again. She whirls and darts up the last steps to where Jacob now leans against the front door, one hand still pressed to his head. Blood drips between his fingers and soaks through the shoulder of his plaid fleece shirt. "Vee," he says to her again. "What the fuck?" His eyes aren't quite focused, but he struggles to fix on her face before his attention drifts past and then he blinks, squinting. "*What the fuck?*"

It's all she can do to grasp the front of his shirt and fixate on the familiarity of him in the maelstrom. She knows the exact pattern of his mussed hair. It loosens a coiled binding within her that she didn't know was there. "Are you okay?"

"...No?"

"Fucking hell!" Colin's voice is ragged with torn feathers and the brown exhaustion of a leaf finally falling. Verity wraps her fingers in bloodstained fleece and cranes her head to look back at the street.

At the steps of the house, Ouroboros is shaking its prey as though the man were a rat.

"Goddamnit, stop!" calls Colin again. The black dog drops the man to the ground and launches itself back into the fray; Jihan has already slipped aside, half a breath ahead, to give it room. The woman drives her knife into one man's gut while she kicks a red-jacketed girl in the throat. Privya's people are down to three.

As Verity turns to face the street, she sees Colin has dropped to one knee beside a fallen body, his twisted leg extended to one side and his cane abandoned in the snow. The trench coat heaves unnaturally around him as his wings spread for balance beneath. She knows he's glowing, but in the smattering of sunlight that creeps through the stuttering snow, it's hard to tell. Only the taste of it is pure and honeyed, cleansing her throat.

At first, Verity can't find Santiago, though she knows he must be near; she spots him pressing to the brick wall of the duplex across the street as he slips behind Privya and Brian. Brian's frosted features are screwed tight in concentration, his skin translucent as ice. The snow whirls around him, eating the street. Privya only stands, bleeding, watching her people die, her lips set and her eyes like black fire. The rest of the street comes to Verity in quick flashes of image: Ouroboros, its head low and its sinuous tail lashing. Bodies on her lawn, beneath the spreading tree. Pools of crimson. The glint of dragon eyes in the snow. Verity's skin burns, but the banister under her hand is cold, and the sensation of Jacob behind her is loose and oddly lukewarm.

Jihan and the dog now rule the front lawn unopposed; the bodies crumpled around them are not all moving. The boy in the camouflage vest is sprawled at an unlikely angle, legs askew, crimson marking the snow in a spray behind him. A whirl of white renders Privya and Brian barely visible at the far edge of the storm; Santiago is lost in a rise of rolling fog. The street is eerily quiet, save for the occasional bubbling groan and the faint silver ring of dragon wings.

With the sun obscured, Colin is aglow; light blooms in his eyes like fireworks or deep-water algae, swirling brilliant and ancient from the depths. His hands are pressed to the neck and wrist of the woman he kneels by. His attention is fixed on her bloody face. He has forgotten the wings that spill from beneath his coat and swoop to either side, slightly raised for balance. They are inky spans against the swirling whiteness; the fraying edges of his feathers gleam with green and gold.

"The hell is that?" Jacob's voice is both unexpected and soft, the syllables slurring.

Verity looks back; Jacob is working to focus past her. A dawning recognition sings in the curve of smile just beginning at the corner of his lips. The other side of his mouth is frowning; it is a slanted expression, both pleased and puzzled, marred by the rivulet of blood that continues to run slowly down the edge of his nose. His lips move slightly, silently, as though he is sounding out an uncertain new word.

Immediately, Verity shifts to block Jacob's view of the street and the angel. "Don't look," she demands, and his eyebrows furrow.

The circling wind pulls at Verity's hair, and the storm strengthens. Several struggling patchwork spots of sunlight are obscured in a flurry of snow and tiny claws. The city dims. Covering Jacob's eyes with her hand, she looks back to see the angel's glow brightening.

In that space of breath where the blizzard struggles to coalesce, several things happen.

Jihan is the one who moves first. From her half-crouch in the trampled, bloody yard, she slices toward the foot of the townhouse's wooden stairs.

An instant later, Brian cries out—a ragged shout of triumph that tastes to Verity like sweat and cayenne. The sound is nearly obscured by a crack of ice both sudden and sinuous. A strand of ice pries itself loose from the walkway, shards twisting together and weaving themselves in bloodied frost. Brian gestures sharply, and the ice spear launches itself toward Jacob and Verity. It looks so much like a striking snake that for one panicked instant, Verity thinks Ouroboros has betrayed them.

Verity grabs Jacob's shirt with both hands and shoves him from the spear's path, blocking his body with hers. He's too tall. His arms go around her seemingly by instinct, though he, too, is making a sound that starts with a grunt and is probably the beginning of a question. She feels his weight press down on her, and she braces herself, boots sliding against the rough wood of the old porch. Trying to wrench them both aside before winter impales her spine, she whips a frantic look at the street.

The storm tastes like panic. She sees snow and rolling fog. Her hair is in her face. Colin is glowing, and in the stillness of his light, Verity catches a glimpse of clarity. The world quiets and slows.

Privya has grabbed at Brian's chill arm—too late, it seems, to stop the spear of ice from launching toward the porch. She is staring at Verity, and her eyes are wide and ringed with white.

Jihan is more than halfway up the stairs; her face is streaked with splatters of blood. Knife in hand, she has angled herself so as to slam sideways into the spear of ice, timed just so; she cracks it with one remorseless elbow and twists to the side, driving her knife into Brian's flashing, frozen weapon so that the ice spear splinters, a chunk snapping off to the side. Flying ice stings Verity's cheek.

She sees Santiago emerge from the edges of the storm, where he has been making his way along the houses at the other side of the street. He takes three long strides toward Privya. He holds one hand low, curled around something hidden. Simultaneously, the dog Ouroboros breaks away from Jihan's side and bolts across the snow-covered pavement, darting toward Brian and Privya from the other direction.

Across the street, Privya turns just in time to raise an arm, partially deflecting the rock that Santiago has clutched in his fist. It sends her staggering backward, away from Brian, as Ouroboros hurls toward the small of her back. The girl grimaces, knocked to her knees. Brian still stands, stiff as the ice statue he now resembles, one hand stretched toward the porch and his features gone to frost within the hood of his coat.

On the porch, Verity manages, "Thank you," but she is hardly stunned when Jihan ignores her; the taller woman steps to the top of the staircase, leaving the bloody ice spear broken behind her, its body still arcing like an ice bridge from the pavement. It is momentarily static, but at its base, the snow ripples inward.

Jacob groans in Verity's ear, his hands moving to grip her shoulders as he gathers his feet under himself. "What," he says, and she is grateful when the press of him alleviates, though he slides as if on ocean waves, lifting and then slipping down on her again. The gash at his hairline has dripped crimson lines to his chin.

"Careful—" Verity isn't entirely certain how she intends to end that, but Jacob isn't listening; Jihan has grabbed his chin, lifting his head, smearing his face with his own blood and the gore of her sticky hand.

Jacob straightens, enough that Verity can see his eyes roll, then settle into focus on Jihan. Confusion pulls the line between his eyebrows, and then something like wonder glimmers on his face, innocent and utterly surprised. "What," he says again. It's an invocation now.

Verity is still responsible for half of Jacob's balance, and she can feel the way his breath stops in his chest before sucking in one great gasp. She can taste Jihan like smoke, and Jihan's bloody fingers, cloaked in granite death. For half a heartbeat, the mad mirrors of Jihan's eyes reflect Jacob's, but then she drops her hand and takes one step to the right, a single sharp wave directing his attention to the street behind her.

"No!" Verity moves to cover Jacob's eyes again; Jihan, without looking, grabs her wrist, immovable and implacable as stone. Jihan is watching Jacob, who, puzzled, is obligingly peering at the mess past his front steps.

Beneath Jacob's gaze, the surge of snow at the ice spear's base quells instantly, a gust of white flakes that scatters in the next bitter breeze. Verity feels Jacob stiffen at the sight of bodies littering the walkway and the bloody marks trampled in the storm; she squeezes her free arm around him, and his fingers tighten on her shoulder, but his attention is all for the massacre in his front yard. His line of sight crosses Brian, at whose motionless feet Privya struggles with black shadows.

"Don't look—" Verity is yanked back; Jihan's iron grip pulls her away, and then Jihan herself has stepped in, sliding her arm around Jacob, keeping him upright. Jacob apparently doesn't notice; he is still staring. Verity twists a frantic glance back over her shoulder to see Privya on the ground kicking her booted foot. Though Privya is small, Santiago goes flying, thrown back ten feet against the wooden siding of the duplex directly across from Jacob's townhouse. Privya rolls, ripping at the long snake that now coils around her; she wraps her fingers around Ouroboros, just below its head, and pries its jaws away from her shoulder. Pushing to her knees in the snow, she holds the snake away left-handed, ignoring the inky coils still squeezing around her.

Brian is nearly solid ice—his hand is outstretched toward the porch, and beneath the winter wool of his coat, his eyes are white and spiked with hoarfrost. Ice grays his skin and hides his eyebrows; where his hood has fallen back, his hair is locked in sculpted waves of snow. Verity can just taste the cold lime of Brian's consternation at the fractured ice spear; snow-covered asphalt stretches between them, but Verity is certain she sees Brian's fingers curl slightly inward, conjuring some new weapon.

Verity lunges back toward Jacob, but Jihan's hand blocks her again, bloody and impassable, holding her at bay. Jihan's attention is fixed on Jacob; as his confused gaze falls on Brian, Brian's frosted fingers tremble and stiffen. Around them all, the storm hesitates, drawing back like the receding tide in the moment before the waves crash in.

Verity can't see any dragons, though the memory strikes her, abruptly, of a sad beast that became a pigeon and died.

Across the street, beneath Jacob's stunned regard, Brian goes still. To Verity, he is suddenly pure: the pillar of him smells of ice, tastes of ice, sends a winter frisson across the skin. The wind tugs at the hood of his coat, but beneath the fringe of fur, his face is carved and perfect. In the break of the storm, a hint of sunlight highlights the inhuman translucence of his cheekbone.

Santiago, shaking his head, is just staggering to his feet, the side of the townhouse splintered behind him.

Privya makes a sound that tastes like the bloody ice spear breaking. She is still forcing away the snake, her thin arm against its inky rippling, but she betrays no strain, only holding the shifting reptile away from her throat. She flashes a single look toward the porch—across the bloody street and the fallen bodies of her people. Her eyes scorch Verity's skin. "Hey!" she spits—it might as well be acid. Verity instinctively raises a hand, ducking.

It isn't Verity whose attention Privya calls, though. She waits for Jacob's puzzled horror. She offers him her best flash of teeth. Then, beneath the fall of his gaze, she sets both hands to the writhing Ouroboros and cracks its neck.

The snake goes limp. Privya drops it. She makes entirely sure that Jacob sees it die.

Santiago makes no sound. Verity hears it clearly.

Vee? A little help here?

```
a noise that was silent i dont know how to tell you
```

Try. I'm going to get this one wrong.

```
loneliness laced in the wings of a dead dragon. a
desert weeping
```

As Ouroboros falls to limp coils, the magician also drops bonelessly, another puddle of ebony in the snow. His fingers spasm as though he might claw his way into the ground.

Simultaneously, a crumpled form on the sidewalk shudders, jerking upward with back arched from where he had fallen across a dead woman's chest. His eyes are electrified, staring at the sky, at nothing; his wings flare ragged and impossible from under his coat, and Verity is stunned—*how did she forget about Colin*—but he was so brittle and silent. Now she sees Santiago's agony rip the very last of the light from his bones.

She is afraid she is seeing the moment when his heart stops. It slices through her as surely as the memory of the knife.

"What," says Jacob again, this time tinted with sugared wonder, and Verity feels the air slacken with his next inhalation. Too late, she thinks again to push herself in front of him, shoving her hand at his eyes and her body between man and angel.

Perfectly timed, Jihan takes one pace back, descending a step from the porch, not bothering to look away or behind herself. As she does, she releases her hold on Jacob, who huffs out his lungful of air and sways once before sagging against Verity. When Verity can't hold the sudden flour-and-sun weight of him, he slides back down to the porch, long legs splaying.

"Are you in a *gang*?" There's blood on Jacob's lips. It still drips from his hair. His voice is both incredulous and blurred.

"You should—" *go inside,* she wants to tell him, because it is safer and because his solidity is jarring in the midst of the snow-winged storm. She wants to break him apart. She wants to hold him in her cupped palms. The snow struggles less when his eyes flutter shut, but the storm is already dying.

Verity keeps a hand on Jacob's shoulder and turns, crouched on the wooden porch.

Colin's wings are mostly hidden now, just poking out from within the folds of his massive coat, but his body slumps over the still-prone form of the woman he failed to save. Verity feels the last of his gleaming settle in her pulse, but she can see only the shattered line of him. He is broken glass, a pile of dried leaves, the husk of a long-dead insect.

The snow is abating; the dragons have gone. Verity watches the wall of white fade and sees a curtain twitch at a window two houses down. Privya still kneels, now at Brian's iced feet, grasping futilely at the coat that wraps the frigid statue that was once a man. The dead snake lies like a coil of rope. Santiago is a fallen mass of black behind them. Bodies are scattered across the frozen street.

Jihan has descended to the foot of the stairs and stands there crimson-spattered, vital fluids caked on her clothing and the smooth steel of her braid. Her blood-wet hands are empty. For an instant, her eyes meet Verity's and there is almost—maddeningly, almost *something*—there, behind the blankly uncaring mirrors of her irises. It shifts, this hint of consciousness, primordial and flinty and terrifyingly alone. Verity finds herself reaching out a hand, but then Jihan's attention (such as it is) slides away, gliding once across Jacob's leggy form before she turns her head and stalks toward Colin.

"Fine." Privya's voice is flat and low, and somehow carries across the sudden stillness of the street.

It isn't fine. The word slices into Verity, just between her third and fourth vertebrae, a blank whiteness punctuated by a low, directionless moan. Verity isn't certain if it's someone in pain or the last remnants of the wind.

Verity freezes, struck, but Privya is already continuing: "This was desperate and stupid. Save them." She pushes herself to her feet, heedless of the blood or the cold or her ragged skirt, and lets go of Brian's stiff hand. Watching Colin struggle, she snarls, "Save *Brian*, at least. It can't be too late."

Colin's wings shiver beneath the folds of his coat as he braces himself against the chest of the dead woman before him. He doesn't answer Privya; he doesn't even turn to look at her. The breath that shudders through him might as easily tear him apart.

"He can't." Verity is the one who speaks. "More will kill him." The knowledge is clear and certain, though the words are cold on her tongue. The fire in the storm has abated, leaving her with memory scorched across her skin. "The storm—people will see you. A car will come. Someone will be calling the police. Colin, your coat...."

Jihan is already there. She drops to one knee, scoops Colin up in one smooth motion, and stands easily again. He makes as if to cling to the body on the ground, one hand grasping. He might choke a denial. One of his wings trails. He curls into Jihan, then, pressing his face to the no-longer-pink sweatshirt that leaves gobs of crimson smeared across his skin.

"These are your people too," snarls Privya. Verity thinks that Privya might leap forward—her eyes are wild and her teeth bared—but the girl looks hard at Jihan before she moves, circling wide, toward the nearest living form: Shauna, dusted with snow, just stirring in a bloodied pile. "These are *her* people too!" She's talking to Verity now. "These were all I had. They gave everything they had to stop her." Reaching the half-animated form of Shauna on the ground, she leans down, grasping the stockier woman by the shoulder. Her hands are more solicitous than the tabasco of her tone. Shauna is shaking her head, hands pushed flat on the red and white ground.

Jihan ignores Privya completely. Still holding Colin, she has half-turned to look away down the street where the lights of the distant intersection are becoming visible, the fading scatter of white flakes pulling back like a curtain.

Verity twists to look at Jacob, who lies with his eyes closed; she can see the steady rise and fall of his chest, so she pushes herself to her feet and picks her way down the steps. Two of them are cracked. "This was a plan? Just ... to fight in the street?" She walks toward Privya, carefully, but her path is winding; she needs to find her way around bodies. The staring eyes of the boy in camouflage are a jangle that stays with her after she has stepped past.

"Do you think that's what we wanted? I—I have had armies at my call. Assassins in the night. These are the last dregs of a dying people. I told them not to, but they were set in their course. Shauna, we have to go." Privya tugs gently but insistently at Shauna's arm and glares across several feet of trampled slush to where Jihan now stands cradling Colin. The other woman is merely holding still, a waterfall of fabric and feathers cascading over her arm and down the side of one leg. "We're reduced to this, you and I. Stupid brute force. Do you even know me anymore? The monster I try not to be? The monster I would hurl at you if I could. *Bring him over and save someone.* Or *come at me.*"

Verity sees lemongrass and the edges of sharp teeth closing. She wonders about the past and its secret ghosts. She half thinks Jihan will simply eviscerate Privya and leave her bleeding out on the ground with everyone else. She breathes the fragility of a moment.

Something twitches across Jihan's aquiline features. She nearly looks at Privya.

Santiago, still on the ground, whimpers. It winds around Verity's wrist like the memory of the broken snake.

Half a breath later, the statue of Brian cracks, a jagged lightning line carving itself through his features. His outstretched arm breaks and falls off, held in the sleeve of his parka, dangling heavily. Privya doesn't make any sound, but her lips go pale and thin. She pulls at Shauna again, this time in a short, smooth motion that lifts the larger woman to her feet and holds her there while she finds her balance on uncertain legs. Leaving Shauna, Privya walks back to Brian and looks up. She traces a finger across the line that now bisects the ice of his features, leaving a copper-pink stain where she touches. Turning toward Jihan and Colin again, she is slim, proud, her skirt covered in blood. She might be a teenaged girl except for the exhausted rage of her stare. "Dangerous," she says. "Useless. The two of you are quite a pair. Do you see what they've done, for fear of you?"

Jihan only stands with her broken armful, gaze drifting over the rigid and shattered Brian; she half-turns to scan the porch where Jacob lies. She doesn't acknowledge groaning bodies or Privya's slender fury. She does pause to look at Verity. Her gaze is both nothingness and gaping maw. The ghost of a woman that was screams silently behind her eyes. Then she nods. It's the barest incline of her head.

Verity almost wonders if the gesture is imagined, but it prickles between her ribs, and she shudders. "You should," she begins, but Jihan has already turned away. If she is not precisely solicitous of the angel she holds, she is at least smooth. She walks unerringly toward the east and the last dying flurries of snow.

Privya's glare presses on Verity with the dulled weight of centuries. "You could have stopped this. You could have joined us."

"I—I haven't joined anyone." Verity has to run her hands up her arms to brush away each clinging year. "People died. What you did at the river. This ... you attacked her. And Jacob." She is trying to watch Privya and look past her at the same time, to where Santiago lies like he, too, had felt Jihan's knife in his gut.

"I couldn't talk my people out of trying. I helped them as best I could. As far as that guy on the river ... there are billions of *them,* and what, two hundred of us? A hundred and fifty? How many made it to the city? We killed the power plant to let a few more of them live long enough to see the Chalice. I don't regret it. I regret *this*—this stupid waste—but that's all."

Verity runs her hands up and down her arms again, then shakes her head. "You," she says slowly, "or her ... I don't understand. I don't know how to 'choose,' or what I'm supposed to do."

"We're all running out of time." Privya surveys the street now, where her people lie dead or bleeding. Some are groaning, moving; her attention lingers on each one. "If you can't help ... well. We all die anyway." The edge of her lips twists. "I can give them a fight. She can give them a stupid, apocalyptic dream. I'm tired and there are no happy endings in this scenario. But do nothing, and all these outside bastards—all the billions of them—they win. They steal our air and make it theirs. And they'll never even know." She sighs and shakes her head. "Look—the dragons have left us."

"You should—um. Someone will call the police, or has." With the storm dying, Verity already sees curtains moving, a pale shocked face at a window. The spot just between her shoulder blades itches with the knowledge that a car will doubtless turn the corner soon.

"Yes." Privya, too, glances around at the surrounding houses and the still-bare street corner. As if on cue come the faint phantom sounds of sirens in the distance, running wailing lines up Verity's spine. Privya mutters something that sounds both old and coarse, then she steps past Verity, toward where Shauna now stands waiting. Shauna has a hand pressed to her bleeding scalp; she is staring at Brian's sparkling remains. "Take the shadowmancer inside. There aren't many left with any real power. It'd be a shame to lose him to some idiot doctor with a wall of machines."

"Can Ouroboros recover?"

"The snake? I don't know. Your man saw it die; I expect it's dead. I suppose I am a little sorry for that. You need to come and find me. This city's practically breathing. We're almost out of time." Privya quickens her steps and reaches Shauna's side, taking her arm again. At first, Shauna ignores her, but at her squeeze, the stocky woman looks downward with a wincing nod.

The sirens squeal like lost children, growing closer. Verity casts a quick look toward the corner, another back toward the unmoving Jacob, and then finally jogs—awkwardly, but as quickly as she can manage—to the spill of Ouroboros at Brian's booted feet.

She bends to lift the snake, but she can already taste that something is wrong. Ouroboros is as still as Brian's broken statue, and as empty. She smells neither flowers nor coal—only the rough-textured scales of a snake that is only a snake, its belly ribbed and its fanged mouth gaping. She is startled at the broken egg-yolk flatness of its eyes. It is not a shadow; no secrets lurk beneath its skin. It is only a dead reptile, already winter cold, its head at a brutal angle.

She picks the snake up, gently, and wills it to curl around her wrist, or her shoulders, but it only dangles. Holding its sloppy coils as best she can, she walks across the lawn to Santiago, hurried but cautious in the slickness of the new fallen snow. Again, she sees a curtain move in the house's front window; she sees only a flash of eyes, but she swallows back a mouthful of confusion and appalled terror. The city's shrieking has rolled to something like a rumble or an ongoing moan.

Against aging brick, the magician is curled tightly, arms around his legs. His tarred eyes stare forward more mindlessly than Jihan's ever have. He is shivering.

Verity is hesitant to touch Santiago, but she crouches in front of him and offers the dead snake. It seems like a long time—she can hear the sirens wail—before he blinks and shakes his head, but his hands are already taking the cold loops from her arms. He presses the snake to his chest. She puts a hand on his shoulder. She is not surprised when his leather jacket feels like fur to her, and his chattering teeth bring the whisper of dry scales around her throat.

She can't think of Ouroboros. She swallows back the sensation. She has no time.

"Santiago," she says.

The magician fails to respond. His long-fingered hands clutch at the dead snake, too small to encircle its girth.

The sirens are yowling closer, streaks of light brightening in front of her eyes, so Verity reaches for Santiago's upper arm and pulls. "*Stefan.* I have to get to Jacob. I'm sorry. I'm sorry about Ouro. Please come." She expects resistance, but the magician only shakes his head again and lets her tug him to his feet. When he stands, she has to pull at him again, yanking him across the street. His stricken eyes are bare. He kneads the snake and its coiled tail dangles at his ankles.

Verity holds Santiago's sleeve and leads him as though he were a child. They step around bodies, and some of them are moving; she can't look, and she has no time for apologies. She looks at Jacob's still form sprawled at the top of the stairs, and quickens her steps.

"Help me," she tells Santiago. She is relieved when the magician cradles Ouroboros to his chest with one arm, then leans down and grabs Jacob's shirt with his free hand. She lets go of Santiago and shoves at the front door. The sirens are screaming, and she tastes the sharp crackle of electricity stinging her throat in the seconds before they pull Jacob's unresisting body inside and she slams the door shut again. It's difficult to set the lock. Her hands are shaking.

"There's a first aid kit. Um, in the bathroom upstairs. Under the sink."

Santiago stares at her, then begins to ascend the staircase. He gets two steps past the landing, but drops to sit with his elbows on his knees and a dead snake spilling across his lap. He rakes his hands through his hair.

Jacob lies where they've left him, puddled on the worn hallway runner, his shoulder leaned awkwardly against the base of the coat rack. He is already stirring; there's blood in his hair, but he groans.

A whirl of red and blue lights comes through the frosted glass of the FLÂNEURS, INC. sign. The colours play in alternating high and low tones that jar against the siren. Verity swallows the vibrant hint of lightning.

"If you cannot find truth right where you are, where else do you expect to find it?" —Dogen Zenji

19

OTTAWA (February 7, 2014)—Police are looking for leads after suspected gang violence left nine dead in the Glebe yesterday afternoon. The victims, currently unidentified, range in age from approximately fifteen to forty.

"A fight broke out two blocks east of Bank Street on Second Avenue," said Constable Georgina Bartheson. "We are still investigating. Multiple stabbings took place. There do not appear to have been any guns on the scene." According to Bartheson, four victims were found alive on scene and were rushed to Ottawa General Hospital, but did not survive. No drugs were recovered, and the exact motives for the fight are not known.

This event is symptomatic of rising incidences of violence in the city, particularly during the recent power outage. The nine victims bring the total number of homicides to twenty-three so far this year, compared to two at this time the year before.

City Council will meet on Monday to approve emergency surplus funding for the police force. "Coming on the heels of this winter's power issues, Ottawa is well over budget for yearly expenditures," warned Mayor Glenn Wickson. "We are already estimating a 4.6-million-dollar shortfall. From snow removal to emergency shelters to heightened police presence, we've been dealing with some significant challenges. Despite this, our priority is keeping citizens safe. If hiring more officers is what we need to do, then that's what we'll do. If it's equipment, we'll bring in equipment. We are already in discussions with the chief."

VERITY

Verity Richards only ever screamed on the day she was born.

She came into the world like most other babies: wailing, covered in mucus and blood, eyes squeezed against the glare. She held her tiny limbs close against her body, already clenched, as if assuming the position could somehow regain her the rhythmic warmth of the womb.

The nurses wrapped her in a pink blanket and handed her to her mother, who was panting and wet on a stained table. "It's a girl!" they said. "What's her name?" The baby's father looked on, beaming. He had only then let go of his wife's hand.

The baby's name was supposed to be Amelia—the issue had been discussed at length—but the tired woman on the table (her name was Letitia) stroked a gentle finger across the red, tormented face of the child in her arms and said without thinking, "Verity." She could never explain quite why, afterward, except that she had the distinct feeling she hadn't been choosing a name so much as just answering a question.

That was when the baby stopped crying—not all at once, but in tiny gasps that gave way to stuttering misery, her bloody lips working, and then nothing. Only then, it seemed, did she dare look at her new world.

"Oh!" said Letitia. "Her eyes are grey."

"That isn't possible, honey," said her husband—who looked, but the baby had already scrunched her face. "Newborn eyes are blue. It must be the light."

"Is she ... is she covering her ears?"

"Of course not. She's only two minutes old."

So Letitia and her husband (Rory) took little Verity home to their house in the suburbs. They put the baby in a nursery with flowers on the walls and lace on the windows and a soft bear in the crib. They fed her and sang to her and rocked her.

But the baby didn't cry or smile. She was a fussy eater. She trembled when her father crooned a lullaby, or when her grandparents made ga-ga noises and waved their fingers in her face. She wept silently when her mother read her a book; her tears ran down her soft cheeks. She only slept when she was alone.

"Something's wrong," said Letitia finally. She sat in the nursery rocking chair, holding the baby that cringed from her hands. "She should be walking. She doesn't try. She looks at me when I talk to her, but then she looks away. She shakes. She's shaking now."

"Nothing's wrong." But Rory's heart wasn't in it. He could see the way his daughter shuddered when he spoke.

Verity's parents were lawyers. They were smart, ambitious people. Their house in the suburbs was clean, filled with plush furniture and elegantly matching drapes. They kept their lawn scrupulously neat and pretended to their neighbours that everything was fine. They pretended their daughter was improving. They pretended to think about having other children. The truth was that it had become suddenly difficult to pretend anything at all.

"What should I make for dinner?" Rory would ask, and Letitia, holding the baby, would sigh, "Just order out now and skip the step where you burn everything."

Letitia, on the other hand, might say, "Should we go visit my parents this weekend?" and Rory would look up from changing the baby's diaper: "You know your mother won't shut up the entire time."

Little secrets they might have kept were out in the open; little lies they might have told were shifted, at the last moment, to bluntness. They were not diplomatic. Their own abrupt honesties caught them by surprise. "I didn't mean to say that," Letitia confessed, one tense afternoon after a particularly harrowing argument about who hadn't done the dishes. She was holding Verity, as tentatively as though her daughter's rigid body were fine crystal. "I just—don't think I can lie in front of her, you know?"

Rory snorted. "Then she can listen to us scream instead."

It seemed to be true, though. Both Rory and Letitia would have scoffed at the notion it was supernatural or strange. It was just that when they were holding the baby, they would start to speak, and then maybe they would look at her downy hair or her squinched little nose, or they'd stroke her tiny fist, and change their minds about what they were going to say.

You look nice today, Rory would be about to comment, then he'd heft his daughter from her high chair and tell Letitia, "I miss the haircut you had when we met."

I'm glad we could spend time together, Letitia would mean to say, but she'd rest her palm on the baby's soft head and sigh to her husband, "I can't wait until we can both go back to work."

They squabbled over chores and families and home decor and what to watch on television. They took turns feeding and rocking a child who wouldn't look them in the eyes.

At night, Rory would stand in her room and stare down at her, his arms folded.

Verity seemed happier in the quiet, which was as well. Her parents, by this point, existed in a state of frosty détente. Letitia was sleeping in the spare room. Still, Rory and Letitia made appointments and went to doctors. They learned words like 'dissociative' and 'sensory processing disorder,' and when the rain of syllables didn't seem to help, they learned more. They hired therapists and read books. They showed their daughter flash cards with pictures of animals, letters, and colours. She looked away.

After a year, Letitia went back to work, with a pinched smile and a quiet sigh of relief. Rory did too, for a few months. They hired a string of nurses and nannies, none of whom remained for long. "She *looked* at me," complained one woman, rushing out the door. "She looked at me, and I just ... oh god. I hate my life."

Finally, Rory sighed, "I'll just stay home."

They worked out the finances. It made sense. Of course, Rory was still an ambitious man. He liked a challenge. He looked at his child, curled silent on the kitchen tile, and tapped his fingers on the table.

When Letitia left in the mornings, nodding coolly, Rory made Verity breakfast. At first, he fed her with a spoon, but after a few weeks, he set the bowl down in front of her and waited for her to find it. "Right there," he would say. "To your left." For two mornings, he let her go hungry. Then she would stare into the middle distance, but her fingers would fumble for the cutlery until she could eat.

In the hours before Letitia returned, Rory would read to Verity. He started with children's stories. He would sit in her bedroom while she shuddered in her crib; he read her fairy tales and stories about princesses.

She tried to bury her head under a pillow. He took the pillow away. "You have to learn."

When he finished the fairy stories, he moved on to the encyclopedia, and then law textbooks, which were swiftly replaced by novels he brought from the library. He was calm and inexorable. He read to Verity for hours each day, and she wept soundlessly and kicked at the air.

"Did she have a good day?" Letitia would ask, running a hand over her daughter's hair, and Rory would consider.

"I think she's improving."

Verity learned to walk when she was five, with her hand on the wall and one small foot always feeling forward to test the solidity of the floor. Her parents, who had not been speaking to each other that week, were ecstatic.

She was at her worst when people talked to her; she would scrunch her face and press her hands to her ears, her eyes welling. Letitia learned to limit her words to simple things: "Dinner" or "bedtime" or "bath." By the time Verity was six, she would pause, cock her head, and then generally wander in the right direction. On a calm, quiet day, she might even accept her mother's hand.

"This isn't working," sighed Letitia. "Not really. We need to find her something else. A better doctor. A different prescription. She's never going to go to school."

"Any kid of mine is a smart kid. She's getting there. It might go easier if you'd even try sometimes."

It came out more snidely than Rory had intended. When his wife stormed from the room, he sighed and put Verity back down on the carpet.

Her father kept reading to her. When his voice gave out, he locked Verity in her room with a radio turned to talk programming and a light that flashed in random colours. She rolled herself into a ball on the floor. He added a second light.

"You can do it," he told her.

She figured out how to unplug the radio. Her father smiled, then added a television on a shelf she couldn't reach.

The first word Verity ever spoke was "lies." She was seven years old. Her parents were in the living room watching the nightly news when she walked into the room, turned the television off, and uttered that single syllable. Her father had time to make a gurgled sound; her mother got three inches off the couch, but then Verity walked out of the room again, arms tightly wrapped around herself. They found her in her closet with her back pressed to the corner of the wall. She sat in the dark and rocked.

It was a month before she spoke again. Letitia came in late one night, shedding her coat and umbrella in the hall. When Rory said, "Everything all right?" she shrugged: "It's pouring out there. Just traffic."

Verity was sitting in the middle of the carpet, stroking her fingers through the fading fibres. But she whispered, "Lies," and hunched one shoulder.

"What's that, honey?" Rory was immediately alert. But Verity only lifted her head and looked straight at her waterlogged mother, who blinked. Kicking off her shoes, Letitia made a beeline for the kitchen. Her daughter didn't speak again.

That September, Rory enrolled Verity in school and went back to work. Letitia found out three days into the school year. Verity hid in the closet during the screaming.

She was still a quiet child, but she could get up in the mornings and dress herself. Rory would make her toast, and then she would go wait for the yellow school bus and go to class.

Her teachers would call. *Verity isn't interacting. Verity is experiencing social challenges. Verity wouldn't do the poetry assignment. Verity hid in the bathroom all day. Verity isn't getting along with the other children. Listen I hate to suggest this, but perhaps you should really consider—*

Rory wouldn't consider. Letitia would. Verity came home each day with tears running down her face and her book bag dragging behind her. She would curl herself into the peace at the back of her closet until her mother returned, and the house became a war zone interspersed with frosty silence.

She did learn to speak in more than single syllables, somewhere between the books and the blaring radio and the schoolyard taunting. She spoke in hurried sentences, with long pauses between, as though each was carefully considered but then blurted as soon as she could get it over with. "Don't make me go," she said to her father one morning, as he inspected the bows she'd tied on her shoes.

He paused. "Why not?"

Verity hesitated for a long moment. "It tastes like bees."

"Hm," he said. "You have to learn," he told her. She mouthed the words along with him and sighed.

She was a bright enough child, if a frustrating one. She often complained that a math lesson had been the wrong colour or that the letters of the alphabet were too loud. The doctors added "synaesthesia" to her list, and "schizophrenia." They gave her more treatments and therapies and pills. She roamed the house like a zombie.

"The words aren't right," she tried to tell her mother. "The doctors, um ... sound like charcoal and stale bread." She sat at the kitchen table with her feet dangling and her fingers steadily ripping apart an orange peel. She was staring at the tile backsplash on the wall. Her voice was little more than a whisper.

Letitia sighed. "That was almost a sentence, dear. Keep trying. And swallow your medicine."

Letitia was not home very often in those days. She told Rory she had to work. Verity would twitch and stroke her fingers along the wall.

The school phoned again after Verity was found hiding in a supply closet. A teacher dragged her out and sat her in the back of the classroom, where she carved LIES in the top of her desk, wearing away at the wood with the nib of her pen. They sent her home.

There were fights. Letitia would slam dishes on the counter and snarl, "This isn't working. The school, the calls. That stupid radio. She is crying *all the time.*"

"She's talking, isn't she? She stopped walking into walls. No one said it would be easy." Rory would go through Verity's textbooks on the living room couch. Still dressed in his suit, he would flip through pages, looking for something to read aloud. "Stop letting her hide in her room."

"Stop *torturing* her."

Finally came the night Letitia didn't get home until almost ten o'clock. She shrugged off a scarf as she came in, and fumbled at the buttons of her coat.

"Why is she up?" she said, gesturing to where Verity lay on the floor by the unlit fireplace, gazing at the coals on the grate.

Rory sighed. "She says the blinds in her room are biting her." He had the television on, but quietly. "Where've you been?"

"Working. The Jameson file blew up." Letitia's lips were thin, as though she expected a challenge. Her husband only looked resigned. But Verity, on the floor, lifted her head.

"*No,* Mommy." The little girl sounded old in that moment—exhausted, exasperated, her patience finally and thoroughly tested. She was a sixty-year-old woman in a fleece onesie. She pushed awkwardly to her feet and walked carefully across the room—a little unsteady, as though the floor were rolling beneath her. Her parents stared at her, but she only reached to wrap her small fingers around her mother's hand.

"Did you want to go to bed?" asked Letitia.

"No, Mommy." The little girl looked upward, her grey eyes for once focused and clear. Her hair was tangled like a nest. She spoke in quiet, precise imitation of her father: "Where've you been?"

"Having sex with Bill Jameson," replied Letitia, blandly.

There was a long pause.

Rory turned off the television.

Verity nodded, apparently satisfied, then let go of her mother's hand. Moving carefully still, she made her way across the living room floor to the hall, then climbed the stairs, one by one, to her room.

She wasn't looking anymore, or she might have seen Letitia's widening eyes; her mother's lips had gone white. It was the moment when resigned indulgence turned to fear and something very much resembling hate.

stop

What am I getting wrong?

~~everything~~

This is the story you told me?

i told it to you wrong words are always wrong all of
this is crawling across my skin when im upstairs i
hear it like a heartbeat

What can I do to make it better?

the house
the tile in the foyer was marble
i used to lie on it when i was a child i would let
my cheek press against it i liked the white streaked
with black and grey it was a little like my first
memories
the fourth tile to the left of the front door was
chipped at the corner
i tell you this but it doesnt capture the exact
shape of the chip or the size of the tiles i dont
know i forget now

The tiles. Okay. Let me go back and work that in.

its not about the tiles
it is but also it isnt
this story is the hardest its mine but its too far
away

look

this is how it ends when the judge asks whom i want
to live with and im nine years old and daddy makes
the world loud and hard but mommy lets me hide in
the closet so i say mommy
and she sends me away and the hospital sounds like
a choir dying

keep going but not this part

20

AGREEMENT FOR SERVICES TO BE RENDERED

The following contract represents an agreement between
_____ (client name) and Flâneurs, Inc. for services rendered
at_____(location).

Representatives of Flâneurs, Inc., agree to appear on
_____(date/time) and perform _____(service)
to the best of their abilities. All necessary equipment will be
provided. Any required uniforms will be worn, but will be provided
by the client.

_____(client name) recognizes that the representatives
of Flâneurs, Inc. have no formal training and are providing the
service free of charge. Representatives of Flâneurs, Inc. are thus
indemnified from any damages and fuck it, I'm not a lawyer. If we
screw up your stuff, we'll pay a professional to fix it for you, but
don't come suing us for extra, okay? We're not MADE of money.

Signed:

_____ (client) _____ (date)
_____ (Jacob Shepard, co-president)
_____ (date)
~~_____ (Verity Richards, co-president)~~
~~_____ (date)~~

FEBRUARY

"Oh my god." Jacob slumps at the foot of the staircase, one hand pressed to his blood-matted hair. "What was—oh my god. What was that? Is she okay? ...Are *you* okay?"

"Yes." Verity crouches in front of Jacob; she tries to take his wrist, to move his hand from his head, but he jerks away.

"Don't touch me."

"I can't see if you're hurt."

"*Yes.* I'm hurt. Fuck, Vee, back off." Jacob closes his eyes, wincing. "And who's this guy? You know what? Never mind."

Santiago sits halfway up the stairs with a dead snake across his lap. Its tail coils crookedly at his feet and dangles over the landing. The dimness of the stairwell cloaks him like a shroud, hiding the vacuum of his eyes.

Verity rises, extending tentative fingers again toward Jacob's matted locks, but he only twists to stare up at her. His face is hollow. A line of blood has dripped from his left nostril and pooled along the line of his lips. He hesitates. They are both illuminated by the flashing red and blue of the lights now revolving in the street outside.

Jacob says, "Did ... did that guy have wings?" His stunned eyes search Verity's face.

Startled, she tastes antiseptic and mildew; she remembers locked halls and paper gowns, and swallows.

Possibility stretches gossamer and insubstantial between them.

"You...?" Verity manages a shocked syllable before a shadow blocks the flashing colours at the front door. Someone knocks forcefully at the glass.

Jacob blinks, his attention jerking to the door. "What—"

"Answer it. Please. The police will have an ambulance. For your head. I, um ... we'll go upstairs." Verity sighs. "Don't tell them."

"You want me to lie?" Jacob is patently incredulous. "*You?*" The knock comes again. They both jump. Only Santiago is motionless.

"I want you to, um ... not tell them. Please." Verity doesn't have time for the coriander uncertainty dripping from her own mouth. She glances nervously at the looming shadow, then ascends the stairs to stand in front of Santiago. Leaning down, she sets her hands on the magician's; his are clammy, curled around the dryness of the snake. The scents of lilac and coal are nearly ghosts.

The knock comes again, sharp and loud—three times, like a gun fired. Jacob and Verity both jump. Jacob winces, wrapping one hand around the stair railing, pressing his other palm to his skull as he totters to his feet.

"What's your friend's problem? Is he high?"

"He is missing half of himself. We—we should go upstairs. I'm sorry."

Santiago is less bloody than Jacob, but he's starting to sweat, his face acquiring an undertone of grey. He lets Verity tug him to his feet and push him up the stairs, Ouroboros cradled in his arms.

"Is that a *dead snake*?"

Verity shoves the magician through into the apartment just as she hears the click of Jacob unlocking the front door. She slips into the upstairs hall and closes the door behind herself as quietly as she can. Santiago stands waiting for her, damp and empty. She pushes him into the living room and says, "Sit," then, "Wait."

She leaves the magician on the couch, staring at the wall, the snake looped across his thighs. He fidgets with a playing card in his right hand, flipping the worn cardboard between his fingers. The light that filters through the blinds stripes the wet, stubbled hollows of his cheeks.

Verity enters the bedroom and fishes a soft flannel blanket, patterned in grey and red stripes, from one of the drawers on Jacob's side. When she carries it out and drapes it over the coffee table, Santiago has dropped the card, which now lies face down on the hardwood, so that he can clutch the dead snake closer, running his thumb over the hard line of the break in its neck. "Here," she says, and when he hesitates, "It's okay." He stares at her for what seems like a long time before he sets Ouroboros down on the blanket, arranging each limp loop, making sure nothing of the long black body slides to the floor. He draws the edge of the blanket over the blank yellow eyes, then drops back, his elbows on his splayed knees and his head drooping. He has already left a smear of blood on the white cushions.

Verity tastes only Santiago's obsidian grief and the throbbing jade of her fading adrenaline. She looks at the blanket and feels her own sorrow distant and cocooned. She goes back to the bedroom and strips out of clothes stained by Jacob and she isn't sure what else. She finds a clean pair of jeans and one of Jacob's shirts. She stands in front of the dresser, the palms of her hands pressed hard to her temples, and imagines she can hear raised voices in the foyer. The world around her is mud. She is subsumed in the dull conglomeration of sirens and snow, corpses and razored dragons. She can taste Privya's rage and the lingering sour defeat of Colin's doom. Jihan's eyes are shards that cut the skin and the incredulous curl of Jacob's lip blooms heavy and pounding beneath her skull.

She leans her forehead against the closet door, staring down at the handle and thinking of the peaceful solitude to be found behind hanging coats and neatly lined shoes. She holds to the last vision of Colin's wings and the glimmer of clarity that still haunts her somewhere just beneath her collarbone. Then, inhaling, she straightens and walks back to the living room, where Santiago slouches unmoving. She sits on the couch next to him. She hears another siren approaching, and the increasing growl of its proximity nearly blinds her.

"There's, um, no one here to see Ouro now—except us. Can it come back?" Verity isn't in the mood to talk. She has to fight to get each syllable past her lips. Still, she tries, and she touches the back of Santiago's sleeve.

The magician turns his head, and Verity has a sudden impression of those untamed eyes in a little-boy face. She smells gin and tastes broken springs. Santiago turns his hand over, wrapping his long fingers around her wrist hard enough to crush, and she doesn't protest because he is a drowning man clutching at a lifeline. It all squelches into the marsh of her perceptions. She knows there will be bruises later.

"You don't know," she says, surprised, and the magician's fingers dig into her flesh. "It's never...?"

"Never." Santiago's voice is guttural. "I don't—I can't—" Verity can't look at him—the shadows of the blinds writhing across him, and the haunted fear that lurks in the caverns of his irises. He says again, "I—they see a snake, he's a snake. They see a dog, he's a dog. He's always mine again, after. He," and his lips twist mutely around the words he can't finish.

"Shh." Verity wants to close her eyes. Instead, she looks down at Santiago's hand, his nails neatly trimmed, his skin swarthy against her pallid beige. Her wrist has gone white around the edges of his grip. His terror throbs in the back of her throat.

She wonders again what Jacob is saying to the police.

"It's okay. Sometimes there aren't words for things." The room beats dully at her temples. Verity sighs. "How did you—the first time, where did Ouro come from? Um. You should know, people who are touching me—they don't lie. Which is, I don't mean I think you—"

"I was a boy. Alone. He was—" Santiago appears to realize the strength of his grip; he relaxes his hand, letting Verity withdraw. His fingers are trembling. "He was the worst thing I could imagine."

"To protect you." Verity doesn't know how she follows that. It's a flare of clarity. She fights the urge to cradle it in her palm before it dies.

Santiago nods. He looks as though he would say something else, but his throat works in silence. His shoulders are flattened.

"Privya said there was power in blood. Maybe...?"

Santiago's nostrils flare. "Privya's power. Jihan's. Mine was ... I just...." He pinches the bridge of his nose. "How can you *think*?" he bursts out. "When there's only one of you? My head echoes. No one answers."

Verity is quiet for several breaths, then she says gently, "My thinking screams at me. Like the city, or the air. Words with textures and scents. Half-complete. In a different way." She has his attention. He is staring at her. She shifts uncomfortably. "I imagine silence, but I can't really ... I would envy you but your eyes are like an out-of-tune piano." She can't actually see his eyes anymore; she sees only the quivering textures of her own voice, melting the air between them. She remembers, though, the jangling caverns of his need.

Verity sighs. "Tell me," she says. "How you called him, or how he felt to you. Maybe we can—I don't know if a shadow can die."

"Why does it matter?"

"All I taste are the sirens. I want to help you but I'm, um, selfish, too, because I need something true. One thing that's clear. I want to—my head hurts. Yours is empty. Mine is full." Verity shakes her head; her words are tripping over one another as she forces them past numb lips. "Tell me. Ouroboros is perfume in a mine shaft to me. Like flowers, but ... smoky."

She has to close her eyes. Against her lids, she sees the slack face of the dead boy in the camouflage jacket. She can feel the fleece blanket brush her knees and can't escape the long chill stillness its folds contain.

It seems that Santiago won't speak, but eventually, he offers, "It was spring. But it was night. There were no flowers. I called him from death and terror."

Verity swallows. "Was he ... the first time?"

"Shadows have always whispered to me. Black things. Possibilities. He was the one who took form. He—people don't understand. He isn't a servant or a trick. We share the same eyes. The same thoughts. You touch him, and I feel you. You take my hand, and you take his."

Verity pauses. "He winds himself in my hair. You...?"

The curve of Santiago's mouth shudders at the corner before the shiver of amusement dies. "Yes. No. Sorry. It isn't—not like—he likes you. We share the same thoughts, but not *all* the same. He does what he wants. More as we both get older."

"Was he the only one? The only shadow, I mean."

"Lately, I can play with most of them, a little." Santiago gestures with his free hand, a graceful waterfall of fingers that leaves him staring with bemusement at the lines of shade falling from the window and across his skin. "At least, I could." His throat works. He is staring at his knuckles. "Nothing speaks to me now without him," he adds, absently. "But to answer your question: he was the strongest and the best. Nothing else has ever stayed." He curls his fingers inward and looks at Verity again. "That girl—Privya—told me in the market that I made her sad, that all I had was a remnant of a memory of power. But Ouro was real. Now she has taken him. I'm half a man." Sweat beads at his temple, running down.

"What did it feel like?"

"What?"

"When your shadow died."

At Santiago's incredulous glare, Verity shakes her head. "I'm not trying to be cruel. I'm only trying to understand."

The magician says, shortly, "Like being decapitated. He was fierce and then scared. And then gone." He almost reaches for the blanket on the table, then curls his hand against his chest. "Colin's okay?"

"Jihan took him."

"We're not going to make it. The Chalice. This concert, or whatever bullshit it is Privya is planning. We're falling. Colin can't save us, and he's going to die." Santiago grinds the heel of his hand beneath his eye, exhaling. "That lunatic—what is she *doing*? She's never threatened us. She didn't have to kill Ouro. She threw her own people against Jihan like she was dropping them into a blender."

"I don't think she wanted to. But she's running out of time. She really thinks Jihan will destroy the world."

"Maybe she's right." Santiago drops his hand and stares at the bare white blankness of the living room wall. "What does it matter?"

"It might matter to billions of people?"

"They're not—" The magician cuts off, then grimaces. "I can't say they're not people. But they're just—they don't *see* us. They're not *real* to me. Just faces watching card tricks. Or your boyfriend downstairs. What's he going to say?"

"I don't know. If they come upstairs, there's—the window in the bedroom goes to the roof. If you drop down the back—"

"I know. Ouro knew." Santiago drops back into the couch, gazing up at the ceiling as his shoulders sink into the increasingly smeared cushion behind him. "It doesn't matter. Let them arrest me. A few more weeks and this will be over, one way or another."

She sees it, then, at the base of his throat: fear beating in fragile staccato. In the bob of his Adam's apple, she tastes despair, dry as a tumbleweed. It is perfect. In his breath, she sees through years to a soiled mattress and silence marred by creaking footsteps.

"Thank y—" Santiago's shaking words slice the moment and then are cut off, interrupted by Verity's soft sound of dismay. She is rigid; she fights to maintain the vision, and her hand flies up almost of its own accord, palm out, fingers taut. At Santiago's widened eyes, she shakes her head—a single, sharp motion—and reaches to brush her fingertips beneath his chin, over the wire of his stubble and down toward his collarbone.

He almost ruins everything with a single bobbing swallow. Verity focuses intently on the skin visible at the junction of his shirt collar, and the sensation of his throat beneath her finger. It tastes of whispering, of a multitude of voices she cannot quite hear.

It's nothing she's ever done before. She reaches within herself for different shadows—for an angel's black feathers, spread tattered in the cold, and the last sensation of his light. Then she gives it up—to Santiago and to the memory ghosted beneath his skin, and the razored electricity of a child's nighttime terrors.

She breathes lilac and coal.

She can almost—

"Vee!" It's Jacob's voice from downstairs, muffled through the apartment door. Verity feels it like a slap; her hand flies back as Santiago, startled, jerks away.

She has lost her focus. The weight of the room crushes down on her. She tastes the couch's plain fibres, hears Santiago's hoarse breath in streaks of grey. He cries out, and his joy is too bright, glaring in her eyes. She knows exactly where the writhing darkness has bloomed in the hollow of his throat; she felt it beneath her fingertips, but now she is blinded and deaf, her lungs thick and her ears overwhelmed by the roaring wind of the hardwood floor.

There's a flash of spreading orange that's familiar to her; she swallows furred, narrow strands and knows that Jacob has called her name again.

There are certain skills that Verity has been mastering since childhood, like the ability to find the flatness of the floor beneath her feet (*sweet sugar on the tongue*) and push herself up from the couch (*a chill like ice cream melting down the back of her knee*). She doesn't speak to Santiago, but instead keeps her chin up and walks the path she knows from memory: four steps from the couch to the hall, six to the upstairs door, where she can fumble for the knob that sounds like a slow gong in a storm. She steps onto the landing, grasps the banister, and slowly descends the stairs. The world rages around her. She gazes at the blur of Jacob's features and does her best to focus past the taste of the railing against her palm. She can't tell if there's still blood on his face. His folded arms are almost lost to the blizzard-blast of the siren that peals anew from the street outside.

Verity swallows. "Are you ... okay? I can't—"

Jacob isn't listening. "I'll skip the 'who is that dude' question and go with: what just happened outside?"

His wounded confusion stops Verity a foot from the bottom of the stairs. Her grip is tight on the banister. She is listening very hard.

She opens her mouth, but syllables struggle and die there.

"Vee." There is no retreat in Jacob.

She says, "Everything is a storm." She hears the pleading in her own voice.

"Uh-huh. You don't get to go hide with this one. First that mess with the river, now—what *happened* out there?"

"You saw it." Verity is blank. "Don't you—" Her head is pounding. Bludgeoned by the creak of the stair beneath her shoe, she nevertheless descends the final few steps. She means to grasp Jacob's wrist; she catches at his sleeve instead, off-target, and slides her hand down until she can touch the skin at the base of his thumb. "You saw the wings," she says.

Verity is touching him; she wills him to the truth. She blinks hard to focus on his face, and the fall at the corners of his mouth. "I got hit in the head, Vee," he says quietly. "Is that what you—did you see wings?" Verity thinks he glances up the stairs; he is a haze of static. "Have you even been taking your meds?"

Verity bites her lip. She thinks she tastes blood. She knows she feels Jacob disengaging from her grip, and that might taste *like* blood.

"I can't—" she begins again, helplessly (*I can't see; I can't breathe; can we talk about this later*), but Jacob has already pulled away.

"Take her. Just—be gentle. She's sick."

Verity doesn't understand, but then tall figures are emerging from the archway that leads to Jacob's office. A scratched police badge rings in her ears. She makes out creased uniforms. Someone grasps her firmly by the upper arm.

"This way, ma'am. Okay, you two take point upstairs. Remember, we don't know if the guy's armed."

Verity wants to protest, but they are pulling her; she stumbles over the hallway rug, then hits the door frame with her shoulder before she is outside and the city roars around her.

Daylight shrieks.

The flash of police lights scrapes across her skin.

Buildings melt into bodies slide into the metal of the cuff someone clicks around her wrist. They are kind; they bind her arms in front. It's the last thing Verity registers before the world swallows her and she can't tell the pavement from the sky.

Inside, she is screaming.

Did I get this right?

no

What's wrong? What can I fix?

```
i cant read it its a wall of black the words are
always wrong when there are no words turn the page
turun the page turn teh paage
t
```

[**IMAGE:** More a doodle, like a page ripped from a sketchbook. Ink blots are running together as shadows regroup into the form of a stylized black dog.]

21

OTTAWA (March 4, 2014)—Amidst the recent tumult in Canada's capital, residents are still managing to find enthusiasm for The Between, set to play the Aberdeen Pavilion at Lansdowne Park tomorrow night. Buzz has been growing around the reclusive band, perhaps precisely because it is so reclusive; ask three fans how many members the group has, and get three different answers.

The Between does not have a website. Its albums are out of print—unavailable at retailers, pirate sites, and even the city's only remaining used music store.

"People have been asking for weeks," said Navid Qadir of Elgin Vinyl and Collectibles. "We don't have any, though. That's a band's band. Heard they were huge in the Boston clubs back in the day. I think it was Boston. Chicago? I'm surprised they're at Lansdowne. It's a pretty mainstream venue."

"There've been some logistical challenges," admitted Lacey Cardiff, the Lansdowne Park event manager. "They're an unorthodox group. But all the contracts are in place, and we're very much looking forward to hosting the show. Ticket sales are good. People are curious."

"They're absolutely one of my favourites." Janet Gunn, 23, a Carleton University student, was one

of a group already setting up camp on the sidewalk outside the venue. "People will tell you they're
impossible to find or whatever, but not for real music
fans. I mean, yeah, they're kind of obscure, but I
was into them ages ago. It's kind of a shame they're
playing such a public show. I never thought they'd be
sellouts."

MARCH

Verity learned to parse the world when she was very young. It was a skill
she built up slowly and with stubborn dedication, before she ever had
words to explain that the bars of her crib were crying, or the carpet tasted
like oranges.

It took her a long time to recognize what oranges tasted like.

Now she finds herself back at the heart of the maelstrom; the world
is a wicked storm that rips at her skin and forces itself into her lungs. She
cannot swallow; she cannot hear; she cannot see. Or rather, she tastes and
hears and sees everything. It is as though she is three years old again, and
everything around her is attacking.

She tries to curl into a ball; she can't tell whether or not she succeeds.
She has the impression that someone is talking to her. Multiple voices
are sweet and sour between her teeth, but the words puddle away. A few
times, she thinks someone is touching her, or the ground is flat beneath
her feet, but these sensations fade before she can grasp them.

She tastes Jacob on her tongue, then he's gone again.

Her head hurts.

She knows she should be alarmed, but the shapes of her thoughts
scatter. She can only endure for whatever time passes before the storm
subsides to a steadier wash of waves. Sensation grows more predictable:
the scent of pine needles, the taste of smoking rubber, the feel of something oily and slick across her skin.

She remembers her father turning on a television, opening a book.
His mouth was implacable. *You need to learn. You'll thank me someday.*

Verity doesn't thank him. She does gather herself.

She begins with the middle finger of her right hand and thinks about
tapping it against her palm, just across the ball of her thumb. At first, she
cannot be certain she's successful, but she concentrates on the rhythm of
it—*taptap, tap, taptaptap.* When it comes to her as little bursts of pepper,
she ignores the taste; she is seeking touch. *Taptap, tap, taptaptap.*

There. She can feel the uncertainty of her own delicate rhythm. That is her right hand.

With that starting point, she can begin to filter through the morass of her exhausted senses. Something is brushing against the hairs of her forearm, and it sings in her ears, but she can think *no, touch* and know it's a blanket or a sheet. There's something unyielding around her wrist— around both her wrists, but her hands are not together. She is lying on her back.

Taptap, tap, taptaptap. She knows the pattern. She learned it against a thousand news broadcasts blaring in her room.

She thinks of feathers and wishes desperately for Colin, knowing that one touch of his hand would banish the throbbing in her brain and settle the air around her into crystal clarity. Instead, she moves her fingers, the rhythm steady. She swallows soap and the lingering scent of palm oil.

Something abruptly gapes and roars—a door? Verity has the impression of a hand on her shoulder. It doesn't last. It leaves her spitting pepper again. She sighs and starts over.

The veins in her eyes are throbbing. She can still see her father's disapproving face.

She reclaims the sensation of lying on her back. She knows her arms are bound. Eventually, she can isolate distant beepings and the static of a voice over a poorly configured speaker system. She blinks iron streaks from her eyes, and her vision resolves to square white ceiling tiles and the track of a hanging curtain.

When she turns her head, she sees an assortment of boxy electronic monitoring devices. The only one blinking measures her heartbeat in silent, irregular flashes. Her pulse has never been steady, but now she can taste it, fluctuating with each throb of her skull.

There is a needle in the back of Verity's left hand, from which a line of narrow plastic tubing runs to an IV stand. She doesn't feel drugged, or at least not with any sensation she recognizes. If anything, it's the crisply utilitarian sheets of the hospital bed that ring familiar, or the metal bars raised on either side of the narrow mattress.

She looks down and is resigned to find herself wearing a pale green hospital gown. It is clean but wrinkled, the fabric slightly stiff. Someone has thrown a blanket over her legs; she can feel the worn fabric against her knees and her bare toes, quietly humming. There are balloon-like plastic sheaths inflating and deflating around her calves, intermittently snug. The blanket heaves over them, breathing.

She is shackled to the bars of her bed. The metal cuffs binding her wrists are padded on the inside. This, too, is familiar; she tugs once, experimentally, and sighs.

Another indecipherable announcement crackles over hidden speakers. Verity closes her eyes and waits for the pounding in her skull to lessen. If she ignores the cuffs, the bed is almost a pleasant change: there are no creeping shadows and no ice is twisting unnaturally towards her. The hospital walls are mundane; there is no space *between* and no single-sided door waiting to be opened.

The doorway from the hall does open, or at least Verity hears a lock click and feels something slither below her collarbone.

"Hello! We thought you might be with us again soon. We've been worried about you." The nurse who pulls back the curtain is a pleasant-looking woman in her mid-forties, with speckled hair in a trendy asymmetrical cut. She's wearing scrubs and her smile is apple-warm.

When Verity doesn't say anything, the nurse continues, "There's a police officer standing guard out there. They've been keeping an eye on you. You must have been busy." She approaches the bed, unhooking a penlight from her pocket. "Can you follow this with your eyes for me?"

"Please don't." It's not a bright light, but Verity turns her face away, averting her eyes from the approaching gleam. Her voice has come out hoarse.

The nurse hesitates, then clicks the light off and returns it to her pocket.

Words catch in Verity's throat. She swallows and manages, "Where are my clothes?"

"We'll keep them for you until—I'm not sure what the process is for you. I can check." The nurse busies herself checking Verity's cuffs. "Can you tell me your name?"

"Verity Richards."

"Do you know whe—"

"The hospital. Um. Ottawa General, probably?" Verity sighs. "I don't know the date," she adds, before the nurse can ask. "It was ... February."

The nurse's glance is quick, but not entirely surprised. "Done this before, hmm? Okay—" She breaks off, looking back in the direction of the hall as the speaker sputters again. A man's static voice, tainted with the elusive flutter of butterfly wings, says, "Ward 2, code violet."

"Honey, I might have to leave you for a bit."

"What's code violet?"

The nurse's thumb is still brushing Verity's wrist, which is probably why she answers absently, "Power outage. Downstairs. Must've blown a fuse." She takes her hand off the cuffs and shakes her head. "You sit tight. Dr. Webber will be in to evaluate you in a little while. Oh, and it's March, honey. The fifth. You remember that for next time."

The fifth. "Don't go down there." Verity says it more urgently than she'd intended. The nurse has kind eyes.

The woman only shakes her head and smiles again, then walks back out into the hall. She doesn't pull the curtain back into place. Verity catches a glimpse of broad shoulders in a uniform shirt; the police badge sounds like an echo underwater before the door shuts.

The flashing machine registers the abrupt pickup in Verity's heart rate. She tastes metal. There's a low ringing in her ears.

She listens intently for the announcement she expects is coming.

"Ward 4, code violet."

She flexes her hands, closing her fingers slowly, feeling the padding shift against her skin. Sudden adrenaline helps push back the low surges of her headache. Her muscles feel like spaghetti. *Weeks,* she thinks. And, *March 5.*

Time seems to stretch, long and slow. All Verity hears is the faint clatter of feet from the hall, punctuated by notes of indistinct conversation and the pinging of machines. She takes a breath and wonders if she is wrong.

"Ward 6, code violet."

Multiple feet pound by outside.

Verity tugs ineffectually against the cuffs. She is trying not to think about Jacob. She imagines the front steps of the townhouse with an unexpected stab of longing, and remembers too late that the old wooden stairs are cracked and stained with blood.

"Ward 7, code violet."

Verity wonders what ward she's in. She is not very good at being loud, but she clears her throat and says, "Police?"

Another set of footsteps goes rushing by outside the door.

Verity swallows. "Police!"

After a few beats, the door opens and a uniformed officer pokes his head inside. He is too young for his moustache. "What?"

On the first try, Verity can't answer. She works her throat to get around the syllables, and the officer almost closes the door again before she speaks. "Don't."

"Don't what?" His hibiscus doubt floats to block her vision.

She shakes her head. "Don't stay. Someone is, um, coming for me. I don't want you to be hurt."

The voice comes over the speaker again, muddled by a burst of static. It has a slightly panicked tone that vibrates across Verity's lower lip. She can just make out the word 'violet.'

The officer smiles, and pats once at his hip. "You don't worry about me. This gun is loaded."

The lights go out. The machines in Verity's room abruptly stop whirring; the flashing monitor of her heartbeat dies. A sliver of light filters in from a window on the opposite wall from the door, somewhere on the other side of the curtain. Behind the officer, the hallway is black.

He swears; his right hand rises to depress a button on the radio he wears strapped to his upper chest. It, too, is silent, and he lets his hand drop. He steps inside the room and starts to close the door.

An instant later, Jihan slides through behind him, as sinuous as Ouroboros, wrapping her arm around the man's neck and tightening her elbow at his larynx. Flailing to reach behind himself, he grabs frantically at the curtain, half ripping it down. The tearing sound shreds the air in the room before the officer goes limp; when Jihan releases him, he crumples to the floor.

Jihan's steel eyes shine jagged, reflecting the light from the window. She's wearing old jeans and the lavender cardigan again, now stained at the collar, lumpy where it's buttoned wrong, and shredding where the left sleeve has been pulled nearly loose from the shoulder. Verity's old, bloody scarf is still tied around her arm, barely a stiff wisp.

Jihan starts to crouch over the fallen man and Verity says, quickly, "He's only doing his job." She isn't certain whether the other woman will listen; Jihan, as always, is as smoothly unreadable as a porcelain doll. The other woman straightens, though, at the foot of the bed, and stands looking at the cop, then at the window. Outside, Verity can see nothing but half-clouded sky, marked by the fading orange of a sunset moving toward twilight.

When Jihan goes too long without moving, Verity ventures, "Did Colin ask you? What's ... what's happening?"

Deerlike, the other woman whips her head around and stares at Verity. For a breath, Verity looks past the swirling haze of the hospital, the fire-and-iron chill of Jihan's presence, and she sees Jihan's shattered eyes, an infinity of broken shards.

She shivers.

The throbbing in her head lingers, but is partially subsiding, forced back by necessity and the pounding of her heart. The sudden dimness of the room is helping.

Verity thinks of the equipment dying all around them and tastes the last hints of ozone electricity. She realizes no one else is coming.

Gently, she says, "Can you get me out of these, please?"

Jihan stands poised in precise balance, fingers outstretched. One of her hands is frozen as though reaching for the weapon she without a doubt has hidden somewhere in the frayed bulk of her clothes. The kaleidoscope of Jihan's gaze slides back to opaque reflection; Verity sees herself, wan and tousled amid moss-green sheets, then the sound of distant yelling washes across her vision and the moment is lost.

Verity says, "*Please.*"

She can't see anymore, but she feels Jihan's calloused fingers on her wrist, doing something quick and definitive to the cuffs. The restraint on her right wrist snaps open, then the left. The tubing attached to the back of Verity's hand rips free as the needle is pulled from her flesh. She winces, then blinks until she can see. She fumbles to free her legs, pulling at velcro, then lowers the bars at the side of the mattress so she can slide off.

When her feet hit the floor, she remembers her bare soles and the uncomfortable whisper of the hospital gown around her hips. "My clothes." It takes her a rushing moment to stand. Her limbs shake. She is relieved to keep the floor steady.

Jihan only moves soundlessly back to the door. She waits while Verity checks the downed officer (who breathes, though it rasps) and the room's only cupboard (which is empty). The second Verity slides her abandoned pillow under the officer's head and straightens, Jihan has opened the door and slipped back into the hall.

Verity finds the ties to the gown and tugs them to the front, pulling them into a rough knot at her hip. She considers the officer's boots, but they are far too large, and the laces elude her in the dim light. She sighs, then follows Jihan.

To the left, the hallway is dark; to the right, the remaining halogen lights die on the ceiling as Jihan passes beneath. The hospital wing is plunged into blackness, leaving only one window at the far end, shining as a beacon. A silhouette crosses in front of it, and Verity freezes before she sees a patient dragging wheeled tubing and the thin line of an IV tower.

She knows Jihan has slipped back beside her because she can taste blood and steel. She whispers, "I can't see," and "Can you stop killing all this equipment? People need it."

A hand closes on Verity's elbow, and she half jumps, but then she's being pulled firmly down the hall and through a doorway. Jihan tugs her against the wall just before another pair of footsteps goes rushing by outside. "Why isn't the generator kicking in?" yells a woman's voice, and a man further down the corridor answers something indistinct.

Another voice, this one querulous, says "Nurse?" from just behind them, but before Verity can muster a response, Jihan has tugged her back into the hall and away.

The floor tiles are cool on Verity's bare feet. Her footsteps sound of soft pine and the tremor of ripples on a pond. Jihan is silent, and her long fingers are strong and unforgiving. Her grip isn't brutal, but neither does she give Verity time to find balance, or to adjust to each new sound or scent. When Verity manages a glance to the side, she catches only the metal sheen of the other woman's eyes, focused somewhere down the hall and—Verity suspects—simultaneously somewhere else, impossibly far.

"Too fast," pleads Verity, but it makes no difference. She is propelled forward. The hall blurs breathlessly around her.

Verity has no idea where they're going—apart from, she assumes, 'out'—but Jihan is assured. Four or five times more (Verity loses count), they pull to the side, ducking into some unlocked doorway just before a member of the hospital staff comes around a corner or emerges from a room just ahead. Flashlights approach them and die before coming in range. Voices curse.

Only once, in the fading twilight that ekes through a window in some sleeping patient's room, does Verity see the shine of the knife in Jihan's hand. The voices outside are close. Someone is complaining about funding cuts.

Greatly daring, Verity touches Jihan's forearm and shakes her head. Jihan stares only at a dead computer on its cart, but she sighs, a slow and deliberate release of breath, then lifts her chin with apparent impatience and slides the blade away within her sleeve.

It is something of an anti-climatic rescue, Verity supposes; they dart through shadows and slide down corridors. They wait what feels a long time in a supply closet before Jihan leads her down an unlit staircase— Verity stumbling, the other woman pulling her with unrelenting insistence—but they don't encounter anyone else. They hear voices on the staircase above them, and someone calls down, "Jessica, is that you?," but Verity doesn't answer, and they keep going.

The main lobby is a babble of voices; they emerge into a crowd and another nearby flashlight winks out. A red glowing sign reading EXIT flares and fades to black. A child is crying. Here, the last of the fading day comes through a glass wall and a set of revolving doors; wheeled cots have been gathered, and nurses are bustling. "The ICU is still running," shouts a woman near the back hall, "and Emerg. Will anyone who needs immediate assistance please report to Emergency!"

Verity tastes the slight gleam of a badge and freezes, but the officer only brushes by in front of her, a short, uniformed woman pushing her way through the crowd. "Everyone remain calm; ladies and gentlemen, we are here to help."

No one is looking for Verity. She thinks of her guard with a stab of guilt.

"Stay away from Emergency," she tells her general impression of Jihan. She can't feel the floor beneath her feet anymore. Every step she takes is cushioned by the slip-slide sensation of angry patients; voices prick her skin. "I can't," she says, or wants to say, but the sound of her own words is lost in a rush of static. She thinks someone bumps into her.

She starts again, one more time: *taptap, tap, taptaptap*, her fingers against her palm. She can barely perceive it, here with a chattering crowd that drips down her skin in cold mustard gobs. She blinks, and sees glass revolving. She blinks, and concrete paving is ridged and frozen beneath her feet. A bevy of flashing red lights nearly undoes her, and then Jihan is jerking her back a step as an ambulance whips past them. She thinks the lights falter as the vehicle comes close, but then the engine roars and it's safely on the street.

More lights denote ambulances lined up and waiting to evacuate off to the side. A wheeled cot is pushed past, a very pregnant woman sweating and wailing in the company of two efficient nurses.

Verity ducks her head and goes in the other direction, hoping Jihan has no need to go too near the ambulances. She's apparently right; they descend a short decline of sidewalk to the street. No one shouts after them.

The chill evening bites at Verity's skin. Night has fallen just enough for the streetlights to illuminate, but a short line of them is burned out just across the road. She is not surprised when they head that way; she is not surprised to see a small white face waiting, glowing with a hint of trapped moonlight, pale as the snow on the ground.

The world comes to her in dizzy waves. She's still tapping her fingers—she thinks she is—but she's lost the thread. Jihan is a razor presence next to her, then behind. A siren peals in the distance and drowns the street in crimson desperation.

The usual evening's traffic congestion is now snarled by emergency vehicles and strobed with flashing lights. There are four lanes for Jihan to pull Verity across, and as headlights fall across them, Verity is suddenly acutely aware of her thin hospital gown, her bare legs and her feet pinched by ice chips and loose asphalt (or by the stutter of an engine stalling; she isn't sure).

Some of the headlights die, and she's grateful. A car horn honks.

She blinks again.

"Crap," Colin is saying, and, "Here."

Clarity suffuses her: Verity is standing on the far side of the road from the hospital, past a snowy snarl of traffic now further complicated by two stalled cars. Jihan is just behind her. Colin has taken her hand; his fingers are small and trembling, fragile as twigs or the wings of a sparrow. She is warm and safe; she is cared for. She can breathe.

It is hard for her to pull her own hand away, but she does. He doesn't try to hold her. Her own shaking has subsided; her headache is gone.

"Thank you." Verity means it, but she hears the remorse in her own voice; the angel is a guttering candle. He stands leaning on his cane, his too-big coat fluttering at his legs in the nip of the evening breeze. His eyes burn like flame shining through sapphires, but his skin is stretched over bone, and even his feathered hair has gone dry. His lips are chapped. He shakes his head.

"Here," he says again. This time he holds out a second trench coat that's folded over his arm. It's nearly identical to the one he's wearing. When Verity takes it, she is careful not to touch him.

Even on her, the coat is too big, its hem brushing the ground and its broad shoulders swallowing her own. She discovers as she shrugs into it that someone has carefully sewn long slits down the back, to accommodate the wings she doesn't have. The coat smells of stale vomit, feathers, and a hint of whiskey.

"Thank you." Verity supposes her conversation is getting repetitive. Colin only shakes his head again; with some awkwardness, he is shrugging a small pink backpack from one shoulder. Jihan takes it, and his lips tighten.

"Pass that off to her, would you? Boots in there," he adds, to Verity. "We're not quite the same size, but it was a bit of a rush. Look, tell me now: did she kill anyone?"

"I—" Verity pulls worn boots from the pack and glances back at the hospital. She sees the top three floors glaringly lit, other windows spotty, some sections black and dead. "I don't think so," she says slowly. "There was a guard. I think he'll live. There were a lot of electronics that failed. Not all. I think she was, um ... being careful." She is pulling at the laces of the boots. It is so easy to do two things at once, with the angel's light in her.

She doesn't touch him again. She only pulls on the boots, which are slightly too small and nibble at her toes.

"Thank Christ." Something loosens in Colin's stance, though he holds himself tensely, chin up, looking across the street as though he's barely preventing himself from bolting toward the main entrance and the line of cots by the ambulance bay. Verity resists the urge to block him, though he isn't actually moving. His hand is rigid on his cane.

"We're done," continues Colin, tersely. "No more fighting, no more—no more of that mess outside your place. I'm sorry about that. I couldn't stop her; I couldn't stop any of them." When Verity would interrupt him, he bulls ahead: "She was the only one who could go in there. All those machines. All that need. We weren't going to leave you, though. Come on. We don't have much time." He extends his free hand toward Jihan without looking; he's already shifting his weight when she steps in to his side, letting him take her arm. He pauses to fumble one-handed at the misaligned buttons of her sweater, quick and practised as he straightens them. "And you," he adds to her, "you keep it up. *You don't hurt anyone.* You remember."

The tall woman cocks her head to the side and extends her free hand to touch Colin's hair with her fingers. For a moment, there's a line between her eyebrows.

Verity sees them look at each other. Holding her own precious clarity close in her chest, she perceives the angel's infinite regret and the lithe puzzlement of the woman he leans on. It almost seems as though Jihan will say something.

"No," says Colin then, roughly. "I haven't forgiven you yet."

It's a lie—Verity feels it scratch against her bones, the first abrupt jarring of her new peace—but both have already turned away from her, walking away from the road and into the park behind. There's a sign:

Lynda Lane. There's a light in the trees that stutters and burns out as they pass underneath. Colin's slight glow bobs unevenly. Between the two of them, only his feet crunch audibly in the winter drifts.

Verity sighs and follows, her own footsteps a whispered crackle. "Is Ouroboros...?"

"He's all right. He and Stefan've gone with the others. They wanted to come here, but they were the best I could send to the stadium. That damn concert, or whatever Privya's—it's definitely going down tonight. Can you feel the air? I've never seen Jihan just fry a building by walking through."

"The Chalice? But I'm here. Doesn't Privya need me?"

"Alan's gone," says the angel, shortly. "Took the little girl with him. Stefan sent Ouro to guard her and found a pile of concert tickets on her grandfather's bed." Trees loom over them. They are keeping to a path, but a fallen branch cracks beneath his foot.

Verity feels her stomach drop. "She's too young. She doesn't understand."

"No shit she doesn't." Colin is limping with haste, balanced between the cane and the silent woman at his side. He crackles despite the fleshless wasting of his body; like Jihan, he is alert, energized. Not only does his pale glow light the path, it casts a warm reassurance that lets Verity focus even as she resists its comfort. Everything is not okay.

"Alan doesn't want to hurt anyone." Of this, Verity is certain. The words are still easy to say; they are ghosted with grey, but there's no undercurrent of oil.

"I don't know what he's doing. I don't know how it's come to this. Look, whatever it is—I don't want you to come with us."

"What?"

Colin glances back over his shoulder; Verity catches the momentary flare of burning blue eyes. When he looks back to the path, he says, "Don't do anything. Whatever it is anyone wants from you—don't do it. Let this cup of power or whatever it is—let it pour out and die."

"But then you'll die too."

"Probably. Look, stop, hold up a minute—thanks." When Jihan pauses, the angel lets go of her arm and turns, bracing both of his hands on the head of the cane. Verity has a sudden impression of Santiago and Ouroboros; Colin and Jihan stand simultaneously still, heads cocked at identical angles, both looking at her. But the woman's eyes are blankly reflective; the boy's are shining.

"We'll die." Colin's voice trembles, but there's strength in the line of his shoulders. "Some have. You saw, outside your house: they threw themselves against her. Like lemmings. I felt them die, and they were terrified—not just of the pain, but before. That's how scared they were of her. That's how real this danger is. So we can't. We can't open up some door somewhere else if it ends everything that's here."

It costs him just to say it; Verity doesn't need the soft clarity of his light to be aware of the tic in his jaw, or the way his hands clench on the head of the cane. The shine of tears in his eyes lodges in her own throat. Colin doesn't look away.

He continues with quiet intensity: "And Privya—she'd kill how many of them, just to give a few of us what, a few more years, or another generation suffering a losing fight? I can't choose us or them, not—we're not *better* than they are. Your boyfriend—he seems nice. It's not his fault he can't see us screaming. So choose peace. I can't tell you what to do, but I'm asking: let it go. We're going to head over there and stop Privya if we can, but that's all. I'll help who I can for as long as I can, and then ... well. The walls will be empty. But no one's killing anyone else, if I can stop it. I sat there on your sidewalk and I felt that poor woman's life slide out of my hands. No more. It was bad, that first day, when Jihan left you bleeding on the floor. I didn't know how much worse it could be. Let it go."

Verity wants to touch him—not for herself, but for the boy in the big coat, standing there with broken dreams littering the ice-slippery pathway at his feet. Jihan is a wordless guardian at his side; her attention falls on him, but then a breeze stirs the trees and she's scanning instead in the direction of rustling branches. So Colin stands alone, and Verity's hand twitches, but she only shakes her head.

"Alethea, um—whoever she was. She maybe understood this, and she failed. I *don't* understand. I—I wish I did. So it's okay. I mean, not okay. But I won't take the risk." She doesn't know she's decided until she's said it, the words coming in a low torrent. "I'm sorry," she adds to Jihan, but Jihan is watching for ghosts in the encroaching starlight.

"All right," breathes Colin, and this time he does look away, blinking rapidly.

"Thank you. For coming for me. Even though I don't know how to help."

"I'm sorry it couldn't be sooner. All those damn machines. I'll be honest: I don't know how this is going to turn out, so we weren't going to leave you there for after." Colin attempts a smile, but to Verity, the expression is a wasp about to sting. The angel only shakes his head and reaches for Jihan again. "I'm sorry we couldn't bring you much. If your boyfriend will let you back in...."

"I don't think he will." Regret is an animal clawing; it hurts more than Verity thought it would. "But I'm going with you. I'm not going to do—whatever Alethea tried. I won't." She jams her hands in the pockets of the unfamiliar coat. "I want to help. And...." She pauses, looking for words, but there is no time and the night is descending. "I want to *see*," she says. "Since Santiago, the first day in the market. Since the knife. I told you all I wanted was to understand. When I'm not with you, everything is grey. I want to know."

It's the truest thing she's said to him. His sapphire gaze flares with the force of her need—as though she had come to him with a tumour, or a gaping chest wound. Colin sucks in a breath. "Christ." There's no vitriol in his tone—only sadness and the terrible grace of his forgiveness. He's already turning. "Then let's go. God only knows what they're up to now."

"Any truth is better than indefinite doubt."
—Arthur Conan Doyle

22

[FOOTAGE FROM PRE-CONCERT FOR THE BETWEEN; LANSDOWNE PARK EXTERIOR, MARCH 5 2014]

[TRANSCRIPT BEGINS **NOTE HAVING A REAL PROBLEM WITH THIS FOOTAGE; CAMERA BATTERY ISSUE?]

JAMES ST JOHN: --you seen the band before?

GIRL IN BLUE SHIRT [**NOTE WHY DO WE NOT HAVE INFO FOR INTERVIEWEES; THINK JILL WAS FIGHTING WITH CAMERA]: No! Their concerts are super rare. That's half the—not even sure—before

[**NOTE FOOTAGE IS CHOPPY; SKIPS HERE]

ST JOHN: -- band before?

MAN IN RED HAT: Oh sure, totally.

GIRL IN BLUE SHIRT: Oh my god, you liar!

MAN IN RED HAT: I have! You wouldn't—was—before they were cool.

[STATIC]

ST JOHN: Seriously, are you getting it this time?

CAMERA OPERATOR (offscreen): I'm trying, but this camera is for shit.

ST JOHN: Okay, let's—the

[STATIC]

MAN WITH BRAIDS: My cousin's ex-girlfriend's sister said she saw them one time, and it was amazing, you know?

ST JOHN: When was this?

MAN WITH BRAIDS: Uh, let me think, when did he break up with her ... I was in college, maybe '98? And—saw—ago

[STATIC]

ST JOHN: —freaking useless—piece—tell Evelyn—goddamn equipment—we're not paid—just shut it—

[VIDEO ENDS]

MARCH

The *between* is humming.

The lights in their sconces gleam brighter than ever, casting their illumination across spotless floors. As always, the walls in the narrow hall rise to darkness above, but even that endlessness overhead seems charged with possibility that shivers across her skin like the promise of a coming static shock.

Verity has never seen this hall before and has to breathe it in. She has followed Jihan and Colin through the side of an older house across the park from the hospital, and she is trying to settle the knowledge in her veins before it fades—the precise way Jihan opened the door that wasn't, twisting it perhaps left instead of right, duplicating Privya's tricks with casually perfect intricacy, a fall of sand echoing.

This *between* is lined with the same faint lights that illuminate the inside walls of McLuhan's, but the long space is ramshackle and eccentric:

wooden boards turn to faded brick become crumbling stucco, each patch-work section of wall holding its own mismatched door. Many doors are marked with neat white chalk letters on fading paint—a tall red set of double doors reading CHÂTEAU LAURIER, a doorknob jutting from a narrow plank of flaking blue paint that says BYWARD, a rich mahogany door displaying SPARKS. Verity tilts her head at a wide oak door with only a rough winged figure scrawled across it. "Is this...?"

"The one we came through, from the theatre. Far as we can tell, this is what Alan was talking about. Doors leading all across the city. Keep going—I'd like to find Stefan." Colin is a little breathless. When Jihan strides silently forward, he hobbles at speed to follow, balanced between his cane and the sleeve of Verity's borrowed coat; he is careful not to touch Verity, but his wings keep opening, half flapping to boost him along, black feathers escaping his coat to brush at closed doorways.

They follow Jihan down the hallway's length, past doors both tall and short, small and wide, plank and painted. They pass a door that says MANOTICK MILL and another reading NOT THIS ONE.

"How far does it go?"

"Got me. I've had all of five minutes in here. Hoping there's a later when we can explore it, if her majesty will bring us back here again."

Verity steps carefully; the floor is like the walls, alternating brick and wood and cracked old tile, though she notices it's free of dust. She curls one hand in the air in front of her, trying again to recapture the exact motion of Jihan opening the door to this place. "It's clean," she murmurs. "The chalk...."

"Yeah, someone's labelled the doors. Gotta figure Privya's people have been all through here. Haven't seen any, though. I'm itching to try some of these knobs." Colin's hand flexes briefly on Verity's sleeve. Ahead of them, Jihan has pulled a leather strap from somewhere and uses it to bind the end of her hair as she walks, before she flips the braid back over her shoulder.

Verity wants to breathe the texture of this new impossible place—to run her fingers along the walls and taste each door, but Jihan is striding quickly, or at least paced just carefully enough that Colin can follow, though his breath huffs with each step. "Has she been able to ..." she shakes her head, redirecting the question to Jihan's bobbing braid. "Did you know how to come here? All this time?"

She is not surprised when there is no response. Colin chuckles breath-lessly at her elbow. "I asked that too."

"Should Jihan even be—" Verity doesn't get very far with that thought because Jihan has shot a look back over her shoulder, one eyebrow nearly raised.

"Good luck with that, also." Colin shakes his head. "I told her we'd be safer if she'd stay away. Didn't get very far with that one. She came with me to the hospital, and now she's doing whatever the fuck she wants." He stops, holding Verity in place just long enough to tilt his jaw back, exposing a small nick red and raised against the pale line of his throat. "That was her."

Verity's spine goes stiff. "She wouldn't hurt you."

"Doubt it. But it's only her gracious attitude that keeps her doing what I ask. Look," Colin adds to Jihan's cool stare, "we're hardly fighting you. And thanks for getting Vee. But slow down a friggin' half-second if you can."

Jihan holds for three beats with only a muted air of impatience before she resumes a pace that is just on the low end of hurried.

Verity looks down at the top of Colin's head. "It's dangerous for you, too."

"Privya hates me, but she won't hurt me as long as I'm helping anyone else. It's not us she's at war with."

"What do we do when we get there?"

"I'd say find that idiot Alan before he finds Privya, but judging by those tickets, we're too late. I don't know. We just ... we stop her. And no one gets hurt. Especially not that little girl."

Between Colin's persistent glow and the sharp insistence that marks the *between,* Verity finds the world almost achingly clear—blurred only by the crimson-copper edge of Jihan's slim form, or the despair and the terrible compassion bound in equal measures between the angel's pinions. She ventures, "Do you think it's possible?"

"I don't know." Colin's voice is tight. "We'll sure as hell friggin' try. How much has gone this far because of people trying to help me? Not Privya—Jihan. Stefan. Hell, maybe you. Stefan wants a way out, but more than that, he wants a way to get *me* out. And I've let him, but we're done."

Their pace doesn't abate, but Verity reaches her left hand across and squeezes Colin's shoulder, lightly, through the worn fabric of his voluminous coat. In the space between hops, he finds the breath to sigh.

Jihan stops by a broad wooden door with an old-fashioned cut-glass knob. The panelling is scratched, fire-scarred at one corner, but a faded '5' is visible in smeared chalk.

Jihan doesn't look back before she slips through; a few steps later, Verity reaches for the knob and brings Colin through with her. Tonight, the transitions are easier than blinking.

She is prepared for the bitter onslaught of the city outside, but with Colin beside her, it's easier; even the streaks and wails of Ottawa in the winter night are little challenge to Verity's senses. She knows she's drawing on the angel, but when she moves to step away, he says, "It's all right. Use it. I'm good for something tonight." His light is dimmer outside of the *between,* but he still glows. His eyes are sparking with inner fireflies.

They are back in the Glebe, on the treed leafiness of Fifth Avenue. The street is lined with townhouses similar to Jacob's: tall, narrow, with wooden steps and fading paint. Night has descended, and the streetlight that illuminates the block dies almost before Verity registers its presence.

"Any way for you to stop that? Damp it down, or—we can't walk into a crowded area if you're going to nuke every piece of tech in sight." Colin's hair is in his eyes. He lets go of Verity's arm long enough to brush it back, glancing down the street.

Jihan looks at him; her face remains inhumanly smooth but she lets one shoulder rise and fall.

"Christ, well that's terribly reassuring. Let's go. I don't think it's far."

They walk down Fifth toward Bank Street; Verity is relieved when the next light they pass below dims but holds. Colin says, "Thanks," but no one is surprised when Jihan fails to respond.

This door has brought them only a few blocks from Lansdowne Park; they turn left on Bank, where a pub in a low mall is marked by a hanging sign that declares 'The Blade and Goose.'

"That's probably us. I'm the goose." Colin is talking to Jihan again. She does glance back at him, then she stills, glaring at a passing car. She waits for Colin and Verity to pass her before she stalks them down the sidewalk.

"She's got no sense of humour, is her problem."

"I'm not sure that's, um, the whole problem."

"Yeah. Well." This stretch of Bank, farther south of McLuhan's, is lined with small storefronts, most of which are closed. They pass a stone-fired pizza parlour; through the window, a group of young men is clustered around a table, laughing. The men don't look over as Colin and Verity pass, though one of them shoots Jihan a bemused stare.

Lansdowne Park is set off from the main street; the stadium looms, seats jutting on either side of a football field, the sloping rows covered by a single long roof that gives the building a jagged, precariously balanced appearance defying its concrete solidity. Beside it, a series of mid-rise rectangular buildings are darkly shining, close together and close to the street. Their windows glitter. Verity thinks she sees a neon restaurant sign struggling bravely, half its letters dying. A traffic signal on the street has burned out, and a man in a police uniform is directing a slow trickle of cars, some of which turn downward into the underground parking lot. As Verity, Colin, and Jihan approach, a car dies on the ramp. Someone blows a horn.

Verity shakes her head; the block's slick modernity slaps at her. Beside her, she feels Colin shiver.

She says, "Really?"

He shrugs. "This is the place. Got a poster in my pocket if you really want to check."

They turn inward, away from Bank and between the close rectangular buildings, walking toward the plaza. Jihan passes in front of them, weaving unhesitatingly around other, slower pedestrians. There are signs: a movie theatre, a bar, a restaurant. Verity swallows logos like seeping tar.

A block in, the looming glass of the new buildings opens; a broad, flat area paved with walkway tiles serves as a wide courtyard before the entrance to the Aberdeen Pavilion. Verity feels Colin suck in a breath beside her and realizes she has been holding hers. The exhibition hall's Victorian curves are brightly lit. It's a long, low building that would have been tall in its day; it has the general shape of a large barn, with a stately dome rising at its centre and smaller silver domes gracing each corner. In comparison, the surrounding buildings are a sleek glass wall, setting the small, pale yellow length of the hall somewhere out of place and time. An excitedly chattering crowd mills around the central double doorway.

"All right, well, here's the bad news." Colin draws to a halt, Verity beside him. "I don't know what we do now."

"Here." Santiago emerges from behind a crochet-wrapped couple much more interested in each other than in him; he glides through the small crowd, his blackness dull in the growing night.

"Glad you got out," he tells Verity, "though surprised you're here," and he's looking at Colin but he holds out a hand to her, as if in greeting; puzzled, she accepts. As she does, she feels the odd, rough weightlessness of Ouroboros enter her sleeve, wriggling its way up her arm. The snake slides down her back, outside the worn hospital gown, and winds its way around her ribs; she feels it getting longer before it comes to a rest. She presses a palm against its slender bulk and feels it contract ever so slightly around her.

"Look at that," observes Colin, pleased. "She does smile. Yeah, she's here. It's all right. The others?" His sparking gaze scans people nearby.

"Most are by the entrance. I sent Rick and Stacy inside."

"I thought you were going to watch out for them?"

"They're fine. I waited for you." The magician conjures a playing card, dancing the four of clubs between his fingers as he turns to look back at the pavilion. "I bought tickets a few weeks ago, thanks to Vee's petty cash, and Alan left us more, but let's be honest; if we could stop anything by going in legit, no one would let us, and we certainly wouldn't be invited. We're trying to check the building, but there's security everywhere. We've made the lights flicker a couple of times. No sign of—does she even have a band? What is she doing? Why are all of these people even *here*?"

"Jacob says it's, um, on the internet—all these rumours about The Between. People saying they've seen them, that they're great."

"Guess we've been laying the groundwork." Colin shakes his head. "We made a rumour, and now it's some indie music legend. People just want to be in on something, I guess."

Santiago looks at Verity. "He tell you about Alan?"

"Yes. Why would—"

"Don't know. We need to find him, fast. No one's seen him, or Privya, or the little girl. Don't think I'm not terrified this isn't one giant distraction and they're all the damn way across town."

"This doesn't feel like—" Verity wraps her arms around herself and feels the snake curled around her torso; she looks at the stadium, then at Colin. "It's all grey," she tells him. "It's based on a lie, but not all a lie. I don't know how to ... Jihan wants you to be here."

Their attentions turn to the tall woman in the ragged pastel sweater, who is somehow positioned with ample space between herself and any passing would-be concert-goer. She stands with her arms folded; by all appearances, she is watching the crowd. Her hair is still neatly braided, in contrast to the thready mess of the scarf tied around her bicep.

"Do you?" Colin asks her, his feathered brows drawing down. "We're not helping you, either. What *are* we doing?"

In response, Jihan turns—her gaze rakes them all without recognition—and then walks confidently across the courtyard toward the bright pavilion. A group of teenagers scatters in front of her like startled pigeons.

"Right." Colin reaches for Santiago's arm this time, gripping the magician at the elbow as they take off after the striding woman. Verity follows, holding the coat closed, conscious of the snake, and her bare legs in the cold, and the uncomfortable pinch of too-small boots.

They find a thin spot in the crowd, or Jihan does, and cross the remaining swath of smooth concrete squares toward the pavilion's curving roof. A few steps further, though, and Santiago slows. Security guards with matching green jackets and folded arms are stationed at regular intervals along the wall, blocking the way.

"The hell?" The magician has paused, the angel and Verity with him; Jihan continues forward.

"Look," says Verity, who points upward. This close, the roof of the pavilion is alive; dragons slither. Spotlights have been positioned in a distant ring to illuminate the building walls—a pale yellow, with white trim—and the long roof curves in a smooth arch, covered in a layer of snow, lit by lights cast down from the stadium. The creatures on it are visible in barest glimpses as they peer off the edge, eyes bright with reflected halogen. As Verity watches, two more flap in to settle somewhere above.

Colin says, "There," and gestures toward a cat with too many legs that is just vanishing around the building's corner.

"I thought I saw a hippogriff circling. Not many of those left. Hope no one looks up. Okay, where is she going?" Santiago is impatient, his motions uncharacteristically jerky, though Verity notices that when he steps after Jihan, he is still careful to choose the clearest path through the gathered crowd so that no one will jostle Colin.

She feels Ouroboros wriggling upward just enough that it can position its head at the edge of her collar. "Can't you use Santiago's eyes?" she asks it, bemused, but it only squeezes around her. Glancing again at the glint of a dragon at the roof's edge, she follows Jihan. It's difficult to move quickly—the crowd of people is a blur of sound, rippling conversations that bring with them tastes and touches and a mess of odd smells. Verity still has a hint of Colin's peace in her chest, though, and she lets the last of it buoy her past the flash of a boy's golden arrogance and a man laughing like smoke. A girl in a paisley coat is jabbing at the dead screen of her phone, muttering.

Jihan ignores the ticket-takers and the line at the main entrance; instead, she heads for the corner of the building, following the path of the many-legged cat. She stops and narrows her eyes at a spotlight positioned to beam down from a restaurant roof; it flickers, but doesn't go out. She chooses her path more widely instead, tracing the edge of illumination.

Along the wall, security people watch her but say nothing.

"She almost had that." Santiago has stopped to wait for Verity, though only barely before she catches up and he resumes his pace, Colin a short and sharp contrast that hobbles pale at his side. Verity realizes they both have shadows: the angel's is long, and the magician's is narrow, a little too short, and slightly writhing. His gaze is oiled with power, and she is barely able to look sidelong at the illusions that cling to his boots. Around her, the snake wriggles with scarcely subdued energy.

"She's been a pro all night," comments the angel, breathless again. "You should've seen her at the hospital. We're all stronger. Matt was sitting up when I left. You can't feel it?"

"I can feel it," confirms Santiago. "Ouro could be an anaconda if he wanted. And there's more: there's a door somewhere around here."

"What? I thought you checked it?"

"I did. Walked around the entire place as soon as those damn posters went up. The building's old enough, but there was no *between*. There is now."

"Yes," agrees Verity, who hadn't thought about it, but is now aware of that subtle vibration in her bones.

There's a group of about eight people clustered around the building's back door; like the others, they are wearing black knit hats and official-looking green jackets, the logo of some company embroidered on the upper right chest. Two are leaning against the wall. At least one more is smoking, the glow of her cigarette butt bobbing as she gestures conversationally to a much taller companion.

"No hurting anyone." Colin's voice is low but sharp, punctuated with gasps as he hurries. "I mean it."

Verity glances over and sees Santiago's lips tighten. Ouro constricts beneath her coat. The magician murmurs, "Remember what's at stake."

"I know what's at stake. We'd be no better than she."

Jihan only strides confidently toward a man who's silhouetted in front of the pavilion door. He's of thin build and middling height; he's not wearing a hat, and his hair is a mess of frizzy dreadlocks slightly too long for order.

Verity perceives his startling familiarity in the instant before he turns. She remembers an afternoon in the kitchen, with sunlight on his laughter—flour dust and the scent of ginger drifting across her skin.

"Hold up," says Jacob. "You can't come—" He stops. He has caught his own reflection in Jihan's eyes.

Verity is surprised he is here. She supposes she is less surprised that of all the guards surrounding the building, Jihan unerringly made her way to this one.

Jacob is caught short, his lips still slightly parted. His breath frosts in the air, unspent. He stares at Jihan as she walks up; she stops two feet in front of him and folds her arms.

At the door, the other people working security have now straightened or turned; they cluster in a loose group, watching. One man puts a hand on the walkie-talkie at his belt.

Jacob stares at Jihan and then looks to Santiago and Colin. There's another flash of recognition across his face; he gives Colin a particularly bemused look, then catches sight of Verity. A number of questions parade across his wide-eyed features and die unsaid. He settles on, "You're not supposed to be here. They're supposed to be helping you."

Verity swallows. "They can't. They never could."

"But how did—what are you wearing?"

Verity feels the weight of the trench coat on her shoulders; it's growing too thin for the frigid night, and she pulls it closer. She feels Ouroboros slide through the fine hairs at the back of her neck. "I, um.... I think we need to get inside."

A burly man with a swath of ginger beard snorts and takes a step in front of the door. "Ticket line's out front."

Santiago gives him a flat look. Beside the magician, Colin runs narrow fingers through the fine ivory mop of his hair. There's a sheen of sweat developing on his skin. He is agitated, watching Jihan, but she only stands as before, staring at Jacob.

Jacob looks back at her, then at his coworkers by the door. Muttering something under his breath, imprecations that puff in the night, he takes Jihan by the upper arm—casually, familiarly—and pulls her away from the door, back toward the privacy of a shadowed piece of pavement.

Colin's breath catches, but Jihan does nothing except walk with Jacob. Her right eyebrow twitches.

They all follow; they end up in a little cluster, their backs turned to any enquiring eyes.

"Vee should be seeing a shrink right now, and you all want to hear *music?*"

"Why are you here?" Verity asks Jacob. "We were already security guards. We tried that in the first month."

"We were going to be roadies. Except you weren't here, and neither is the damn band. No one's showed. Right now, we're counting down until the guy out front calls it, and then we see if anyone riots." The normal puppy-enthusiasm of Jacob's smile is missing entirely; his ebony freckles stand out accusingly against the sienna of his skin, even in the shadows. Verity sees lines at the edges of his mouth that she's never seen before; they taste of rancid milk and something sharp in her gut. He still has a hand at Jihan's shoulder, and Colin's eyes are growing wilder with each passing moment.

"Look," begins Santiago, but Jacob cuts him off.

"I'm not interested in what you say, or in what you've got Vee involved in. Leave her with me and I won't call the cops. How's that?"

The snake tenses around Verity, harder than before; she exhales at the sudden constriction, then pokes a thumb into the side of her coat and has the satisfaction of seeing Santiago flinch. Her focus is on Jacob, though. She chooses her words with care. "We need to get inside. There's a girl who's going to hurt a lot of people."

"Okay. Then *you* call the cops."

"That won't—"

Jihan is the one who moves. Her stillness cracks completely and without warning; she is faster than Ouroboros, and faster than Colin's choked sound of protest when she slides her hand behind Jacob's neck.

Verity experiences a moment of sick vertigo where *she sees Jacob's neck snap and the sound of it is sharp as dry-cracking timber; it is red in her nostrils and despair across her tongue,* but when the sparks of fear dissipate, Jacob lives, and Jihan has pressed her lips to his.

They stand interlocked, Jihan an inch taller, Jacob broader across the shoulders and frozen in abject startlement for the second time in as many minutes. She leans into him, and the instant he remembers to breathe is almost palpable; he slips an arm around her waist and leans in, kissing her back.

Ouroboros wends around Verity's neck, a shadowed choker. She is watching Jacob—Jacob melting and reshaping, Jacob *finally* whole—but she reaches up one hand and brushes her fingertip very lightly across the top of the snake's head.

When Jihan steps back, she raises both hands to cup Jacob's face. She looks him straight in the eyes—she waits for him to blink and focus. He only stares at her for a long, bright-eyed moment. A hint of his easy grin plays along his lips before he says, "I'll come with you."

Her hands drop; his smile goes out. Jacob sighs.

"All right," he says. "You do you. Just go."

He gestures toward the door with one loose hand; Jihan slips past him and strides forward. Santiago and Colin are almost rigid, but then the angel shakes his head and they follow.

Jacob catches at Verity's arm. She raises her chin when she turns to him, but he only looks puzzled. "Your friend," he says. "The kid. Is he ... kind of shining?"

Verity blinks. "Yes." But she has no time. She pulls her sleeve free and hurries after Santiago.

"Hey," calls the burly man at the door, folding his arms as he jerks his chin toward Jacob. "Rookie. Letting your buddies sneak in isn't part of the deal."

"I'll match your night's pay." Jacob sounds, abruptly, exhausted. "It looks like there's no show anyway. Just shut up, Gary. Let 'em through. I'll make it up to you." At that, the security group is suffused with a sudden onslaught of shrugs.

As the guards peel away, the spotlight shining on the door finally blinks and then dies. "Aw, for ... someone wanna check that light?" Gary thumbs his walkie-talkie, then presses the button again. "I'm not going up there. Is this even on?"

"Leave it," comments the smoking woman. "That thing was killing my eyes. The band doesn't like it, they can complain themselves." She opens the door and bows sardonically; Jihan sweeps through as regally as any queen. Santiago and Colin follow; Verity takes the rear and resists the urge to look back. She can feel Jacob's stare pinning her shoulder blades.

Inside is blissfully warm and rocked by a coasting hubbub of sound that comes to Verity in waves; she is momentarily mid-ocean before Colin brushes his fingertips against the back of her hand and the building around her solidifies. Everything echoes; the broad, long pavilion is all open space inside, and there is clearly a crowd, though Verity can't see it. She finds herself standing just inside the door at the back of the hall, behind long black curtains that separate the small backstage area from what sounds to be the audience seating at the front. The curtains drape along the back of the low stage that's been set up, and security guards stand here, too. Some look bored, others agitated ("What do you mean, no one's called?" "Seriously, no opening act?" "How long are we supposed to stand around here?"). A few shoot suspicious looks at the new arrivals, but Jihan and Santiago in particular move with sublime confidence, stepping immediately to the left and following the line of the wall around toward the rear of the building. Colin holds to Santiago. Verity sets her shoulders back and follows. Within her coat, Ouroboros wriggles up to her shoulder and winds itself around her right bicep. "That's very distracting," she murmurs, and the snake holds momentarily still.

It's murky backstage—a sharp contrast from the glaring spotlights outside—but there are theatre lights set up for the crew to work. Verity is relieved to see them stay lit, though a few have already begun strobing.

The rumble of the crowd continues to wash around Verity's feet like a low river; she is careful not to tread in the currents of impatience. The complaints flow restlessly. Above, tiny winged figures flap amongst the narrow metal rafters that support the hall's high roof. If she doesn't look, she can catch other creatures wriggling at the corners of her eyes—not the cat this time, but something scurrying with a tail like a broken disco ball, and something else even smaller that only lurks beneath the back corner of the stage, visible as a single broken-clawed, mangy paw and flat pink teeth.

Jihan is lost against deepening shadows, but Verity follows Colin's soothing peace and Santiago's darkness. The air in the pavilion is close, warmed by breath and sweating bodies, and Verity feels a line of moisture run down the back of her neck that she is fairly certain is actually wet and not an echo of the rippling noise.

The space between curtain and wall is narrow, not unlike navigating the hallways *between*. Now that Santiago has called attention to it, Verity too can feel the doorway that waits somewhere ahead and to the right.

They round the corner at the back and there is only one figure waiting there—ten feet away, half-sitting in what is partly a crouch and partly a slump. She wouldn't be tall even if she were standing. She has the look of a beetle that's been stepped on. There's a light above that doesn't quite land on her, focusing instead on the bare floor beside her. It brushes the curled fingers of her hand.

It's probably Colin's pale bobbing that catches her attention; when the figure turns her head, Verity sees her round face and the whiteness of the teeth gnawing at her lower lip. It's Shauna, her breathing strenuous as she draws in her heels and struggles to her feet, one hand against the wall. Orange lines run under her skin, outlining the veins of her throat and hands like slow-running lava. It occurs to Verity that she doesn't know what Shauna does, or could do, on a night when power thrums in the air.

Santiago gestures, and the shadows roil. Verity feels Ouroboros slide toward the end of her sleeve.

"Don't," snaps Colin, and Jihan whirls to face him, her knife already in hand. She is a portrait of perfect movement, her glare unmistakeable. It is abruptly clear, human, and eminently frustrated.

The angel adds, more quietly, "Please." The shadows at least subside, and Ouroboros settles for wrapping itself around Verity's wrist; Jihan doesn't put up her knife, but she holds in place.

Shauna glowers, but also coughs, then spits a gobbet of blood on the ground.

"Jesus." Colin gestures Santiago to stay and hobbles forward alone, leaning on his cane. He touches Jihan's hand on the way past.

"Don't you come near me."

"I'm not going to hurt you." Colin stops, though, and stands there with one hand outstretched. Verity can only see the back of his voluminous coat, flaring with the twitch of his wings, but she can imagine his gaze, its glitter called by someone else's pain. "She didn't really leave you here? Alone?"

"I volunteered." Shauna spits again, then wipes the back of her hand across her mouth. "I'm the last."

"You're hurt."

Shauna's attention lashes toward Jihan, then back to Colin. "Yeah. Well. You're still not getting through here."

"Let me help you."

"Fuck off." Shauna's face is hangdog, her ember eyes yellowed, harsh lines of pain etched into her flesh. Her lips are smeared with red; she is more visible in the glow that Colin casts. The angel is brighter in the presence of need.

"Let me help you," says Colin, patiently. "You can fight us after that, if you really want. We're not enemies. We're all just unlucky assholes. If you know me, you know I don't have a knife or a dog. I've never punched anyone in my goddamn life. All I do is heal people. So take my hand."

Shauna stares at Colin for a long moment, then her attention shifts again to Jihan, and to Santiago. She lingers only a moment on Verity before she looks back to Colin.

It occurs to Verity that she doesn't know anything about Shauna— where she's from, what her life has been like, whether she has children or a pet or a job. Her accent is mid-east North American. Her face is ashen now with blood loss. Her hair is brown, but specked with white, and she doesn't look like a warrior but she holds herself with confidence, straightening her shoulders and forcing that glowing orange *something* through her veins.

Indecision flits across Shauna's face, but she's locked eyes with the angel, and with one abrupt motion she reaches out and grabs Colin's hand.

Verity is expecting a flare of light; she sees only a strengthening of the glow that escapes Colin's coat, and blue reflected on Shauna's slack and wondering face. Colin only holds on for a moment. When he pulls his hand back, the woman lets him go; Shauna's cheeks are wet with tears.

Santiago takes two steps forward, but Colin waves him back. "It's all right. A good night for healing, I guess."

Shauna's voice is rough. "Thank you. And I'm sorry. You still can't pass."

"Chrissake, lady, what are you going to do?" Colin shakes his head. "We're not going to break anything. We're not going to fight you. We just need to stop Privya. You really want her to kill, what? Thousands? A hundred thousand? More? What's it going to help?"

Santiago and Jihan stand alert, waiting. Verity can feel the snake wrapped around her wrist. Its tongue whispers against the back of her hand.

"It's us or them."

Colin sighs, spreading his hands. "Yeah, maybe. But they don't know that. They aren't hurting us on purpose. Haven't you been listening to that crowd? Are you just sitting here, hearing them laugh, knowing how many of them are about to die?"

Shauna has tears running down her face; she makes no effort to wipe the moisture away. The orange in her veins dims as Colin hesitates.

"That's your life I just gave you. Don't burn through it just so someone else can take a run at genocide."

Shauna flinches in another flare of sullen orange; she shakes her head. Closing her eyes, she draws in a long breath, then glances again at Jihan. "She can't go down with you."

"Well, I'd stop her if I could, but she only does half of what I ask on a good day. Look, she'll carve you in half. That's not a threat, I promise. I've been terrified of her for the better part of a decade. I'm terrified for you." Colin spreads his hands, palms out, fingers outstretched. "I can tell you we've got Verity with us, and Vee's not going to help anyone. Jihan included."

Shauna looks to Verity, who only shakes her head.

"Who's Privya got with her?" Colin continues. "That little girl of Alan's? Can't speak? She doesn't know what the fuck's going on. Is that what we've come to—using children? Look, you're right. You've all been right. Whatever door we might open, it's not worth the risk. But mass murder isn't the answer, either."

Shauna stands, loose-limbed, and stares at Colin. Verity stays still. She thinks she sees Santiago and Jihan shift; she thinks Ouroboros slips toward the cuff of her sleeve, but the sounds of the crowd are growing edgier, and the surge threatens to swamp her in mustard impatience.

A flashlight cuts the shadows at the far corner of the wall, and two security guards come into view. The beam shines directly in Verity's face before someone shouts, "Hey!"

Verity is never sure whether Jihan cuts the lights or whether it's Santiago's illusions that slither to drop darkness down. Either way, the curtained hall goes pitch black, save for the lingering impression of muted orange and a kindly white-sapphire gleam. Ouroboros erupts from her sleeve, latching onto her wrist with its tail. She feels a shift, and then they are *between*.

Shauna doesn't stop them.

The crowd is abruptly silenced.

Verity feels the ground solid beneath her feet and the familiar press of Ouroboros—a dog now—against her leg. She can see only the ghost-glow of Colin's face and the disembodied spark of his eyes. There's a pause before he says, "Anyone have a light?" His voice is low.

"Is there a lamp? Vee, check the wall to your left. Just by the door." Santiago sounds tense, but not alarmed; Verity feels the dog alert at her side. She reaches to the left, and behind herself; she encounters only rough stone.

"No. Do you think she'll come after us?"

"No." Colin's starlit gaze shifts side to side as he shakes his head. "Hell. I should've remembered. Privya had a lantern last time."

Light flares—not a match, but the quicksilver gleam that usually occupies the lamps of the *between*. In this case, it issues from a fist-sized rock Jihan holds in her left hand. Straightening from a fluid crouch, she offers it to Colin.

"Thanks—oh, Christ, you've bled all over it, haven't you." It isn't a question. Colin sighs. "We need to talk about this system of yours." He reaches for the rock, but doesn't take it; he grasps Jihan's bloodied wrist instead, and his light flares slightly as he heals whatever cut she's made.

He doesn't let go; he only holds her there, looking up at her.

"There's not much time," he says. "I don't—are we just reading things in to what you do? Assuming you'll do the same thing you tried before? You never tell us. I don't know what you want. But you haven't killed anyone tonight. You got Vee out. Thanks. But I need to know—really, truly—that when we go down there, you're not going to snipe Privya and open some portal to hell. You've been here. You've been listening. It's not worth it."

Santiago snorts. "You want to avert an apocalypse by asking nicely?"

"We're through fighting." Colin's voice is both steel and exhaustion. He doesn't look away from Jihan.

She meets his gaze, and the line between her eyebrows deepens, then melts away. Reaching forward with her other hand, she touches Colin's cheek—leaving a smear of wet darkness—and leans down, pressing her lips gently to his forehead. When she steps back, she leaves him holding the rock, its white glow somehow unmarred by crimson. For a single breath, the quirk of her lips is wry. Then she looks away, expression shifting to marble.

Colin's sparkling stare is briefly brighter than the light he nearly fumbles. "That ... holy shit, first. But also, that is maybe not as comforting as you imagine."

Jihan reverses her grip on her crack-bladed hunting knife and turns to proffer the weapon, hilt-first, to Verity.

Verity says, "Um."

Jihan only stands, precise and patient, continuing to offer the knife.

Hesitantly, Verity takes it. It's slightly heavier than she expected, but also smoother; the chipped hilt is well worn in her hand. Just the heft of it tastes of hot violence. She drops it awkwardly in a side pocket of her borrowed coat and wipes her palms against the lapel.

Jihan bows almost infinitesimally, takes three steps to the side, and vanishes into blackness.

"Damn it, now where's she—I'll take that as a promise." Colin bites at his lower lip. "And you," he adds to Santiago, quietly.

"I'll do what you want." The magician's voice is strained.

"Yeah. Well." Colin briefly transfers the lamp-rock to his cane hand and shrugs at his own coat. "A little help?" When Santiago helps him get the trench coat off, his wings rustle and flex; the angel breathes a sigh of relief, but he's already raising the light up to look around.

They are surrounded on three sides by a wall that is partially the pale cream yellow of the pavilion, and partially uneven brown stone; the mix of the two is oddly organic, as though they'd been liquefied and then frozen together again. The space is not as narrow as the *between* Verity has become accustomed to; it is not large, but they have room to stand a little spread out, and when Colin's wings stretch outward, the edge of a feather tip only brushes one wall. The angel is still aglow, but his light is dimmed in contrast to the brilliance of the stone in his hand. Their shadows—even Santiago's—are long on the walls. The door back is plain and yellow, with a metal knob. The *between* ahead is blackness.

"Well," observes Santiago. "Guess we go that way."

"Jihan obviously has." Colin frowns. "It'll be a staircase soon, if I remember. But also ... there's someone else up ahead? I can feel it." He doesn't sound certain, but he moves forward anyway, holding the rock out. His cane makes a clicking sound on the half-stone floor.

"Here. Let me go first." Santiago is already moving.

"I've got it—Jesus!" Colin's wings beat twice at the air, propelling him a step backward and filling the strange cave with wind. The light from his hand falls across the face of a young woman who sits splayed against the wall, her legs barring his path. She is wearing a security polo shirt over jeans and runners. Her skin is white, her black hair artfully straightened; strands of it dance in the play of feathered air. She blinks reflexively at the light and the wind, but her lips are slack and her chin is wet with drool.

Ouroboros has sprung forward, its teeth bared in a silent growl; its head low, it crowds the space between the angel and the staring woman. Verity, abruptly alone, steps toward Colin so she can take the rock and hold it high. Its shining surface looks rough, but against her palm, it is cool and clear-cut as a diamond.

"Thanks. Ouro, don't." Colin hands his cane to Santiago, then sets his hand against the wall and lowers himself carefully to kneel in front of the girl, his bad knee stretched out and his wings spread for balance. "She's barely here. She isn't here. Feels like someone miles away."

"Privya did it." Verity keeps the light steady. Looking at the stranger's empty face, she is acutely conscious of the weight of the knife in her pocket. She doesn't touch it. Ouro has returned to her side, and she breathes in the shadow-scent of the fur pressed against her bare legs.

"I know." Colin's glow brightens as he leans in close to the girl's face, tracing his fingers across her skin. His tone is tired. "Haven't seen it before, but—Privya's very old. She's used so many lives. It's no wonder she's so easy with death. Come on, sweetheart, can you hear me?"

The girl doesn't blink again. She only stares at nothing. The drool on her chin is fresh, though, and her shirt rises and falls with her breath.

"She's ... is she, was she, one of you?" Verity isn't sure whether to say 'us.'

"No. But she isn't anything, now. Easy enough for Privya to bring a shell *between*." Colin sighs. He squeezes the girl's shoulder, then stands, waving off Santiago's assistance. "I'm guessing Privya wanted to be strong for whatever's next. I can't do anything. Shit."

Santiago shakes his head. "I'm sorry for the girl, but we have to go. We can come back for her."

"Yeah." Colin is an open wound. He only steps over the girl's legs, carefully, then holds his hand out to take the rock back from Verity. This time, Ouroboros flows out in front of him, vanishing into the darkness before the angel can protest. Verity catches a glimpse of golden eyes before the dog is gone.

"Staircase ahead," reports Santiago. "Going down." Verity glances at him; in the faint light of the stone, his lips are thin with tension. He moves after Colin; Verity goes with him. Both are careful not to disturb the injured girl. "It's strange in here," he comments. "Besides the obvious, I mean. This shadow is none of mine. Ouro and I can't speak to it. It's old. It watches."

"It tastes like licorice," offers Verity.

Santiago snorts. "Red or black?"

"Black. Aniseed. But it's kind of, um ... fuzzy."

"You are *some* help."

"This is why I don't tell people things."

The magician conjures what momentarily looks like a snake, but is in fact a black scarf. He flourishes it, making the end dance a little, then tucks it in a pocket. "Stairs about ten feet ahead," he notes to Colin. "Ouro's waiting. There's more light below."

"Right." Colin's footsteps, already faster than he's generally prone to, pick up, irregular but speedy. The rhythm of his cane taps an eccentric beat on the ground. He flaps his wings, helping himself along, though he curses once when his feathers scrape the wall. "Here it is. Look, I've been here, or somewhere like it. The stairs'll lead down to a tunnel, and the tunnel to a cavern, and god only knows what Privya or Jihan is—do you feel that?"

The air in the hallway shivers.

"Yes." Santiago follows as closely behind Colin as he can without getting in the way of flapping wings. Ouroboros, still a dog, melts out of the darkness ahead and positions itself at Verity's side again. She drops a hand to its shoulders, letting it guide her. Ahead of her, Santiago sets his palm against the base of Colin's wings as though he might lend the angel further speed.

The floor does give way to stairs; they are smoothly cut from the same brown rock, descending gracefully in a spiral. No hint of the pavilion's yellow remains here. Everything is stone, and it grows rockier as they descend.

Verity expects the air to be musty, but in fact, it has a silvery fresh quality—as though it is new, and no one has ever breathed it before. She realizes the silver is light, getting brighter; she brushes the wall with her fingers and feels the coarse texture of faintly glowing lichen.

"Something here." Colin pauses, where a series of sigils and whorls is smeared dark and intricately dripping across the step and down both sides of the wall. It extends upward past sight. "Blood. Friggin' of course. What is it with those two?"

"What is it?"

Santiago leans around Colin, trying to get a better look at the ground. The stairwell is tight. "My guess is Privya left something to slow us down, and Jihan's broken it."

"So we can step over it?"

Santiago hesitates.

Verity murmurs, "Tell me it's safe."

Colin turns, craning his neck as he looks back upward. "Sorry?"

"Tell me it's safe. Like you mean it."

"It's safe."

Verity considers that—cider and fog—then nods. "Marbled, but not a lie. Keep going."

"Thanks." Colin taps his cane down on the next step; encountering no apparent resistance, he proceeds downward. Santiago follows, then Verity, with Ouro crowding at her.

"You could be a snake again," she suggests, but the dog only looks up with laughing yellow eyes, and she sighs. The streaks of blood brush her skin as she passes, spiked but soft. "Did Jihan cut—I have her knife."

Santiago snorts. "I'll eat Ouro if she only had one."

"Just come on." Colin's wings are beginning to take up too much room on the increasingly narrow stairs; the black feathers block the light in his hand, making Verity hesitate on the uncertain footing. She's grateful for the dog, even when it pushes impatiently at her knee.

The steps give way to rock as the curling stairwell levels out into a straight tunnel. "Almost there." Colin hefts the gleaming rock and pauses in front of another mess of bloody marks blocking his way. "Well, she's gone past, so." He steps past and nothing happens. Santiago, Verity and Ouro follow with caution.

A few steps further, the corridor begins to open up; Colin sighs with relief as he can stretch his wings. The walls ahead are illuminated by some other blue-white light that spills across the rocky floor; the angel hesitates.

Somewhere up ahead, a child laughs.

[**IMAGE:** Aberdeen Pavilion at night, lit by spotlights from surrounding buildings. It's late winter. A crowd has gathered in the courtyard.]

23

I'm not sure how to write this part.

youve come a long way

It's still for you. I know you want people to know.

thanks
when youre finished take the pages away
keep them safe
dont let me burn them

Will you read to the end?

once

All right. Before I finish: did you ever understand, about Jihan? Even a little?

jihan
we were exactly where she wanted us to be

You've tried to explain it. I just don't follow. She'd go days without looking at me. She carried that knife like it was her only friend. Then, one time, she watched a raindrop run down a window, and maybe I almost saw her smile.

jihan was a real person
alethea was a real person
i didnt know them none of us did except privya and
privya wouldnt say

What do you mean, real?

thats the problem a good question maybe i mean ~~real~~
maybe i mean they had childhoods and favourite
colours
jihans favourite colour is death not because she
doesnt care (she would have once) but she forgot how

you ~~wrote~~ typed the story about colin in the cavern
in san francisco

Yes?

Vee?

okay stop interrupting this is hard
leave me a few days between sentences

okay
imagine
~~hypothetical~~
two women one tried to open a door but it was a chasm
to swallow the earth
an accident
the other one stopped her but *stopped*
together
they broke the door
they stopped
for a century for ever they were
together
all their pieces scattered over time and possibility
even time has a *between*
colin had a choice gather one in let one go
imagine trying to come back from that
from everything everywhere
and be someone who spoke words and remembered your
mother
if you are part of eternity once can you ever not be
isnt that what eternity means

I think I understand now.

colin would never torture anyone on purpose

THE END

"Wait." Santiago presses himself against the wall and Ouroboros flows past, sliding sinuously beneath Colin's raised wing before it whips ahead and vanishes around the curve.

Colin flashes Santiago a look that manages to be indulgent, impatient, and terrified all at once; his irises spark sapphire, then he follows the dog. Santiago and Verity are close behind. Verity feels the weight of the knife in the pocket of her borrowed coat, heavy against her thigh.

The cavern that opens up in front of them is vast. Lichen gleams faintly, illuminating shapes and shadows, but the walls spill away to either side and the ceiling vanishes above. There are narrow stalagmites rising from the floor, and stalactites that descend from some hidden darkness to drop like ghostly swollen fingers toward the ground.

The floor of the cavern slopes upward, toward what is presumably the centre; at the top of this low, lumpen hill, a beacon burns that dwarfs the faint glow from the walls or the steadily shining rock in Colin's hand. Verity has to blink and raise one hand to shield her eyes from the crystal-bell ringing.

She can just make out a stalagmite that is thick at the base and broken off where it begins to taper, rising perhaps four feet from the ground. It's from the top that the light spills. Blinking into the beam, Verity can inhale colours rising in a rainbow braid, tinting the air with pastel that tastes of forged steel. Privya stands on one side, up to her wrists in light. She is wearing a loose red t-shirt over a ragged grey skirt and boots; the clothing is incongruous, her girlish features now set in lines of ancient, stubborn concentration.

On the opposite side of the low stone column, Alan stands, holding his granddaughter up with his withered hands cupped around her middle so that she can brace her tiny feet on the stalagmite's edge. She is smiling and bright-eyed as she reaches for the lines of shining colour.

They are surrounded by a circle of small, crimson-glowing sigils, interspersed with dry scattered leaves and white sparking grains of sand. Jihan kneels here, her back to the tunnel entrance and her hands working feverishly at the ground.

In the vast cavern, Ouroboros is a dog, then a wolf, then a massive beast that stalks toward the glowing column, gliding its way between stone formations. Its teeth are bared. Santiago stalks behind it; he would pause to help Colin, but the angel waves him off as he limps hurriedly toward the centre of power. Verity trails behind, moving carefully, sensitive to each sweep of wings ahead.

"Oh hi," says Privya, pleasantly. "You made it. You didn't hurt Shauna, did you?"

"No." Colin is panting as he moves. "We're not the ones hurting people."

"Tell that to my guys you left lying in the street." Privya's tone is less pleasant. She doesn't look over as Ouroboros reaches the boundary of herbs and sand on the floor; Verity hears the markings sing as the massive dog rears back, stung. "I couldn't stop them. That's how scared they were. They knew they couldn't win, and they still tried."

"I'm sorry." Colin is only halfway up the sloping climb, his wings flapping awkwardly as stalagmites catch at his feathers. He has to pause to talk; he leans with both hands on his cane. "I tried to help them. The woman in the red—"

"Nadine." Privya continues watching the pool of light in front of her; her brows are furrowed in concentration. "You did try. Thanks for that. Nadine died in the ambulance. All those ... needles. Computers."

"I'm sorry."

"It doesn't matter how sorry you are. I do appreciate that you made the effort. It's more than you did for my Alethea."

The little girl Sanna motions with her hands; to Verity's eyes, she shifts one of the strands of light-within-light just a few inches to the side, where it winds around another. There's a chiming sound and a waft of roasting chestnuts. Something small snaps into brilliant focus within the larger column, part of a shining whole.

"I couldn't save her," Colin says. "I wish I had. She felt kind."

Ouroboros ripples, growing longer and more sleek. Scales undulate across its shadowed form, and it settles into the shape of a sullen anaconda, sliding restless along the borders of Privya's barrier circle. It weaves through stone columns; it doesn't touch Jihan, though it intermittently obscures her from outside view as she works like a gardener bent over weeds.

"She *was* kind," snaps Privya, without shifting from her position at the stalagmite pool. Ouroboros's writhing momentarily blocks any view of Privya, Alan, and the little girl, leaving only the column of light extending upward to seemingly black oblivion. "She wanted the best for us all. She wanted truth and clarity. She had the strongest hands I've ever known, and she laughed like a bull. Tell me, angel-boy, why you chose so wrongly."

It is no surprise to Verity that Santiago is pacing the circle as well, feral in the braided column's glow. He walks counter-clockwise to the snake. She wishes they would both stop. She almost trips over a rough ledge of stone, but catches herself, trailing after Colin's flapping ascent.

"Who would you have saved?" asks the angel, hoarsely. "Knowing neither. The one with the blade in her stomach, or the one with the hilt in her hand?"

The braid of light is yet incomplete, but Verity feels another strand slide into place; she hears another bell, pure and sparkling. Again, the child laughs.

Verity chokes, "Don't."

"Keep going, sweetheart." Alan holds his granddaughter securely; he looks toward Verity over the scales of the sliding snake. His blue eyes are bright. "Is she doing it right? Whatever she's doing. We can't tell, you know."

"Indeed. Thanks to you, Vee, we're now gambling everything on a five-year-old playing in a sunbeam. Does what she's doing make sense to you?" Privya shakes her head. "It was like this before. I remember light, and Alethea's hands weaving something I couldn't see. This power is too old. It's the wrong shape for this time and place. It needs someone who sees both worlds, to balance it out and guide it to being. At least, that's what she told me. Go on, little one. We're almost there."

"Alan. For Chrissake. What are you doing?" Colin reaches the edge of the sigils, just behind Jihan and outside the river of writhing snake. Ouroboros slows and coils, clearing room.

The light of the column has turned Alan's white beard nearly incandescent. He holds Sanna with care. "This seems like a betrayal, doesn't it? I'm sorry, my boy. I trust you implicitly. But I remember Jihan in San Francisco. She was beautiful when she was real, but just as deadly. They died screaming in those walls."

Sanna barely touches one pale pink strand of possibility; Verity hears its tone like a gong. It seems to her that she can hear a cascade of voices beneath it. When she looks behind herself, back into the receding darkness of the cavern, she sees ethereal faces glimmering past the stone formations.

"What's that?" Santiago and Ouro have both paused to stare, the snake's head rearing up and its slitted golden eyes narrowing. Colin turns, frowning. Even Alan and Privya glance briefly over. Only Sanna and Jihan remain focused—the little girl on her braid of translucent brilliance, and the woman still kneeling before the glowing circle on the ground.

Verity is close enough to study the sigils now; she doesn't recognize the shapes, but blood is delicately dripped, interspersed with the dried herbs and grains of sand whose sparkling light is now drowned out by the searing column at the cavern's centre.

Jihan's forearms are also wet and black with blood. Verity can't see Privya's, but she expects they are the same. She wonders how the girl can ooze so much, then she remembers the slack, staring face of the body far up the tunnel. She shivers.

"I thought you wanted a different path," she says to Alan. "Something new."

"I do." The old man smiles at her, a little sadly. The lines that crease his features are fissures trembling. He looks at Colin, then back to the little girl concentrating so hard, her face screwed tight. "I gave everything I had for that dream, years ago. Go on, honey."

"Goddamnit! You don't have to do this!" Colin's wings spread wide and beat down hard as he propels himself forward toward the circle. Santiago intercepts him. The magician grabs Colin around the waist, forcing him back from the glowing line.

"Careful," notes Privya. "Your shadowmancer has the right idea. That line will burn you ... what's the saying? Something fierce? It's going to be a minute before Jihan gets through." She tilts her head, looking at the light. Even she is squinting. "What do you see, Vee? I'm honestly curious. All this power. There's something very complex in here."

Verity advances far enough that one of Ouroboros's massive coils lies seething at her feet. "I see Sanna's almost finished," she says. "There's a pattern, like a puzzle falling into place. It looks like a rainbow and tastes like poison. I want her to finish. Please stop her."

"I expect it's beautiful. The last legacy of those who came before. I wonder who they were. I bet my father knew. Alan, are we ready?"

"We're getting there. You know, I've never done this." Alan studies the distant ghosts over Verity's shoulder, and he smiles. Taking one hand off Sanna, holding her securely still, he dips his fingers into the pool of light. For the first time, brilliance sparks in the blue of his eyes, like sapphires, or fireflies. The murmur of the phantom crowd grows stronger; it's marked with wonder and excited anticipation. "Oh, there's so much power here. I can breathe this air."

Sanna smiles brightly and touches a thin strand of red with her fingertip. It snaps into place. Verity can feel the vibration in her chest, the echoes of a rumble too low to perceive.

"Stop!" Colin lunges again, and Santiago holds him back, but Ouroboros throws itself against the invisible barrier, only to be hurled away once more. The giant snake rears up, white fangs exposed, smelling of singed fur. "*Alan*. What are you doing?"

"I told you I was a builder, didn't I? I carved impossible spaces. I was one of the last. It's been such a long time since I could touch it." Alan lifts one hand to adjust a strand of Sanna's hair, smoothing it down, then wrapping it affectionately just around the tip of his finger. "I didn't think I ever would again. There's a specific art to the undoing." Verity notices that his feet are bare; his toes are pale, the nails long and yellowed, curling into the rock and the dust. He takes his hand from Sanna's head and sets it at the edge of the broken stalagmite, where the pool of light is glimmering and brilliant with the growing promise of release.

Jihan's blood-slicked hands are leaving wet streaks all across Privya's patterns. Jihan doesn't stop or look up. She presses her palm to the ground and the grains of sand flare. The marks of the barrier shift, melting into new shapes.

Ouroboros whips forward and is repelled again. The snake's mouth goes wide, but Santiago is the one who cries out. The magician is still holding Colin, who would launch himself across the line if he could, but now twists to stare back at the growing pale faces of the murmuring ghosts. His wings, stretched to fullness, heave with each panicked breath he takes.

The faces in the crowd are gaining solidity as the stalagmites and stalactites of the enormous cavern begin to fade from view, replaced by growing hints of tall curtains. Something flutters above; Verity looks up and sees translucent rafters, and flocking dragons that both are and are not there.

She shudders with the weight of impossibility and hears the space around her crackle and contract before it blows open. Her skin expands with it, and walls flex around her, heaving. The cavern is not gone—they stand at its centre, at the top of the curving hill—but simultaneously, they stand on a low, flat stage, faced by a crowd of people who are neatly lined up, seated on cheap folding chairs. The crowd is watching and startled; delighted smiles fade in and out of opacity. There comes the sound of applause.

"There we go," breathes Alan, and though his knees shake with strain, there is joy in his voice. "Both at once. Here, there, and everywhere. They can see us. I told you—I told you I could. Come on, sweetheart. Grandpa can't hold this forever."

"You're a smart girl, aren't you? Come on now." In the brightness that washes over her features, Privya is older and thinner; grey streaks her hair. The bones of her skull show pale through her cheeks, and the blood on her arms has started to clot. Her teeth are sharp and shining.

The applause is louder now, cutting through Verity's bones. She is torn between staring at Sanna, willing Jihan to greater speed, and turning to look at the audience. She thinks she sees Rick, off to the side, his whiskered face a study in flummoxed surprise. She thinks she catches a glimpse of Jacob's freckles.

Colin screams, "Run!" at the phantom audience, and his voice is lost under their rising chant.

"Be-*tween*. Be-*tween*. Be-*tween*."

There is music. Verity is startled—*there is no band*—but she hears a rising harmony, and tastes it like honey on her skin, only the sweetness is laced with arsenic and the wings of dead flies. She turns, denial on her lips, and sees the rising light of the Chalice wending almost perfectly, strands humming chords that only she and Sanna can hear. Only a single faint buzz remains, bringing with it an off-key hint of diesel. A wisp of yellow drifts slightly outside the pattern.

Sanna reaches forward and strokes a finger across the sunlight line.

Privya smiles.

Jihan slams her fist into the ground, which has become some impenetrable blend of stone and stage that squirms from the eye. She rolls forward, the sigils that blocked her flaring and melting into meaningless smears. Ouroboros rears up and hurtles one more time at the line, fangs bared and golden eyes narrowed. This time, there is no barrier. The black coils of the anaconda block everything as Ouroboros throws itself between the little girl and the stalagmite pool, knocking Alan backward and obliterating any other view.

But the column of light rises now in a tight, precise braid of colour and sound; Verity, staring at it, can feel it ripple across her skin and knows that its balance is perfect. Tiny dragons launch themselves from half-corporeal rafters, flapping toward the gathered power with ragged, delighted wings.

They are in the cavern; they are on a stage. Whatever it is the audience sees, there are screams, and gasps of delight.

Colin roars at them again, a tiny prophet held back solely by the worn determination of the man in black. The angel's own wings are still spread, his eyes like the ocean on fire.

The braid of light snaps open like a flower. To Verity, it's the first notes of a symphony played on electric strings, at first a slide of all-engulfing harmony that fills something hollow and ravenous within her just as it shifts slightly discordantly, each instrument wandering individually out of tune. She tastes it like acid and feels it as tiny razors slicing across the skin of her face; she has to close her eyes so the power won't cut through her corneas, but she can still see all those tiny individual strands lashing outward. She sees them latch onto the people who are and aren't present—a teenaged boy wearing a plaid shirt and holding a baby; a laughing girl with red and purple spiked hair; a security guard leaning, arms crossed, against the main door; a man with a long, wiry beard poking with irritation at his presumably malfunctioning phone. She sees those people shiver; the boy almost drops the baby.

When she opens her eyes again, the pavilion has grown more solid around her, but she can still see the remnants of the poison light roiling. It's a gleam in the eye of the boy who breathes on the baby; it lingers on the fingers of the bearded man who passes his phone to a friend. The security guard is coughing, a hand to his throat as he chokes. He is not the only one. He sprays spittle on the woman who rushes to his assistance.

It is a strange thing, standing in an impossible cavern on a stage that isn't there, watching death spread through people who are just sitting on chairs, some starting to choke and sneeze, others staring open-mouthed, clapping their hands beneath rafters and a blackly infinite sky. Verity doesn't know who can see the lights. Distantly, though, she can hear individual cries beneath the chanting:

"Play something!"

"This is a weird concert."

"Shit, are you okay?"

"Is that snake *real*?"

"Can we get some *help* over here?"

And behind her, Colin: "Oh Christ oh fuck oh god oh shit—Stefan, let me *go*."

Under it all, she hears Privya laughing.

When Verity turns, Ouroboros lies in great coils that presumably encircle Alan and Sanna. The snake's head is reared, its teeth still bared; it has developed a hood reminiscent of a cobra. Below it, Jihan and Privya face each other across the broken stalagmite and the pool of light that is even now fading, leaching to the hollow grey stone of an empty basin.

Jihan is taller. She stands empty-handed and bloody; Verity's scarf flutters stiffly from her upper arm.

Privya still grips the stalagmite's broken edge with both gore-covered hands. Her chin is high and she chuckles, shaking her head. "Come at me," she says to Jihan. "You bitch. It's done now. Kill me for a month, or a year—hey, forever if you can. It's the only thing I'd ever be grateful to you for."

"Do something!" Colin, released now by Santiago, almost trips in his haste to cross the former barrier, but he catches himself with wings flapping sharply.

"Oh, that is way cool," says someone from the crowd.

Jihan stands perfectly still. Colin is a foot shorter, white as old bone, grabbing at Jihan's arm. As the light from the column slowly dies, the light from the angel is rising; it spills from his eyes, his hands, the skin beneath his thin white shirt. His glow touches Verity, and she feels her fingers unclench from her palms, the sting of welts fading even as she registers them. Even his frantic desperation brings a warm, clear comfort; she knows it's wrong. A thousand people have just been doomed in front of her. She can't help but feel her shoulders relax.

"Jesus—do something! What the hell are you for?" Colin clutches at Jihan, reaching up for her shoulder; it is as though he is trying to move a statue. Panic makes his eyes blue lightning.

"She can't." Privya smiles; she is worn and skeletal, but somehow the expression is still girlish. "No one can. The Chalice is draining. These people will go home, and kiss their loved ones, and death will spread. Let it go, angel. This is good for our people. We'll have room to breathe again."

"It's too late." Santiago is resigned. He would put a hand on Colin's wing, but the angel jerks feathers away, furious. Ouroboros has turned to regard the increasingly restless crowd; it has lost the cobra hood, and the tilt of its head is despondent. Its coils loosen as it unwinds, revealing the old man standing at the heart of its black loops. Alan is unharmed; he holds Sanna gently. His bare feet are firmly planted on the stage and the light in his eyes is dying.

"I can't hold it," the old man tells Colin. "The cup is emptying and my power with it. These spaces will separate in a few more beats of your heart. Do it now."

Colin is so focused on the crowd he barely registers Alan. "What are you talking about?"

"I did this for you. Take what's left." Alan gestures with his free hand, toward the dying light of the braided column. "Before the moment's gone. You were made for a purpose."

A long beat passes before Colin goes rigid. Turning, shining eyes wide, he stares at the old man. "What?" In the perfect comfort of his glow, Verity traces impossibilities—she wonders whether the audience can really see him, or whether the stage is lit by some spotlight that doesn't pierce the cavern. But she hears chatter—ripples and waves of sound cresting behind her.

"You're the other path." Alan cuddles Sanna against his shoulder; in Colin's light, the little girl smiles. Alan is smiling, too, but the last sparks of power in his eyes are fading. "I gave everything I was to you, a long time ago. Carved a *between* of flesh and bone. Carved the impossible. Made the kind of miracle they have words for. Go on, Icarus. Save them. Let them believe again."

Colin stares at the man and the girl, then he whirls to look out at the restless crowd. Someone has started booing. A few are getting up, staggering, or dragging choking friends toward the door. Plague drifts with them, a smoky curse already exuding invisibly from their every pore.

The angel's free hand curls, quite slowly, into a fist.

"Oh, fuck you," Colin breathes. "You made me a fucking martyr. My whole life." He stands, leaning one-handed on his cane, his wings spreading. Without the shield of his massive coat, he is only a slim, short figure in a loose-buttoned white shirt and torn, stained jeans. The power of him spills through the thin shirt, illuminating the blue-green-purple highlights of his feathers.

Santiago has to squint, raising a hand to shield his eyes. "What are you doing?"

It's Privya who hisses, "*No.*" Crimson wells in her eyes; she takes a step toward Colin. Jihan, in one quick and economical motion, elbows her in the throat.

Privya falls to her knees, Jihan standing over her. Someone in the crowd cheers: "Fight!"

"Don't!" barks Colin, not looking. "Don't make it worse. That's one more damn thing I have to heal." He has the audience's attention. Countless eyes are locked on him, as though suddenly hypnotized. In this space of *possible and not possible,* Verity sees some people fighting with their mobile phones, but others with their phones raised, cameras directed at the brilliant boy with the graceful wingspan. The boy with the baby has darkness running from his nose, and his mouth is gaping.

Verity hears screams—immediate as though someone is right next to her; soft as the echoes of the dead. They come in gurgling waves: "He can't breathe!" "Is there a fire?" "Help!" "She's bleeding!" Beneath them are the gasps of the ones who can't take their eyes off Colin.

"It'll be okay," he promises them. His light is reaching out; his glow falls across the faces of the people in the first few rows. Verity sees Rick, unbloodied and weeping; she sees the boy with the baby suddenly take a sharp breath.

"No," says Santiago, sounding strangled. Ouroboros hurtles forward, leaving Alan and the girl behind as it interjects its massive form between the angel and the edge of the stage. "You can't. There are too many."

"I have to. There are too many. Ouro, you're in my way." Colin's wings spread impossibly wide, then beat downward, lifting him a foot in the air before he drops awkwardly back down. He releases the cane. The next beat lifts him again, and he has both hands outstretched, casting his glow as far as it will possibly reach. He is a pillar of fire. Behind him, the broken stalagmite that holds the Chalice is dark and empty; it doesn't matter. Colin is incandescent. His glow touches Verity like a childhood blanket or a summer wind.

His warmth fills her chest with that particular, perfect clarity, and she could weep for it. Verity wants nothing more than to step forward and wrap her fingers around his. Instead, she tells him, "There are one thousand and six outsiders here."

"And they're poisoned. And they'll spread that poison. Oh, Chrissake, I can't reach them all. The ones at the back—Ouro, help me."

The snake's eyes narrow, but it's Santiago who answers: "They're not worth it!"

"Of course they are." Colin's wings beat again; it's awkward, arrhythmic, and does little to gain him any height. He almost loses his balance when he comes down, booted feet sliding. "I'm sorry, Stefan. We were going to get out of here, weren't we? I wanted it too. Ouroboros, you *brute*, if you're going to be this big, make it good for something."

All Verity wants to do is look at the angel flapping like a wounded moth; he is searing and soothing all at once. He is the most beautiful thing she's ever seen. The sounds around her have become silent; the world is still.

In that last moment of Colin's perfect grace, Verity is utterly aware of those nearby: Alan standing well back, holding his smiling granddaughter; Privya, kneeling with her hands around her own throat and her eyes savage; Jihan, half-turned, her steel gaze on Colin and her smooth features touched with rare, regretful lines at lip and brow; Ouroboros, its great curves looping loosely around the space where Colin struggles to rise aloft; and Santiago, the dark magician, now just a plain man with thinning hair and a soft paunch, his attention locked on the angel and his mouth a study in despair. Verity saw Santiago break once; now she sees it again, deep and raw, as the snake ripples.

Colin's attention is all on the crowd. They've gone silent now, except for the sounds of choking, and beneath that, someone weeping. "Hang on," whispers the angel, his arms open and his wings beating. "Hang on. I love you all. Even you, Alan—you asshole. Sacrifice your own damn self. Ouro, *please*." Black feathers whip the air. His is the only light left, apart from the impossible starlight now glittering above, and the equally impossible glow of bobbing cell phone screens as they film. He illuminates a hundred faces.

Santiago covers his face and the snake dives downward, flowing and stretching, impossibly vast. For a breathless second, it seems as though Ouroboros will simply swallow Colin; its gaping maw yawns, and the stage goes pitch dark as the living shadow strikes, as vicious as a real snake hunting a trapped bird.

Someone screams.

Verity takes a breath.

Colin explodes from blackness like a silver sun, soaring upward, his wings spread vast and strong. Shadows cling to his feathers, building and stretching; shadows *are* his feathers, the span of them nearly brushing the sides of the walls-that-aren't. Two golden eyes mark the joints of his wings, symmetrical and slitted, like the markings of a moth. Ouroboros bears the angel upward; Colin's light casts down and reaches all the way to the back of the pavilion hall. His light illuminates a thousand.

Verity doesn't want to take from him, but she can't help it; she, too, turns her face to his glow and feels her blistering feet soothed and her aching hand healed. She can trace the lines of the places Alan has brought together: the terrible space of the cavern and the narrow old walls of the pavilion. They are faced with a screaming crowd. They are alone. Both of these things are true, and the weight of it is easy on her bones as long as the angel shines down.

The little dragons leave their perches on the rafters and swoop delightedly around Colin. He flaps his shadow-wings once, twice—there is joy in it, the joy of a dandelion seed in the wind, or a small boy leaping finally from a cliff over the ocean. Colin flies, and where his light passes, the people below stop coughing; they take their hands away from their bloodied noses, and blink, not only able to breathe, but suddenly, blissfully safe. Verity sees faces, smiling upward; she sees childhood dreams. She herself tastes cotton candy and remembers, quite abruptly, the startled ecstasy on her father's face the very first time she learned to say his name.

Santiago whispers, "Oh, god." It is likely louder than he intends, on the stage, in the sudden stillness.

The angel banks and swoops. He is a star with wings, and then he is a supernova. The light grows brighter and brighter. Verity has to close her eyes, and something inside her weeps even as it flowers.

The world shifts again, and everything goes silent and black.

Verity almost reels back, but she is uncertain of the slanted stone footing, and she stands unmoving. She is bereft. Her boots are pinching her toes again, and her legs are cold. The old coat she's wearing smells of sweat and citrus bile. Still, she has the last taste of Colin's grace inside her, and she holds it beneath her ribs. She wants to hold it forever.

Someone is cursing, hoarsely and steadily. It flashes red and blue in Verity's sight, vivid with the darkness as backdrop.

She waits until she's quite sure, and then she ventures, "Privya."

The cursing stops, then is replaced with a bitter laugh. "Is this what you wanted? The Chalice is empty—and worse, wasted. Your damned angel died for it."

"No," says Verity, softly. "It isn't what I wanted." She can't taste the stage anymore. The crowd leaves only a vibrating memory. The cavern stretches invisibly around her, and she hears a stone rattle. "Who's here?"

"Is it just us? I think we lost Alan. Which is for the best ... I could strangle him myself." Privya's rasp is growing closer. Verity hears a skidding footstep; another stone skips across the floor. She is acutely aware of the emptiness between her shoulder blades.

"What happens now?"

"In the wider scheme of things? I expect the last of the weak will die, slowly. I don't know how much longer I have left. Being myself, I mean. You know, I used to go months without taking a mind. Now it's days. No one even understands I do it to be kind." Privya chuckles. It's an old sound; too old for the girl with the ragged skirts and the quick, sunny smile. "Speaking of. Listen, it's not personal. I'm furious at you, sure. But if I don't do this, it gets a lot worse for some pretty random people. At least, judging from past experience. Nice people. Jerkoffs. Kids. Whomever. The monster doesn't care."

"If you don't do what?" Verity takes two careful steps to the side. A thin column of stone barks her shin.

"You know, he actually tried to fix me? Just now. I felt it. It's a shame; I wish he had." Privya's voice is closer. It is acetone and sugar on Verity's tongue. She wishes it were lilac and coal; she thinks of Santiago. Another breath and all she wants is Jacob's hand in hers. "I at least wish he had killed me," continues Privya. "For real, I mean. For good. For a second, I thought maybe he could, and I was glad. How sad is that?"

Verity takes a breath to answer and feels Privya's hand come around her throat in the dark—a small hand, short rough fingers. The girl's grasp is hot and unyielding, like an iron poker left too long by the fire. It sears Verity's nerves as Privya pulls her closer from behind. Questing fingers slip through her hair.

Verity throws back an elbow and feels it crunch against thin bone, but the hands holding her don't waver, and she pitches herself forward with futile desperation. She reaches up, clawing at Privya's wrists, and Privya murmurs only, "I'm so much stronger than you think." Her regret steams against Verity's shoulder.

Verity drives her heel back and encounters only stone. The fingers in her hair are settling, pressing lightly but firmly, finding rainbows in her skull. A twist of her shoulders gains her half a breath. She thinks of the shy grin of Jacob's secrets. *Tell me something true.* "If you want to die," she chokes, and feels the arm barring her air give, just a little, "why fight? Why any of this? What do you care if Jihan destroys us all?"

Privya hums, low and raw and too close, but her hands are on Verity's skin now, tight enough to bruise, and she answers: "I've tried death. It just gets worse. You don't know what agony is. You don't know what it's like to have all your pieces scattered and screaming. It doesn't ever stop. Maybe the world ends and I don't. I can't bear that. Not the cold alone forever."

Verity swallows vinegar and grief. "You aren't afraid for them. Only for you."

The laugh huffs again in her ear. "I forgot what this was like. Alethea in my arms and my whispers in her hair. No lies between us, hmm? I live because I must. I would have kept them with me, if I could. Now I only hope to fade with them. If not—well, I suppose the world will still be here, even if it's cold and grey. Oh, you're right, I *am* afraid. You don't know what I could become. Hold still. I will show you the pressure points that best foment the transfer of thought."

Light blooms somewhere behind them, unexpected and soft. It brings with it the promise of flowers and new beginnings. It is *Colin* on Verity's skin, and hope flares in the exact instant she makes out a river of perfect shadow leaping past her and high, a line of pure canine purpose that knocks her ear and tears a claw into her shoulder on its way past, driving into Privya. The arms around Verity release her, but the force of it pulls her back; she falls roughly on an elbow, feeling her shoulder crack against unyielding stone.

Privya howls, but the dog is silent. Verity twists, frantic, and in the newly blooming glow, she sees Privya lunging back through the dark cavern toward her. The girl is wizened, her teeth bared; the whites of her eyes have gone dark-veined. It's only a flash; Ouroboros leaps from the side, yellow glare and white fangs in a sea of black fur, hurling itself into Privya again as they both fall back, rolling from sight.

The light is still soft and forgiving. Verity staggers up and would run to the angel, but she sees no black wings or starlit eyes. Instead, Jihan stands perhaps ten feet away, behind the broken stalagmite at the top of the cavern's mounded floor. The glow comes from the stone pool at the top of the shattered pillar. It grows with slow, steady warmth that plays across Jihan's aquiline features and reflects from her steel eyes with more affection than she herself has ever shown. Colin's love shines from her face, and even refracted, it makes Verity pause.

"The Chalice is empty," says Verity quietly—not to Jihan, really, so much as just testing the sound of it across her lips. It buzzes like a gnat, and she shakes her head. "It isn't empty," she corrects. "He filled it. He filled it again?"

Jihan looks at her—once more, straight at her, and Verity looks back. There is no shattered darkness in the other woman's eyes; nothing is lost, or alone. Jihan sighs—a human sound, palpable, rich with sorrow and weighted by infinity. Then she plunges her hands into the pool.

Light rises in tentacle beams; possibility shifts in the pool's impenetrable depths like a kraken awakening.

The ground rumbles.

From somewhere in the darkness, Privya screams like a wild thing.

Verity, shivering, takes several hurried steps forward and up, to scramble to the side of the column across from Jihan. She realizes it's where Alan and Sanna stood moments before.

"Don't. Don't—it isn't—we promised Colin." That gnat buzz pricks her skin again. "I promised him."

The tentacles shift and twine. They are smaller than before, and at first only Colin's white gleam, but as Verity watches, she can find traces of colour—blue, green, purple—that remind her of an oil spill, or the highlights on the angel's wings. They're emitting a sound that rumbles off-key somewhere just at the lower edge of her hearing. It tastes like wet earth.

The ground shivers again. Verity grips the edge of the stone column with one hand and finds it cool and rough to the touch.

Tentatively, she reaches one fingertip forward and nudges one of the beams of power just slightly to the left. She can touch the light. It almost curls around her finger, a feather brush as the discord of the harmonics eases slightly.

When Verity looks up, Jihan is smiling.

Verity says, "This isn't safe."

In response, the other woman takes her bloodied hands away. The pool of light flares alarmingly, tendrils shooting up toward the cavern's hidden ceiling. The ground shakes harder; a cracking sound echoes sharply from somewhere to the left. Verity is forced to grab the stone with both hands before Jihan puts her own back.

Verity swallows. "It's too late. Again." She doesn't need the hint of apples or cinnamon to tell her that she speaks the truth.

She hears a wet rending, and a shriek that melds anger and pain. She knows Privya and Ouroboros are still behind her somewhere. There's nothing she can do to help the dog.

She says only, "He didn't want this." But there is nothing to be done, so she looks at Jihan and strokes her hand across another questing strand of light. She feels it shift and settle.

It's not something she can explain later—how light has a life and a texture, or how Colin's last breath inflects a radiant pool, or the soothing ways in which she knows precisely where an ancient pattern should fall, because *this* goes a little to the right, and *this* one is first, and *this* one smells like peaches, but the other one whistles like the wind in winter. But she knew it when Sanna was doing it, and now she does it herself, with exquisite care, crafting a braid of silver and shifting jewel tones. This one is smaller than the first, but infinitely more intricate. She can't follow the pattern with her eyes. She only *knows*.

"It was very old," she says once, much later, fumbling for words. *"We're*

very new. The context changed. It had to be re-shaped." It is just before she burns her first page.

Verity loses track of time and the shivering of the ground. She forgets about the dog and the girl in the dark. She is crafting perfection. She thinks she should be frightened, but an angel's forgiveness is curled warmly around her, and she only knows precision and need.

When the pattern in front of her resolves, it shines atop the stone as though it were sculpted of glowing crystal. She can hear it singing. Its points extend in a circle; it is an impossibly delicate star. Light pulses in a tiny marble at its heart. Verity doesn't dare breathe on it.

Jihan reaches down and cups the braided ball of light, somehow without touching it; it rises just above her palms, and when she lifts it, the column of stone beneath is left barren and plain. She looks once at Verity, and the star is twinned in the mirrors of her gaze.

Jihan lifts the pool of light to her mouth and breathes it in. At first, it only stretches, each tiny strand like a spider's web caught in a breeze. Then the gleaming twists vanish between Jihan's lips, and the cavern would be dark again except that now the glow blossoms in her eyes and at the base of her throat, travelling somewhere deep down in her chest before it spreads, following the lines of her veins, tracing her as she is: the outline of what used to be a woman. Brightness stretches out gracefully from her shoulders, just briefly, painting the momentary shapes of Colin's wings.

For a moment, she is purest possibility.

The cavern rumbles again, more drastically than before. Verity is almost thrown to the ground before she can grab at the shattered stalagmite. She finds herself choking on a cloud of dust.

She whispers, "No."

A stalactite falls from somewhere above and shatters, narrowly missing Verity. Another falls just behind Jihan, who stands alight, arms spread as though she were Colin offering his benediction to the pavilion.

"Stop her." Privya is a panicked face in the dark, all sharp teeth and a reaching, clawed hand, before blackness bowls her over and she's lost to a dog, or a snake, or whatever shape faces her in the shadows. A crack opens in the ground and ripples toward Verity's feet. A crack opens somewhere above, and rocks fall, bringing with them unexpected moonlight and the snapping electric doom of the city.

Verity, stricken with horror, stares above and sees, somehow, the lights of Ottawa screaming.

She knows the star was as perfect as she could make it.

She coughs on dust and looks frantically toward Jihan.

Jihan stands calmly. Colin's light spills from beneath her skin. It is darker, bolder—spiced with his love, still, but also with iron peace, focused into something rife with a hundred thousand possibilities. The other woman smiles, still—truly smiles, slow and bright with joy—and reaches forward with one glowing hand to brush her fingertip to Verity's lips.

Everything

Stops

She sees nothing and everything, feels feathers across her skin, hears a hundred bells chiming a thousand different notes.

She swallows whiskey and coal and a butterfly's song.

Verity clutches the last of Colin's gift within her and feels, solid against her leg, the knife in her pocket.

She knows exactly what she is supposed to do; she has the precise scar herself, invisible, a memory edging above her hip. She knows the angle and the depth and the weight of the blade.

She doesn't think.

Sliding her hand into the pocket of the coat, she grips the hilt of the knife and draws it forth, driving it in one smooth motion into Jihan's body. Just above the last rib, on the right, angled up and toward the centre. She knows.

Turning the knife, she opens the door.

[**IMAGE:** Jihan and Verity, in the dark. They are close together, each leaning into the other, and Verity is driving a knife between Jihan's lower ribs. Verity is shocked. Jihan is smiling very slightly. They are staring into each other's eyes.]

24

OTTAWA (March 6, 2014)—Emergency teams have been dispatched to Ottawa from both Toronto and Montréal after an earthquake measuring 6.8 was recorded in the centre of the city last night, rattling buildings and knocking out power in a 20-block radius around south Bank Street.

While the subsequent power outage is another hit to a city that was without electricity for much of the winter, and authorities have only begun inspecting buildings for damage, most attention is focused on Lansdowne Park, the site of the Between concert located at the epicentre of the quake. Aberdeen Pavilion was badly damaged, though most concert-goers escaped unharmed and many are crediting an "angel" for saving them.

"Screw the quake," said Marcus Price, 32, of Kingston. "There was some kind of damn bioweapon in there, or—terrorists, or—I don't know. People were bleeding from the eyes! First the band almost didn't show up, then there was this crazy-ass giant snake on stage, and—oh my god, the angel. You didn't see the angel. If you didn't see him, you won't understand."

"He was the most beautiful thing," added Suki Knapton, 21, from Kanata. "They say angels don't exist. I saw a miracle. I couldn't breathe, and then he just ... have you ever felt love? I mean real love?"

Frank Whiteside, 29, says he has given footage from his phone to the police, and will soon be releasing it to news networks. "You'll understand when you watch. There's wonder in the world. I went into that concert with a broken collarbone. Now it's great. He just reached in—like, not reached reached, he— were you there? You have to watch this."

Early video from multiple cameras shows a winged human figure flying over a crowd of concert-goers, shortly before the building starts shaking. Multiple people have already reported watching the footage and experiencing an overwhelming feeling of well-being.

Representatives from The Between could not be reached for comment. Lansdowne Park officials have released....

WHAT COMES AFTER

Verity steps quietly through a door that doesn't exist, into rubble that was once a Victorian pavilion. She feels the way close behind her as she passes.

She is an odd sight: a nondescript woman with mousy hair and rock dust on her skin, wearing a loose navy coat over bare legs and too-small boots. She's hardly dressed for winter. Her hands are in her pockets. She has blood smeared down one temple, and even though it's not hers, her eyes are not quite focused. No one notices her.

One of the pavilion's long walls has fallen in, and people with flashlights and blankets are climbing over the wreckage, picking through chunks of broken ice, mashed snow, and a sea of fallen chairs. Curtains are ripped down. The low stage at one end is in shambles, swarmed with uniforms. The roof is open to the sky, where dawn's cold light is just starting to peek through.

Verity ducks her head and peers at the floor, picking over and through the mess. She walks by a security guard who gives her a very close look, as though she's familiar, but she stares at the ground. His eyes are wet with tears. He can't seem to stop smiling. He doesn't stop her.

In the shadow of one wall, Verity closes her eyes and pauses for a long time. Her nostrils flare.

Outside, the ground is cracked, paving stones heaved up and great swaths of earth erupting along the courtyard. A chasm bisects Bank Street. Emergency vehicles swarm on either side, lights flashing.

Verity holds her borrowed coat closed with one hand. It smells of birds and hope—and still, somewhere underneath, of stale liquor. She walks carefully through the pavilion's broken remains, moving with slow deliberation toward the street. She passes two men huddled in a blanket, a girl rocking a child, an ambulance attendant staring at a cell phone and crying. Despite the distant sirens, she hears only hushed whispers, and a hesitant, wondering laughter. There's dust in the air, and the frost of her breath, but everything feels particularly clear. The city is light on her shoulders.

"...Vee?"

Verity turns to see Jacob standing uncertainly on broken stones. His jacket is ripped along one sleeve, and his hair is even more of a mess than usual. In the rising daylight, she can see the cut on his forehead has been stitched and long scabbed over, but it's going to leave a scar.

Verity only stands. Jacob stares. Eventually, he ventures, "What happened?"

Verity looks at him. Her eyes are grey and steady. When he has to look away, she says gently, "I opened a door. I unlocked it, and they went through."

Jacob's Adam's apple bobs in his throat. "Is...." He hesitates again, then forges onward. "Is she coming back?"

She answers him as if he were very young: honestly, but with kindness. "I don't know if she can."

Jacob winces. He doesn't look surprised, though. Instead, he turns to look back at the ruins of the pavilion, then he straightens his shoulders and walks up to Verity, close enough to touch her. He doesn't actually touch her. "Were those ... is that a dragon?"

He's pointing. She doesn't have to look. She can hear the flapping overhead, prickling just beneath her skin. "Kind of."

Jacob swallows again and stands there staring before he looks back down. He rubs his hand over the back of his neck. "Was ... that a real angel?"

Verity is the one who hesitates. Finally she says, "What is 'real'? He was Colin. You saw him. They all saw him." A balding man in a blue down coat wanders slowly by, his thick moustache not enough to obscure the awed, dreaming curve of his smile. Verity watches him pass, then adds, more to herself than anything, "I think that's what Alan wanted. There's space for them, now. Possibility. But now they've left."

Jacob asks again, "Is she—are *they*—coming back?"

"I don't know. They might."

"How do you know?"

Verity turns in a careful circle, looking at the cracked buildings and the growing pink light of dawn. Off to the side, she can see a young girl praying. She pauses, then lifts her chin to look up at Jacob once more. Lifting her right hand, she shakes back the worn sleeve and shows him the tiny black snake wrapped around her wrist like a bracelet. It is narrow, curled tightly. It stares at Jacob with golden eyes.

"We're not alone," she says, then offers Jacob her hand. "Let's go home."

Jacob blinks down at her, and, dubiously, at her wrist-snake, which looks back up at him and flicks a forked tongue in challenge.

Jacob takes Verity's hand, and she leads him toward the street. She picks her way with great care over the paving stones. They taste like shattered glass.

"I think," she tells him, "we should try running a theatre."

Should I finish here?

For now, I mean? What's left?

Are you still reading?

Vee?

[**IMAGE:** An old-fashioned typewriter, with a white page half run through it. On the page is typed 'FIN.' A small black snake is curled around the typewriter, looking out at the reader.]

ACKNOWLEDGMENTS

This book would not have happened without years of encouragement and critical support from my writing group: Diana Knapton, Anne Price, and Dan Whiteside. If you like something in here, there's a good chance they liked it too. Remaining mistakes—factual and otherwise—are mine.

Elaine Spencer was the first to read the whole draft and be excited—emphatically, repeatedly, as many times as I needed to hear it. She is why this book isn't buried ten feet deep in the yard.

Jenna Butler believed in this project *so hard*. She offered not only vocal and generous enthusiasm, but also copious amounts of professional advice. She heroically put up with my stressing through the submission process, and then she committed to editing the entire manuscript. She is entitled to at least two of my bodily organs.

Much gratitude also goes to Matt Bowes, Claire Kelly, Isabel Yang, Kate Hargreaves, and the readers at NeWest Press.

The little girl who wanted to write stories thanks Daryl Bissell.

The teenager who tried thanks Erin Rother.

For as long as I can remember, Marilla Bain has wanted to know when I would write a novel. Here it is, finally! And thanks for asking.

I honed a lot of my creative writing skills in the darkest, MUXiest corners of the internet, where some of *In Veritas*'s character seeds first germinated. I never knew all the names of the writers I encountered there—and I've lost some, too—but if you were one of them, I thank you. Shout-outs to Jennifer Andreani, Mike Athey, Tara Atkisson, Gordon Delp, Gina Donahue, Elissa Dukes and Larry Isen, Melanie Edmonds, Amber Fox, Jason Franks, Todd Harper, Angela Hawkes, Andrew Jones, Abby Laughlin, Rob Lipson, Aaron Maracle, Barry McKelvey, Karla

Moon, Siobhan Morris, Mark Porter, Caroline Pryde, Erin and Adam Schroeder, Daphne and Gordon Sleigh, and Kelvin Wong. Amy Poon Shibasaki gave me the idea for a synesthetic character. Jason Cline gave us our best and most enduring home. And Theresa "Kate" Campbell, my most imaginary friend, has listened to me mutter about word count more times than I would have thought humanly possible. Thanks!

Friends who have supported me in myriad ways also include Gwen Larouche and Milks Milks, José Pou and Sarah Picard, Andrea Principe, Dave Principe, Mike Prince, Matt Webber, Nancy Batty and Glenn Russell, Andy Colven, Jackie Cowan, Tera Dahl-Lang, Holly Ellingwood, Jamie Fletcher, Stephanie Gilbert, Reesa Herberth, Kim Horne, Jane MacNeil, Heather Marcovitch and Larry Steinbrenner, Jim and Margaret Martens, Adam Mugford, Adrienne Orr, Elaine and Chris Parker, Val Pérez, Stéphane Perreault, Jamie Prowse-Turner, Susan Richter, Cindy See, and Jennifer Terry.

I am perennially grateful to—and for—my astonishing family: James and Elizabeth Lavigne, and Erica, Pedro, Elsa, Mila, and Davi Pereira.

Finally, I've thanked coffee in every acknowledgment I've ever written. I'm not about to stop now.

C.J. Lavigne was born in Kingston, ON, but grew up all over Canada, from Comox, BC to Barrington Passage, NS. Since 2007, she has divided her time between Ottawa, ON, and Red Deer, AB, where she currently resides and works as a professional communications scholar who writes on television, gaming, and popular culture; at other points in her life, she's been a barista, tech support supervisor, marketing manager, freelance editor, and—briefly—radio DJ. *In Veritas* is her first novel and is part of the Nunatak First Fiction Series.